Praise for Josephine Myles's
Junk

"If your favorite thing in the world is watching the sweet, delicious dance of souls showing their vulnerable sides in hopes of connecting—then this book is for you."

   ~ Heidi Cullinan, author of Love Lessons

"...very pleased that these two got their happy ending, they were that adorable together..."

   ~ Dear Author

"*Junk* is everything I was hoping for. [...] It's exactly the type of character-driven romance I expect from Josephine Myles."

   ~ Reviews by Jessewave

"Once in a while I'll come across a romance that lives in my mind long after I finished reading the book. Junk by Josephine Myles is one of those books."

   ~ Top2Bottom Reviews

"This is the complete package for me as a reader, the only problem I had was it ended. Very highly recommended."

   ~ Gay List Book Reviews

"An emotionally rich and compelling story of two men striving to clear the clutter, literal and metaphoric, to make room for true love. [...] Junk is a must read for fans of contemporary romance."

   ~ Fresh Fiction

Look for these titles by
Josephine Myles

Now Available:

Barging In
Handle with Care
The Hot Floor
Screwing the System
Merry Gentlemen

The Bristol Collection
Junk
Stuff

Junk

Josephine Myles

Samhain Publishing, Ltd.
11821 Mason Montgomery Road, 4B
Cincinnati, OH 45249
www.samhainpublishing.com

Junk
Copyright © 2013 by Josephine Myles
Print ISBN: 978-1-61921-955-7
Digital ISBN: 978-1-61921-755-3

Editing by Linda Ingmanson
Cover by Lou Harper

First Samhain Publishing, Ltd. electronic publication: August 2013
First Samhain Publishing, Ltd. print publication: August 2014

Dedication

For everyone who's ever bought a book they know they'll probably never get around to reading...

I had an awful lot of feedback on the second draft of this story, and those fearless pre-readers have helped me shape the final novel into something I'm really proud of. Thank you so much to Jennifer, Stella, Kristin, Tavdy, Shelagh, Lillian Francis, Kira Delaney, Prue Tremayne and Susan Sorrentino: you're all stars!

And finally, as always, my heartfelt thanks to JL Merrow and Lou Harper: great friends and fantastic crit partners. And to my editor, Linda. Working with you is a true pleasure.

Chapter One

There was still an area of clear space left in the middle of his kitchen, but even that was gradually being encroached on.

Jasper dropped his bag onto the uncluttered section at the end of his dining table and pulled out his latest acquisitions: a book on postmodern film theory and the latest editions of the *New York Times* and *Engineering Monthly*. The newspaper was easy to file, and it joined the stack over by the breakfast bar. That particular pile had almost reached the top of the work surface, so soon he'd have a wall developing between the cooking and dining sides of the room. Would that constitute a fire hazard?

He should move the stack somewhere. Fire and paper most definitely didn't mix. Well, they did. Too well, actually; that was the problem. But after looking around the crowded room, Jasper had to admit defeat. There weren't any other stacks he was willing to add to right now. Some of them were looking decidedly unstable. No. Safer to stick to these lower ones over by the breakfast bar. What he'd do when those reached the ceiling, he had no idea. Call that clutter-clearing company? The very thought of someone else seeing what a mess he'd made of the place was enough to make him queasy with nerves. Besides, they'd want to throw things away, and everything he'd collected was important. They'd never understand that, would they?

More to the point, no matter how many times he read their advert, he'd never pigging well pluck up the courage to call them.

Jasper sighed and picked up the magazine. *Engineering Monthly* was more problematic than the newspapers. Since he'd filled the dining room, finding spaces to fit magazines was increasingly challenging. In the end, he'd started some new piles by the back door, but they were already making it difficult to get outside. Still, he added it to the neat tower, then shuffled carefully back to the oasis of space around the table.

The book. Jasper fondled the cover lovingly. He wasn't actually planning to read it, of course. He'd already determined that fact back at the library during his tea break. But he couldn't have left it languishing there on the sale trolley, unwanted and unloved. He knew just the place for it.

Jasper trod carefully through the hallway, turning sideways between walls of books piled three or four deep, until he reached the lounge door. It didn't open all the way anymore, but there was enough room for him to slip through. He flicked on the overhead bulb—a small amount of light still filtered in at the top of the window, but it didn't reach far into the room—then followed the pathway between towers of books on gardening and crafts, history and philosophy.

Cultural theory was located behind his sofa, and recently over the seat too. Jasper added the new find to the growing pile on the end cushion. He couldn't lie down anymore to watch TV, but that was okay. He couldn't watch TV anyway—not since the extension cord had blown a fuse. Theoretically, he could replace it if he could ever remember where the wall socket was behind all the books.

But who needed television when you had a whole library at your fingertips?

On his way out, Jasper ran his fingers up the spines of a stack near the door. So much knowledge buried within. Far more than one person could ever hope to learn in a whole lifetime of reading. The thought made him smile, made him push against the books ever so slightly, the better to feel the friendly comfort they offered. Their solid presence.

Maybe not so solid in this case, as the whole stack shifted. Jasper exited hastily, closing the door behind him with more force than usual. And that's when he heard it. The unmistakable sound of an avalanche of books.

Oh God. Not again.

Jasper tried the door. He rattled the handle and pushed against the weight of all those words. But it was no use. Another room cut off from use. All those books, out of bounds forever.

He leaned his forehead against the door and held back the tears until his eyes stung. What a stupid bloody loser. Not even able to enter half the rooms in his house anymore. Too embarrassed to invite anyone around. His entire social life reduced to the interactions at work and his occasional Internet hook-ups.

No, this was no use. He couldn't carry on like this.

He pulled out his phone with shaking hands and called up the number for the clutter-clearing company. Could they really help him overcome his hoarding issues like their advert promised? It sounded too good to be true.

It sounded...challenging.

Before he could chicken out yet again, Jasper pressed dial.

"Wonderland Clutter Clearing. Carroll Miller here," a chirpy voice announced.

"Oh, I uh..." The words dried up somewhere between Jasper's larynx and his mouth.

"What can I do you for, love?"

"I'm so sorry to trouble you," he said, "but I think I might need a little bit of help."

Chapter Two

"Here we are," Carroll said as she pulled up outside the house. "And what a fine example of a standard hoarder hedge."

Lewis stared up at the overgrown, shaggy monstrosity, which all but shielded the house from onlookers. He could only see one of the upstairs windows, a large bay one, but there was a telltale bulge of stuff piled up behind the closed curtains. Oh yes. Once you knew what to look for, you could spot a hoarder's house from the street. You could even pinpoint them on Google Maps sometimes, by looking for gardens piled with rubbish. Every town had them, and a city the size of Bristol had enough to keep him and his twin sister in business all year round. Not that you could cold-call on hoarders you'd spotted via satellite. No. Frustratingly enough, you had to wait for them to come to you. Maybe they should try leafleting them, though. Lewis made a mental note to suggest it to Carroll after they'd finished with the client.

"Can you check his name?" Lewis asked. Carroll had taken the call yesterday afternoon, only filling him in on the bare bones on the drive over from Ms. Priddy's place. She hadn't been able to remember the potential client's name—typical Carroll fashion—but he'd learned that the man had lived in the house all his life and had said he needed "a little bit of assistance with keeping the place tidy". Words to that effect usually meant they'd need to hire a skip for a whole week to empty the house, but you never knew. One person's terrible mess was another's cosy and lived-in.

Carroll thumbed at her phone. "Jasper, that's it. Jasper Richardson."

Lewis's stomach gave a funny lurch. "Couldn't be, could it?"

"Couldn't be who?"

"The Jasper Richardson we went to school with."

Carroll scrunched up her nose like a demented rabbit. "What Jasper Richardson? The name doesn't ring any bells. Jog my memory?"

"I don't know if you'd have noticed him. He was kind of...nerdy, I suppose. Tall, skinny, big nose. Wore thick glasses, messy black hair." Hair that the fifteen-year-old Lewis had yearned to run his fingers through almost as much as he'd craved kissing those sensual lips. When he hadn't been mooning over his drama teacher, anyway.

"I dunno. Doesn't sound like my type. This Jasper's thirty-three, I think. That the right age?"

"Sounds like it. He was three years above us."

"Was he fit? Must've been. Yeah, you've got that look on your face."

Lewis pursed his lips.

"Nah, now you just look constipated. I prefer the dreamy look. You used to get it whenever Mr. Blewitt over the road mowed his front lawn without a shirt on. Don't you dare try and deny it."

Lewis tried to give Carroll a forbidding look, but the trouble with having a twin was they knew you back to front. Carroll just laughed, kissed him on the nose and opened the door of the van. "Come on. Let's go see if your teenage hottie's aged well, or if it's all just a horrible coincidence."

Lewis slammed the door of their van, giving it that special wiggle it needed to engage the lock properly. One of these days they'd be able to afford a new van, but for now the garishly painted "Wonderland Clutter Clearing" vehicle would have to remain.

The houses in this up-and-coming part of Southville were turn-of-the-century stone semis. It had been gentrified, but Weston Road still sat right on the border with the more multicultural and down-at-heel Bedminster. The houses sat back from the street behind what were mostly well-tended front gardens. Number sixty-four was another matter, though. Vegetation exploded out of its confines, leafy trees dangling their branches possessively over neighbouring gardens and all but blocking half of the pavement. There was a low stone wall with a peeling gate set in the front, and Carroll pushed it open.

"Oops." The gate crashed onto the ground, and Carroll picked it up, showing the rusted hinges to Lewis before propping it against a tree trunk.

"God, I kind of hope it isn't him, you know," Lewis murmured, looking around at the junk accumulated in the gloom under the trees. Piles of broken hand tools rusted away next to heaps of cracked terracotta pots. Somewhere at the back lurked what looked like a kiddie's plastic slide, but the colours were muted by the greenish mould covering everything. At least it was all garden-type stuff, though. Lewis always held out hope for the clients who could at least categorise their hoard and store it appropriately. Ah, to hell with it. He held out hope for all hoarders. It might be tough, but nearly all of them could be helped. The selective combination of Lewis's gentle approach and Carroll's perky energy and wit usually sorted them out.

Carroll was already up on the front step, knocking on the door, so Lewis hurried after her. The house itself could be attractive if cleaned up a bit, what with the large bay windows and the stained glass around the door. The sheltered porch, however, was a more worrying indication of what they might find inside, seeing as both sides were stuffed with newspapers. Newspaper hoarders were some of the worst, their teetering piles of junk paper giving Lewis nightmares of being buried under them.

"Coming!" a voice called from inside the house. "Might take me a minute."

"Sounds like he's got goat trails," Carroll whispered as they listened to the sound of shuffling footsteps followed by scrabbling around on the other side of the scuffed and peeling paintwork.

"Sorry. It's not usually this hard to open the door," the voice continued. Despite the nervous quaver, Jasper's voice had a cultured accent and a pleasant timbre, but Lewis couldn't for the life of him tell if it was *his* Jasper. He'd barely heard him utter a word back at school.

The door cracked open, and a dark eye peered out at them from the gloom within. "Carroll?"

"That's right." Carroll stepped forward, smiling in that dimpled, close-mouthed way that seemed to put everyone at ease. "And this is my brother, Lewis Miller. We work together."

"Oh! I...umm, I didn't realise." The eye winked.

Winked? Was Jasper flirting? He sounded too nervous to flirt.

"I did mention I'd be bringing my partner," Carroll said.

"You did?"

Carroll nodded.

"Buggeration. I should have remembered. I'm so bloody forgetful sometimes." Jasper winked again, and now Lewis saw the movement for what it was, a nervous tic. As tics went, it was a pretty cute one, but he'd far rather get Jasper to relax.

Lewis moved forward, trying to get a better look at the owner of the voice and the eye. "Hi, Jasper. And don't worry about it. I find it difficult to remember things when I'm feeling stressed."

"I was a bit anxious. Haven't had anyone else in here since... Well, *since*. I'm not sure there's going to be room for everyone inside."

Lewis and Carroll exchanged a glance. "It's useful for us to see your home first," Lewis began, before Carroll butted in to finish his sentence.

"But if you'd rather we go somewhere else and talk, that's fine, too."

The door cracked open another inch. Recognition pinged through Lewis's awareness. Oh yes, that was his Jasper

15

Richardson all right. And hadn't he grown up handsome? Despite the blatantly English surname, he must have had some foreign blood in him, because his skin had a permanently tanned hue to go with the Arabic nose and dark hair. It was hard to get an idea of the adult Jasper's body from the slice Lewis could see, but he got the overall impression of untucked scruffiness and lean height.

Jasper's eyes widened as he took the two of them in properly, but if he recognised them, he was keeping it to himself. "I, uh, yes. I think I'd prefer that. There's a café down the road. The Copper Kettle. Could we go there?"

"Of course. I think we passed it on the way here." They'd driven past a row of local businesses at the bottom of the street, crowding near the junction with the main road. Lewis had noted the coffee shop with all the longing of a man who'd spent most of the day at Ms. Priddy's, drinking dishwater-weak tea made with slightly off milk.

"Okay. I just need to get my things. Might take me a few minutes. I can meet you there."

Lewis and Carroll exchanged a glance. "We can wait," Lewis said.

"Oh, uh, okay. Umm, I just don't want you to get bored. They do good coffee there. And cake. Really nice cake. Could you ask Yusef to save me some baklava, please?"

It sounded like they'd been given their marching orders, in the most polite way possible. Lewis decided to admit defeat. "We'll meet you there in ten, then. But make sure you don't take too long," he said, waggling a finger and grinning. "You wouldn't want Carroll here to eat all the baklava, would you?"

"As if," Carroll protested. "I'm on Atkins, remember?"

"Oh, you really should be careful," Jasper said. "It's not healthy to cut out all those foods for too long, you know. There's an osteoporosis risk. I was reading about it just the other day."

"Don't worry about me," Carroll said breezily, although Lewis knew how much she hated being given advice. "I'm bound to trip up and scoff a cream cake sooner or later. Now come on, bro. Let's walk. I could do with the exercise. See you in a minute, Jasper."

Lewis allowed Carroll to yank him down the garden path but shook off her hold when they were out of sight of the house. "Oi, you'll crease my shirt. This is a Paul Smith."

"Like Jasper is going to notice. Did you see the state of him? Poor love. Still, at least his house didn't stink too bad. Not as bad as the Kopcheks' place."

"Ugh!" Lewis shuddered. The Kopcheks had hoarded out-of-date food along with everything else and had a major roach and rat infestation. They'd had to wear face masks just to check the place out. In the end, they'd had to hand the case over to the local council, who sent in their team in Hazmat suits to chuck the whole lot out. Lewis had been there purely as moral support for the elderly couple. Poor Mrs. Kopchek had been in floods of tears when her precious, ruined possessions were carted out. "I wonder if they've started up again?"

"I don't even want to think about it. So, tell me, was it your Jasper?"

He could have denied it to avoid any teasing, but there wasn't much point. Carroll had always been able to sniff out his lies. "Yep. That's him all right. I wonder what happened to turn him into a nervous wreck of a hoarder?"

"Maybe you can weasel it out of him over coffee."

"Hey, I never weasel!"

"Yeah, right." Carroll gave him the *whatever* sign, creating a W with her fingers, probably because she knew how much it drove him up the wall. "Call it what you like, you're a master manipulator. You'll have him eating out of your hand by the end of an hour, knowing you. So, you think he's into blokes?"

"Don't know. I hope so. No, wait! I don't hope so. He's a client. And I'm sworn off relationships for a while."

"Oh, come on. It's not going to be unethical if I handle his case, is it? And anyway, you've been single for three months. That's some kind of record for you, bro. You must be dying to get out of Mum and Dad's place and into the next love nest."

"I don't need a love nest. And anyway, I love Mum and Dad." Even if they did sometimes drive him up the wall.

"Yeah, so do I, but you wouldn't catch me moving back in with them if things went pear-shaped with Matt."

"I didn't have enough money for a deposit anywhere."

"That's because you spent it all on fancy clothes and presents for that eejit absentee ex-boyfriend of yours."

"Carlos wasn't an eejit. He was just too focused on his career." And unfortunately, his career as a troubleshooter for a major chain of carpet retailers took him all over the country at a moment's notice.

"That makes him an eejit, if he didn't spend enough time with you. And it makes you one for putting up with it. Talk about being a doormat."

"Hey, I stood up to him. Gave him an ultimatum and everything."

"Yeah, eventually."

Unfortunately, Carlos hadn't taken more than a moment to decide when given the "me or the job" challenge and had chosen his career, leaving Lewis homeless yet again, as he seemed to be after every significant relationship ended. He should probably stop moving into other guys' places, but then again, it always made sense as he was the one still kipping at his folks' house.

All the more reason to wait. Take it slow. Get to know someone before rashly cohabiting. Maybe even save up to get his own place first, although the idea of having to save brought him out in hives.

They'd reached the bottom of the road, where an odd mix of retailers huddled in the shelter of the hill. A newsagents and a fireplace shop sat on either side of a rather run-down-looking charity shop supporting the local cats-and-dogs home. A small pharmacy—with the window proudly displaying a range of support stockings and incontinence pads—flanked the hairdressers, and at the end of the row was the café. The Copper Kettle might have had a traditionally English name, but the decor inside had a distinctly Middle Eastern ambience with terracotta walls and fretwork lamps hanging from the ceiling.

There were cosy booths along one of the side walls, with the bar taking up the entire back wall. At this hour of the day, it was empty apart from the heavyset, dark-skinned man behind the counter—Yusef, presumably—but it looked like a well-loved place with plenty of flyers for local events pinned up and a scruffy but lived-in vibe.

Lewis took a window table while Carroll ordered coffee for them both. "You think he's going to show?" Carroll asked as she plonked herself down in the seat next to him.

"I hope so."

"You want to do the chattering-twins thing to put him at ease? Or do you think we should go for reserved and professional?"

That was a tough one. Lewis's instincts were always to go for the more professional approach, but he'd come to realise that many clients actually preferred Carroll's casual and chatty way of starting a session. "Let's see if we can ease him in with some banter. Just don't go telling him all my childhood secrets. You're worse than Mum with a photo album sometimes."

Carroll poked her tongue out at him, but Lewis could see her thinking things through. She might come across as slapdash to those who didn't know her, but there was a lot of wisdom hidden away in that head of hers.

"Reckon he's OCD?" she asked. Because of his psychology-degree background, Carroll usually deferred to him on the more diagnostic side of their work, while she took charge of the practical stuff. It was an arrangement that suited them both.

"OCD? Possibly." The nervous tic and categorised hoard might indicate that, but it was too soon to tell. "If so, could take him a while to get here. I don't think they're in any danger of running out of baklava, though."

Carroll eyed the display of sweet pastries in the glass case with a look Lewis knew well. "Oh, those look fantastic."

"Not for you, though, Ms. Faddy-diet." Lewis checked his sister out more closely than usual. While Lewis's skin was wrecked by acne scars and Carroll's remained flawless—except for the holes she'd voluntarily had pierced—they'd both inherited the same middling height and pale blond curls from their mother and were obviously related. However, Carroll had their dad's tendency to put on weight at the drop of a hat, whereas Lewis remained as wiry as ever. At the moment, though, she was looking pretty trim. "I reckon it might be working. You're looking good."

"Thanks!" Carroll glowed. "I've lost a stone in the last month."

"Don't let Dad hear. He'll want to feed you until you put it all back on again."

"Bugger that. If I wanted to scorch the inside of my mouth, I'd start taking those fire-breathing lessons I was telling you about."

Lewis thought back to the eggs he'd been served for breakfast, adulterated with more than a dash of Tabasco sauce to add what his dad referred to as "vim". "I reckon the fire-breathing would be milder than Dad's cooking."

His stomach gurgled in agreement.

Chapter Three

Jasper peered through the little peephole in his door until the two visitors had disappeared behind the trees. Two of them! He couldn't fit two in here. He'd have to ask only one of them to come next time. The man, perhaps. He'd looked familiar, somehow. But where from? He certainly didn't work at the university if he was a professional clutter clearer, and he didn't look much like one of the students who used the library where Jasper worked. Too neatly dressed, for a start.

Dress. That was a good point. Jasper glanced down at his own ragtag outfit. Should he get changed before going out? No. Not enough time. It was going to take long enough finding his bag and keys. Silly, really. He should be able to remember where he'd put things. Especially the stuff on the top. So why was it he could perfectly picture the stuff that lay behind the piles, but the contents of the stacks themselves were largely a mystery? Memory loss. He was turning into an old fart way before his time. Next thing he knew, he'd be wearing elasticated deck shoes and complaining about the youth of today.

He shuffled his way sideways back through the narrow passageway to the kitchen. His bag had been there last, surely? Somewhere behind one of these piles was a perfectly good coat rack, which would be a perfect place to hang his bag if he could get to the blasted thing.

Eventually, Jasper made it down the hallway and into the kitchen, the most functional remaining room in the house. His gaze homed in on the kitchen table. There was a clear spot at one end, just big enough to fit his laptop. Should he take that with him? Yes, probably. You never knew when you were going to need computer access. And there was his phone, plugged in to a USB port so he could use the 3G connection to get online. There was a Wi-Fi router somewhere around here, but the signal had died a few months back, and he hadn't been able to locate the pesky thing to try to figure out what was wrong.

Jasper gazed around the room again, wondering if this time he'd spot the small black box lurking somewhere. He didn't, but instead glimpsed the leather strap of his messenger bag, poking out from under a pile of newspapers. Oh yes. He'd only been given those ones this morning. Must have put them on the bag when he got home from work. Stupid idiot. He'd forget his own head if it wasn't screwed on.

He added the papers to the top of the stack by the back door before checking the contents of his bag. Magazines? Right. He'd forgotten about those. There were five copies of *British Deaf News*, which the university had decided it wasn't going to keep in hardcopy now they had an electronic subscription. Seemed a shame to throw out all that useful information, though. Not that Jasper knew any deaf people, but he might meet one in the future. Probably not today, though, so he wouldn't need to take them with him. He added the magazines to a teetering tower on one of the dining chairs.

The rest of the bag was filled with his usual emergency kit: a Maglite torch, first aid kit, various colours and types of pen and paper, Swiss Army knife, spork, aspirin, travel-sickness wristbands, energy bars and a half-empty bottle of water. Jasper filled the bottle up at the sink, then decided to leave it there. Yusef had water on tap after all, didn't he? And it wasn't like Jasper was going to die of dehydration on the way down the hill.

But what if he ran into someone who needed water? A red-faced, panting jogger on the way up the hill on this hot June day? Jasper couldn't live with himself if someone died of heat exhaustion simply because he'd wanted to spare himself a bit of extra weight.

He picked the bottle up and put it back into the bag before adding the laptop. His phone could go in his pocket. The bag now bulged dangerously, and he couldn't get the zip closed, but at least no one could accuse him of not being prepared for every eventuality.

Jasper shuffled sideways back down the hallway, holding his bag out in front of him so he wouldn't risk knocking anything over. Maybe if that cute blond—what was his name? Oh yes, Lewis. Maybe if Lewis could help him get his hallway clear, then that would be a good start. He didn't need all the rooms, after all. Some were better left blocked off. One in particular. But it never helped to start thinking about Mama again.

No, don't think. Time to get going. Jasper reached the front door and began the increasingly difficult manoeuvre involved in sweeping aside the ever-growing pile of junk mail under the letterbox, opening the door and then insinuating himself through the tiny gap, without causing any of the papers that had built up behind it to fall.

Done. Jasper breathed a huge sigh of relief, his shoulders shaking. He locked the door, ran his hands through his hair and set off down the pathway under the trees.

Had he locked the door? Yes, he was almost certain he had. Better check anyway.

Jasper jiggled the door handle, pleased to see he had in fact locked it as usual, and sauntered down the garden path feeling strangely optimistic. It had been a long time since he'd actually looked forward to seeing someone.

The oddly buoyant feeling was still lingering when Jasper reached the Copper Kettle, and the sight of those two blond heads bent together in his favourite window table made him smile. They reminded him of Easter chicks, all fresh with sun-kissed cheeks like they both spent lots of time outside. Their hair was bright and fluffy too. He wondered if Lewis used dyes or bleach to get that colour. He hoped not. Lewis might look all dapper in his blue shirt and tailored trousers, but he was way too good-looking to need any artificial help.

But if his sister had the same hair, that meant it was natural, right? Well, the pink-and-green streaks in hers clearly weren't, but Lewis was a different matter. Lewis had...class.

Jasper didn't realise he'd been staring through the glass like a kid outside a cake shop until Lewis turned to him and gave a brilliant smile. Carroll beckoned impatiently, the bits of jewellery in her face glinting in the sunshine. It would be hot at that table, but it would make a pleasant change from the perpetual cool of his house.

Jasper was still pondering Lewis's hair when he got inside, which was probably why the first thing he said was, "Your parents should have called you Alice instead. Your hair is just the right colour." Unfortunately, he was still staring at Lewis.

Lewis gave him a bemused smile. "Alice? Are you sure?"

"Oh, I, uh, I saw the van. With the White Rabbit painted on it? I hadn't twigged about your names until then. But no, I meant Carroll, not you."

Carroll rolled her eyes. "Actually, the van's called Alice, and it's my middle name. Mum's got a PhD in Victorian Children's literature. She knows pretty much everything there is to know about Lewis Carroll and his freaky stories."

"I reckon we do too," Lewis chipped in. "They were the only bedtime stories we ever got read to us."

"Not true. I remember *Peter Pan* too."

"Yeah, but that was really weird."

"And *The Water-Babies*." Carroll smirked.

"Must have blocked out that memory."

"You used to love it. I remember, sunshine. I also remember

you stealing my Ken dolls whenever you got a chance."

Lewis gave Jasper a crooked smile, which made one of his cheeks dimple. "He had much better clothes than my Action Man did."

"Yeah, but what about that time I caught you making the two of them—"

"Anyway, we really should be talking about Jasper, shouldn't we?" Lewis interrupted, with a hint of colour to his cheeks.

"I'd prefer to listen to you two," Jasper said, surprised at his honesty. "I mean, I never had a brother or sister."

"Do you have any remaining family?" Lewis asked.

"Not that I'm in contact with." Why did they have to start with that one? Would they change the subject if he didn't volunteer anything else, or would he have to give them something more?

Fortunately Yusef chose that moment to deliver his usual mochaccino with caramel syrup and plate of baklava. "Thanks, Yusef. How're the kids doing?"

"Oh, same old, same old," Yusef replied, tucking his apron over his large belly. "You know teenagers. Don't want to tell their poor old dad anything. Still, at least they're keeping their grades up. Yasmina still has her heart set on dentistry."

Jasper had known the Othmans since the kids were still in nappies, when the recently widowed Yusef had first taken over the café. Jasper had even babysat occasionally when Yusef needed a night out and the usual girl couldn't make it. "What about Derin? Is he still going to be an animator in Hollywood?" You certainly couldn't fault those two kids for ambition. Unlike Jasper himself, who was probably never going to make it past senior librarian and didn't particularly care.

"Oh yes. And apparently I have to buy him some software that costs eight hundred quid just so he can practice. Eight hundred! He's going to be working extra shifts after to pay me back."

When Yusef had returned to his favourite stool at the end of the counter and picked up his latest knitting project, Jasper realised he was being stared at by two pairs of bright blue eyes. He stirred his coffee to have an excuse to drop his gaze. And you had to stir, anyway, or the thick syrup all sank to the bottom and made the last couple of mouthfuls unbearably sweet.

"So, this is a favourite hangout of yours?" Carroll asked.

"I've been coming here ever since it opened. I think that was in... What year did this place open, Yusef?" he called.

"Nineteen ninety-five," Yusef replied, not looking up from his knitting.

"Wow. A genuine twentieth-century establishment," Lewis said.

"I always think of it as more *fin de siècle*," Jasper mused. "There's something about it that comes across as Parisian decadent. I can imagine Toulouse Lautrec and Debussy downing absinthe at the bar."

Yusef snorted. "Wouldn't stock the stuff. It's revolting."

Lewis was staring at Jasper, a quizzical tilt to his eyebrows. "What is it you do for a living, Jasper?"

"Me? Oh, nothing interesting. I'm just a librarian at Bristol University."

"You're a bibliophile, then? I'd say that was pretty interesting. More respectable than clearing people's houses."

"Oi, no one forced you to do this," Carroll said.

"I didn't mean it like that. I'm just saying that being a librarian is a pretty smart job. Especially at the university. Hey, you might even know Mum and Dad. They both lecture at the other place, but I bet they use your library sometimes. It's the best in town, isn't it?"

"We do have a particularly well-stocked literature section," Jasper agreed, "but it concentrates on early literature. Chaucer, Beowulf, that kind of thing." Jasper stirred his drink meditatively and scooped up a spoonful of sweet froth to eat. "Mmm, this is really good. You two should try some." They both had black coffees, he'd noticed, which really wasn't the same thing. Not even with five packets of sugar stirred in, and he didn't see any empty paper packets on the table.

Lewis smiled and raised his espresso. "I'm fine with the pokey stuff, thanks. Now since we've all got to know each other a bit better, how about we talk about why you called us out?"

"Oh, that. Yes, I suppose... Where to begin?"

The siblings exchanged a look. "How about the point when you started noticing your possessions were causing you difficulties?" Lewis asked.

Jasper thought long and hard. "I'm not sure, exactly, but I remember the first winter the radiators stopped working properly. I couldn't get to them to find out if there was a problem with the pipes or if they needed bleeding, so I ended up turning the whole system off."

"And how long ago was that?" Lewis asked.

"Umm, well, it was about..." No, there was no *about*. He knew exactly. It was the third winter after... "It was four years ago," he mumbled to his coffee, and stuffed a baklava in his mouth so he didn't have to say anything else for a moment.

"You've been without central heating for four years?"

Jasper nodded miserably, barely tasting the pistachio-laden pastry as he swallowed it down. "But I have heaters for the rooms I use. Electric ones." When he hadn't been able to reach the plug sockets, he'd ended up using extension cables from the hall sockets. Even those were now blocked off, but at least he had access to a four-socket extension lead in his bedroom, and the kitchen wall sockets above the counter.

"And how many rooms do you still use?"

"Does the hallway count?"

"If you want it to."

"Four. The kitchen, the bathroom, the hallway and my

27

bedroom."

"I see," Lewis said, his tone amazingly patient. "And why did you stop using the other rooms? Those houses must have four bedrooms, surely?"

"Yes, but one of the bedrooms is only a box room. Couldn't fit an actual bed in there, even when it was empty."

"But they're full now?"

Jasper stuffed another baklava in his mouth and nodded.

"Just how full are we talking about?" Carroll asked. The two of them made a great interrogation team. "Is there any floor space left at all?"

"I don't know," Jasper muttered through a mouth full of pastry, before swallowing it down. "I...I can't open the doors. Sometimes piles of books fall over and block the way. Newspapers are even worse. And magazines. I think it's the slippy covers."

"So is most of your hoard paper goods? Or do you collect all kinds of things?"

"Paper, mostly, but I don't exactly collect anything. Not like a proper collector would. It's just stuff that could be handy one day. Books and papers people are throwing out, sometimes. I hate seeing them going to waste."

"So which do you think you're most in need of help with at the moment?" Lewis began. "Learning how to resist bringing more stuff home, or help in getting rid of what you already have?"

Jasper stared down at the crumbs on his plate and ran his finger through a blob of sticky syrup before sucking on it. "Both," he mumbled around his finger, still not daring to look up at their faces in case he saw condescending sympathy. It made him feel so useless, being pitied. This was why he didn't tell anyone. Didn't invite anyone back to the house. "I want a life again," he said, before he lost his nerve. "I want to be able to invite everyone at work around for dinner. And Yusef's family."

Yusef grunted, clearly listening in on every word. "You'll

definitely have to tidy up, then, lad. That place of yours is a disgrace. Why d'you have to carry home so much rubbish every day?"

"I don't know. I don't like things being wasted, that's all."

"I've seen you, poking around in people's recycling bins for newspapers. That stuff's old news. No good to anyone now."

"It might be. You never know what's going to be useful. You don't— You just—" Oh God. Jasper could actually feel his eye twitching. He must look like he was having some kind of fit.

"Hey, it's okay." A hand landed on his. A strong, male hand. Jasper stared at Lewis's fingers lying pale across his own. He froze and let his hand be clasped. "We can help you with this," Lewis continued. "It's what we're good at. We can help you to clear your house, and in the meantime work on some strategies to help you resist bringing new things home."

"I'd like that," Jasper whispered. And before Lewis could pull his hand away, Jasper squeezed tightly.

Lewis returned the pressure, only then letting go of Jasper's hand and picking up his espresso again. Jasper wanted to grab the hand back again, along with all the calm reassurance Lewis offered. The man understood. He was going to help. He risked a quick glance up at Lewis's eyes. So warm and kind. Yes, he could trust a man with eyes like those, couldn't he?

"I have some pictures I'd like you to take a look at," Lewis said in that soothing tone. "Pictures of people's homes, and I'd like you to estimate which is closest to the situation in your house." As he spoke, Lewis laid down a set of eight laminated photographs on the table top between them.

Jasper stared. The pictures were all of cluttered homes, and if you followed them from left to right they read like a history of his own situation, beginning with a room that had too many ornaments, stuff piled on a table and numerous bulging plastic bags tucked into gaps between the furniture, all the way up to a wall of stuff that almost reached the ceiling and carpeted the floor.

He swallowed hard and willed his finger not to tremble as he pointed to the card on the far right. He glanced up briefly, but rather than the disgust he half expected to see on the Millers' faces, they were both nodding as if it was fine.

"It hasn't always been like that," Jasper babbled. Couldn't have them thinking he was entirely hopeless. Especially not Lewis. "A couple of years ago it was only here." He pointed to the situation two cards back, where the walls were only half covered and there was still some floor space. "And about, erm... Well, when Mama was still alive, we were here." He pointed at the first card. The house had always been somewhat cluttered, he realised, but then again, Mama had had so many projects on the go all the time. She'd taken up new hobbies with alarming regularity, and all of them seemed to involve buying, begging or borrowing a significant amount of equipment.

"How long ago did your mother pass away?" Lewis asked, and again, there was a brush of his fingers over Jasper's, as if the man couldn't help reaching out and touching other people. He probably did it with everyone, but even that thought couldn't diminish the comfort Jasper gained from the warmth of his skin.

"Seven years ago. I was twenty-six."

He braced himself for more questions about her, his stomach knotting tightly, but instead Lewis's fingers tapped the photos again. "I'm not sure if you noticed, but these are actually in the wrong order. You see, these are all of the same room. A client of ours. When we first visited it looked like this." He pointed at the most extreme picture. "But over the time we worked with her, she managed to clear it all."

Jasper stared, entranced. Of course. Now it had been pointed out to him, he noticed the features of the room behind the mess. There was the same faded wallpaper and threadbare curtains. The fact the pictures had all been taken from slightly different angles had prevented him from making the connection at first, but now all was revealed, like one of those magic pictures of dots that sprang into 3D when you squinted just right.

Hope clutched at his heart. Could it really be possible to get his home back to something respectable? How did you even begin?

"How long did it take?" he whispered.

"About six months all in, although most of the progress was over the last few weeks. Once she got going, she was ruthless. But that's not all." Lewis smiled a mysterious smile and took another photograph out of his folder. He handed it over to Jasper.

This was laminated like the others, but for a moment, Jasper couldn't see any other connection between the pictures. The living room in this one looked like it had come straight out of one of those fancy interiors magazines, all tastefully coordinated sofa cushions and duck-egg blue walls. Then it hit him.

"No way. Are you really— Are you saying this is..." He couldn't seem to push the words out of him and looked up in mute appeal.

Lewis grinned, his cheeks both dimpling as he flashed his teeth. "It's the same room. She celebrated finishing the job by redecorating. Had both of us round for a meal. It was the first time she'd entertained visitors in over a decade."

The hopeful feeling that had crept up inside Jasper now threatened to choke him. He wanted this. Oh, how he wanted it. And Lewis seemed to be telling him it was within his grasp. All Jasper had to do was work with him. And that would be no hardship, would it? He stared at Lewis's hands just in case he gave himself away. His hands were attractive, slender like those of a musician or artist, but with a wiry strength evident in the corded veins and tendons. He already knew what they felt like on his own hands but had a sudden urge to feel them elsewhere, clutching at his naked flesh.

"So, we need to talk rates and what you can afford," Carroll said, cutting through his pleasant thoughts. "Do you have a particular budget in mind? We generally prefer to work out a weekly sum you can afford and then fit our hours to that, rather than a fixed sum for the whole job."

"Oh, why's that? Everyone else seems happy to give quotes. You know. Plumbers and carpenters."

The Millers shared a look, and Lewis spoke next, his gentle tones calming Jasper's racing brain. "This is a very different sort of service. We're dealing with the vagaries of people's psychological makeup, and all clients vary in how long they need the support. It's not that we're trying to fleece you out of more money, but we discovered early on that if we set a fixed term, many clients wouldn't then begin to make any progress until the time was nearly up. The one in these pictures? Like I said, she only started making significant progress once she realised our sessions were nearly over."

"Are you implying there's a connection? That they were self-sabotaging?"

Lewis seemed to sit up straighter. "What makes you say that?"

"I've done some reading on the subject. I do a lot of reading. Books are kind of..." Could he say it? He glanced up and could only detect kindness in Lewis's gaze. "Books are my life," he confessed.

Lewis nodded slowly, and Jasper gulped back the swell of gratitude that the ready acceptance called up. Stupid, getting emotional over something like that. Lewis would end up thinking he was in need of serious psychological help if he went all drama queen whenever anyone seemed to understand him.

Carroll came to his rescue this time. "You've got a lot of books in your house, then? You already mentioned them before."

"Books, papers, magazines, leaflets..." If it had potentially useful information on it, he'd pick it up and take it home. "You must think I'm cracked."

Carroll chuckled, and the sound was warm just like her brother's voice. "Not at all. You should see the stuff some people hoard. Seriously, paper's good. We like paper. It doesn't smell and it can be recycled. You don't have any pets, do you?"

"No… I don't know. There might be a mouse somewhere, but that doesn't really count as a pet, does it?"

"Shouldn't think so," Lewis said. "Not unless you're intentionally feeding it." Jasper shook his head vehemently. "Good. So, next steps. If you need more time to think through how much you can afford, that's fine, but we're still going to need to come and see what we're dealing with at the house. Can we arrange a time tomorrow for one or the other of us to come and have a look?"

Jasper would have promised him anything right then, but tomorrow was no good. He couldn't let down the library when they were already short staffed. "Sorry. I have to work. Unless… I finish at four on a Thursday. I'm usually back here by five." He held his breath waiting for the dismissal. No one wanted to work at that hour, did they? It was why Jasper had ended up volunteering for three late shifts each week.

Lewis cocked his head to one side. "Five? Sounds doable for me. What about you, Carroll?"

"Nope. I've got my woodcarving class tomorrow evening, but I could do it on Friday morning."

Jasper's gaze shot up to Carroll. Had he imagined the warning tone to her voice? But she was staring back at him with wide, kind eyes. Shame the row of three piercings in the right eyebrow kept distracting him.

"Looks like you've just got me, then." Lewis's voice wrapped around him, just like his hand had earlier. "Don't worry, though. I'm the sensible, responsible twin."

"Twins?" Jasper must have sounded incredulous, because now they were both staring at him with bemused little smiles. "I'm sorry. I just assumed you were younger," he said to Carroll.

"Don't let the piercings fool you. I'm thirty, same as him," she said and winked. "Although Lewis is definitely the mature one in terms of being a boring old fart."

"You look older," he said to Lewis, then realised how that could be taken. "Oh, I'm so sorry. I don't mean in a bad way. Oh pigging hell." Heat crept up Jasper's cheeks. He'd actually assumed Lewis to be older because of his skin, but now he stole a more careful glance, he realised the craggy texture was some kind of scarring.

Lewis smiled, but there was now something guarded about his expression. Crap-crappity-crap. He was probably sensitive about it, wasn't he? Just like Jasper with his stupid bloody twitching eye, which was currently going crazy.

"Christ on a bike, will you look at the time!" Carroll exclaimed, staring at her oversized pink plastic watch. "We've gotta go in a few minutes or I'll be late for archery."

"Oh, I'm so sorry. I didn't mean to make you late. I just... It takes me so long, sometimes, to get out of the house."

"It's fine," Lewis reassured him, and the return of his hand on Jasper's was the calming influence he needed. "We've had enough time to get to know each other, and that's what's important. Now, I usually end the first session by handing out a few worksheets to get you thinking about your attitude towards your possessions. Do you think you'll have time to look at them before tomorrow? I don't need them all filled in, but just reading through the questions should help prepare you for the home visit."

"I can certainly look," Jasper promised. Lewis handed him a fairly thick stack of sheets, but, after flicking through, he could see plenty of blank space to fill in answers. "Yes, more reading matter. Just what I need. You realise you've just added to the sea of paper, don't you?"

"Maybe just keep this in your bag, then. Wouldn't want it to get lost among all the rest." But the way Lewis grinned took any sting out of the words. Okay. It looked like the two of them were fine. No offence taken at Jasper's tactless remarks.

Jasper shook both their hands, surprised by the double hand clasp Lewis used. The man was tactile, that was for sure. Jasper's skin buzzed from the brief contact, and once again he had the urge to grab hold of Lewis and hug him tight. But instead he watched them both head out the door and past the window, Lewis giving him a cute finger wave, and then walked to the counter and wrestled out his wallet.

"I'm not taking your money, *canim*," Yusef said.

"Why not?"

"All this help you're getting. It's expensive, no? So this one's on me, all right?"

"Thanks," Jasper said, nonplussed. In all the years he'd known Yusef, this was the first time he'd refused payment.

"Just don't go expecting it all the time. I have a business to run. Now be off with you before I change my mind."

Jasper grinned and headed out the door. Just a quick stop at the charity shop to check out the books, then he could walk back home and fill out those sheets for Lewis.

Chapter Four

Carroll pulled the van up outside their parents' home. "So, when are you getting the Duchess back on the road, then?"

Lewis gave his beloved dark green Mini Cooper a wistful gaze. "The mechanic said she needed the engine replacing."

Carroll whistled through her teeth. "Shit. That's gotta cost a bomb."

"And then some. He said it would probably be cheaper to buy another old banger."

"But you're not going to."

She knew him so well. "I'd never find another one like her." She was a beauty, built in the early eighties with cream leather upholstery. Not an old banger at all, no matter what the sneering hulk of a mechanic had thought. "I couldn't go from that to a modern car. No way."

"Yeah, but you might be able to get one with more leg room that way."

"The Duchess has plenty of leg room. I prefer her being snug and cosy."

Carroll huffed. "I swear, you're getting as bad as a hoarder. You know that's what Albert said to me last week? That the piles of stuff made him feel cosy. I said he should try moving into that sheltered accommodation they offered him. That'd be plenty cosy enough, what with only having three small rooms."

"Carroll! I was working on that. You could have set me right back."

"Take a chill pill, bro. He laughed. He likes me. Thinks I'm full of spunk, apparently." She imitated old Albert's nasal Aussie intonation perfectly, even pulling one of his apparently innocent smiles. Quite a feat, considering Carroll hadn't been even remotely innocent for a very long time. "I've no idea how he could tell I'd breakfasted on Matt."

"Shut up!" Lewis grinned despite himself. "Thought I was meant to be the one making gross jokes."

"Yeah, well, since you never do, someone has to keep up the side. Besides, I'm older."

"By a whole twenty minutes."

Carroll shrugged. "Makes all the difference, apparently."

She had a point. When they'd been growing up, Carroll had always been the first to find things out. While Lewis had been a good boy, working hard at school and keeping his nose clean, she'd been the one gossiping and hanging out with the wrong crowd. The wrong crowd turning out to be the right crowd if it was illicit information you were after. Fortunately for him, Carroll had passed on all the juiciest titbits, sneaking into his bedroom after lights out and scandalising him with her talk of deep throating, butt plugs and rimming. At first he'd been shocked to discover it was the talk of men doing things to each other that gave him a deliciously squirmy feeling inside, but having liberal academics as parents meant neither of them had any ingrained homophobia.

Indeed, it had been a shock to Lewis to discover that others did. He wished he'd realised just how deep it ran in some of his peers before announcing he was gay to his whole class. Still, what did twelve-year-olds know about the way the world worked? In hindsight, he'd been glad to be out and proud at school, even if it had exposed him to some merciless teasing and occasional roughing up. Nothing too bad, though. Cotham Grammar just hadn't been that kind of school. Besides, it was character building or something. That's what his mum had always told him whenever he complained, anyway.

"Thinking about Jasper, are we?" Carroll said, a smile lurking behind her deadpan expression.

"No. Should I be?" Of course, now Carroll mentioned him, Lewis's head filled with memories of just how handsome his teenage crush had turned out.

"Well, he is our newest client so yeah, I reckon you should be thinking about him. Lots. Probably obsessing about him, knowing you."

"I don't obsess about our clients."

"Really? Could have fooled me. You definitely obsess about your boyfriends, anyway."

"Jasper isn't ever going to be my boyfriend," Lewis insisted.

Carroll arched her eyebrows, making her piercings glint. "He couldn't keep his eyes off you."

"He barely made eye contact."

"Maybe, but he kept looking at your hands—especially when you grabbed his. Hardly spared mine a glance, and with all the effort I made." Carroll waggled her habitually bitten nails and pouted, although she couldn't hide the dimples that gave her away. "A girl could feel hurt."

Lewis snorted. "The princess thing really doesn't suit you, sis."

Carroll's expression reverted back to its usual cheeky smirk. "Okay, but you have to admit, he wanted you to come and do the home visit. That's got to mean something."

"What it means," Lewis said, opening the door to get away from the direction the conversation was taking, "is that I'll have to be on my guard against our client forming any kind of inappropriate attachment to me. If he does, I'll have to hand him over to you."

"Yeah, right. Well, I'm ready to take over whenever. Face it, bro, you'll be packing your bags and moving in with him as soon as you've got his place livable."

"Bye, sis. See you tomorrow morning." He stepped down from

the van and closed the door firmly. Not firmly enough, though, and he ended up having to open it again before doing the old slam-jiggle trick. "Speaking of getting vehicles serviced, this old heap of junk is in dire need of some TLC."

"Nah. Alice is fine. You just have to know how to treat her right." Carroll revved the engine and shot him a bright smile through the window. "Oh, and bro, if you dream of Jasper tonight, make sure you show him a good time."

Lewis shook his head. "I'm not that cheap. He'd have to wait till the second date at least."

Carroll stuck out her tongue, flashing the silver stud there. The van peeled away on squealing rubber, drawing disapproving glances from a couple of yummy mummies in designer track suits jogging along behind their three-wheeled baby strollers. Lewis gave them an apologetic shrug and turned to the house.

Another night alone in front of the telly while his parents were gadding about. Why, yes, there really was something wrong with this picture.

However, when Lewis pulled the front door open, he was assaulted by mariachi music playing at full volume, and the familiar scent of pan-fried chillies. He tried sneaking past the open kitchen door, but his dad's hearing was uncannily sharp.

"Lewis! Hey, fancy trying some of this? I need a willing victim."

Lewis stuck his head around the door to find his dad naked except for a frilly apron, holding out a wooden spoon full of something dark and evil looking.

"Is it going to take all the skin off the inside of my throat like that last lot did?"

"Oh, don't be such a baby. And no, these are only habaneros in here, so you should be fine."

Only Alan Miller could refer to habaneros like they were baby food.

Lewis stepped into the room. "What is it?"

"Chocolate-and-lime truffle mix."

"With chillies in."

"Of course. Come on, taste it. I need to road test whether it's going to work for Christmas presents for the history department."

"Christmas? Dad, I don't know if it's escaped your notice, seeing as how you keep the heating on full blast all year round, but it's June right now."

His dad just folded his arms smugly. "What can I say? Organisation is my middle name."

"I thought you were called Alan 'Shameless-naked-chilli-fiend' Miller."

"Nice one. Stick a professor on the front of that, and I think I'll have it on a plaque on my office door. Now come on, give it a try."

Lewis screwed up his nose and touched his tongue to the gooey mixture. "Okay, it's passed the first test. No third-degree burns just yet."

His dad looked at the ceiling as if to say, w*hat did I do to deserve a son like you!* so Lewis girded his loins and scraped a small mouthful off the spoon with his teeth. He'd learned the hard way not to get his dad's concoctions on his lips if he could possibly help it. The velvety chocolate melted over his tongue.

"Actually, that's all raa-a-a-arrgh!" His mouth on fire and his eyes watering, Lewis ran to the sink and stuck his head under the tap. He fumbled with the mixer until cool water began flowing, washing the devil's own truffle mix off his tongue.

When he'd just about recovered the use of his tongue, Lewis turned round to find his dad waiting with a towel, a decidedly sheepish smile on his face. Lewis took it and dried his face.

"So, still too hot, then?"

"You could say that. Dad... I know it goes against everything you believe in, but how about you make some Christmas truffles without any chilli in them? Most people haven't destroyed all their capsicum receptors like you have."

"Nonsense. Chilli and chocolate are the perfect combination. I just need to get the dosage right. I'll halve it in the next batch."

"Or how about starting with just a tiny bit and working your way up?"

"Now, now, Lewis my boy. Where's the fun in that?"

"It's fun to burn the roof of your mouth off?"

On his way to the stairs, Lewis passed the lounge door and peered in. His mum was lying on the sofa, reading a book. Could have been like anyone else's scene of domestic harmony, if it weren't for the fact she was stark naked and reading a book called *Hellenism and Homosexuality in Victorian Oxford.*

"Hey, Mum, I thought you were going out tonight," he said when she finally noticed him standing there.

"Oh, there you are, darling. Yes, we were meant to, but Shona McBride ended up muscling in on it, and I just couldn't face spending any more time with her and her sense of self-righteous indignation." Shona was an up-and-coming lecturer in Gender Studies and his mum's main rival for head of department when the current incumbent retired at the end of the year. "She's civilly partnered to a disabled Indonesian woman. How am I meant to keep hold of my liberal credentials with only one gay son in the family? I'm considering taking on a girlfriend to bolster my languishing bisexual identity. I'm sure your dad wouldn't mind."

"I so hope you're joking."

She winked at him. "I'd let him watch."

"Mum!"

"Don't you *mum* me. It makes me feel old. Anyway, if you don't want me to do anything disgracefully bohemian, you'll have to help me out. How about Brandon? Is he single yet?"

"I don't think so. He's still with Jos, last I heard." Lewis should call Brandon, he knew. It was a challenge to keep friendships going sometimes when relationships interfered, and Brandon and Jos were tighter than a pair of shrink-to-fit Levis.

41

"Oh. Shame. You'd look adorable together. And I know for a fact the board choosing the next head of department has a healthy mix of ethnicities and sexualities represented. They're like a multicoloured QUILTBAG explosion. Alan and I look like a couple of middle-aged, middle-class fuddy-duddies in comparison. Keeping my maiden name is so old hat. I need something new to impress them."

"You could always try turning up to work starkers and seeing how that goes down," he teased.

"Don't think I haven't considered it."

Lewis stared in openmouthed horror.

"Oh, don't give me that look. There's nothing wrong with the naked human form." She gestured down at her body, and Lewis couldn't help his eyes tracking the motion. He shuddered. There were some things a man shouldn't have to know about his mother, and whether or not she shaved her pubes was one of them.

Best change the subject before she really did take his suggestion seriously. "I'm not going to start a relationship with someone just to improve your chances of being promoted."

"No, of course not. It's just you're the kind of man who needs someone in his life. And I've always liked Brandon. Nice boy. Very...committed to social causes." Her face brightened. "How's about you just invite him around next time I have a dinner party? You don't have to actually kiss him or anything. Just, you know, make out you're in an open relationship or something. Or a ménage with this other man. He could come too. Actually, yes, that's a fabulous plan. Polyamory is so in right now. I could invite a few gossips from the uni, and word would soon get out."

"I'm not going to lie for you."

"Oh, come on. It wouldn't be the first time. What about that Christmas when you pretended to have chicken pox just so we could get rid of Alan's awful brother?"

"You still owe me for that!" His parents had been so

uncomfortable after having to spend an entire week clothed around the house, they'd staged an elaborate ruse to send Uncle Rudi back to Australia a whole two weeks early. It had involved some brilliant makeup work from his mum and a fair bit of play-acting from Lewis. Carroll had refused point blank to waste a day of her Christmas holiday sitting around in bed, but Lewis had always gone along with things to keep the peace.

"Just have a think about it anyway. You don't want your poor old mother languishing on a lecturer's salary for the rest of her career, do you?"

The sad thing was, Lewis would probably end up agreeing if it weren't for the fact Brandon would almost certainly refuse. "Night, Mum," Lewis said, shutting the door firmly behind him.

As he climbed the stairs he wondered, not for the first time, how he'd managed to survive growing up with his sanity pretty much intact.

He could do it. He could throw something away all by himself.

Jasper sat up in bed and stared resolutely at the walls of stuff around him. He'd read through the worksheets Lewis had given him the previous night and rated his attitude to various aspects of hoarding. As far as he could tell, he had difficulties related to both acquiring and letting go of objects. Letting go of them seemed the obvious place to start, though. He absolutely had to clear some more space in the house, and after the first good night's sleep he'd had in a long time, he felt ready to start.

He'd begun piling up fiction in the bedroom, as it seemed like the sensible place, seeing as how he loved reading in bed. Unfortunately, now the stacks of paperbacks surrounded his bed on all sides. He couldn't get to his wardrobe, so he kept his current collection of clothing piled on the end of his bed. In winter, he could pull it up over him like an extra blanket, but in summer, it was a liability, prone to getting tangled around his feet. Some nights he'd give up on the stuffy room and go and sleep outside in the hammock. Waking up in the garden to the sound of birdsong was always a great way to start the day, even if he did invariably end up with a crick in his neck.

But this morning he was glad he'd spent the night up here, because now he was in the perfect position to choose something to throw away. A book. Surely he could get rid of one book. Not throw it away, of course, but pass it on to another reader. Perhaps he could find something Lewis might like to borrow.

No, not borrow. Have. *Keep.* A gift. Jasper could give something away. Of course he could.

The stacks next to the left-hand side where he slept were all twentieth-century classics, and he'd read every single last one of them. If he wasn't so sure of a book's literary merit, it ended up on the other side of the room until he'd had a chance to read it and make his decision. There were many more books on that side, it had to be admitted. Books that he ended up classifying as light genre reads made their way out onto the landing, seeing as how he'd completely filled the spare bedroom with them a few years back.

Jasper picked up Heller's *Catch 22* and read the blurb. The memory of Yossarian's wartime exploits filtered back in flashes of colour, but he could no longer remember the whole storyline. No, not that one, then. Not until he'd had another chance to read it and fix it in his memory.

Ulysses presented the same problem, as did *The Sound and the Fury*. Even EM Forster's *Maurice*—a book he must have read at least five times during his teens and which had helped him in so many ways—was little more than a frustrating set of isolated images and feelings. What the hell was wrong with his mind?

It would have to be one from the other side of the room. But when he crawled across the bed and examined the first stack, Jasper knew it was futile. How could he possibly decide to get rid of a book he hadn't yet read? There could be useful information in there. Even the most unpromising-looking books contained hidden nuggets of truth and beauty.

Even Jeffery Archer must have his good points, although he couldn't think of one off the top of his head.

For a moment, Jasper seriously considered offering Lewis a copy of Stephen King's *The Stand*, as he was sure he'd seen it somewhere else in the house at some point. But who was to say Lewis would appreciate being offered a brick-sized tome of post-apocalyptic weirdness? No, safer to wait until Jasper had read it first, and then he could decide whether or not it would suit Lewis. He wouldn't want to give the man nightmares.

Perhaps not a book, then. A magazine? Or a newspaper? But no one in their right mind would give one of those as a gift. Lewis would sneer at him, Jasper was sure of it. He'd never realise just what it had cost Jasper to lose even one paltry magazine.

As the familiar headache started up behind his eyes, Jasper gave up on the task. Better just get washed and dressed, then head into work. At least he could promise himself not to bring any more magazines home today, couldn't he?

Yes, that would be something. An achievement, of sorts.

The bitter irony that his biggest achievement of the day would lie in not doing something didn't escape him, however, and Jasper's steps were heavy as he negotiated the crowded trail between his bedroom and the bathroom.

Chapter Five

By the afternoon, Jasper's mood had lifted—the result of a happy couple of hours in the back room entering new books into the system. He loved that job, with its comforting ritual of entering the data on the computer. And best of all, he got to open the boxes to unleash the scent of fresh books. Being the first one to lift them out of the packaging was always a buzz. This particular supplier used the concertina-cut cardboard packaging, which he always found pleasing. It might not have the fun potential of bubble wrap, but he loved the way they could turn a waste material into something useful simply by scoring a lattice of cuts into it.

He was using a letter opener to carefully slice open the tape holding the packing paper around a book from the final box, when Brenda shuffled over to his desk, her arms weighed down by a stack of periodicals that reached her chin.

"Got some room there, love?" she asked, dumping the papers on his desk before he'd had a chance to respond. "These are all on their way out. Would you mind? I'm meeting Imogen for coffee, and I'm already late. Don't want her thinking I've stood her up."

"No, that's fine. I'll take them out when I've finished this lot." It was a short walk across the quad to get to the university's recycling facilities, but he knew how much Brenda hated even that much exercise. It wasn't that she was overweight or anything, but she had the lifelong bookworm's instinctive distrust of anything approaching physical exertion. Jasper seemed to be the anomaly among his coworkers, what with his love of running.

"You are a sweetheart." Brenda leaned over the desk and kissed Jasper on the forehead. "How come you're still single, eh? Bet I could find you a good man if you'd let me know what you're after."

"How about someone who loves all the same books I do, who can quote Shakespeare, and who doesn't mind the state of my house?"

"Could be doable. How bad is your house anyway? Can't be worse than Immi's. That girl's a total pig."

Jasper just shrugged, remembering the spread of photographs Lewis had laid out on the table. No, there was no chance of anyone sticking around once they'd seen his place. That's why it was safer to stick to online hook-ups. He'd always made it clear in advance it had to be at their place rather than his. Most of them probably thought he was cheating on a partner at home, but that was infinitely preferable to them discovering the truth.

Just lately, though, he'd been sticking to seeing Mas, a young man with a big smile who was an energetic and enthusiastic bottom. It wasn't that Jasper was particularly toppy, and he certainly didn't want to be the sugar daddy Mas was searching for. It was more that he hadn't wanted to go through that whole rigmarole of sounding someone new out first. At least he liked Mas, and they were mostly compatible in bed.

"I'm happy with my life the way it is." He crossed his arms and glared at Brenda.

She was still studying him, her arms folded on the top of the magazine pile. The woman clearly couldn't take a hint. "Hmm, give me a bit of time to test the waters, and I'll see who I can find."

"I'm fine with being a bachelor. Books are better company than people. They don't hog the bedclothes or mess with your things."

Brenda just gave him an infuriatingly smug smile. "Ah, well, you say that now, but how would you know if you just haven't met the right bloke yet? He's out there. And I'm going to find him for you. Ciao for now, babes." She blew him a kiss as she trotted off towards the library's main exit.

What was it with the happily coupled woman's urge to matchmake? Since she'd paired up with Imogen, Brenda had gone from engagingly cynical about love to the world's soppiest romantic. Actually, it wasn't just the women either. One of the engineering postgrads had been in the other day threatening to set up a blind date for Jasper with some mate of his boyfriend's. Did Jasper have a sign on his forehead saying "lonely" or something?

He wasn't lonely all the time. He could forget about it for hours while running or reading. And he didn't need a boyfriend to satisfy his need for intimate contact either. Jasper pulled out his mobile and texted Mas, asking *Are you free tonight after eight?* Mas could be relied on for a no-complications shag at his city-centre flat. It was simpler that way. Simpler than messy emotional entanglements.

No. He definitely didn't need to get embroiled in some relationship where someone expected too much of him. Wanted him to open up and share things.

He was never going to show anyone the guilt eating him up inside.

Five minutes later, his phone buzzed. He checked the message inbox.

8 is gd, but just a quickie im gng out.

No expectations. No mess. Shame the prospect of a quick and dirty encounter with Mas didn't excite him nearly as much as just the rub of Lewis's fingers across his had done.

Friday brought a long morning of clearing the Lehrmans' place, which involved Lewis and Carroll getting all hot and sweaty parading a bunch of junk past the elderly siblings while they sat outside in camping chairs, and the Lehrmans deciding they couldn't possibly live without any of it. Actually, that wasn't fair. Gladys Lehrman was ready to let things go now. It was her stubborn brother who refused. It was no coincidence that this was the man who also refused to stick around for the counselling sessions.

Frustrated, Lewis decided to spend his afternoon off at the pool, swimming length after length. He became so absorbed in the hypnotic glide through the water that he lost track of time, only glancing up at the clock at half three.

Crap. He'd been meaning to get home and change into something more attractive before heading out to Jasper's place, but it looked like he'd end up late if he did. Lewis hurried through to the changing rooms and did his best to wash the smell of chlorine off his skin before throwing back on the plain old T-shirt and cargo shorts combo. He looked a bit like a GAP model with his chunky leather sandals, but it couldn't be helped. Anyway, he wasn't trying to impress Jasper with his natty dress-sense, was he? The man probably didn't even notice clothes. You only had to take one look at Jasper's rumpled, mismatched wardrobe to figure that out.

The bus dropped Lewis off at the bottom of the hill, and it was a long walk up with the late afternoon sun beating on his back and the day's stored heat radiating off the tarmac. By the time he reached number sixty-four, it was a relief to be able to slip under the cool green shade of those overgrown trees. Jasper could have a beautiful garden if he cleared the place up a bit.

As to how much of a challenge awaited them inside... Well, that remained to be seen. Lewis rubbed his hands together and knocked on the door.

No one came. Lewis checked his watch. Yep, he was on time. Just how long could it take Jasper to negotiate the junk in his house? He rapped on the door harder this time. He even tried stepping back to call to the upstairs windows, but one look at them made him realise the futility of Jasper hearing anything that way. Both sets of curtains were pressed back against the glass with the weight of whatever lay behind them. Mildew had stained the linings, and more of the green algae that coated everything in the garden grew up the glass.

This could end up being one of his toughest challenges yet. Perhaps an insurmountable one, if Jasper was too nervous to show for the appointments.

Unless he just couldn't get to the door. What if he was trapped under a pile of fallen paper? It happened. Hoarders died that way every year. Admittedly, it was mostly the elderly who didn't have the strength to dig themselves out again, but even a young and healthy man like Jasper could be in serious trouble if enough heavy stuff went over.

Paper was heavy stuff.

Keeping the panic at bay with decisive action, Lewis forced open the letter box and called for Jasper. He held his ear to the gap but couldn't hear any response from within. He was just wrestling his phone out of his pocket to try the man's mobile, when a voice from behind him made him jump.

"I'm sorry. I'm so sorry. There were road works in town and a huge traffic jam, and I got stuck outside Cabot Circus for twenty minutes. I should have rung, I know, but I don't like to use my phone in the car. I mean, I know everyone else does, but the law is the law, even when you're not moving. I hope you didn't get put off by what you can see through the letterbox. It's better in the kitchen, I promise." As he babbled, Jasper shuffled closer, his keys held out in front of him almost like a weapon he was afraid to use. Lewis realised what his pose must have looked like.

"I wasn't looking; I was listening. I thought maybe you might..." His face heated as he continued. It sounded silly, with Jasper standing in front of him, all vibrant eyes and nervous twitches. "Sometimes people get trapped in their houses when things fall over. I wanted to make sure you weren't in there, needing help."

For a moment, he thought Jasper might bristle, might feel patronised, but instead a smile broke slowly across his face, tilting the corners of his eyes in a way that made Lewis's heart flip. "Oh.

Thanks." The sincere way he said it suggested maybe he wasn't used to having people look out for him, and once again, Lewis found himself wondering just how many friends the man really had.

"Not a problem," he said gruffly, still a little embarrassed at having been caught out. "It's just one of my recurring dreams. Being buried under an avalanche of stuff."

"You have nightmares too?"

"Don't we all?"

"I don't know. I thought you seemed so...together. Not like me." Jasper took a step closer, and Lewis could smell him then. A hint of soap mingled with a larger dose of sweat. But fresh sweat, so not unpleasant. Not by a long stretch.

Lewis's eyes drifted closed for a moment to better concentrate on Jasper's scent. Lulled by the drowsy heat and the distant buzz of traffic, he drifted for a moment, almost content.

Then his eyes sprang open. Jasper was closer now, staring down at him with a quizzical tilt to his left eyebrow. For a breathless moment, he held eye contact, and Lewis could make out the flecks of amber in his eyes. They were like a glass of dark rum held up to the sunlight, rich colours swirling within.

"Are you okay?" Jasper asked.

"Fine, fine. Sorry. I was up late last night. Probably should have got more sleep." Now why did he say that? He didn't want Jasper thinking he was some kind of party animal. "I mean, I was up playing Trivial Pursuit with my folks; then the heat stopped me sleeping." What a wild life he led.

"Oh yes, I know. Sometimes I have to sleep in the hammock. Can't open any of the windows in the house," Jasper added, his eyes darting away again in their habitual dance.

The house. "Are you ready to show me the inside now?"

Jasper folded his arms around himself, and for a moment, Lewis expected a negative. But when it came, although quietly voiced, the "yes" sounded firm and sure.

It was only when Jasper stepped around him to unlock the front door that Lewis noticed the triangle of sweat turning the back of his faded shirt a darker shade of green. Nerves, or simply a result of the heat?

The lock seemed to give Jasper some trouble, but after a few muttered curses, it opened a foot or so, and Jasper slipped through the narrow gap. "Come on in," he called from inside.

It was a good thing Lewis was slim. As it was, he had to brush against the table piled high with junk mail sitting just inside the door. A pile of envelopes slid to the floor. A floor that was carpeted with more of them. As Lewis raised his gaze, he commanded his face to stay expressionless. After the number of cluttered homes he'd seen in his eight years working with Carroll, very little still shocked him, but he'd learned to be careful.

He was glad he had.

The hallway was dark, but enough green-tinged light filtered in through the stained glass above the door for him to see the brooding stacks of books that lined both sides of the narrow corridor. Ahead of him were two paths to take: on the left was a passageway towards the back of the house, on the right, a staircase. The staircase appealed the most as a shaft of sunshine lit the upper risers, but the path up was obstructed by yet more books. Dog-eared paperbacks with lurid covers sat next to plastic-covered textbooks. There were old, leather-bound spines butted up next to ones that looked like they hadn't yet been cracked. Like the corridor, both sides of the staircase had been conquered by the books, so that only a foot or so of clear wooden boards were on show in the middle.

Jasper Richardson's home looked like it had had the entire contents of a library jammed into it for temporary storage, and the Dewey decimal classification system had been utterly abandoned.

Lewis scanned the room again, noticing how high the stacks had reached. Not quite up to the picture rail, and he could see the tops of some frames peeking out above the makeshift book skyscrapers. There was even an old-fashioned wooden coat stand lurking back there, with an incongruous lacy pink scarf just visible. Somehow he couldn't see Jasper as a cross-dresser. The wallpaper behind them was covered in blowsy roses, and from the texture, it looked like expensive stuff.

"So was it your mother who decorated the place originally?" Lewis asked, pleased at how matter-of-fact his voice sounded. Jasper started visibly, but in the dim light, all Lewis could make out behind his glasses was a dark shadow.

"No, well, er, yes. But I don't remember mentioning that to you." Jasper's eye started twitching. The motion of that, at least, was visible in the gloom.

"You didn't in so many words," Lewis soothed. "I just couldn't see you picking out that wallpaper, that's all."

"Oh! No, of course. Well, I expect it probably needs replacing by now. Not that I imagine I'd ever be able to decide on a design. Or even a simple sodding paint colour. And that's if we ever manage to get this lot under control." He cast a woeful look around him and his shoulders slumped, as if the house was sapping him of all his excess nervous energy. Clutter could do that to you if you let it take over.

"It's *when* we get it beaten, not *if.* You'll see." Lewis rubbed his hands together as if relishing the notion of getting going, although even he had to admit a hoard of this scale was daunting. "Right, then, how about you show me the other rooms first, and in the meantime you can start thinking about where in the house you'd like us to start."

"Down here," Jasper said, so emphatically Lewis blinked in surprise.

"Okay, that makes sense. Getting this clear first will make it much easier to work on the other rooms."

Jasper nodded, but something in his facial expression didn't sit right. He appeared relieved, which could be explained simply by Lewis's approval, but the pinched look remaining around his eyes suggested he was hiding something.

Still, there would be plenty of time to discover all Jasper's little secrets once they got working on the house together.

"I'll take you to the kitchen first," Jasper said, turning to shuffle his way to the back of the house through the drifts of junk mail. They rustled like autumn leaves, making Lewis shiver. Watching his footing carefully, he followed.

The kitchen wasn't quite as bad as the hallway had led him to expect. To the right of the main doorway was a U-shaped kitchen that had mostly escaped the tide of paper. That wasn't to say that the worktops weren't full of random utensils and items that would normally live elsewhere in a house, like a tool kit and a laundry basket, but at least the floor was clear and the area around the gas hob and sink bore evidence of recent cooking. Lewis took a cautious breath, but the room smelled acceptable, if a little musty. Clearly he wasn't dealing with a rotten-food hoarder, thank God.

The other side of the room was more like the hallway, but this time with piles of newspapers rather than books. A wooden dining table was half buried in the melee, with three of the visible chairs piled high with yet more papers, but the end of it was clear, and an empty chair sat there. Beyond the table lay the door onto the back garden, and through the dirty pane, Lewis could see a jungle of plants and riotous flowers.

"This would be the periodicals room, then," he quipped, holding his hand over a paper from the nearest pile just to gauge Jasper's reaction. "Mind if I pick it up?"

Jasper frowned. "Of course not. Why would I?"

"Just checking your boundaries. Some hoarders are so protective of their stuff, they don't even like me touching it. To begin with, anyway. It's often the first thing we have to work on together."

"Oh. I'm not like that. It's fine for you to pick up anything you see. Just make sure you put it back in the same place, that's all I ask."

"It would bother you if things were out of place?"

"I have a system. I know it probably doesn't look like it, but I do."

Jasper sounded so defensive, Lewis decided to change the subject. He glanced at the paper in his hand but couldn't even make out the title as it was all written in those crazy Arabic squiggles. "Can you even read this?"

"Only a little. I'm afraid I'm rather rusty now. It's one of the more left-wing Egyptian papers, I know that much."

Okay, that was unexpected. Lewis examined the paper some more, noting the red ink stamp from the university library. "Did you grow up in Egypt?"

"No. What makes you think that?"

"You look like you might have some Middle Eastern ancestry."

"My mother was Egyptian," Jasper muttered, so low Lewis had to strain his ears.

"But I'm guessing your father was British, then. From the surname," he added, when faced with a blank gaze.

"Oh. Yes, of course. Sorry. I thought maybe...maybe you knew something about me. I don't know. Maybe you did research or something."

"I haven't been snooping into your past. Don't worry. I'll rely purely on what you decide to tell me when you're ready. But I do have one confession to make. We've met before."

"We have?" Jasper closed the space between them, staring down the two or so inches he had on Lewis. "No. I'd remember someone like you. Your hair..." He reached out his hand as if to touch, then withdrew it suddenly. "I'd remember," he maintained, a stubborn set to his jaw.

"It was a long time ago, and maybe saying we met is stretching it. I was at Cotham Grammar too. Three years below you. That's probably why you never noticed me." Lewis gave a mirthless laugh. "Even if I was the favourite topic of gossip in my year." First for being out and sort-of-proud, then for the whole shagging-the-drama-teacher scandal, which had never been as hushed up as the headmistress had imagined, despite Mr. C being relocated to another school way up north.

"I never listened to gossip," Jasper muttered. "No, wait. Hang on. I remember... I do remember a blond boy. Always neatly turned out. Wore one of those AIDS ribbons on his blazer. Kind of..." He mimed a swooshing fringe over his forehead. "Kind of foppish hair."

Lewis grimaced. "Yep. That was me. Used to straighten my curls back then. Not my most flattering hairstyle, it has to be said."

"That was you?" The amazement in Jasper's voice made Lewis look up. He'd stepped forward again, and all Lewis's body prickled with the awareness of how close he was standing to his teenage heartthrob.

"I didn't think you'd ever noticed me."

"How could I not have?" Jasper's hands twitched, wanting to grab hold of Lewis, so he shoved them into his armpits instead. "You were... You were my hero."

Chapter Six

Silence crowded them, jostling into the space between their bodies. Jasper squeezed his eyes shut. What had he just said? Oh God, Lewis was going to think he was completely hopeless when he explained himself. He cracked his eyes open to find Lewis gazing up at him, the glimmer of a smile haunting his face. Lewis wasn't going to laugh at him, was he? Jasper didn't think he could bear it if he was mocked.

Lewis tilted his head to one side. "Your hero?" he murmured. "I've never done anything remotely heroic."

"You were out when you were at school. I'd call that pretty heroic."

"I don't know. If I'd realised how it was going to go down, I might have kept my big mouth shut for a few more years."

"I'm glad you didn't."

"You are?"

Could he say this? Jasper turned away to face his kitchen, but all he could see was the defiant face of a fifteen-year-old Lewis walking past a bunch of sniggering lads with his head held high, despite the taunts of "gaylord" and "poofter". Someone had even drawn a crude cock and balls on the back of his blazer in chalk, and Jasper had wanted to run down the language block steps and tell him. To help him rub the offending picture off. To tell him he wasn't the only queer at school.

Jasper hadn't fallen in love at first sight or anything. As a teenager, Lewis had been all bones and awkward posture, his face blighted with acne. No, Jasper hadn't even fancied him back then— not like he did now. The scarring on his tanned cheeks gave him a rugged, outdoorsy look, like an explorer in one of the adventure books Jasper had devoured as a child. And like those heroic men, Lewis had grown into his body and gave an impression of great energy held in calm reserve.

No, back then Jasper hadn't found the teenaged Lewis attractive, but he'd felt an instant rapport. A recognition of another who was like him.

Or perhaps not like him, because Lewis was ever so much braver than Jasper had ever been.

Time to emulate that bravery and come clean.

"I didn't notice you until the last few months of my A-levels. Never did find out your name. And I don't remember Carroll. Was she at a different school or something?"

"Nope. But we didn't spend much time together back then. She was usually out in the car park getting stoned with all her weirdo mates."

"Ah, I see. And you weren't like that."

"Neither were you."

"I was a nerd," Jasper said decisively. "Teachers' pet. No friends. Always had my head in a book. I only noticed you because I was on my way to the library one day and I saw you had this...er, this giant pink cock and balls. On your back!" he squeaked, at Lewis's mischievous smile. "Someone had chalked it on your back."

"I would say I remember that day, but it happened a few times, so I can't be sure which it was."

"Well, this bunch of lads were making fun of you outside the language block, but you just carried on walking with your head held high. One of them asked you to, er, service him." Oh God, he sounded like such a prude. The swaggering thug in question had in fact ordered Lewis to suck his cock like a bitch, since he was a one of them dirty benders. "You told him you wouldn't touch his nob if he paid you because you didn't know where he'd been sticking it."

Lewis's grin spread all over his face. "I think I might have put it more crudely than that, but yeah, I remember now. You were watching?"

"I was watching. You were so brave. I couldn't have done that. Couldn't have told anyone. That I was gay, I mean."

"There's no reason why you should have. Everyone comes out when it feels right for them. Hey, it's okay. There's no rule book for these things."

"Maybe there should be," Jasper said, surprised at his own ferocity. "I mean, it might have been easier to know what to do then. I left it way too late. Especially with Mama."

Lewis laid his hand on top of Jasper's. "But you told her in the end, didn't you?"

Oh, he'd told her, all right. The expression on her face still haunted his nightmares. She'd come round after a few days and told him it was fine, and she didn't mind really, but it could never erase the memory of her devastation. "I waited until she was having a good spell. I'd somehow convinced myself she'd take it okay. But she went downhill again after that. Barely got out of bed again from then on."

"She was ill?"

"Leukaemia. She'd had it for a while. It started getting bad when I was in my late teens. Dad died when I was a kid, so I was her sole carer. It's why I never moved away." He could say it in such a matter-of-fact tone now. He'd almost convinced himself it hadn't hurt like hell to give up all his dreams of moving to a new city. Somewhere he'd have been able to start afresh and be someone different. Someone confident and proud of who he was.

Instead, he'd stayed here and stagnated.

"Was she a hoarder herself?" Lewis asked, the question surprising Jasper, even though he probably should have expected it. That was what Lewis was here for, wasn't it? Talking about Jasper's hoarding problem. Not going over their schooldays.

"She had lots of stuff. Not books. Hobbies. Crafts. That kind of thing."

"And is that all still here, behind your stuff?"

How did Lewis know these things? Jasper nodded mutely.

"It's probably going to be tough on you when we get things cleared back to that stratum. All hoarders react differently, but all of them find it emotionally draining."

"Why are you telling me this? Sounds like you're trying to put me off."

"I just want you to go into this with your eyes open. It will be difficult, and you'll need to be brave, but you can do it, I know."

"You don't know anything about me really. I'm not brave. I'm a coward. Always have been."

"I don't know. You've taken the first step and admitted you have a hoarding issue. That takes guts. Asking for help takes even more."

"I spent weeks with your number programmed into my phone." Jasper exhaled an almost-laugh at the memory of his vacillations. "Every day I'd look at it at least five times, daring myself to touch the screen. In the end it was the book slide in the living room that made me call. I just couldn't bear living like this anymore."

"I'm glad you did call," Lewis said, smiling just as a shaft of sunlight lanced in through the back door glass and lit up his face. His eyes glowed like a pool of water, small flecks of lighter and darker blues in his iris only adding to the effect. Everything about Lewis looked wholesome and outdoorsy, from his sun-bleached hair to the light tan across the bridge of his nose. In comparison, Jasper felt sallow and drawn, even though he knew his skin was actually darker than Lewis's.

"Did you want to see the back garden?" Jasper asked. Lewis would fit in just right there. He was all wrong surrounded by the stacks of unread paper. "It's kind of stuffy in here."

"Sounds great."

Jasper led the way to the back door and opened it onto

brilliant sunshine. There were trees in the back garden too, but fortunately they were dwarf fruit trees and planted far enough away from the house not to shade it out. There was a shallow veranda along the back, something his dad had apparently added to make Mama feel more at home after moving to England. Between that, sheltering them from the view of the neighbour's upstairs windows, and the high stone walls overgrown with plants, it was an intensely private place.

Out of the corner of his eye he saw Lewis step next to him and pull a bottle of water out of his bag.

"Oh, I'm so sorry. I didn't offer you a drink. Where are my manners?"

Lewis took a long swig, then offered him the bottle. "No worries. I'd rather that than be force-fed lukewarm, stale-milky tea from a dirty cup like I do with some of my clients."

"Ugh. No, no dirty cups here."

"I saw. It's fascinating how differently everyone approaches hoarding. You, for instance, don't seem to have any trouble keeping some areas clear." Lewis gestured around the veranda, empty apart from the hammock swinging between two rafters.

Jasper took a quick swig from the bottle, imagining that was the warmth from Lewis's lips he could still feel on the plastic. He handed it back.

"This wouldn't be a good place to store books."

"Oh, I don't know. I can think of a few you might want to store out here. Margaret Thatcher's autobiography, perhaps? Or maybe George W. Bush's?"

"Not a fan of right-wing politicians?"

"How did you guess?" Lewis quirked a smile at him, then stepped to the edge of the veranda, where the steps led down into the jungle below. "This is an amazing garden. Seriously beautiful."

"It's overgrown," Jasper said, giving the response he felt was expected of him when faced with the lawn that had turned into a meadow, and the rampant flowerbeds. "I should probably get a gardener in to come and clear it all."

"Don't you dare! It's perfect the way it is."

"You really think so?"

"Of course. It's like Hodgson Burnett's secret garden or something. You'd need to find a gardener like old Ben Weatherstaff to respect it. Or just leave it how it is."

"Dad planted it for Mama. Growing up in Egypt, she'd always dreamed of an English rose garden." Strange, how easy it was to talk about her with Lewis. "She loved it out here."

"And so you've kept it clear of clutter. Unlike the front garden, I mean."

"Yes. She never liked that one so much. Too dark, what with it facing north." A memory of her sitting out on the veranda in the old steamer chair crept up on him. Where on earth had he buried that chair? It would be great to see it back where she'd used to sit. But a twinge of pain warned him off pursuing that thought any further. He turned from the empty veranda to where Lewis stood, now at the bottom of the steps. "I thought you'd be a fan of trendy modern gardens. All gravel and abstract sculptures."

"Sounds like my folks' place." Lewis shook his head and pulled down a branch of rambling rose to sniff at the blooms. "Don't let the day job fool you. I'm not a neat freak, really. Well, I am about my clothes, but not everything. I don't find tidiness particularly desirable in others." Lewis gave him a lingering look that burned onto Jasper's skin like the late afternoon sun. Jasper took a step forward, down into the garden, so that the leaves of the grasses brushed against his bare ankles.

One more step, and he could be kissing Lewis. An idea as appealing as it was dangerous. What's more, Lewis seemed to be inviting him, tilting his head back and staring with a sort of lazy flirtatiousness.

A dog barked in a nearby garden, startling them both.

"We should get back inside," Lewis said, turning away and walking briskly up the steps. "There's still the rest of the house to see. Do you mind if I take some photographs? It's useful for clients to look back on at later stages in the process. Reminds them just how much progress they've made. Jasper?"

Jasper realised he'd been zoning out, standing there with his fingers resting on his lips. Lewis hadn't been making eyes at him. He was a professional. He probably just couldn't help sending out that kind of signal, being an open, friendly sort of person.

Thank God, Jasper hadn't embarrassed himself by leaping in, lips first.

Chapter Seven

Showing the upstairs wasn't as excruciatingly embarrassing as the downstairs had been, but that was only because Jasper now knew Lewis wouldn't show any shock at the state of the house. Instead, Lewis stood in a shaft of sunshine slanting through the landing skylight, picking up books from the tops of stacks and asking Jasper if he'd read them or why he'd brought them home.

"That one?" Jasper eyed the lurid cover of a Mills & Boon bodice ripper. "It has a certain kitsch value, don't you think? And there was something about the hero." The hero in question was a blond hunk, but he could see the passing resemblance to Lewis. "He has your eyes." Shocked at his own boldness, Jasper led the way to the bedroom. He shoved the door open and stood aside. "There isn't room for two," he mumbled as Lewis edged past him.

As he leaned back against the books and watched the light of Lewis's camera flash reflected in the gloss paint of the open door, he wondered how he'd explain having blocked all the other rooms off up here. Mind you, Lewis hadn't batted an eyelid at his inaccessible living and dining rooms. Jasper was no closer to coming up with a plausible reason when Lewis appeared at the doorway again.

"So, this wing of the house is out of bounds, I see." Lewis gazed around the cramped landing as if trying to calculate where the doors were behind all the books.

"You can still get into the bathroom," Jasper said, pointing the way.

Lewis reappeared after a few more camera flashes. "No books in there, I see. Plenty of other stuff, but no books."

"Paper doesn't like damp."

"No." Lewis stared at him for what felt like an eternity. "It's interesting. The way you've categorised your hoard. You're pretty organised, you know."

Jasper shrugged it off. "I'm a librarian. It's second nature."

"Hmm. So how would you feel if I were to take one of these books from here... May I?" Jasper nodded, and Lewis picked up a book from the pile next to him. "And put it on top of one of the downstairs piles?"

Jasper took a deep breath. His palms sweated. "You can't do that."

"Why not?"

"Because..." Oh God, this was going to sound ridiculous. "Because these are the ones I plan to read myself one day, and the ones downstairs aren't."

Lewis's cheeks dimpled, even as his expression stayed mostly serious. "You're keeping books you don't intend to read?"

"It's not so strange. I don't plan to read every book at the library either."

"No... But most people don't give up substantial amounts of living space to something they don't intend to ever make use of. Oh, don't get me wrong. I'm not criticising. I'm just trying to understand what your motivation is. What are you keeping all those books for, Jasper?"

Okay. This was the point where Lewis abandoned him as a hopeless crackpot. But he wasn't going to lie. Not about this, anyway. "It's insurance," he muttered.

"Insurance against what?"

Jasper fingered the spines of the books, looking at them to avoid the intensity in Lewis's eyes. "Insurance against the collapse of Western civilisation. Someone needs to archive all our information, our culture. There's knowledge there that could be lost forever if I don't save it. Knowledge that could be useful to people. Help them rebuild society, you know?"

"But there's the Internet and proper libraries out there for all of that. Why do you need to archive things in your own home?"

"Libraries can burn! They're targets for rioters. The Internet, that's only good as long as we have functioning servers and electricity to run our PCs. It's not a stable form of data storage. Not really. Hard copies are safer. That's what I'm doing. I'm saving the hard copies. For the future." There. He'd said it, and now Lewis really would think he was nuts. He'd probably call the men in white coats to take him away.

"Why not keep them in a rented storage unit, though? Why here, in your home?"

"I need to look after them. I'm their...custodian." That was much better than admitting they were his only real friends, wasn't it?

"I see."

Jasper almost didn't look up, afraid of what he'd see on Lewis's face. But when he stacked up his courage and did so, Lewis's smile surprised him. "You are definitely the most organised hoarder I've ever encountered. I love that you have a plan."

"You don't think I'm mad?"

"Mad? Who's to say what's mad? You could have a point. There are plenty of theorists warning us about the collapse of Western civilisation."

"So...all this..." Jasper gestured around himself. "All this is okay?"

"The answer to that doesn't lie in whether or not the reasoning behind hanging on to all these books is valid. Only you can answer whether or not it's okay. Are you happy with living in a house that's been taken over by books you're never going to read? That's the question."

"Happy?" Had anyone ever really asked him whether or not he was happy? Jasper laid a hand on the nearest stack of books.

These books had made him happy, once, when he brought them home with him, but now they were in the way, forcing him to turn sideways in order to get to his bathroom. Irritation surged down his arm, and he shoved them hard. There was nowhere for them to go, though, wedged in as they were by so many other books. "No. I'm not happy. I can't get into my living room anymore, and I can't find anything I want. I'm too embarrassed to invite anyone around here because they'll see how hopeless and weak-willed I am. Did you know, you're the first person other than me to set foot in this place for more than six years? I'm not happy. I'm lonely. That's what I am. I'm really fucking lonely." The expletive shocked him. He never swore. Mama had washed his mouth out with soap and water the one time he'd unwittingly cursed in front of her.

But Lewis didn't look shocked. He seemed to be taking it all with the same maddening calm. "Good," he said.

"Good? I tell you I'm lonely, and all you have to say is good?"

"That's not what I meant. It's good that you're strongly motivated to change. You can work with that. Get this hoarding beat. And I'm going to help you through it, I promise."

"Are you going to stop me feeling lonely too?"

Some indecipherable emotion flickered across Lewis's face, and he turned away, starting gingerly down the stairs. "I'm always there for you, at the other end of the phone. How about I book you in for a session early next week? I can do Monday mornings at nine. And we could stick with this Friday session too, if you like."

"Mondays are good. I'm on the late shift then, so I don't go in till twelve."

"That's sorted, then. Two hours on a Monday morning, and two on a Friday afternoon. We charge twenty pounds an hour for one of us, and thirty for the two of us when we get into major clear-out mode. You think you can afford that?"

Jasper mentally calculated based on their hourly rate. "Yes, that's fine. I was expecting it to be more, actually." In truth, he had enough savings to pay for Lewis to be round all day every day for the next year, but the man probably had other clients depending on him too. Besides, asking for that would look kind of weird and needy.

"Brilliant. I'll make sure I get that down in the diary. To keep you going till then, though, I'm setting you some homework."

"Homework? I did your worksheets already." He'd completed the main questionnaire during his lunch break. "They're in my bag. See? Amazingly enough, I actually know where they are."

"Excellent. But this is an extra assignment. I want you to select a book you're ready to let go of."

"I already tried that."

"Oh yes? When?"

"This morning. And I couldn't do it." Panic clenched Jasper's stomach hard. "I'm not ready."

"Okay. You weren't ready this morning, but you've got the whole weekend ahead of you. I want you to find something in this house that you're ready to get rid of."

"What, throw it away? I don't think I could do that."

"No, not send it to landfill. Just to release into my safekeeping, and let me decide what to do with it."

"Will you send it to landfill?"

Lewis just smiled. "That depends on whether it still has any use for anyone else. Not if I can help it, no. I don't like senseless waste any more than you do."

Oh.

"Will you do it?" Lewis asked, moving closer and giving Jasper a smile that made him want to promise Lewis anything he wanted, just so long as he kept looking at Jasper in that way. "Just find one thing you can hand over to me next week?"

"I'll do it," Jasper promised.

It was only once the front door had clicked shut behind Lewis that Jasper realised the enormity of what he'd promised. Somewhere, in this house full of paper, he had to find something he was willing to let go of. But with so many potential options, how could he ever possibly decide?

Chapter Eight

They'd almost kissed, Lewis was sure of it. As he sat on the bus on the way back home, he played the scene over and over in his head. He'd been standing there in the garden. Jasper moving closer, a question in his eyes. There was no doubt in Lewis's mind at that moment, spellbound by the sun-drenched, fragrant garden buzzing with insects, he'd have welcomed that kiss.

It would have been intensely stupid, and precisely the kind of thing he had to avoid. That was how all his failed relationships had started: with Lewis unintentionally flirting, capturing the attention of someone he didn't yet know well enough. And then he'd sleep with them, and if they worked well in bed together, then he'd move in a few days later just to get out of his parents' unofficial nudist camp. And before he knew it, he was embroiled in a "serious" relationship with a bloke he didn't necessarily have anything in common with. Oh, sure, the sex was always good, but you couldn't build domestic harmony on the sole basis of compatibility between the sheets. Compatibility in the rest of the house was every bit as important.

And Lewis most definitely wasn't compatible with Jasper's house. The place was a nightmare. He flicked through the photographs on his phone. You couldn't even tell it was a house. Each picture just looked like a wall of books or stacked newspapers. He paused on the one of Jasper's bedroom. The bed with its rumpled sheets and pile of clothing was hemmed in by stacks of paperbacks. Even the windowsill behind the bed was piled high, so only a crack of light filtered in at the top.

No. There was no way Lewis was going to have sex with Jasper on a bed like that. And they couldn't do it at Lewis's parents'. And besides, he definitely shouldn't be thinking about shagging a client. Especially a screwed-up, hot client with an adorable nervous tic.

Maybe he should just go to the pub. Reconnect with some old friends. And until then, he'd lose himself in the homework questionnaires Jasper had filled out for him. Yes. That was bound to help him forget all about the man.

Lewis sighed and scrubbed at his forehead with his fists.

"So, do we have a full-blown case of OCD on our hands?" Carroll asked when Lewis called her as he stepped down from the bus.

"I don't think so, no. He doesn't seem to have any rituals that I can see. He even let me pick up a book, although I wasn't allowed to move it."

"You sure? He seemed pretty twitchy to me."

"Plenty of people get twitchy when they're nervous."

"Yeah, I suppose..."

"What is it? Come on, sis. I know that tone."

"Have you thought about which of us should handle the case?"

"Definitely me. He trusts me now, and he's got some serious attachment issues with his hoard."

"You sure?" Carroll asked, but Lewis could hear the relief in her voice. "You've got more clients than I have at the moment."

"I can fit him in okay, and we'll need your help when he gets stuck into serious clearing." Lewis pictured the narrow corridors through walls of paper. "It's the most extreme case I've ever seen in terms of quantity of stuff. He's filled his house. We'll probably have to hire a storage unit and move it all there temporarily so he can begin sorting through it all."

"Wow. Haven't had to do that in a while. Right. I'll get looking for somewhere nearby. And maybe a removal van. Won't hurt to have it all set up for him when he's ready, will it?"

Lewis chuckled. Carroll was such a whirlwind at times. It was just what some clients needed, although he felt Jasper would be better off with his more gentle approach. "Okay, but it could be a couple of months before he's ready to get rid of anything. I'm going to be working on his acquiring habits first. He can't seem to resist picking up old books and newspapers."

"Bit of a problem for someone who works in a library."

"Exactly."

"So, you still finding him just as sexy after seeing his house? His bedroom?"

"I'm not getting involved with a client."

"Don't remember suggesting it, bro. Just wanted to know if it was off-putting for an anal retentive like you."

"I'm not anal about mess."

Carroll just snorted. "What was his bedroom like? Oh, go on. You know I'm not going to tell anyone else."

He was about to inform her it was confidential, but they always shared this kind of stuff, didn't they? Yes, best not to start thinking of Jasper as in any way different than one of the other clients. "His bedroom was like the rest of the house. Piles of books surrounding the bed on all sides. It's a total death trap."

"Not somewhere you'd want to have wild monkey sex, then. If he wasn't a client."

"Carroll!"

"Take a chill pill, for fuck's sake. I'm talking hypothetically. God forbid I suggest you do anything normal like shag someone you fancy."

Lewis took a deep breath, glad to have reached home and have a good excuse to ring off. "No, that whole house is a health-and-safety hazard. I wouldn't want to have sex anywhere in it, hypothetically speaking."

"Gotcha. You'll just have to sneak him into Mum and Dad's when they're out. That's what I used to do with all my boyfriends when I was still living at home. Not that Mum and Dad would have minded, but I didn't want the boys all getting scared off by them in their birthday suits. Still, who knows. Maybe Jasper would find it a turn-on. D'you think he's kinky? The quiet ones often are."

"I'm not listening to you anymore." Lewis hung up and unlocked the front door. Time for a soak in the bath, then a night out with people who had no idea Jasper Richardson even existed.

An hour later, Lewis boarded the night bus into central Bristol. When he'd called Brandon earlier, his old university friend had sounded pleased to hear from him again, and Lewis's conscience twinged. Yes, he'd probably neglected Brandon while seeing Carlos, but then again, Brandon had been equally wrapped up in his Dutch boyfriend, along with his interminable urge to save the world via the medium of tea and biscuits with other right-on Bristolians.

They were meeting in the Spyglass—some new place down on the waterfront by Millennium Square that apparently stocked a good range of continental beer. However, he could see from the outside that the owners had apparently forgotten to create any atmosphere while they were planning the interior. Instead, they'd decided the high ceilings and wall of windows would be best teamed up with purple-and-green lighting, and blocky, blond wood tables. Just like every other supposedly trendy bar in town.

Lewis scanned the crowded tables. The two of them shouldn't be too hard to spot, what with Brandon's afro and Jos being a blond giant, but the sultry evening meant the place really was packed, even at eight thirty. Eventually, he saw them waving at him from an outdoor table, so he headed on over.

"Great to see you both," Lewis said, hugging first Brandon, then Jos. The tall Dutchman practically crushed the life out of him, and not for the first time Lewis found himself wishing for a few pounds of extra muscle.

"About time too," Brandon scolded, but there was a warm lilt to his voice. "Jos, would you mind getting the next round in? Some of that lovely Trappist beer we had last time, yeah?"

Jos left after giving Brandon a peck on the cheek, and Lewis took a moment to study his friend. Yep. Being in love clearly suited him. He'd always thought Brandon had a kind of strained look about his eyes, but that was all gone now. He looked healthy and happy, lounging comfortably in his chair. "You're looking great. Jos must be good for you."

"Like you wouldn't believe," Brandon said, winking. Winking! Brandon never winked. "What? He's the One. Seriously. We're like a hundred times better together than we are apart."

"That's cute. And also kind of sick-making."

Brandon just beamed even more widely. "So go on, then. Spill the beans. What happened with carpet man?"

"Carlos? Oh, nothing much. We just drifted apart."

"Cheating on you, was he?"

"No! Well, I don't think so. I never caught him at it, anyway." Although what with the way Carlos's job took him all over the place for weeks on end, he could have quite easily had a man in every town and Lewis would have been none the wiser.

"Hey, cheer up. I always reckoned he was a stuck-up wanker, anyway. Reminded me of some of the arseholes I have to deal with on the city council. Only interested in backing policy changes that are likely to inflate their house prices. Never mind that there's folk sleeping rough just yards away from where they park their fancy cars."

"Carlos wasn't like that," Lewis began, then thought about what he was saying. Why was he defending the man who had been more interested in earning money than spending time with him? "Okay, maybe he was a bit like that, but he had his good points too."

"Kept them well hidden, then."

"Not in bed, he didn't," Lewis said, raising his eyebrows suggestively.

"Oi! I don't want to think about the two of you at it, thank you very much."

Lewis smiled to himself. Brandon always had been a bit of a prude, bless him.

"So anyway," Brandon began, glancing over to the bar where Jos's head was clearly visible above a group of girls in pink, the bride-to-be with the obligatory hen party L-plate on her back. It looked like they were sexually harassing him en masse, poor bloke. "Jos knows this guy at the university who's single right now. He's a bit of an odd one and doesn't get out much, but I reckon you'd like him."

"You're not at work anymore, mate."

"What's that got to do with anything?"

"I mean, I'm not one of your charity cases. You don't have to try and fix my life."

"Hey, I'm just trying to help you find a man with a bit of integrity this time. If you'd rather go for the one with the nicest car or biggest dick, that's your call. Just don't come sobbing to me when it all goes tits up."

"But you've got such nice shoulders for crying on," Lewis said, throwing an arm around said shoulders and clasping Brandon to him. Brandon grinned, and the atmosphere eased. Just then a group of three tall pilsner glasses landed in the middle of the table, lager slopping over the sides. Lewis let go of Brandon and glanced up guiltily, but Jos had a knowing grin on his face.

"So, Brandon told you about Jasper, yes?"

"Jasper?" What the hell?

"My friend at the university. Sexy librarian man. You two, you will love each other. I know this. Both kind and gentle souls. You're made for each other."

Lewis's eyes felt ready to bug out of his head and land in his pint glass. He took a swig of the strong lager, barely tasting it, but the cold fizz cleared his head a little. "Are you talking about Jasper Richardson, by any chance?"

"Yes!" Jos clunked his glass enthusiastically against Lewis's. "You know him already? This is great, ja?"

"Er, no. He's a client of mine. I mean..." Oh sh— *sugar*. He'd broken his long-standing policy of never speaking about clients unless cloaked in anonymity. "Well, we're working together, anyway. And besides, I want to be single for a while."

"Oh yes? You're keen to play the meadow?"

"The field, sweetheart," Brandon said. "It's play the field."

"It doesn't matter. Lewis knows what I mean."

Lewis nodded, then caught the raised eyebrows. "No! I don't want to play the field. Come on, I'm thirty years old. I think I can cope with a few months without sex. It'll be good for me."

Jos shrugged. "I do not think so. Not if it means storing up all your urges inside, until they burst out of you and make you wild. I made stupid mistakes like that. Took up with bad men." Jos got this strangely cowed look about him then, and Lewis wondered what on earth anyone could have done to intimidate the gentle giant.

"Shhh, you're okay now," Brandon said, hugging Jos to him and ruffling his hair in a strangely paternal gesture. "I'll look out for you."

What was that all about? Admittedly, Lewis hadn't seen much of the two of them interacting since they'd first hooked up, but that was weird, watching Brandon doing the whole Nurturing Parent thing. Or was he a Controlling Parent? It'd been way too long since he'd read up on Transactional Analysis theory. Not since he'd taken his counselling qualification. He should probably brush up on some of that. Might help when dealing with Jasper.

But when Jos looked up again he seemed totally confident, and definitely in an adult headspace. "So Jasper, he is one of your hoarders?"

"I never said that."

Jos's forehead scrunched up like a ball of paper. "Oh, but I thought you said he was a—"

"Look, I shouldn't have said anything. Hoarders are usually ashamed of their living conditions and do their best to hide it. Promise me you won't say anything to him."

"Okay, that's fine." Jos was clearly thinking it through. "But do you think I should still be giving him my old copies of *Professional Engineering*? I mean, if he has too much stuff already."

"He takes magazines from you?"

"Lots of the students give their old course materials to him. Even if the library already has enough, Jasper says he can find a good home for them."

Visions of the narrow passageways through teetering stacks of books filled his head. "Maybe just don't give him any more until I've figured out what the issue is. So long as you can do it without letting him know you know, if you know what I mean." How many "knows" did a sentence need, for crying out loud? Lewis took a deep draught of lager. Time to steer the conversation away from Jasper.

"So, are you two going away anywhere this summer?"

As Brandon and Jos launched into an enthusiastic rundown of their plans to hike through the Loire Valley, Lewis did his best to shove thoughts of Jasper Richardson to one side. The world might seem determined to push the two of them together, but that didn't mean he had to cooperate.

In the end, Lewis made tracks after his third pint, leaving the two lovebirds to carry on feeling each other up. It was starting to make him feel jealous. Carlos had been delightfully tactile when he'd actually been around, and that had been one of the things that made Lewis keep hanging on, even once it became abundantly clear they were terminally mismatched. Unfortunately, the night bus seemed to be full of couples too. Or maybe it was just the one straight pair, sitting down at the front and eating each other's faces off in full view of everyone farther back. That was just rude. Talk about rubbing it in.

Lewis took out his phone and played Angry Birds instead, but even when he'd beat his high score, there the happy couple still was, touching foreheads and whispering drunken nonsense. Lewis sighed, then called up his Tumblr dashboard and started browsing porn instead. Even his right hand needed a little extra inspiration now and again.

Unfortunately, none of the blokes he found on hot_geeks could give Jasper a run for his money. Looked like Lewis was going to have to break his personal ethical code and have sex with a client.

In his head, at any rate.

Real life was an entirely different matter.

Chapter Nine

Jasper lay back on the rumpled bed sheets and watched as Mas made his way to the tiny adjoining bathroom. He heard the shower water start running. Now would be a good time to make his excuses and leave, but he couldn't bring himself to be so rude. Not that Mas expected him to hang around after sex or anything, and he'd told Jasper he was on his way out clubbing in a moment, but leaving without at least some kind of postcoital conversation felt wrong.

Instead, he hauled himself up and dealt with the used condom. The nearest bin was in the bathroom. Perhaps he could say his good-byes while Mas was under the water.

Steam was billowing out from over the top of the shower curtain. Jasper made as much noise as he could treading on the bin pedal, then went to rinse the lube off his fingers under the sink tap.

"Ow-ow-ow! Fuck's sake, Jasper. Turn it off! That's fucking freezing." Mas pulled away the end of the shower curtain to glare at him. It looked comical, considering how cute he was with his heart-shaped face and Cupid's bow lips. His looks bordered on angelic, although he couldn't really pull off innocent too well. There was a certain slinky sexuality that oozed out of every movement he made, and a permanent tease in his large, grey-green eyes.

"God, I'm so sorry. I forgot." Jasper turned off the offending tap and sank down onto the toilet lid. "I'm an idiot."

"Yeah. Good thing you're a big, lovable one, isn't it?" Mas reached over to ruffle Jasper's hair before letting the shower curtain fall back into place.

Jasper picked up one of Mas's bottles of product from the shelf behind the sink. "Glossing serum." What the hell was that?

"So, who's this Lewis, then?"

Jasper nearly dropped the bottle into the sink. "Lewis?" He hadn't said anything about Lewis, had he? He'd barely been in the door when Mas had told him they didn't have long if he was to get to The Retreat while it was still happy hour and begun stripping off his uniform from the fancy department store where he worked.

"Yeah. *Lewis*. The one you were imagining you were fucking. You called out his name when you shot your load."

Oh. Was that jealousy Jasper could hear? The bottle of glossing serum slid out of his hands and hit the sink enamel, cracking and spilling oily liquid everywhere. "Oh God, I'm so sorry."

"Hey, don't worry about it. For what it's worth, I was imagining you were Professor Brian Cox." The noise of the water abated, and the shower curtain rattled on its rings. "I've got a thing for hot nerds. You remind me of him."

"I don't look anything like him." The Mancunian TV physicist might have similar colouring, but Jasper was nowhere near that pretty, and he certainly didn't have those luscious lips.

"I dunno. It's a vibe. That kind of sexy-scientist thing you've both got going on. Makes me want to bend over a lab table and demand you do all kinds of naughty experiments on me."

"I'm a librarian, not a scientist. My degree was in English Literature."

"Yeah, yeah, but you're a right brainbox, aren't you? Bet you could beat Stephen Fry at Trivial Pursuit. Anyway, you're changing the subject. Who's Lewis? I'm hoping he's totally cream-your-pants hot if he's that distracting. Don't want to think I'm losing my charm already."

"He's...he's my..." What was Lewis to him, exactly? Therapist? Hired help? Declutterer? "He's my friend," Jasper settled on.

"Right." Mas stepped out of the bathtub and grabbed the

threadbare towel hanging over the door. "I'm guessing not a friend with benefits either, if you're over here rather than with him. But you want him to be more, yeah?" The words were muffled as Mas towelled off his hair.

Yes. Jasper wanted Lewis to be more. So much more. "But we've only just met, really." He couldn't count their school history. They'd never even spoken back then.

"Sometimes you just know. You meet someone, and it's like, *Kapow! Take me now, cowboy. I'm yours.*" Mas's smile appeared strained, somehow, but then it changed into a frown as he took in the mess of serum and broken glass in the sink. "Shit! That stuff was expensive."

"I'll buy you some more."

The frown melted, quickly replaced by a lopsided smile. Mas's moods flitted from one to the next like a butterfly on crack. "Nah, it's all right. I can always grab another bottle from the stockroom at work. Just, could you do the honours with what you've got on your fingers?"

"This? Oh, er, okay. I've never done this before." Jasper clumsily brushed his oily hands through Mas's mop of chestnut ringlets. Did Lewis do this with his curls? Would Jasper ever get a chance to help him out?

"First time for everything," Mas said archly. "Oi, that's enough! We want glossy, not greasy. I don't want to look like I've just finished a shift in a chippie."

"Right. Sorry. I'll just... I'll clear up this mess, and then I'll get going." Jasper gestured at the sink.

"Nah, leave it. I'll sort it out in the morning. You should go find this Lewis bloke you're so strung up on and make him yours."

"Mine? I couldn't do that."

"Why not? You're sex on legs. He'd be a bloody fool to turn you down. Oh." Mas pouted. "Straight, is he? Well, most straight blokes are happy to accept a blowjob off you, even if they don't want to return the favour. Sometimes they'll even fuck you up the arse if you're not too hairy. You might have a problem there, but I could always help you with a back, sac and crack wax, if you wanted."

"Umm... He's not straight."

"In a relationship?"

Jasper shook his head.

"So..." Mas strolled through to the bedroom and began searching through a drawer, naked, hairless arse in the air. "It must be you who's in a relationship, then."

"No! We're both single. Seriously. You didn't think I was cheating on someone, did you?"

Mas started pulling on a pair of bright green skimpy underpants. "Other guys do. I seem to be their 'slut on the side' of choice."

"You're too young to be cynical."

Mas stood and stared with his hands on his hips. "I'm twenty-two."

"Way too young."

"And you're old and crusty enough for it to have settled into a permanent way of thinking, right?"

"I'm not cynical!"

"Then go find this Lewis bloke you're hung up on, and let him know how you feel. What's the worst that can happen?"

The ground would open up and swallow him. Or maybe a pile of books would fall on top of him instead. Yes, that was much more likely. "He could laugh at me."

"Trust me, that isn't going to happen. He'd have to be stark raving bonkers to turn you down. You're hot, intelligent, and you've got your own place." Mas raised an eyebrow and posed coquettishly. "I think I'll have you myself if he can't see what a catch you are."

"You've already had me," Jasper pointed out.

"You know what I mean." For just a moment, Mas's mischievous expression slipped, and Jasper saw the longing lying behind it. Oh. He hadn't realised. He'd assumed the man-tart was impervious to falling in love. If he'd known he was toying with Mas's heart, he'd have stopped seeing him a long time ago.

"Mas, I..." But he didn't know where he was going with that. How to bow out gracefully from a one-sided relationship. So he ended up saying what he always seemed to end up saying. "I'm sorry."

"Ah, don't worry about me. I'm young, I'm fit, and I've got the sexiest bum in the whole of the South West. I'll find me a hot nerd all of my own one day. Hey, you got any numbers of professors at the Uni? I'm well up for some teacher/naughty student role playing."

Jasper found himself smiling, despite himself. "None of them look like a certain TV physicist, if that's what you're after."

Mas tutted. "Shame. Now go on, tiger. Go get this Lewis fella, and make him see just how lucky he is."

Jasper walked out of Mas's Stokes Croft building and headed back towards where he'd left his car, deep in thought. Mas's advice was all well and good, but how on earth did Jasper "get" Lewis? He didn't even know where the man lived. Could be just round the corner, for all he knew. Jasper glanced up at the brightly coloured mural on the wall opposite. This part of the city was covered in them, every other building sporting its colours proudly. Would Lewis choose to live in an area like this? It was on the up, but still only in the early stages of urban regeneration. For all Jasper knew, though, Lewis lived in some genteel little village on the city outskirts.

He pulled out his phone and navigated to the screen displaying Lewis's mobile number. Would Lewis be annoyed if a client phoned him at nine thirty in the evening? He had said anytime, but wasn't that just one of those things people said? They never meant it literally. Lewis had never mentioned there being a twenty-four-hour call-out service included in the weekly plan they'd drawn up.

Two sessions of two hours each week. And Jasper was paying for them. No. This wasn't a friendship. This was a business transaction, and he wasn't about to make Lewis into some kind of whore by expecting him to conform to Jasper's every whim simply because money was changing hands.

Jasper would just have to wait until their next scheduled session together and try his best not to make a total fool of himself.

Chapter Ten

Choosing a single book from amongst the hoard was impossible. After spending the whole weekend working his way through every last stack in the entrance hall—the accessible ones at the front, anyway—by Monday morning Jasper had narrowed it down to a selection of five. It would have to do. If Lewis was angry he hadn't followed his instructions exactly... Well, Jasper couldn't actually imagine Lewis getting angry. He seemed totally unflappable. This was the man who'd resisted the urge to lash out at bullies. Did anything ever shake that calm?

The knock at the door made Jasper jump, even though he'd been listening out for it for the last ten minutes. But when he opened the door, he had another surprise. Lewis stood there, drenched from head to toe.

"You're wet!" Yep, talk about stating the obvious. Jasper could hear the drumming of the rain now the door was open. Could even see it sheeting down if he craned to look over Lewis's shoulder. "I didn't realise it was raining."

"Like cats and dogs. Not that I'm sure what the connection is between them and water, anyway," Lewis said, then sneezed.

"Oh God, you'll catch your death. Come on in. I'm so sorry. I shouldn't have left you standing there."

"Not your fault. I should have remembered my umbrella. Had to bus it over today as Carroll was busy with the van this morning."

"You don't have a car?"

Lewis pulled a sad smile. "I've got one. She just needs a whole new engine, and I can't really afford that right now."

"Ah. I suppose... It's really none of my business and I don't like to snoop..."

"Yes? Go on." Lewis sounded amused now.

"Well, you don't seem to charge much for your services. I was thinking about what your overheads must be with the van and advertising, and I can't see how the two of you are able to make much more than minimum wage."

"It's not quite that bad, but put it this way, if I weren't living with my parents, I'd qualify for Housing Benefit."

"But that's ridiculous! You're a smart man. You could be earning a small fortune."

"You'd be amazed how many unemployed Psychology graduates there are out there. It's a cut-throat field."

"Seriously?"

"Like you wouldn't believe. I started working with Carroll just to get some relevant work experience. You kind of need it even to get considered for a postgrad course. But then I loved it so much, and I couldn't abandon my clients once I'd started working with them, so I signed up for the same part-time counselling course Carroll had done, and, well, here I am."

"Didn't you want to be in something more high-powered? Better paid?"

"I don't think I'm all that ambitious, really. Besides, there's more to life than money," Lewis said, then sneezed loudly.

"Bless you!" Why had he said that? Made him sound like an old dear. Next thing he knew, he'd be saying Lewis would catch a cold standing around all sopping wet. "I suppose...I could lend you some dry clothes. They're clean, I promise, but they might not fit you all that well."

Lewis stared at him for a long moment, as if considering the offer. Jasper forced himself to return eye contact, even though he could feel himself twitching and it made him want to scurry away and hide behind a wall of books. Eventually, Lewis's cheeks dimpled; then the rest of his face followed in a slow smile. "Thanks, I'd really appreciate it."

Jasper led the way upstairs. "They're in the bedroom, but there's not much room to get changed in there and if you're all wet... Oh dear. I don't think I have a clean towel right now."

"That's fine. I don't mind using one of yours."

"Yes, but..." Oh God, after his morning wank, had he wiped himself off with the bathroom towel? He couldn't remember now, but it wasn't outside the realm of possibility.

Lewis blinked, and when he spoke again, his words sounded carefully chosen. "If you'd rather I didn't use such an intimate item, that's fine. We all have different personal boundaries about our possessions."

"It's not that! I'm not... God, I don't have a hygiene obsession or anything. Far from it. I just, erm. I might have used it to...to...you know, erm...clean something up..." Jasper's face burned, but fortunately, Lewis came to the rescue.

"It's fine. I'll be all right with just some dry clothes, honest."

Jasper nodded, dizzy with the rush of oxygen to his brain. "I'll get them for you. Hang on."

The bathroom door would no longer close properly, and Jasper knew he should head downstairs to give Lewis some semblance of privacy, but when he started round the corner of books leading to the stairs, Lewis called out to him.

"How did you get on with the homework assignment?"

"I sort of... Well, not so good, really."

"You couldn't find one? It's okay. You'll get there eventually."

"No. I couldn't find one, but I've got five."

"Five?" Lewis stuck his head around the door, revealing a slice of naked chest. His body was pale and sinewy, just as Jasper had imagined, but with a delicious fuzz of golden hair spanning between his pebbled nipples. Oh, he looked delectable. Made

Jasper want to lick his lips, but then he'd be rumbled for ogling, assuming he hadn't already been.

Jasper made himself look up at Lewis's face. Uh-oh. Lewis was smirking. Not a full-on grin, but one of his cheeks sported a tell-tale dimple and his eyes sparkled.

"You said five," Lewis said as Jasper stood there with his mouth open.

"Erm, yes. Five. Right. Oh yes, five books. Sorry. I know I was only meant to find one, but I'm sure you can help me decide which of these is *the one.*"

"That's the kind of thing I'm here for." Lewis disappeared back into the bathroom, and when he next opened the door he was fully clothed, much to Jasper's simultaneous disappointment and relief. It was strange, seeing him in Jasper's own clothes, his hair all wet and mussed up like he'd just taken a shower. The T-shirt was a little baggy on Lewis, but the jeans seemed to fit him well, so perhaps they weren't so far apart in physique. This was how a boyfriend would get to see Lewis, Jasper realised with a pang. Swapping clothes and seeing him in all kinds of disarray. What would those golden locks look like first thing in the morning? What would it be like to wake up beside him?

More to the point, what would it be like to wake up beside another man? Thirty-three years old, and Jasper still didn't know. How sad was that?

"You all right, Jasper?"

"Yes. No. I don't know."

"Well, that just about covers all the options."

Jasper screwed his eyes shut in embarrassment. "You must think I'm terminally indecisive. I couldn't even decide on one single sodding book over a whole weekend."

"Hey." Lewis's hand landed on his arm and squeezed. "There are worse things than being indecisive about clutter. It usually just means you're an intelligent and imaginative person who can see hundreds of different uses for things the rest of us dismiss as useless."

"That's definitely true. About the different uses for things, anyway." Jasper snuck a peek at Lewis to see if he was making fun of him, but he looked earnest. Did he really believe Jasper was intelligent and imaginative? "But at the moment, the main use all these books are being put to is building blocks, and that isn't right, is it?"

"Why do you say that?"

"It's obvious, isn't it? I can't find the ones I want anymore. They could be anywhere, buried behind or under others. I had a system. I'm trying to keep it going, but there's too many to cope with. And every time I think about clearing a room out and sorting it properly, I get exhausted. Where am I meant to clear them out to anyway? There's nowhere for them to go. I'm not using the kitchen because I know... I just know—" Jasper swiped at his eyes with his fist. He wasn't going to cry over this, because that would really cement him as pathetic, wouldn't it?

"What would happen if you put them in the kitchen?" Lewis asked, his nonjudgmental voice quiet enough to calm Jasper down.

"I'd lose that room too. I wouldn't be able to cook or even make a cup of tea. And all the food in my cupboards and fridge would rot because I couldn't find the energy to move a few heaps of stupid books."

"Do you often get tired when you think about sorting them out?"

"All the time. It's exhausting." He looked around at the books on the landing, and it hit him. This wasn't a home anymore. This was a burden. The weight of all those hidden words, dragging him down until he could barely find the energy to read a sentence, let alone file a book correctly. "Just being here is exhausting. I go out running in the evenings just to get away from it. Funny how much more energy I get as soon as I'm out of the house. Can we do that now?"

"Go for a run?"

Was Lewis teasing him? "I meant get out of the house. Maybe down to Yusef's?"

"Good idea. Looks like it's stopped raining, so we can take the books down there with us and talk them through." Lewis smiled, and gestured at the stairs. "You'll have to go first. There's no passing room."

"Mama used to say you should never pass on the stairs." Uh-oh. Where had that come from? He didn't want to start talking about her again. Jasper turned and started down the stairs, hoping Lewis would forget the subject.

No such luck. "She was superstitious, then?"

"A bit. Sometimes." A lot, really, but he didn't want to pique Lewis's interest. No doubt it would all go towards explaining why Jasper was so monumentally screwed up, but he wasn't ready to hear that just yet.

But perhaps his tone had been sufficiently forbidding, because Lewis didn't ask anything else, other than a brief enquiry about the books. "Shall I carry them, as you've already got your bag?"

Jasper hefted his overstuffed bag over his shoulder, almost knocking over a pile in the process. "Erm, are you sure? You shouldn't have to."

"It's fine. I'm stronger than I look, honest."

"You look pretty strong to me."

"Thanks." Lewis beamed. "I never seem to bulk up however much I work out, but I like to think I'm not a total wimp."

"Not at all." Jasper admired the breadth of Lewis's shoulders and the wiry musculature visible in his forearms as he lifted the pile of bulky textbooks. "After you."

Jasper had to squint when they got outside as the sun was now reflecting off the wet pavements, dazzling them both.

"Blimey, that's bright." Lewis shifted the books into a one-armed grip against his side and shaded his eyes with his free hand. "Wish I'd remembered to bring my shades with me."

"Wish I knew where mine were. I think I might have some kind of goblin infestation."

"Goblins?"

"Something keeps stealing my stuff, and I can't see mice having any use for a pair of prescription sunglasses."

Lewis chuckled, and as they fell into an easy conversation on the various bad habits of goblins, Jasper kept on sneaking glances at Lewis's arms. His muscles bulged enticingly, just begging to be touched. Shame Jasper would never have the nerve to reach out and do it.

When they got to the café, Yusef was clearly having one of his grumpy days, but his face softened as he saw them both. "Jasper! You've come to eat some baklava, I hope. I hate having to throw it away at the end of the day. And you," he said, turning to Lewis. "You need something to put some meat on your bones. None of this black coffee nonsense today, you hear me?"

"But I like it black."

"You'll like it more with milk. Trust me. I do it properly. None of this overcooked rubbish you get in your Starbucks or your Costas, where the milk gets scalded and they have to cover up the taste with all those nasty syrups. No, with Yusef you will get a velvety-rich milk, naturally sweet. I'll do you a latté."

Lewis shook his head a little but smiled sweetly and agreed.

Compliant. That was kind of endearing, but worrying. The idea that someone might take advantage of Lewis's urge to please. Yes, that was worrying. Jasper scowled as he ordered his usual.

"Yes," Yusef continued, pointing at Jasper. "Here is a man who likes everything loaded with sugar. Perhaps you can work on that too with him. I hate to think of him getting diabetes because of my cooking."

"I'm not a project," Jasper said, annoyed. "I'll look after my

91

health myself, thanks."

"You make sure you do, young man. I don't want to lose another of my old friends."

"Another?" Lewis asked.

"I had a letter this morning. My oldest friend, Murat. We were like brothers growing up. Closer than brothers as teenagers. He held a piece of my heart all these years."

Oh God, Yusef was about to cry. Tears had begun welling up as he thumped his fist against his chest. "I'm so sorry," Jasper began, but already Lewis was heading around to the other side of the counter and hugging Yusef. To Jasper's amazement, Yusef hugged him back and sobbed into his neck.

"We weren't brave enough to be together. And I loved my wife so much. But sometimes when I think of what could have been—" Yusef broke down again, his words incoherent.

So Yusef had loved another man too? That explained a lot. His easy acceptance of Jasper's sexuality, for one thing. Jasper wished he could just walk around there and join in the hug, but he wasn't like Lewis. He couldn't just put himself forward like that. Best to stick to words, but it was so difficult to find comforting ones in a situation like this. Lewis wasn't talking either. Just making gentle hushing noises, his eyes closed. Jasper couldn't help but stare, mapping out the boyish contours of Lewis's face. Now Jasper had got used to the texture of his skin, Lewis didn't look his thirty years, not with his eyes shut. It was only when you could see the beatific wisdom shining out of them that you realised he was older than he appeared.

With a start, Jasper realised Lewis was returning his gaze. *Come here,* Lewis mouthed, beckoning.

Could he? Yes, of course he could. Especially if someone else was making the decision for him. Jasper stepped around the end of the counter and laid an arm over Yusef's shoulders. Oh God. Now Yusef was sobbing into his neck. Jasper froze, then patted the big man's back. That was how you comforted someone, wasn't it? Hopefully he wasn't doing it too hard. It wasn't like Yusef was choking or anything.

Jasper was just starting to relax into the hug, when an arm wrapped around his waist. Not Yusef's arm.

Jasper froze again. Lewis was hugging him.

He was officially taking part in his first group hug.

Tentatively, he moved his other arm up to round Lewis's shoulders. He felt tiny compared to Yusef's bulk, but warm and vibrant. Positively thrumming with energy. And now Jasper could smell him too. Some kind of earthy spice aftershave, or perhaps it was the scent of his shampoo, because now Lewis's head was snuggling into the other side of his neck.

Oh God. How did this end? Three gay and/or bisexual blokes in a three-way hug. There'd better not be kissing. While the idea of kissing Lewis was extremely appealing, the thought of puckering up for Yusef made him want to run away. And Lewis kissing Yusef? No, that would be very bad indeed. What was the etiquette for extracting oneself from a group hug without causing offence? Jasper contemplated faking a coughing attack, but that didn't seem terribly hygienic when standing behind the counter.

In the end, it was Ivy who saved him. Jasper recognised her as a regular customer in the charity shop, who always seemed to leave with a full basket. She bumbled into the coffee shop, setting off the bells over the door and giving them all time to separate and get themselves back on their respective sides of the counter while she fussed with her wheeled shopping basket.

"Here, let me help you," Jasper offered, grabbing hold of the handle and lifting it up the two small steps by the door. The basket felt like it was full of bricks, and he glanced in the top to see an assortment of bric-a-brac, including a ceramic tiger. Whoever needed a two-foot-tall ceramic tiger?

"Oh, bless you. You are a dear. Oh, and you're that young

fellow I see in the shop sometimes, aren't you? You remind me of my Daniel, you know." She patted him fondly on the cheek before heading over to the counter and querulously enquiring about the soup of the day. Yusef seemed to have cheered up after their hug, and although his eyes were still suspiciously bright, he flirted with Ivy in that brusque way he always did with the female customers.

Jasper turned to see Lewis sitting at the corner table and went to join him. He didn't want to talk about the hug, about the feelings it had stirred up, but fortunately there was the stack of books. Jasper laid them out on the table. "So, I have to choose one of these, do I?"

"If you want to. You could always choose more if that's too difficult."

"Get rid of two books?"

Lewis's cheek dimpled. "*Re-home* two books. We're not getting rid of anything. We're moving it on to somewhere it can be better appreciated."

"Yes. I suppose so." Jasper stared down at his selection of titles.

One was a hefty anatomy textbook. The library had replaced it with a newer edition, as this one was looking pretty tired and dog-eared. There were a couple of statistics texts, filled with graphs in eye-strainingly small type, a book on self-sufficient gardening, and Sun Tzu's *The Art of War*.

All useful. All books he'd brought home for a reason.

Jasper looked up into Lewis's patient gaze.

"I'm so sorry. I don't think I can let go of any of these."

Lewis smiled sadly, and Jasper's heart broke just a little.

"Please," Jasper whispered. "Please help me."

Chapter Eleven

"Please. I can't do it on my own," Jasper said and began cracking his knuckles.

Lewis leaned across the table and took Jasper's hand. No, he probably shouldn't keep touching him—overstepping therapist/client boundaries and all that, but seeing how he'd already jumped over them all with that hug...

Besides, the knuckle-cracking thing was seriously irritating.

"Of course I'll help you. That's what I'm here for."

The panic seemed to ease. Jasper's shoulders dropped and his breathing returned to a normal rate.

"Okay, I want to try a little thought experiment," Lewis began. Best if he took charge at the moment, guiding Jasper into healthier habits of thinking. "We're going to use a scale of discomfort. One hundred is the most distressed you've ever felt, and zero is absolutely fine and dandy."

"The most distressed?" Jasper blanched, his tan skin turning sallow.

"Or the most discomfort, if you prefer. Just think of a time when you really couldn't bear what was going on, and use that as your baseline."

Jasper nodded, his lips tight and his eye twitching like crazy. Whatever that memory was, it was a traumatic one. Perhaps at some point he'd tell, but Lewis certainly wasn't going to press for that now. Not when the aim was to get him to relax.

"Let's start with right now. I've just asked you to choose a couple of books to let go of. What's your discomfort rating at this moment?"

"Erm…" Jasper licked his lips and swallowed like he had something stuck in his throat. His hand convulsed in Lewis's grip, but he wasn't about to let go. "I'd say about fifty."

"Can you tell me more? What are you feeling right now?"

"I'm nervous, and I don't like having demands put on me."

"What are you nervous about?"

"That I'll disappoint you. I won't be able to choose. I've got reasons for keeping all of these."

"Okay. Let's talk about those reasons, then. This one." Lewis picked up *The Art of War*. "Why do you want to keep this book? You told me yourself you don't plan on reading any of these."

"It's a classic." When Lewis didn't respond other than to nod encouragingly, Jasper continued. "It was listed in the Times as one of the most influential ancient books."

"We're in the twenty-first century now."

"I know that. But it's a piece of history. It shows us something about humanity. How we've got to be where we are. What's shaped our thoughts."

"So would you say you feel a certain reverence for it?"

"Reverence? Yes, I suppose so. Yes, that's a good way of putting it." Jasper's lips curled a little. "Now you put it like that, it sounds a bit silly. Like I'm treating it as a holy book or something. Or a Shakespeare, at least."

"Hey, no dissing the Bard. *Hamlet* is my holy book."

Jasper's mouth was a perfect O. Eventually he shook his head as if to clear it, before speaking. "*Hamlet?* But everyone dies."

"Okay, I know the ending isn't exactly upbeat, but there's so much wisdom and drama on the way there. You know, I love his sonnets and his comedies too, but Hamlet does have a special resonance for me. I sort of…" How much of this did he want to confess? It wasn't exactly a professional thing to share personal information with your client, but then again, he was asking so much of Jasper, it felt right to reciprocate. "I'm a bit of an amateur dramatics fiend. Always have been. And I played Hamlet when I was in the sixth form. That play's responsible for my sexual awakening."

"But you were out already."

"Yes, but I'd never done anything about it till then."

Jasper fiddled with the book in his hands and avoided Lewis's eyes. "I suppose there was a dashing Horatio who swept you off your feet or something?"

"Or something. But not Horatio. It was the director. Mr. Cartwright."

"The drama teacher?"

Lewis couldn't tell if Jasper's obvious shock masked a censure or acceptance, but he wanted to tip it into the latter, at the same time demonstrating to him that everyone made mistakes. "I let him seduce me. I encouraged it, to be honest. And he treated me well. Respectfully. Could have been much worse. At least I didn't have to fumble around with another nervous virgin."

"But still... He was your teacher."

Lewis shrugged. "He was lonely, and I was a very available and up-for-it young man he ended up spending a lot of time with. I don't think he made a habit of sleeping with his students. It all got hushed up anyway, and he had to move schools."

"I can't believe you slept with Mr. C." Jasper shook his head, but the shocked expression had a hint of amusement in it now, so Lewis relaxed.

"He was a nice bloke. Used to quote sonnets to me when he was feeling randy. I still get shivers when I read some of those early ones to W.H."

A frown of concentration marred Jasper's brow; then he cleared his throat. "Then let not winter's ragged hand deface in thee thy summer, ere thou be distill'd."

Lewis stared, dumbfounded, before whispering the next lines.

97

"Make sweet some vial; treasure thou some place with beauty's treasure, ere it be self-kill'd."

A smile quirked Jasper's lips. "Didn't realise I'd actually read some of my books, did you?"

"And memorised them too."

"I love Shakespeare. Wish I'd been confident enough to take drama at school." The wistful expression on Jasper's face evaporated with a wry chuckle. "Although maybe it was for the best, considering what happened to you."

Lewis grinned back at him. He wanted to quote "'Tis better to be vile than vile esteem'd" and watch Jasper's reaction, but it would have felt too much like seduction, and that definitely wasn't what they were here for. No, they had these books to deal with. He took *The Art of War* out of Jasper's hands. "Okay, back to work."

"Do we have to?" Jasper said, a tease in his voice.

"Yes, we have to. Thinking back to that hundred-point scale, what level of discomfort do you feel when considering donating this to a charity shop?"

Jasper looked like he wasn't going to play along for a moment, but then his expression collapsed into serious mode. "Erm...seventy? Seventy-five, maybe. Yes. Seventy-five."

Quite a bit of discomfort, but not unbearable. That was promising. "Taking it further, what do you imagine would happen if you gave this to the charity shop to resell?"

"It might sit on the shelf for a long time."

"Why's that?"

"Most people don't read this kind of thing. It's hardly a JK Rowling or an EL James, is it?"

"And how would it make you feel if you saw it on the shelf in a month's time?"

"I'm not sure. Sad, I suppose. Sad that nobody else cherished it like I could."

"What if I were able to find someone who really wanted to read it. How would you feel about letting go of it to them?"

Jasper bit his lip, and his hand tensed. "I don't know. I wouldn't be able to get it back then, would I? Not if it was in their house."

"On the scale?"

"Oh, an eighty, I'd have thought."

"So you see the charity shop as a preferable option, because you can always buy things back."

Jasper ducked his head. "Dumb, isn't it? There's me, saying the reason I should keep a book I'm probably never going to read is because I would cherish it, yet I'd rather give it away to a shop than to someone who'd actually read it."

"It's not dumb. It's just that we're figuring out the unconscious thought processes determining your attitude towards your books. They're likely to be emotional rather than rational responses to the problem, or you'd never have accumulated so many books that you couldn't use your house properly."

"Hmmm." Jasper sat for a while, apparently deep in thought, while their coffee arrived.

Yusef tipped Lewis a wink he'd almost categorise as a come-on. "Enjoy the milk, young man. You need your energy for the job ahead, yes?"

Energy? As Yusef made his way back to the counter, Lewis stared at Jasper's ducked head. Yes, they probably did need excess energy. Jasper appeared to need an infusion of it.

But then Jasper met his gaze for a brief moment and cleared his throat. "I suppose that the books here I feel the least emotion about would be the ones to, erm, move on to a new home?"

Lewis nodded.

Jasper pulled his hands away and laid them on the two green-covered statistics books. "These two. They're not classics. I suppose they could be useful in the future, but maybe they'd be more use to someone now. I think... No, they're not likely to sell in the charity shop, but they might sell from the library. Students sometimes want stuff like this."

"But isn't that where they came from in the first place?"

"Yes. I, erm... I saw them on the cart, marked down for sale. Only one pound each. I couldn't resist." He mumbled the last sentence in the direction of his coffee and pastry.

They definitely needed to work on this acquiring problem before they tackled the main hoard.

"Okay, using the scale again, what level of discomfort would you have felt just walking past the cart so someone else could have had a chance to buy them?"

"An eighty. No! Eighty-five. Definitely. Like having my toenails pulled off. That kind of discomfort."

Lewis winced. "That's pretty painful." Then it sank in. "You're working somewhere where you have to face that kind of decision every day. Wow. No wonder you—"

"—have so much stuff," Jasper said, finishing Lewis's sentence. "Yep. I bring stuff home every day. There's always a newspaper being chucked out, or second-hand books for sale."

"And where else do you acquire things?"

"It's charity shops mainly, but I pick up free papers in places too. Only if they look like they have an interesting article in them, though. I don't collect the ones that are just advertising."

"But you have a hard time throwing away your junk mail?"

Jasper flushed. "You must think I'm such a hopeless case."

"Not at all. I have huge hopes for you. We'll get this all figured out. Together." Lewis grabbed Jasper's hand again. "Just you wait and see."

The wistful smile on Jasper's face made him want to reach out and crush the man to him in a tight embrace. Instead, he grasped Jasper's hand then made himself drop it, to pick up the battered anatomy textbook. "Right. You've chosen two, which is brilliant, but I still want to find out about the other books. Why is this one so important for you to keep?"

"It has good pictures. Take a look if you don't believe me."

Lewis picked it up and did the spine-flop trick. It fell open on a page with detailed drawings of the male reproductive system. A rather well-endowed and shapely male reproductive system, he had to admit. "Okay. Good pictures. I agree."

"It was like that when I got it. Honest."

"Uh-huh. I believe you. Thousands wouldn't. So tell me, besides the pictures, what reason do you have for hanging on to this?"

Jasper looked at him. Really looked at him, then got this mischievous smile on his face. "It's in case of a zombie apocalypse. I want to be able to research anatomy then. Figure out how best to kill them. Actually, it could be pretty handy with all kinds of monsters. Knowing where all those arteries and things are."

Lewis glanced down at the page again. "I've got a fairly good idea where these sorts of *things* usually are. Shouldn't think you'd need a textbook for that." Oh blast. Was he flirting? It was so difficult not to, with Jasper being so adorably nerdy and shy.

But the heated look Jasper gave him was anything but shy. "Oh no. I definitely don't need a textbook for *that*."

How the hell was he meant to stop himself returning a smutty remark? But Lewis railed against temptation. He made himself look at the books, zoning in on the only one they hadn't yet discussed. "And the self-sufficiency one? Actually, I know someone who might be interested in this one."

"Oh, well, that's obvious, isn't it? I mean, when the apocalypse does come, we're going to need to start growing our own food. This one has huge survival value."

"Unless we become zombies ourselves. I think they have an all-brains diet."

"I'm not letting the zombies get you," Jasper said and the ferocity of his tone made Lewis look up. "I know karate. They're not getting anywhere near you. I'll kick their heads off first." He scowled, but the frown quickly melted into a grin.

Oh my. That was sexy. That possessive machismo. It was like Jasper had tapped directly into Lewis's fantasies and taken all the best bits. Not only was he a gentle, kind soul who loved books—loved Shakespeare, no less—but he could do the alpha-male thing to protect the people he cared about.

If Lewis wasn't careful, he'd be a goner.

Chapter Twelve

Jasper sat at his workstation and stared down at the two books on the counter. *Discovering Statistics*, and *Geostatistics in Action*. Lewis had trusted him to bring them into work and return them to the sales trolley, and Jasper wanted to be worthy of that trust.

Only problem was, he could see from here that the trolley was half-full already. Brenda had been busy clearing out the medical section that morning to make way for new stock. Okay, there probably wouldn't be anything there too tempting for him, but could he resist looking?

Jasper steeled himself and got to his feet. He could do this. His heart hammered like it was trying to punch a hole through his ribs, but he walked over to the trolley and dropped the two books onto the top shelf.

Definitely an eighty-five on Lewis's scale. Felt like he was having forks stuck in his legs by malevolent dwarfs. The thought made Jasper smile, though, and that eased it down to an eighty. By the time he'd walked back to his desk, it was perhaps a seventy-five.

Hmm...interesting.

As the hours of his shift rolled past, Jasper had occasion to walk near the trolley several times, and each time his anxiety spiked, but when it fell again, he realised it dipped a little further back towards normal each time. Well, whatever normal was for an inveterate worrier like himself. He doubted he ever reached a perfect zero on the scale, although Lewis probably lived there. Permanently relaxed, like a cat stretched out in a patch of sunshine. What would that be like? He'd have to ask him.

At seven thirty, Jasper looked up to find a skinny girl standing at the counter. "Are these really just fifty pence each?" she asked, as if she couldn't believe her luck.

Jasper noticed the small stack of books she'd selected, his two returned titles on the top of the pile. "That's right. You've got yourself a bargain there."

"It's just what I needed. Thanks."

Jasper rang up her purchase. She gave him a braces-riddled smile as she picked up the books. "I just checked on my phone, and these are going for a tenner each on Ebay. I'll be able to pay my rent on time after all."

That hadn't been the idea. They were meant to be going to a student who wanted to read them. But as Jasper sat there and felt his anxiety drop, he had to admit, at least someone was getting some use out of the books. Keeping penniless students from being kicked out on the streets—that had to be a result.

Perhaps there were others who could make better use of his books than he was. After a quick glance around to check none of the other staff were likely to interrupt him, Jasper called up the browser and started searching.

"I want to try a visualisation exercise today," Lewis said, settling himself cross-legged on Jasper's veranda. It was their third week of working together, and as yet Jasper hadn't managed to let go of anything other than those first two books, despite the regular homework assignments asking him to do that very thing. This, even after he'd admitted his discomfort level about them had gone down to about a twenty-five. Knowing what he now did about Jasper, twenty-five seemed to be pretty much the normal state of affairs when he wasn't wound-up about anything specific.

Although Lewis rarely managed to convince a stubborn

hoarder to let anything go in the first few weeks, it was frustrating when he could see just how much insight Jasper had already gained. He was a quick study, and Lewis was starting to win over the rational part of his mind. It was the emotional side he was still experiencing problems with, and it was also this part of Jasper that intrigued him the most. What lurked under that unassuming exterior? What parts of himself had Jasper locked away from the world, buried under a heap of books? He looked up and met those wary dark eyes.

"Visualisation?" Jasper asked. "What, like some kind of hypnotism thing?" He stood over Lewis—all six foot two of lean body—and Lewis really needed to concentrate on the whole therapy thing rather than that enticing bulge in Jasper's jeans. He made an effort to pull himself back to the job in hand.

"Not hypnosis, exactly. I'm not going to go all Derren Brown on you, so you needn't worry. You can think of it more like guided meditation if you like. It's just a chance for you to relax and focus on your goals for the future."

"Okay..." Some of the tension melted out of Jasper's shoulders.

"Come on. Down here." Lewis patted the sun-warmed boards in front of him and watched in amusement as Jasper folded up his long legs in awkward imitation of Lewis's pose. "Just sit however you feel comfortable. You don't need to copy me."

"Oh. Okay. No, this is fine."

"If you start getting a dead leg, I want you to move. I don't want to be sued for giving you pins and needles."

"I'd never sue you," Jasper said, his lips quirking into a lopsided smile.

That smile tugged something deep inside Lewis. He yearned to reach out and take Jasper's hand. But that was bound to be misinterpreted, and he was determined not to take advantage of someone so vulnerable. No. Stick to the therapy. A talking cure.

That was safest. "Visualisation, then. This is an exercise to help you concentrate on what we're aiming for here, so first I need you to close your eyes. That's it, now take a deep breath. In...out...in....out.... And as your breathing slows, you feel yourself here in the garden, with the bees buzzing and the breeze stirring the air around you."

Okay, so he hadn't been strictly honest about the hypnotism thing. There was definitely an element of that involved in helping Jasper to relax, but this was therapy, not stage magic, and Jasper so urgently needed to unwind.

Lewis continued in the same soft monotone. "And as your eyelids grow heavy and you listen to my voice and feel the sunshine warming your skin, I want you to picture your house in the future, after we've finished all our sessions and you've moved things on to new homes. Everything is going to be just how you've always dreamed about it. The perfect house for you, and you're about to walk me through it, proud to show me everything you've achieved. We're going to start at the front gate, and you're meeting me there. Now you're going to take me to the front door and describe what you're seeing on the way."

The silence stretched out for what felt like minutes, but Lewis didn't mind when he was sitting in the drowsy July sunshine, watching Jasper concentrate. With Jasper's eyes closed, it was impossible not to notice how lusciously thick his eyelashes were, and how strong the lines of his face were in repose.

Eventually Lewis had to nudge. "You're walking me down the front path, and I need you to tell me what you're seeing."

"Oh. Right. Of course. Sorry, I got lost in there." Jasper's body tensed again, and his left eye twitched.

Lewis instinctively reached out to take his hands. Damn. Hadn't meant to do that. Still, Jasper's breathing slowed again, so maybe this was just the way it needed to be. Some people relaxed best when in physical contact with someone else. Lewis worked on keeping his arms and hands supple and limber, so as not to transmit any of his misgivings to Jasper.

"That's fine. Just talk me through what you're seeing in your front garden now."

"The garden? Oh, it's nice. Erm, pretty. Lighter. I've pruned the trees, and the ground underneath them is covered in soft moss, with daffodils bobbing around in the breeze. It's how it used to be. When I was little."

"And the front of the house?" Lewis prompted when Jasper fell silent again.

"It looks good. The curtains are all open. The windows gleam. All those green stains are gone. You can see into the rooms. You can actually see inside."

"You're going to walk me up to the front door now. What colour is it?"

"Red," Jasper said, decisively. "A rich, warm burgundy kind of red."

"Sounds cheerful." And worlds away from the scuffed and peeling navy it was at the moment. "How do you feel, waiting by the door to show me inside?"

"I'm... I'm nervous. But just a little. Happy nervous. Not like I was the first time you came inside. I think I must be... Yes, I'm excited." Jasper's words came in a breathless rush, like he couldn't believe what he was feeling. "I'm going to open the door now. The lock turns easily, and the door opens all the way inside."

"What can we see now? What furniture is inside your hallway?"

"A hat stand. Somewhere for you to put your coat, and the table by the door's still there, but it's just got a bowl on it for my keys and wallet. Nothing else. I've got one of those wire baskets on the back of the door to catch all the letters and junk mail. But I don't get much of that anymore."

"Why's that?"

"I filled in a form and took it to the post office." Jasper's eyes sprang open. "I did that. I really did it. Last week. I meant to tell you when you got here, but I forgot."

"That's great." So they were making some progress after all, at least in terms of stopping new paper coming into the house, anyway. "That's a really good step to take. Now, I want you to tell me what you see on the floors and the walls."

"The floor is polished marble. It really is, you know? It's under there somewhere. Kind of cold, but there's a colourful carpet to soften it. One of those Persian rugs, all warm colours and patterns."

"And the walls?"

"Covered in books."

"In books?"

Jasper smiled then. A cheeky little smile tugging at the corners of his lips. It suited him. "Books. Everywhere. But they're on shelves now. And I know where they all are. They're all ones I'm looking forward to reading. Fiction. I've moved unread fiction down to the hallway."

"Okay, so you're starting to decide where you want things to end up. That's great. What about the lounge? What's it like in there?"

"There's a sofa and a couple of armchairs. Brown leather. And the fireplace is working again. I've got logs burning in there. It's cosy. Other than that...it's bookshelves again. Floor to ceiling on every wall but the outside one. I've got the old books in here. Leather-bound ones. Looks really classy with all those rich colours and the gilt on the spines. You can smell them. That sweet, old-paper fragrance." Jasper opened his eyes again and gave Lewis a fiercely defiant look. "I'm still going to need lots of books around me."

"That's fine. No one's saying you shouldn't have your favourite things around you. I like the idea of bookshelves. What kind are they? Built in or freestanding?" The more detail in which Jasper could picture this, the better he'd be motivated to work towards it. That was the theory, anyway. If Lewis were being brutally honest with himself, though, he was just enjoying listening to him talk. The way Jasper's face lit up when he pictured his house in working order again—that was magical.

"The shelves are wooden. Built in. I must have hired a carpenter, because I don't know how to do all that kind of thing. Can barely rewire a plug. Should have learned, really, but by the time I was old enough, Dad had died."

Lewis's heart melted at the plaintive tone in Jasper's voice, but it was time to steer him away from negative thinking. "Okay, it's fine to get help with the things we can't manage ourselves yet. Carpenters need customers too. But tell me more about the room. When do you use it? What do you like to do in here?"

"I come in here every morning after breakfast to drink my coffee and read a book. I like to sit in the armchair by the window. There's good light there. And in the evening... In the evening, I spend time in here with my...my..."

"Your friends?" Lewis prompted. Jasper needed a social life.

"With my boyfriend," Jasper said, his eyes springing open. "With you."

Lewis stared, his heart hammering wildly, as Jasper leaned forward and cupped his jaw. He should move. Back away. Laugh it off.

He should do something sensible and act like the therapist he was.

But he was flesh-and-blood too, and he wanted this. God, how he wanted it.

Lewis's id told his superego to go take a long walk off a short pier.

Jasper's lips touched his. Tentative. Soft and searching.

Lewis moaned and opened his lips to deepen the kiss.

Chapter Thirteen

The moment spun out in time, an eternity crystallised in the press of Jasper's lips, the sweep of his tongue and the breathless sounds in his throat. Lewis wanted it to stay that way forever. Suspended in perfection, rather than crashing back into the everyday world.

The world where he had to find a way to let Jasper down without crushing his fragile confidence.

He drew back a little to catch his breath, letting it out in a shaky laugh. "Okay. I wasn't expecting that."

The tenderness in Jasper's expression was going to break Lewis's heart. "You knew. You must have. You seem to be able to read me like a book."

"I knew you were attracted to me, but I didn't want to make a big deal of it. It's very common for clients to transfer erotic feelings onto their therapists."

"That's not what this is."

But Lewis continued, steeling himself against the hurt visible in every line of Jasper's face. He kept hold of Jasper's hands, though, hoping that by rubbing them he'd help to mitigate some of the damage. "It can't be helped sometimes. You're going through a difficult process. Dredging up emotions and memories and needing someone to attach them to. We call it transference."

"We? Who's we?"

"Therapists. Counsellors. Whatever you want to call what I do."

"I thought you were a clutter clearer."

"Jasper, I trained for this. I know what I'm talking about."

Jasper glared at him. "You've no idea what's going on in my head."

God, the man could be stubborn when he wanted to be. Lewis suppressed a huff of frustration. "You just told me I could read you like a book."

"Some of the pages are torn out. You haven't seen those ones." Jasper pulled his hands away and began cracking his knuckles.

"Please, don't—" Lewis reached to take Jasper's hands again, but he yanked them away and jumped up.

"You want me too. You can't keep your hands off me most of the time." Jasper leaned back against the veranda railings, his arms folded across his chest.

Crap. He'd known that was going to come back and bite him in the bum. Lewis stood and moved over to Jasper. "I'm just... I'm a tactile person. Can't help it, and you looked like you needed a bit of human contact. You shouldn't read too much into it."

"I don't know. I... Are you really saying you don't fancy me? Even a little bit?"

Oh double crap with chilli sauce on. The look in Jasper's eyes was so hopeful, and Lewis didn't even want to lie to him. "It's not that. I think you're sexy as hell and I wish I'd met you under some other circumstances, but this really isn't a good time for us to start anything."

"Why not? I want you. You want me. We're both spending lots of time together. Seems like the perfect time." Jasper was tenacious when he wanted something—Lewis had to give him that.

"I'm not after another relationship right now. Look, I've spent most of my adult life going from one relationship to another. I've not spent more than a couple of months single before hooking up with some new bloke, every time convinced he was going to be 'the One'." Lewis made air quotes. "I need to spend some time alone. I need to figure out what it is I need out of a relationship. I can't keep getting involved with blokes, hoping I'll be able to change them into what I'm after."

Jasper unfolded his arms, and his face softened. "What are you after?"

And there was the million-quid question. "If I knew that, it would be simple, wouldn't it? I could just write myself a lonely hearts ad or join a dating agency."

"See. We're made for each other. You're just as messed up as me on the inside, aren't you? We can help each other." Jasper smiled then, a fond expression that made Lewis want to close the distance between them and tackle him to the ground. Why did Jasper have to be so kind? Made it impossible to push him away as firmly as Lewis knew he should.

"I think we're all a bit messed up inside. Part of the human condition."

"But we can get better," Jasper insisted.

"Of course. It takes time, though. And work."

"I want to get better."

Lewis sighed. "I know you do."

"I'm going to do it. I'm going to get my house in order. And while I'm doing that, you can figure out everything you need to figure out. And then, when we're both ready..."

"No promises," Lewis said, forestalling him. "You just need to concentrate on reducing your hoard right now. You've made progress in stopping new items coming in, which is great. Now how about letting something else go? There's a charity shop down at the end of the road. I bet they'd like more donations."

"I could..." Fear flitted across Jasper's face, but his expression quickly settled into a grim determination. Damn, he looked good like that. Strong-jawed and tough. Just the kind of looks Lewis was a total sucker for.

"Let's do it," Jasper said. "Five books? We'll try the paperback fiction on the stairs. That was the last lot in."

"Okay. Sounds good."

"Come on, then." Jasper headed back into the claustrophobic interior. "No time like the present."

Lewis followed after him, edging through the hallway just in time to see Jasper pick up a small armful of paperbacks from the third step, then turn to the front door.

"Whoa! Aren't you even going to look at them?"

"I know what they are. I brought them home last week. Come on. I want to get them to the shop before I change my mind." Jasper patted down his pockets. "I've got my keys. I could leave my bag, couldn't I? Just this once." His eyes met Lewis's with a kind of mute appeal.

"Of course you can leave your bag. It's only a short walk back if you find you need anything in there."

"Okay..." Jasper's gaze slid in the direction of the kitchen, where Lewis had seen him leave his overstuffed bag. "Yes, I'm sure you're right. I'm hardly going to need my laptop just to go to the charity shop. But what about if we need money? I should go and get my wallet."

"Why would we need money?" Not for more books, please.

Jasper wouldn't meet his gaze. "A coffee? I could go for some baklava."

"I'll get you a coffee. We can carry on our session in the café. How does that sound?"

"Sounds good." But Jasper still vacillated by the front door.

Lewis wanted to make the most of the impulse to leave. "Let's go. I've been meaning to schedule in a trip to the shops with you anyway. It's going to be useful to see how you usually go about acquiring new books."

"Oh, right. Of course. Well, I suppose we'd better go, then. Does this mean I'll be allowed to look at the books there?"

"I'm going to insist on it."

Jasper's face lit up, then fell. "But I won't have any money if I see something I want."

"That's kind of the point."

"Oh, of course."

"Come on, out the door."

With a last wistful glance in the direction of the kitchen, Jasper let himself out the front door.

The walk down the hill was too short for Jasper to say good-bye to the books properly. He had an absurd urge to take out his phone and photograph them before they were lost forever, but when he confided this to Lewis, he just smiled.

"That's pretty normal behaviour for people who hoard. I had a client once who had to make up poems about every object she got rid of. Took me three months to wean her off the habit. After that, she was able to move away from the individual items and make up poems about whole bags, and even a vanload of stuff."

"She sounds crazy."

"She was definitely a more extreme case. She didn't have as much stuff as you do, but it wasn't remotely organised, and she was incredibly attached to every last piece of it. Lots of soft toys and clothes that didn't fit her anymore. Everything had a sentimental memory." Lewis trailed off, sounding thoughtful.

"I don't really have that problem. Maybe with a few of the books I've read and loved, but I'm planning to keep those."

"On your fancy new bookshelves."

"Right."

"What about the stuff behind the books?"

Jasper halted, frozen to the spot. "What stuff?" How did Lewis know?

Lewis turned back to face him, tilting his head to one side.

114

"There's furniture behind it all, isn't there? And your mum's things. You told me in our first session."

"I did? Oh. God, I'm so forgetful. Why can't I remember things? I can never bloody well remember anything. I'm hopeless. That's what I am."

"You seem to remember a pretty normal amount of stuff. We can't all have photographic memories."

"Yes, but I can barely remember a thing. I have to make lists when I go shopping or I forget something basic like milk."

"That's pretty normal too." Lewis shrugged. "I make shopping lists all the time. Well, I did. Before I moved back into Mum and Dad's." His body seemed to sag.

If Jasper could steer the conversation in this direction, perhaps Lewis would forget his previous line of questioning. "So why did you move back in there?" He started walking again. The sooner they got into the charity shop, the more distractions there would be.

"After my last relationship ended, I didn't have any money or a home."

"That's terrible."

"Not really. At least Mum and Dad have enough room in their place and we get on well enough. I mean, I'm not homeless."

"No, but still... How come you didn't have any money? You seem so organised. I'd have thought there'd be savings somewhere." He glanced over to see a wry smile on Lewis's face, quite different from his usual sweet ones.

"I've never been any good at saving. If I'm not buying presents for people, I'm expanding my wardrobe." He gestured down at his jeans, which to Jasper's uneducated eyes didn't look like anything particularly special, although they did hug Lewis's arse agreeably closely. "These were custom made. Cost a small fortune, but worth every penny."

"I'll say." It popped out before he'd had a chance to censor himself, but Lewis's smile now reached his eyes.

"Didn't think you cared much for clothes."

"Not on me I don't. Doesn't mean I can't appreciate them on others."

Lewis chuckled, shaking his head. "You know, I had to resist the urge to buy a shirt the other day. It was on sale. This deep rusty red colour. Would have looked fabulous on you, with your colouring."

"You were going to buy me a shirt? But I've got enough money to buy my own shirts."

"I wasn't exactly thinking rationally." Lewis's smile twisted out of shape again. "See what I mean? I understand the shopping compulsion. I just don't tend to keep most of the stuff I buy."

"Oh. I never would have thought..." Jasper walked along, his steps suddenly buoyant, like the pavement had been spring-loaded. "You really wanted to buy me a present? Why?"

Lewis was looking anywhere but at him. "It would have suited you. With your skin and hair, you should go deep and bold. Wishy-washy doesn't work on you."

Jasper got the feeling Lewis was evading the real question just as he had himself earlier, but they'd reached the shops now and the time for revealing conversation was probably over. Still, the idea that Lewis had been thinking of him... Had wanted to buy something he thought would look good on him... That wasn't the kind of thing you did for someone you didn't care about, was it?

Jasper grinned as he pushed open the charity shop door. "Morning Rose," he called to the woman with the overdone blue rinse sitting behind the counter. "You're never going to believe this, but I've actually got something to donate."

He plonked the books down on the counter and glanced over to Lewis. His heart was racing, but he wasn't entirely sure if that was down to giving up the books or Lewis's proximity. *Seventy*, he mouthed, knowing Lewis would understand.

Lewis nodded and moved back to look through a rack of men's clothing.

Yes, it looked like they did both have their own little shopping addictions. Strange that the thought could make him so absurdly happy—that they shared a psychological weakness.

Once he'd finished exchanging pleasantries with Rose, Jasper went to join Lewis. "See anything you like?"

"Hmm? Oh, not for me. But this..." Lewis lifted up a dark green shirt. "This would look great on you. I think it's your size."

"Aren't you meant to be stopping me from buying things?"

Lewis's cheeks flushed. "Yes. Sorry. Right, books. Let's go look at the books."

So now Lewis was the one apologising. Interesting. Jasper kind of liked seeing him flustered. Seeing that unflappable calm ruffled up just a little. It made his eyes brighter and his cheeks pinker.

He followed, watching the back of Lewis's head and the set of his shoulders. It was a view he didn't think he'd ever tire of.

"So, tell me what goes through your head when faced with lots of books like this," Lewis said.

Jasper ran a fingertip along the row of spines. "I'm excited. So many possibilities. There could be something fabulous lurking in amongst this lot."

"Define fabulous."

"I don't know. A book I don't already have. Something rare or unusual. I like finding ones that have gone out of print. Ones with beautiful covers."

"So you'd consider yourself a collector?"

"Oh, well, not really. I mean, I don't go to auctions or antiquarian bookshops or anything."

"Why not?"

"Why? Erm... I suppose it just seems so expensive. I mean, I could find a first edition of something like *The Little Prince* for maybe a few hundred. I don't know. Perhaps more. Think how many books I could buy here for that money."

"So that's the aim, is it? Economy. Quantity rather than quality."

"Well...when you put it like that. Pigging hell! Is that what I've been doing? That's so stupid. Like I need that many books!"

"So, maybe we could start coming up with some guidelines for acquiring."

"Guidelines? Like what?"

"When I'm tempted by something, I have a set of rules I go through to help me decide whether or not I really need to buy it. Unless I can answer yes to at least five of them, I leave it in the shop."

"What kind of rules?"

"All sorts of things. When I last bought clothes, how many other of that type of garment I already have, whether it goes with my existing wardrobe, whether it's a breathable fabric..." Lewis fidgeted with one of the books, sliding it halfway out of the row and then shoving it back into place. "Not that my rules are all about clothing. Most, but not all."

"And yet you still managed to make yourself broke?"

Lewis coloured some more and stared at the books. "Sometimes the system breaks down. Especially if I'm under stress. I have a tendency to try and buy people's affection when I'm feeling insecure."

"You? You feel insecure sometimes?"

"Don't we all?"

"I never knew." Jasper reached out and touched Lewis's hand where it rested on the book. "You have nothing to feel insecure about, believe me. Any man would be lucky to have you."

"I wish you'd been around to tell my ex that," Lewis

murmured. But then he gave a brittle smile. "So, enough about me. This is your time. Your rules we need to be thinking about. Do you have any ideas?"

Jasper had all kinds of ideas. Ideas about Lewis, and how Jasper was going to show him just how good they'd be together. How he'd cherish him more deeply than he cherished his piles of books. But one way to do that was to work on this whole acquiring problem, wasn't it?

"Anything you want to suggest?"

"Perhaps we could start with whether you're actually going to read it. How would you feel about a rule that you plan to read the book yourself?"

"But what about if I saw something someone else would love? I could buy it for them."

"You could. But how are you planning to keep a cap on that? I bet you know people who'd get something from loads of the books in here."

"Erm... It would have to be someone I was going to see in the next few days. Someone like Yusef—he likes mysteries—or Brenda at work. She's into pretty much anything historical... Or you."

Lewis tilted his head and smiled. "I don't need any books, Jasper."

"No, but you might be interested in them."

"I can always get them out of a library. I mostly read on my iPad these days, anyway. It's easier, and I don't have anywhere to put books at the moment. I don't even have my own place."

"No. Of course. I should have thought of that."

"It's okay. You're thinking of it now, and that's what counts. Perhaps you also need to think about whether people are going to want these gifts, and how often. The occasional one might be okay, but what if you saw ten a week you knew Yusef would be into?"

"Yes. Sorry. I didn't think of that. I don't think he reads that fast. Maybe limit it to one a week per person?"

"Sounds like a workable rule. I like it."

Jasper glowed inside. "Okay, so I have to plan to read it myself sometime in the next year, or to give it away to someone else within the next week. And only one book per week for those people." A thought occurred to him, making his heart skip a beat. "What about me? Should I set a limit on how many I can have for myself each week?"

"How many books can you read in a week, Jasper?"

"Fiction?"

Lewis nodded. "Let's start there."

Jasper mused. Just how long had he been reading his current evening tome? And then there was the one he liked to pick up in the morning too. "That's one of those how-long-is-a-piece-of-string questions. It depends on the length of the book." He scanned the shelf in front of him. Perfect. A copy of *Anna Karenina*—more brick than book. "Tolstoy, for instance. I read *War and Peace*, but it took me a good month. Maybe longer, whereas a Terry Pratchett might only take a couple of evenings. And I don't just have one on the go at a time. I have morning and evening books. And sometimes a weekend one too. I like different kinds of reading at different times of day. Nothing too heavy-going late at night. Gives me bad dreams. God, I'm babbling, aren't I?"

"That isn't babbling. It's explaining, and you don't need to apologise for that. Does it make you nervous, the idea of limiting your book acquiring?"

"Yes. It shouldn't, should it? I should be more worried about the idea of getting buried under a pile of paper. I mean, what exactly is going to happen if I tell myself I can only bring home...say three new books a week? Fiction, that is. We're not talking nonfiction here. I dip into loads of those every week."

"And what is going to happen?"

"What do you mean?"

"If you limit your acquiring. If you set a number on it, like three a week. How would that affect you?"

Jasper stared at the shelves in front of him. He was used to taking home whatever he fancied, but this would prove a serious challenge. "I'd have to choose much more carefully. Take my time over it. Make sure the books were really, really special." He pictured himself browsing the charity shops, trying to find just one or two gems among all the used paperbacks. But talking about gems... "Hang on. If I set those limits, I could afford to buy more expensive books, couldn't I? Like, new ones, or really old ones. Proper antiques. Oh my God, I'm a total idiot. Why didn't I see that before? I could be a real book collector, with nice shelves to put them on and keep them safe. Maybe even get some glass-fronted cabinets for the really valuable ones." He pictured the spines standing to attention behind glass. Of spending happy evenings curled up on an armchair by the fire, reading a beautiful old tome he'd selected from his own shelves.

"And you'd like that?" Lewis was grinning now, his face mirroring the enthusiasm Jasper felt inside.

"I'd love it!" He gave into impulse then and hugged Lewis to him. "Thank you. Thank you so much. You've given me a... This is going to sound stupid, but it feels like an epiphany."

"I didn't do anything. This is all you."

"Couldn't have done it without you."

Lewis let himself be embraced for a few moments longer, but eventually he pushed back. "Come on, then, epiphany man. Let's think about a few more acquiring guidelines. How about over coffee?"

"Sounds good to me."

And hopefully, one day soon, Lewis would ask Jasper out to coffee when Jasper wasn't paying him for his time.

Jasper touched his lips, remembering their fleeting kiss, and smiled.

Chapter Fourteen

Later that afternoon, Lewis met up with Carroll for their weekly mission to help the Lehrmans clean out something. Anything. Normally it got him down, what with Mr. Lehrman's relentless inability to let even the smallest item out of the house—especially when he could see how desperately his sister wanted a clean and clear home.

But today was different. Today he felt hopeful.

Carroll noticed it straightaway. As they went to get their first baskets of stuff from the dining room, she nudged him with a pointy elbow. "So, why the secret smile, bro? You break your self-imposed celibacy pact yet?"

"Not yet, no."

"It's only a matter of time, though, right? I can see it in your eyes. You've gone all dreamy again."

"I don't know what you're talking about." Lewis grabbed a bundle of mismatched knives and forks, still held together with an elastic band, dangling price tag attached. "Did we already show them this?"

"Don't think so. And don't change the subject. How's book-boy doing?"

"Well. Really well. I think we had a breakthrough today. He took five books back to the charity shop."

"Five? Not bad. Still a ways to go, though." Carroll picked up a toy rubber duck and frowned at it. "What the hell reason is he going to give for keeping this piece of crap?"

But Lewis didn't want to think about Mr. Lehrman's quirks. "That's not all. Jasper's starting to visualise a life without the clutter, and making up rules for acquiring." They'd come up with a small list for fiction, and Jasper had promised to work on the one for nonfiction in his spare time. It was a real pleasure to work with a client who had Jasper's degree of insight and intelligence. Once the emotional barriers were worked through, he should have few problems dealing with his hoard. "I've got a really good feeling about this. He might be ready for the big sort out sooner than we think."

"Cool. Well, the storage rental nearest his place is all pretty full except for the tiny units, but I found a warehouse in Bedminster. It's bigger than he needs, but it's on his route home from work. Think that'd do?"

"Sounds great."

"So, no OCD, no depression. Any idea what got him started hoarding in the first place?"

"I didn't say he wasn't depressed. He feels down in the house. Exhausted." A bit like Lewis did looking up at all the crap the Lehrmans had accumulated. Why on earth did the two childless elderly siblings have a broken Barbie playhouse?

"But not clinical depression."

"No. Doesn't seem that way. He cheers up easily enough when he's away from the house. But as to what got him started... I don't know. He won't really talk about his mother, but it sounds like she was a bit of a magpie. Possibly a control freak too, but I don't know for sure as he always changes the subject when I mention her."

"Uh-oh. Another gay man with mother issues. What a cliché you both are."

"Shut up." Lewis picked up a threadbare cushion and bounced it off Carroll's head. "I haven't got any mother issues."

"You sure? I think I have." Carroll screwed up her nose. "I might love her, but the woman's a major pain in the arse. She was on at me to do something constructive with my life the other day. As if what we're doing here isn't constructive."

"Actually, sometimes I think it's more destructive." At Carroll's quizzical look, he expanded. "Well, look at it this way: they've spent all these years building up their piles of stuff, and then we come along to tear it all down."

"We're making their lives better."

"Not denying that, but it's like the process I take some of them through. It can hurt, knocking down all those ingrained thought patterns and habits. And sometimes they have to work through past traumas on the way." God. He hoped Jasper didn't find it too tough when they got to the root of whatever his problem was.

"Don't worry. He's got you to hold his hand."

"How do you do that? Reading my thoughts?"

Carroll shrugged. "I dunno. Creepy twinny psychic bond?"

"There's no such thing." He knew that for a fact, after years of them testing it out with all manner of experiments.

"All right, then. It must have been the way you got that soppy yet terrified expression on your face. I know that one. It's the I-want-to-get-involved-but-don't-know-if-I-dare one."

"Rubbish. I most definitely don't want to get involved." Which was a bald lie, and Carroll must have seen through it, but for once she didn't challenge him, contenting herself with a noncommittal hum. Lewis pulled a plastic bag full of balls of yarn down. "Do either of them knit?"

"Don't think so, but I'm sure he'll come up with some reason. Maybe he hopes to own a kitten one day."

"God forbid. Can you imagine the stench?"

"I don't have to. Remember old Alfie's place?"

Lewis shuddered. "Don't remind me." Hoarders with animals were the worst clients to work with. If the place was too unhygienic, they had to pass it on to the local council enforcement team, as was the case with Alfie and his five dogs, who'd been allowed to do their business pretty much wherever they liked. Clients like that, they got him down. The ones who were unwilling

124

or unable to change. But Jasper—he was a model client, eager to please. A dream client. The best client he'd ever had.

Oh God. What if he was experiencing counter-transference?

Or worse yet, what if he was genuinely falling for Jasper?

Lewis chucked a broken shelf bracket and a couple of loose cassette tapes into his basket. Better distract himself from the whole Jasper situation. They still had a long way to go before he was rehabilitated. But as to what happened then, when their client/therapist relationship ended? Lewis's stomach fluttered.

Yes. That could be interesting. Bring on the recovery.

He'd just have to hope that whatever it was Jasper was hiding, it was something Lewis had the skills to steer him through.

A week after his epiphany, Jasper felt ready to start on the newspapers in his kitchen. He told Lewis as much when he arrived for their usual Monday-morning session.

"I thought we could take them out onto the veranda a stack at a time and sort through them there," he said. "It's way too hot and sticky in here."

"It's pretty humid out there too." Lewis wiped at the strands of hair that had stuck to his forehead. "Ugh. I hate this kind of heat. How do people cope with living in the tropics?"

"I don't know. Give me dry heat any day." Jasper went to pick up an armful of papers from the stack that was most annoying him, as it prevented the door from opening fully. "I'd rather roast than steam."

"Is that what it's like in Egypt?"

Jasper froze momentarily, then straightened up slowly, papers in his arms. "I don't know. I've never been there."

"Oh, sorry. I assumed having family out there, you would have visited."

"Family? I don't have any family." It came out sounding much more bitter than he'd intended.

"Does your mother not have any surviving relations, then?" Lewis moved forward, his eyes soft with concern. "I didn't realise you were all alone. That must be tough."

"Tough? I don't know. It's all relative, isn't it?" It was hard to shrug nonchalantly when you had your arms piled high with newspapers. Even more difficult when you felt anything but nonchalant. But while it would be easier to say nothing, to change the subject, he felt he owed Lewis some kind of explanation. "I've got used to it. And her family are probably still around, but they cut Mama off when she married outside her religion. What would I want with a bunch of fundamentalist Sunni Muslim relatives? I'm better off pretending they don't exist."

"I see. And there's no one on your dad's side?"

"Nope. He was an only child, and my grandparents are both dead. It's just me now."

Lewis's smile was more melancholy than a smile had any right to be. "I'd happily give you some of mine. There's more than enough to go round. And they drive me up the wall at times."

That was hard to imagine, with Lewis being so calm and level. But it was easier to turn it into a tease than to voice that thought. "You want to palm off your annoying relatives? Thanks."

"Don't mention it. You can have my folks if you like. They're good people, but they've got some pretty weird habits. You'd never believe I share their DNA."

He wanted to ask to meet them, to be welcomed into this family he'd already heard so much about, but it would have sounded ridiculously needy. "Come on. Papers. I'm doing all the heavy lifting here."

Lewis lifted his own armful and grinned. "Righto. Let's get to it."

Half an hour later, as Jasper flicked through a copy of Le

Monde from 2009, Lewis interrupted his thoughts. "I was wondering, do you have a set budget for this sorting-out process?"

"Not really. Well, I have savings. Haven't really had much to spend my salary on, and the mortgage is all paid off." But his savings were precious, his insurance for the future... Not that they'd be any use if civilisation did collapse. "I don't know. I still want to be careful with them... Why? What are you thinking?" Please, God, not some kind of intensive residential camp for recovering hoarders. He couldn't imagine anything worse than being stuck in a room full of strangers, forced to do therapeutic exercises and spill his guts.

"It's not too pricey. Don't worry. It's just something we've done once or twice before when there's a large hoard to sort through. I was thinking, there's no room inside to sort, and we can only do it out here while the weather allows, so why not hire some extra space? There's a warehouse we could rent nearby, and we could take things there to sort through them."

"What, like empty the whole kitchen in one go?" The idea made him shiver. Did he really want to see the skeleton of the room exhumed?

"Kind of, but think bigger. We could empty the whole house. And while it's empty, get everything fixed up and some carpenters in to build your bookshelves while we get sorting off site."

The whole house? Even upstairs? Even Mama's room? "No." Jasper wrung the newspaper he was holding until it began to crumple and tear. "No. Definitely not. I couldn't do that."

But Lewis continued, relentless. "I know the idea's daunting, but it really speeds up the process, and you're going to need shelves to store the ones you plan to keep. This way, you could find out exactly how much shelf space was available and make sure you don't keep any more books than that."

"No. Sorry, but no."

"You don't need to make your mind up yet. It's just an option

Josephine Myles

to consider. Keep it in the back of your head in case you feel ready later on." Lewis's hand landed on his shoulder, but Jasper wasn't in the mood to enjoy it.

"I said no! N. O. What part of that is so hard to understand?" Jasper dropped the newspaper and pushed the hand off his shoulder, the gesture more violent than he'd intended. God. What had he done? He didn't want to alienate Lewis.

Far from looking upset, though, Lewis was regarding him with his head tilted to one side, that way he always did when he was thinking. "Can you tell me what it is that upsets you about the idea?"

"No." Jasper began cracking his knuckles, barely aware he was doing so. All his attention focused on avoiding thinking about the answer.

"No, you don't know, or no, you don't want to?"

Jasper refused to answer, cracking his knuckles one by one until the noise made even him wince. In the end, Lewis stilled his restless hands by grasping hold of them. Jasper let himself be held, even though the muggy heat made them both clammy.

"Okay. I'm not going to ask you again because I can see how much it's upset you. Just let me know when you're ready to share." Lewis sounded so confident. So sure of himself. But how would Jasper ever be ready to share something he was determined not to think about?

But he tried to smile, and when Lewis squeezed his hands, he returned the pressure.

Chapter Fifteen

Two days later, on a bright evening, Lewis was sweating buckets on his local tennis court, thoughts of Jasper temporarily banished by the effort required in beating his dad at his favourite sport. Considering how much extra weight Alan Miller carried around, he was still surprisingly good at the game he'd excelled in as a youth. This time, though, Lewis bested him in only three sets.

"Game, set and match to Lewis Miller!" Lewis crowed, tossing his racquet up into the air and catching it neatly. "Good game, Dad."

His dad gave him a wry smile from his stooped position, his hands resting on his knees. "Think I might be getting too old for this. Can't even win a single bloody set anymore."

"You won a few games, though." Lewis joined him on the other side of the net and peered anxiously. His dad didn't usually take this long to recover, and he was worryingly red in the face.

"Yes, *few* being the operative word."

"Are you feeling okay? Need to take any of your meds?"

His dad straightened up with a groan. "I'll be fine. Honestly, I think it's just this clammy heat. Far too bloody humid for my liking."

"Why don't we sit down for a bit before heading home. I'll get you a drink." Lewis steered him towards one of the benches facing the courts, and to his surprise, his dad didn't protest at being treated like an invalid. Worrying, really. He'd been denying the severity of his angina ever since it had been diagnosed, and Lewis had taken his words at face value. After all, his dad never acted like he had a health condition and had carried on as active and hearty as ever. Seeing him suffering was like being drenched in ice-cold reality.

But by the time Lewis returned with a couple of cans of iced tea, his dad looked far more his usual self. He even grimaced at the tea. "They still haven't listened to my requests for lager in the vending machine, then?"

"Doesn't look like it," Lewis answered, clicking cans when his dad held his out. "Cheers, Dad."

They drank in silence for a while, Lewis gazing up at the treetops while his dad apparently ogled the two young women in short skirts who'd taken the court after them. It was unoccupied moments like this that were dangerous, Lewis was discovering. These were the unguarded times when thoughts of Jasper snuck up on him and refused to leave. Memories of their conversations and their kiss were swirled in with a kaleidoscope of fantasies, from the domestic to the downright sensual. What would Jasper look like when he...

Lewis sighed. No, he shouldn't torture himself with those kinds of questions.

"Want to tell me about it?" his dad asked.

Lewis glanced over at him. His gaze was fixed on the court, but Lewis had a feeling he was still being closely observed. Did he want to talk? Perhaps it would help to get it all out there to an impartial listener. Dad had proved good with this stuff in the past. "It's one of my clients," he began, then didn't know quite how to continue.

"Is this one more obstinate than usual?"

That called up a chuckle. "You could say. And not just about his hoard. He's got major transference going on. Thinks we're made for each other."

"And are you?" It was hard to tell what his dad was thinking from the tone of his voice.

"I don't know. I do like him. A lot."

"In a sexual way?"

"In pretty much every way." Lewis drew his fingertips through the condensation on the side of his can. "He kissed me last week. I shouldn't have let it happen, and I'm on my guard now. But... I don't know. I've got feelings for him. Must be counter-transference, I reckon. He's a model client in nearly every way. He's gaining real insight to his problems."

"Not like the usual stubborn old bastards, then?"

"Not really. Well, sometimes he is. No one's perfect."

The two tennis players high-fived each other over the net, and Lewis slouched back against the bench, tipping his head back farther to watch the last rays of the sun lighting up the treetops. "I suppose I should hand him over to Carroll, really, but it's not like I want to start a relationship with someone when they're going through all this, anyway. It would be taking advantage of him when he's in a vulnerable state."

"Do you think Carroll would be right for him? She's got a very different approach to you. Something of the bulldozer about her, I've always thought."

"She's really good with some clients. But I don't know. Not with Jasper, I think. Not yet, anyway. Maybe when he's further into the process it would work."

"So what are you going to do about this Jasper's crush on you?"

"What can I do? Just carry on like this, I reckon. And make sure he doesn't kiss me again. Have you got any tips? You must have had students try it on with you in the past?"

"In the past? I'm not over the hill just yet, I'll have you know." His dad huffed and straightened himself up. "Honestly? It's always so bloody flattering when it's this pretty young woman making eyes at me, and I get why so many of my colleagues can't seem to help themselves, but it just isn't ethical. I'm in a position of authority, and it's up to me to be the responsible one. You've just got to stick to your standards like glue and order your body to behave. Of course, being married helps. I've got the thought of Cassie skinning me alive to keep me on the straight and narrow."

"So you think I'm right to insist on a professional distance?"

"Of course." His dad grunted and leaned down to start massaging his calf muscles. "There's only one person you're answerable to, and that's your client. His needs come first. And I don't mean the needs he thinks he has, but the actual ones. He needs you to be his therapist, not his lover. You're much more use to him that way."

"Yeah, I know you're right." Lewis watched the leaves above him rustle as a pigeon came home to roost. His dad had just told him everything he wanted to hear.

So how come he didn't feel any more content?

Jasper sat cross-legged on the veranda and stared at his phone. It would be so easy to call Lewis—just a simple touch of the screen—but then what? Begging to see him again would be beyond pathetic, and he didn't want to come across like the needy, desperate obsessive he really was. Besides, all Lewis would say was that they'd be seeing each other in the morning. It wasn't like he had a valid reason to call on a Sunday.

But he couldn't take another day of being alone with his books. They'd gone from being comforting to disturbing. Inside the house, he was constantly assaulted by their presence, the accusing fingers they pointed at him. Maybe a run would be in order, although the muggy heat stole any enthusiasm for that idea.

No, what he really wanted was company. Someone to talk to. If Lewis was out of the question, that left him a grand total of...

Jasper scrolled through the contacts on his phone. Yep, just a few workmates, his doctor's surgery, and Mas. What a life.

He stared at the headshot of Mas, grinning dreamily after Jasper had just screwed him senseless. Looked like it would have to be him.

Mas was standing where he'd promised in his text, leaning on the railings overlooking the Avon outside the Watershed arts centre. Jasper joined him and stared out at the boats. On their side of the river, rows of small white cruisers were neatly moored, one of them flying a rainbow flag, which was nice to see. The other side of the river was lined with narrowboats and the occasional floating restaurant, and in the distance, he could see the white masts of larger boats.

"So," Mas began, "if this isn't a booty call, what have I dragged my arse out of bed for at this ungodly hour of the morning?"

"It's half-past eleven." Jasper watched the strolling shoppers and tourists crossing the river on the footbridge, dwarfed by the weird metal trumpets that grew out of it, like giant lilies reaching for the sky. "Look, the world is up and awake. It's hardly early."

"Any hour of the morning is ungodly on a Sunday. Never could understand why Mum used to insist on dragging me to church then. I told her God would be having a lie-in after watching all the sinners at it like rabbits on Saturday night. He's like the ultimate voyeur or something. Watching your every move. Reading every dirty thought you ever have. I must keep him busy twenty-four/seven, I reckon."

"You told your mum all that?"

Mas waved a hand dismissively. "Just the edited highlights. No point trying to reason with her. Not since the JW's brainwashed her. She's pretty much disowned me now, although I do still get cards on birthdays and Christmas."

"I didn't think Jehovah's Witnesses were allowed to celebrate Christmas."

"They're not. That's what makes those poxy little supermarket cards so special, isn't it?"

So Mas had pretty much lost his mother too, by the sound of it. They had so much in common, the two of them, and they were good in bed. Life would be so much easier for everyone if Jasper could just fall for him instead of Lewis.

But wishing was futile. He'd learned that lesson a long time ago.

"Come on," Jasper said. "I'm treating you to coffee, and if you're really good, you might get cake."

"Ooh, is this a date, then? Kinda doing things backwards, isn't it? I always thought you were meant to get all that kind of stuff out of the way before you started shagging. Mind you, I could never see the point of waiting. I'm pretty cheap, you know. You needn't go the extravagance of buying cake to get me to put out. You'd have been quite welcome to come round and hop into bed with me."

Jasper ran his hand along the railing, searching for the right words. "Mas, I don't think that's going to h—" He came to an abrupt halt as a hand slapped over his mouth.

"Don't say it. Let me keep on hoping, yeah?" Mas's eyes were the same colour as the river, and it was hard to resist the way they implored him.

Jasper peeled Mas's hand away gently and held on to it in the same way Lewis held his hand. Now that he was doing it himself, he realised with a pang how the act was purely comforting, not sexual. But that didn't change the fact he had to be honest with Mas. "I don't want to mess you around. I'd like to stay friends, though. I don't..." He turned to stare at the sun glinting off the water. "I don't have many of those."

"Yeah?" After a long moment, Mas's fingers tightened around his. "I've got tons of friends going spare. You're welcome to a few if you want."

"Doesn't sound like you need me for anything, then."

"Hey, I'm always happy to find room for another friend. Besides, they're all pub-and-club mates. You can be my elevenses friend if you like. The one man I'm willing to drag my arse out of bed for before noon on a Sunday."

Jasper squeezed Mas's hand back. "Thanks. That means a lot to me."

"No worries." Mas dropped his hand and grinned. "Just remember, I'm only a penniless shop assistant so you're buying. Can't even afford to get myself new clothes on sodding eBay at the moment. Got outbid on a pair of jeans yesterday. I swear, the price of second-hand glad rags is going through the roof."

"Just wait. When you get your first paycheque from modelling, it's your round," Jasper said, aiming for gallant flattery, but Mas just pulled a face and laughed dismissively.

"Yeah, right. They told me I didn't have the physique for it, the bastards. Too bloody skinny apparently. That's all right, though. I could always hire myself out as an escort for a bit of extra cash. Mind you, I don't reckon I'd be all that into desperate middle-aged men pawing all over me." Mas smirked. "Still, there's always a demand for cute twinks in porn. I could make myself a bloody fortune and shag more sexy men than I've had hot dinners."

Jasper stared, aghast. "I hope you're joking. You know how risky the sex industry is, don't you?"

"Yes, *Dad*. God, you're worse than having a conscience. Tell you what, how about I just find myself that sugar daddy I've been talking about?"

"Sounds like a better idea."

"Right, then, let's go for coffee. I can scope out the wealthy men, and you can feed me cake. We spot anyone likely, I'll fake an orgasm like that chick in that eighties film I saw the other night. When Someone Met Someone or other. That's bound to catch their interest."

Jasper shook his head and couldn't help smiling. "Just make sure you don't swear as much as you usually do."

Mas threw his head back and moaned filthily. "Oh, Jasper,

fuck, that's it, right there. Harder, do me harder!"

Cheeky little blighter. Jasper cuffed him in the shoulder, and Mas collapsed into a sniggering fit.

An unfamiliar feeling rose inside Jasper. Something warm and comfortable, and quite different from the confusing way Lewis made him feel. Yes, being friends with Mas was definitely the right choice.

It just remained to be seen whether things would ever be this easy between him and Lewis.

Chapter Sixteen

The next couple of weeks proceeded just as Lewis had hoped. Jasper made some progress with the newspapers in his kitchen and eventually agreed to take a carload of them down to the recycling centre. It was time-consuming work, as Jasper had to look through every single paper first—the English-language ones, anyway. He was making separate piles of foreign-language ones out on the back veranda.

"Just while the weather stays nice," he explained. "I'll take them back in if it looks like rain."

"Or we could just take them directly to the van. Why are you keeping them, anyway?"

"In case...someone might want them. A language student. They'd be good practice material."

"Really? I would have thought that with foreign-language websites, people had easy enough access to that sort of thing these days."

"I suppose..."

Lewis pressed his point. "This is old news now. Don't you think a language student would rather practice on fresher papers? Maybe you could put up a sign in your library or something, and they could come and collect the new ones."

"Hey, that's a brilliant idea. And then I wouldn't have to bring them home, would I?"

It was hard to bite back the comment that Jasper didn't have to bring them home, anyway. He had his reasons, warped though they might be. "What if no one wants the old papers? What's the normal thing to do with them at work?"

"Normal? I suppose...on days when I'm not there, they get thrown in the recycling."

Lewis kept his voice light, nonjudgmental. "Do you think you could do that yourself next time there're old papers going spare?"

"I don't know. I wouldn't want to. I'd want to save them. I always want to. Drives me nuts when I can see them at the bottom of the recycling bin. I'd fish them out, but it's too high for me to reach in."

"Why do you think they need saving? Isn't being pulped and turned into something new a good use for them?"

"Yesss..." Jasper didn't sound convinced. "It just seems wrong. Destroying all that information."

"And you want to save it all from destruction, like a curator."

"Exactly."

"But we live in a world overflowing with information, don't we? There's more out there than anyone could hope to absorb in thousands of lifetimes." Lewis paused, choosing his words carefully. "Surely the real goal for curators is in carefully selecting the information that's valuable and discarding the rest. If we keep everything, it just gets drowned out in the white noise."

"I'm no good at making those kinds of decisions. I just want to keep it all. Save it all."

"In the way that you couldn't save your mother?"

Jasper went silent then, and Lewis studied his face carefully. The emotions ran deep and were normally well hidden, but he could see the pain and distress in his eyes.

Eventually, Jasper spoke, his voice quiet but firm. "I can see what you're saying, and maybe you're right. I don't know. There's probably a connection. It was tough. Being her carer when I was so young. I just coped however I could."

"You did a great job of coping."

Jasper scowled. "Yeah, right. I filled my house with crap."

"Not crap. Information. Books. Things that gave you comfort."

"And now you think I can just let go of them? That I don't need that comfort anymore?" Jasper glared at him then, the paper in his hands tearing as he twisted and pulled at it.

Okay, time to back off. "That's something only you can decide. For now, though, I was just going to suggest we work on some acquiring guidelines for papers and magazines."

"I don't need rules for everything." Jasper shoved the paper down onto a nearby pile, which teetered and fell, scattering papers across the veranda. "Pigging hell!"

God, maybe it was the heat making Jasper crabby. It was certainly having an effect on Lewis. The sky was clear, and the August sun stood almost at its zenith, blasting the garden with a stultifying heat. Made it tougher and tougher to keep up the professional facade. To maintain the distance Lewis knew he needed to keep.

Jasper was still glaring at him, but unfortunately for Lewis, the expression suited him. Anger only increased his attractiveness—darkened his eyes and intensified his features—unlike Lewis, who got sweaty and red in the face.

Jasper slammed his hand down on the pile of papers. "I'm not some kind of weak-willed moron."

"I never said you were. Listen..." Lewis couldn't resist the temptation to reach out and place his own hand on Jasper's. The scowl melted off Jasper's face to be replaced by a hungry expression. Oh God, he should be resisting the urge to touch—he knew how it would be interpreted—but Jasper's hands felt so good. "A set of acquiring guidelines is a tool, not a crutch. You come up with them, and you remain in control of them. If they don't work for you, then you can change them."

Jasper looked away into the garden, and when he looked back at Lewis—a fleeting glance that lingered just a little longer than usual—his eyes were sad. "I'm going to need to use them for the rest of my life, though, aren't I?"

"It will get easier, with practice. Eventually you'll internalise them so most of the time you won't even have to go through it as a conscious thought process."

"Is that what it's like for you? When you're clothes shopping?"

"Most of the time." He didn't think it would help Jasper to share just how challenging he'd found it to walk past his favourite Park Street menswear boutique just the previous day, even though he already had a new purchase from farther up the hill hanging off his arm. Easier to blame his weakness on the heat than admit how tempted he was to buy things for Jasper. "It comes and goes with different moods. But yes, most of the time I don't have to think it through consciously."

"So that isn't a new shirt, then?"

"This?" Lewis fingered the crisp fabric guiltily. It was covered in a pattern of Swiss cheese plant leaves in soft blues and greys, and he hadn't been able to resist at that price. "Well, yes. But I'm allowed to buy some new things, aren't I? Just like you with your books. It's about setting a level that's manageable. I'm allowed to get something every week."

"Fifty-two new garments every year? Your wardrobe must be overflowing. I don't think I even own that many items of clothing. And that's including socks."

"Now why doesn't that surprise me?" Lewis eyed Jasper's threadbare old T-shirt. With the holes at the seams, it really was only fit for the bin, but Jasper still somehow managed to look sexy in it. Maybe it was that whole *who cares?* attitude he exuded when it came to his appearance. "That T-shirt ought to be condemned."

A look of mischief dawned on Jasper's face. "You want me to throw it away? Yeah, I suppose I could do that. I'll have to take it off first, though."

Before Lewis could protest, Jasper was lifting the shirt over his head, revealing a lean torso. Lewis couldn't tear his gaze away, no matter how much he knew he ought to. Jasper was hairy. Not excessively so, but a pelt of dark hair swirled around his nipples and arrowed down towards his groin. Although the olivey skin there was paler than his face and forearms, he was still at least two shades darker than Lewis at his most tanned. What's more, his physique was toned without being overly developed, which made an intoxicating change from the gym bunnies Lewis usually went for.

"See something interesting?" Jasper asked, and Lewis flushed to have been caught staring. Distraction required. Right. His gaze fell on the rumpled ball of cotton fabric Jasper had so carelessly tossed aside.

"Yeah. This." He grabbed the T-shirt. "You said you could get rid of it."

Jasper crossed his arms. "Yesss..." he started.

"No time like the present, then. I vote it goes on the compost heap. No good for anything else."

"Well, hang on. I could... I could use it for cleaning rags."

"You've got plenty of cleaning rags." Lewis had encountered a whole drawer of them when looking for a teaspoon one time. "Compost. Come on. Betcha can't catch me." And with that, he took off, bounding down the steps into the garden.

For a moment, he didn't think Jasper would be capable of unwinding enough to follow, but then there it was—the sound of Jasper's bare feet slamming down the steps. Lewis glanced over his shoulder. Jasper was making short work of the distance between them, but while his chaser might be faster, Lewis would bet he was more agile.

He headed towards the mini orchard and swerved around a stand of fruit bushes, yelping as he narrowly missed having his arm lacerated by a rambling blackberry cane. Wouldn't want it to hurt Jasper.

Lewis halted, turned, and the full weight of Jasper crashed into him, knocking him to the ground.

It took a dazed moment of catching his breath for Jasper to realise what had just happened. He was lying on top of Lewis, face-to-face, and somehow his glasses had been knocked off in their tumble. He raised himself up on his arms, relishing the sensation of his lower body pressed against Lewis's, their legs tangled together. It was cooler under the shade of the fruit trees, and the grass grew lush and juicy, tickling his bare calves.

Jasper blinked, adjusting to the shade. Good thing he was short- rather than long-sighted, meaning he could still make out every freckle on Lewis's cheeks, every lock of his hair gleaming like gilt against the long grass. Their eyes met, and instead of the apprehension Jasper had expected to find, Lewis radiated a desire to equal his own.

Lewis's hands moved against him, went to wrap themselves around his waist. It was all the invitation Jasper needed.

They met in a crush of hungry mouths. Lewis tasted fresh, like toothpaste. Jasper licked the flavour out of him, trying to get at the real taste hiding beneath.

Lewis moaned and arched his back, pressing the whole length of his body against Jasper's. Jasper could feel every button on Lewis's shirt digging into his chest. He wanted to rip it off, but it was new, and Lewis loved his clothes. Instead, he pushed it up, his hands exploring Lewis's ribs.

Lewis wriggled. Ticklish? Maybe. Jasper made his touch firmer, dragging his fingertips down towards Lewis's waistband. Lewis was hard too; he could feel their erections bumping together as their bodies moved.

Any minute now, Lewis was going to tell him they couldn't do this. That it was unprofessional. But it felt so right. Jasper pushed his hand lower, under Lewis's waistband, delving into humid heat. Lewis made a sound in his throat. Protest or bliss? Jasper couldn't tell from the sound alone, but Lewis's hands were engaged in their own dance down to his arse, pulling Jasper to him, groin to groin.

Too much clothing in the way.

Jasper pushed up onto his knees, keeping Lewis pressed to the ground with his relentless kiss. There wasn't a moment to waste. This had to happen before either of them had second thoughts.

He scrabbled with his zip. With Lewis's. The first touch of their swollen cocks made his breath catch. Jasper wrapped a hand around them both, too urgent for finesse. But Lewis kept kissing him. Kept groping his arse. Kept making those gorgeous, needy sounds in his throat.

Jasper wanted to make it last, but every moment they lingered gave Lewis a chance to back out. He picked up his pace instead, lost in the sensation of them rubbing together, skin on skin.

Wet heat burst across Jasper's hand, his chest, Lewis gasping into his mouth. Gliding on Lewis's come, Jasper rutted against him. Everything intensified. The breeze across his back. The buzz of insects and the rustle of leaves. The scent of Lewis's release exhilarating him. Impossible to hold back.

A sunburst of colours wiped out his mind as a rush like champagne fizzed from his balls to his dick, spurting out between them.

Breathing heavily, Jasper propped himself up on his hands. He watched Lewis's face, memorising the way he looked after orgasm. Eyes half-lidded, swollen lips parted and spots of colour high on his cheeks. The sheer beauty of it made him want to write a poem. To capture the moment and keep it forever, locked in the perfect arrangement of words.

It was because he was studying Lewis's face so intently that he saw it. A tightening of his lips. A focusing of his eyes. A wary drawing back.

The moment Lewis started to regret it.

"We shouldn't have done that," Lewis whispered.

Chapter Seventeen

Jasper rolled off him, trying to ignore the pain in his chest. He wanted to lick his fingers clean. To discover how Lewis tasted and savour what should have been postcoital bliss. But instead he wiped his hand on the long grasses, wincing as the edge of a blade cut his finger. He wasn't about to bitch about it, though, because if he let out his frustration, he'd probably end up saying something he regretted. Something sure to drive Lewis away for good.

So instead he looked around, blinking. Where the hell were his glasses? He pushed himself up on one hand, feeling a disquieting crunch underneath him. "Oh, bugger."

"What's the matter?"

"Nothing." Jasper picked up his glasses and examined them. The lenses were intact, which was a relief.

"Are they broken?"

"Nothing that can't be fixed." Unlike the way Jasper felt inside. One of the slender wire arms was bent at an angle, but he yanked it back into place and shoved them on his face. They had a smear of grass sap obscuring his vision and weren't sitting right, he could tell, but at least he could now see well enough to locate his discarded T-shirt. He wiped his belly clean with it before handing it to Lewis. "Here," he said, his voice alarmingly rough.

"Thanks."

Jasper turned to face the fruit bushes while he tucked himself away and zipped his shorts up. He could hear the rustlings of Lewis doing the same behind him. He could even feel the weight of Lewis's gaze against the back of his head.

"Tell me what you're thinking," Lewis said.

"Why?" he snapped. "Is this part of our session? Because I don't think it should be counted." Sex with Lewis while he paid for the privilege of his time felt wrong. And it shouldn't have been wrong. Damn Lewis and his stupid scruples for spoiling a good thing. A beautiful thing.

"No. You're right, it shouldn't be counted, and it shouldn't have happened. Sorry. I'm as much to blame as you are. It's just... It's been a while. You're attractive, and I wasn't thinking straight. It's this heat. Makes my judgment fuzzy."

"And that's supposed to make me feel better, is it?" Jasper barely recognised his own voice beneath the acidity. The fruit bushes blurred into a watery green mess. Jasper sniffed hard. Not in front of Lewis. He was buggered if he was going to make any more of a fool of himself than he already had.

A weight landed on his shoulder. Lewis's chin. Jasper stiffened, but Lewis's arms wrapped around him anyway.

"Jasper, I'm really, really sorry. I never meant to hurt you. That's what I meant when I said it shouldn't have happened. I know you want more from me than I'm able to give you right now."

"All I wanted was a chance to lie there and kiss some more," Jasper whispered, the fact Lewis couldn't see his face somehow making it easier to confess.

"Really? That's all? I thought you wanted a relationship."

"I'll take what I can get." Whatever scraps of affection Lewis was willing to share. Now he understood what Mas must have gone through. God, he hoped he'd never made him feel like this.

Like his heart had been ripped out and chucked carelessly onto the compost heap.

Thinking of which... Jasper looked around and located the offending T-shirt, now draped over the branch of an apple tree. He shook off Lewis's arms and walked over to it, lifting the soft black cotton, now splattered with their come. Part of him wanted to keep it as a memento, but it would be a bittersweet token, stirring up as much of the hurt as the passion. No. Better to let it rot away and turn into something useful.

He marched off to the compost heap.

"Jasper? What are you doing?" Lewis sounded like he was struggling to keep up with him as Jasper dodged around the familiar obstacles of Mama's vegetable patch.

"What you said. I'm getting rid of something I don't need."

"Listen, Jasper, I really am sorry. Truly. Please, will you just look at me?"

"Why?" Jasper spun around, angry now. "So you can get a look at how screwed up I am? Pining after a man who doesn't want anything to do with me? I'd rather keep that to myself, thanks."

"I do want something to do with you."

"Yes, but what? Just a working relationship, right? Nothing meaningful. Nothing closer."

"I want us to be friends."

"Friends? How do you think that's going to work? I hang around mooning after you, waiting for you to notice me? We could be so good together. You've just seen it. Felt it. Or was that just me and my crazy brain again, imagining things that weren't actually there?"

"There was something there. I'm not denying it. I'm just saying you need to wait. I can't rush into a relationship like this. I can't build a life with someone who's going through so much change. You might be a different person in a couple of months' time."

"It wouldn't have to be a serious relationship." Felt like ripping a scab off a wound, revealing his naked desperation. "I'd settle for friends with benefits."

"You shouldn't have to settle for anything. You deserve to be with someone who thinks the world of you."

"And as we've already established, that isn't you."

"Jasper—" Lewis's hand landed on his shoulder again, but this time Jasper shook it off savagely and stepped away from him.

When Lewis next spoke, his voice was uncharacteristically subdued. "I think I should get going now. I'll be back on Monday, but in the meantime, if you want to talk about anything with me—I mean anything—just call me."

Jasper didn't answer. Didn't trust his voice not to break, and eventually he heard the sound of Lewis trudging back up through the garden. Only then did he let the tears stinging his eyes roll down his cheeks.

Books were no comfort for a broken heart, Jasper was beginning to realise. Oh, he could probably find something here that would offer some solace if he could bring himself to focus on the text, to string together the phonemes into words and sentences that made sense and filled his mind with pictures. But he couldn't even do that. The words danced away, teasing him.

He'd spent his Saturday alone and now he needed a person to talk to. Someone who knew him and could listen. Or even just sit there with him, silent together.

He chucked his book back on the nearest pile he could still reach the top of and headed out the door.

He was halfway down the hill when he realised he wasn't carrying his bag. Bizarre. He hadn't missed it. What would Lewis ask him right now? He'd probably want to know where Jasper was on that anxiety scale he loved so much. So where was he?

Maybe a thirty. For the bag, anyway. The whole general situation was about as close to a hundred as you could get, but the bag no longer seemed terribly important.

Maybe he'd just needed something to put it all into perspective. For God's sake, how bad could it really be to see his house emptied of all those books again? It was what he wanted, ultimately, wasn't it?

He reached the Copper Kettle and peered in. Good, almost empty. It was that Sunday morning lull when the morning coffee customers had left, but before the lunchtime rush. Yusef was sitting on his favourite barstool, and rather than head over to the middle of the counter like he usually did, Jasper perched on the one next to him. Yusef glanced up for just a moment, his thick fingers still dancing away with his knitting needles and fine, bright pink yarn.

"I just need to reach the end of this row and then I'll get your coffee. The usual?"

"Sounds good." Jasper watched Yusef's fingers some more, marvelling at how deftly they could move. "What are you making?" It looked like a fine cobweb of pink lace, and quite unlike the usual chunky, earthy-coloured things he worked on.

"I wanted to make a pretty scarf for Yasmina. A going-away present. She got in at the Royal Dental College. Starts in September."

"That's wonderful news! She must be over the moon."

Yusef gave a lopsided smile. "She's trying to play it cool like teenagers do, but yes, she's excited. I can tell."

"Little Mina, all grown up." Jasper shook his head, hardly able to believe it. She didn't seem old enough to be moving away from home. Oh. He looked closer at Yusef, noticing the sadness mingled in with the parental pride. "You'll miss her."

"Of course. But I knew it would happen one day. Children leave the nest and fly out into the world."

"I never did."

"You had reason to stick around. You're a good man, Jasper."

Was he? Jasper considered it carefully while running his fingers along the woodgrain of the counter. "I don't feel like it. Didn't, even at the time. I resented her for stealing all my chances. For pressuring me to have grandchildren."

"I think all parents want to see their children settled in a family. It's only natural."

"Not if you're gay."

Yusef tutted. "Being gay shouldn't stop you, if that's what you want."

"I'd be an awful parent."

"You were a great babysitter."

A memory of jumping on the sofa with two small, giggling children hijacked Jasper's mind. Okay, maybe he'd been good with Yusef's kids, but that didn't mean he wanted his own. "It's too much responsibility. I feel guilty about everything as it is. I feel guilty for not being straight like Mama wanted. I feel guilty for hating the way she screwed up my chance of a normal life. I meant to move away, you know? I had plans."

"But that's what makes you a good man, you see? You could have still gone away, but you chose to stick around. There was no law saying you had to stay on as Layla's carer. She would have understood."

"How could I have left her? She was sick."

Yusef set down his knitting and got down from his stool with a groan. "Like I said, you're a good man. Not every teenager would stick around to nurse a sick parent. You should be proud of yourself, not wallowing in your grief."

"I'm not grieving anymore."

"Then why do you live like you've given up hope? I've seen your house, Jasper. I walk past it every day. That's the house of someone who's depressed. Who doesn't have the energy to try anymore."

"I...I have been trying. Recently."

Yusef turned away to tend to the coffee machine. "This Lewis," he called out over the noise of the grinder. "He's been helping you?"

"Yes." When Yusef didn't respond, Jasper raised his voice. "Yes, he has. He's full of good ideas."

"But your house still looks the same."

"It's taking a while."

"He's too slow. It's been months now. You need to get this sorted by the winter."

"It hasn't been months. Six weeks. That's all."

"Six weeks is almost two months, and in another six weeks, we'll be halfway through September. Could be getting cold by then. They say we're in for another hard winter, and I don't want to see you scurrying in here with blue fingers and toes again. This Lewis, he needs to get a move on." Yusef stopped talking for the time it took to steam Jasper's milk, but he wasn't finished yet. When he plonked Jasper's coffee cup down, he delivered the thing that had clearly been bugging him. "I'm worried he's just dragging things out and taking your money. Why can't he just hire a skip like they do on the telly? I could close this place and come help. The children too. We'd have your place cleared in a day."

"I doubt it."

"Two days, then. A week, whatever. Why hasn't Lewis done this yet? He's meant to be clearing your clutter. Not sitting around drinking coffee and gossiping with you all the time."

"We don't gossip. He's helping me. I've stopped bringing new books home, so that's working." Maybe that was why he wasn't so attached to the bag anymore. He didn't need it to carry home new acquisitions.

"This is all well and good, but you still have a house full of rubbish. Time to get it cleared out, yes?"

Jasper took a sip of coffee, mulling it over. Yusef's advice did sound dangerously close to Lewis's suggestion. "He wants me to move everything into temporary storage. Empty the house so I can get it fixed up with bookshelves, while I'm over at the warehouse sorting out the things I want to bring back."

"You can't just throw it all away?"

"No! It's not rubbish."

"The things in your front garden are. All broken and dirty. You'll get rats if you don't tidy it up."

What was in his front garden? Lewis hadn't brought that up as a priority yet, and Jasper had stopped noticing it all years ago. He certainly hadn't added to any of it in a long time. "Okay, so maybe I need a skip for all that. But not the things inside. They're useful. Books and things. Someone might want them."

"Okay. So when are you doing this move, then? I'll come and help."

"When? We're not."

"Why not? You just told me this would be the best way for you to sort things out."

Why not? Jasper knew exactly why not, and Yusef might even understand. "Because—" His voice cracked, and he cleared his throat before trying again, this time in a voice so low it was almost a whisper. "Because I'd have to go back into her room."

He stared down into the swirls of milk foam on the top of his coffee. The stool next to him creaked as Yusef shifted his ample bulk onto it. A warm hand landed between his shoulder blades and rubbed. The touch wasn't as gentle as Lewis's, but Jasper began to melt under it anyway.

"If you want me to, I could clear out Layla's room for you. Save you the pain."

Jasper dipped a fingertip into the foam, drawing out the darker swirls into a spiky pattern. "I appreciate the offer, but I should do it."

"There's no should about it. If you're not strong enough, let me help you. She would have agreed. It's a parent's duty, to help their children."

"You're not my dad."

"No." Yusef sighed, his hand seeming to grow heavier on Jasper's back. "But if Layla would have had me, I could have been."

151

"What?" Jasper started, shoving the stool around so he sat facing Yusef. "You knew Mama in Egypt? She never said."

"No, not back then. I met her here, when I first moved to the area. You were what, fourteen, fifteen?"

"Fifteen."

"Right. I remember. My Selen had died the year before, leaving me with a baby and a toddler, and here was this beautiful young widow come into my life. I thought we were made for each other. I proposed within a week."

"But she wouldn't have you."

"No. No matter what I tried. At first she thought I was out for a wife just to have someone to help out with the business and the children. But that wasn't the reason she kept turning me down." Yusef picked up his knitting again and wound the yarn around his fingers like a cat's cradle.

"Why did she?" Jasper asked when the suspense had grown too great.

"I think her love with your father was a once-in-a-lifetime thing. She'd left her family, her country and her religion for him. Nobody else could ever compare. And later I discovered she already knew about the leukaemia, even then. I don't think she wanted to be a burden on anyone either."

She knew? Jasper sat in stunned silence. But she'd found out when he was seventeen, surely? He remembered the day she told him. Her measured tones. Her unnatural calm.

Oh God. Of course. She'd known for years. It made perfect sense. That wasn't shock keeping her voice level. It was acceptance. She'd kept it from him. But why? So she could use it like a weapon when he was ready to leave home? Or so she could save him from the anguish of knowing?

That was it. Jasper blinked back the tears that threatened. She'd coped with it alone all those years so he could be happy. Meanwhile she tried to distract herself by trying out all the crafts she could while she still had time. Yes, that must have been it.

Whether it made sense of her last days... Well, that wasn't something he was quite ready to think about just yet. But maybe, just maybe, with Lewis by his side, he might be able to. Whether they were friends, lovers or even just therapist and client, it didn't much matter.

Just so long as Lewis was there.

Yusef was still talking. Something about how he'd always viewed Jasper as the stepson he'd never had, but the words washed over him. Jasper slid down from the high stool and blinked. "I'm sorry. I've got to go. Things to do. But thanks." Yusef frowned as if Jasper had hurt his feelings. A sudden impulse made him reach out and hug the man, just briefly, around the shoulders. "You'd have been a great stepdad, you know. I'm sorry she didn't give you a chance."

As he walked to the door, the floor turned bouncy. The sunlight glinted off a broken bottle outside, dazzling him. Yes, the world was a beautiful place, and it was time to start living that truth.

"Where are you off to?" Yusef grumbled.

Jasper spun round, grinning like a lunatic. "Phone call to make. Left my mobile at home, didn't I?"

The swinging door silenced the sound of Yusef's grumbling, and Jasper took off at a run.

Chapter Eighteen

Lewis was eating a Sunday roast with his family when the call came.

Carroll had popped round, like she usually did when there was a non-chilli-based dish on the menu, and she raised her eyebrows in a pointed manner when his phone started buzzing on the dining table.

Lewis's internal organs started doing gymnastics inside him when he saw Jasper's name come up on the screen. They hadn't spoken in two days, ever since Lewis's awkward leave-taking in the garden. Lewis had the feeling he should probably be the one to call and check up, but he still couldn't figure out how to explain the way he felt any better than he had on Friday.

But now Jasper had been the one to take the initiative. It had better not be another plea for them to be together. Lewis didn't have the strength to fend off one of those right now. He'd probably cave in. Agree to everything, no matter how much he was setting himself up for another broken heart.

"Sorry, I've got to take this," he muttered, answering the call as he walked from the room. He strove for light and casual. "Hi, there. What's up?"

"I'm ready. Oh my God. I'm definitely ready."

"Ready? Sorry, mate, you'll have to be a bit more specific than that."

"For the clear-out. You know, you said you could hire somewhere. Take all the books out of the house in one go and sort them there. Well, I was talking about it with Yusef, and I decided I'm finally ready."

"Seriously?" Oh God, that sounded sceptical, but only because Lewis had been expecting something entirely different. "That's brilliant. What made you change your mind?"

"Well, this might sound stupid, but I got to thinking about Mama."

"Yes?" Lewis held his breath, waiting for Jasper to continue.

"I just kind of... Well, it's not like I believe in ghosts or an afterlife or any of that rubbish, but I imagined how she'd react if she could see the house now. I could even hear her. Scolding. Asking me if that was any way to treat her beautiful home."

"I see. And that helped."

"Yes. I don't know why. Like I said, it's dumb because it's not like she's anywhere to see over it all. Maybe the whole clutter thing wouldn't have happened if I could believe in her spirit haunting the place, but I can't commit intellectual suicide. She's not around anymore."

"She's around in your head. Your memories. The things she taught you."

"Yesss... I suppose."

"Jasper, if keeping her memory alive can help you, then see it as a gift from beyond the grave. I'm sure she wouldn't have wanted you to live the way you've been doing. If she was anything like my mum, she'd only have wanted the best for you." Not that Lewis's mum's version of the best bore much relation to his own, but he appreciated the sentiment.

"Yes. You know, I think you're right."

"I know I'm right," Lewis assured him, trying to project more confidence than he really felt. He had no idea what Jasper's mother had really been like, and you didn't generally get screwed up like Jasper had become unless there were some issues with your parents.

They chatted for a few minutes longer, mostly to arrange a convenient time to begin the move. "You might find it best to take a week or two off from work. That way you can really get stuck into either the sorting or doing whatever repairs need doing to the house."

"Yes. God. Of course. There'll be all sorts of things, won't there? Erm, like what, do you think?" The nervousness was back, and Lewis sought to soothe it away.

"Nothing we haven't dealt with before. You can expect mildew on outside walls, and soft furnishings might well need replacing. Sometimes carpets too. You might have to dig into your savings a bit."

"Oh, yes. And... Well, this is going to sound silly, but do you have reliable workmen you can recommend for doing everything? I've never had to use any before, and I don't want to be ripped off. Brenda at work, she had a guy come round to fix a radiator that was clunking, and he ended up flooding her whole kitchen."

"Don't worry. Carroll and I will sort you out with all the contacts you need."

"Well, if it's no bother, I'd be ever so grateful."

"Jasper, this is what we do. Of course it's no bother. We love helping people get their homes back in working order. I promise you, in a couple of months' time, you'll be living somewhere you can be proud of."

"I do hope so."

"I know so," Lewis reiterated, trying his best to ooze confidence, so it would seep over the airwaves and infect Jasper.

When he finally got back into the kitchen, his entire family were staring at him over their empty plates. It was like a silent interrogation, but made even more unnerving by the fact two of them were stark naked. "Yes?" he asked, taking his seat again. Ugh. Cold gravy. He pushed his plate away.

"Was that Jasper?" Carroll asked, her tone dripping with smugness.

Lewis rolled his eyes. "Yes. It was Jasper."

"Phoning on the weekend now, I see."

"It was a work thing. He's changed his mind about the warehouse. Think you can get it sorted sometime in the next week?"

"Yes!" Carroll high-fived him. "Nice one. I'll get on the phone first thing tomorrow. Shouldn't be a problem."

"This Jasper, then," their dad began. "Is he the one Carroll said you used to have a crush on at school?"

"For God's sake! Can't anyone have any secrets in this family?"

"Of course not." His mum leaned forward, her breasts brushing the edge of the table. "What a terrible idea. Now, since you two are getting along so well, why don't you invite him along for Sunday lunch next week? I'm sure it's been a long time since he's had a decent meal, if his house is in that kind of state."

"Mum, we're not fraternising with our clients."

"You sure?" Carroll butted in. "Coz I had the impression you and Jasper had already been *fraternising* pretty intensively." The way she managed to shoehorn that much innuendo into one word was masterful.

"I don't know what you mean." Lewis's cheeks heated, betraying the lie.

"Ha! Busted. I thought as much. Nice one. Knew he'd knock the starch out of you eventually."

"So you are a couple?" his mum asked. "He definitely needs to meet the family, then."

"No! We're not a couple, and he definitely doesn't need to come round here."

"Why ever not?" his dad asked. "You're not ashamed of us, are you?"

"No. Not exactly. But look at you both." Lewis gestured at the naked flesh on display above the tabletop. "What's he going to think? It's really embarrassing when you wander around starkers in front of guests."

"Only close friends. We'd put clothes on for someone new. I promise."

"I'll believe it when I see it."

"Right, then. That's settled. We clearly need to prove ourselves to you, so let's have this Jasper round next week. Carroll tells me he's of African descent."

"He's not a multicultural trophy, if that's what you're thinking."

His mother put on her best "Who, *moi?*" face.

"His mum was Egyptian, but he grew up over here. He's as English as they come."

"How do they *come?*" Carroll asked, the mock innocence of her tone not fooling Lewis for a moment. "The English, I mean. I've been doing my research, but I could always use some extra input."

His mum cackled. "Alan used to come like a geyser, but not anymore. These days it's more like a water fountain. A few gentle spurts and it's all over."

"Mum!" Lewis and Carroll protested in unison while their parents cracked up.

"If you start talking about ejaculation when Jasper's here, I swear I'll disown you," Lewis said, only half joking.

"Oh, so he is coming after all? Excellent. It will be great to finally meet a boyfriend of yours your sister likes. Although actually, maybe I shouldn't take that as too high a recommendation, judging by some of the specimens she's dragged home over the years. I'll never forget that one who spent the entire meal droning on about animal rights, then wolfed down that trifle like it was going out of fashion."

"You let him think it was vegan!"

"I did no such thing. I set him right at the first possible opportunity—"

"—and then he threw up all over the dining table," his dad finished. They had this tale down pat now. "Come on, you've got to admit he was a sanctimonious dick."

"Actually, he had a very nice dick. Probably the only reason I started going out with him," Carroll mused.

"I think I'll divorce the whole lot of you at once," Lewis said, looking from one smiling face to another. "Jasper's not used to this kind of talk. He'll probably self-combust in embarrassment."

"Nonsense. He'll be craving a nice cosy family environment. Just you wait and see." Cassie Wilde folded her arms, looking remarkably mumsy, despite the lack of clothing.

"I hope you're right," Lewis muttered.

But all the doubts in the world couldn't destroy the spark of happiness Jasper's phone call had resulted in.

They were really getting somewhere. Work wise, anyway. What their personal relationship was doing was anyone's guess.

Who did the therapist go to for advice when his family were all insane?

Time to phone Brandon.

Brandon was busy getting ready for haymaking, so he said, but Lewis could meet him at the City Farm and then they'd walk back to his place together. It wasn't the unbroken period of his friend's close attention he'd been after, but at least they'd be able to chat without Jos being there. Not that he didn't like the man, but he really wanted to find out what Brandon thought without any interruptions. However, he agreed to the offer of a meal at their place afterwards, seeing as how he'd only eaten half his lunch.

Lewis hadn't visited the City Farm since Brandon first started working there in the spring, and he was unprepared for how much more lush everything looked. Vegetable plants trailed out over the straw-lined footpaths, and the tang of fruit bushes filled the air.

Despite the glimpses of the railway lines and a graffitied bridge from between the trees and the rumble of traffic, it was just that little bit too much like Jasper's garden for comfort, reminding him of the hurt he'd caused.

Caused to the very last person in the world he wanted to harm.

After wandering around the vegetable plot, he eventually located Brandon sitting on a straw bale in the shade of an apple tree, sharpening a scythe. With his bright red Carhartt hoodie, baggy cut-offs and lime-green All Stars, he looked like a street version of the Grim Reaper.

"Hey, mate," Brandon called out and patted the bale beside him. "Take a pew. This is gonna take me a while." He went back to rubbing the blade with a stone. Each long, sharp stroke made a metallic zing.

Lewis eyed the bright, wicked-looking edge of the blade. "Umm, I think I'll take this one. Don't want to get my leg cut off." He pulled another bale out from where it was half buried in the undergrowth. One end was disintegrating, but the other would support him.

"So, what's up? Long time no see. Again," Brandon said, but tempered the harshness of his words with a grin.

"Yeah, yeah. I know. I'm a bad friend, but you're the ones who've been away." Lewis held up the bottle of merlot he'd raided from his parents' cellar. "Brought you a bottle of red to go with the meal. It's meant to be a good one."

Brandon screwed up his nose. "Cheers, mate, but wine? What happened to the usual beers?"

"I don't know. Figured you two had gone all sophisticated now, after your trip to France. How was it, by the way?"

"Amazing. You should go. The scenery is just stunning, and the French know how to live. All local produce. Loads of tiny smallholdings everywhere. It's perfectly normal to have little fields with donkeys, geese, pigs and sheep all living together over there, you know? Like proper rural fucking harmony. I kept thinking I'd wandered into a kid's picture book or something."

Lewis just nodded. Now Brandon had gone off on one, it seemed pointless to remind him that Lewis had been to the Loire plenty of times on family holidays. If Brandon hadn't been listening the last time he told him, chances were he wouldn't be this time either.

"We could learn a lot from them here. I'm working on a proposal for mixing it all up more. Get some livestock. Not gonna let the pasty lentil-munchers block me again. Looking after animals would be a really positive experience for some of the people who visit here, and it's not like the veganic bunch would have to eat them, is it?"

Lewis just nodded, and after a few more grumbles from Brandon about "bloody hippies" and "entitled trustafarians", decided it would be up to him to steer the conversation in the direction he wanted.

"I need to ask you something."

"Yeah? Out with it, then. Ain't gonna get any easier to ask the longer you sit around squirming."

"I'm not squirming!"

"Are too. You're acting like Jos does when he wants something but doesn't know whether I'm going to agree to it." Brandon broke into a leer. "It's fucking sexy. On him, I mean. Not on you. You just look like you're busting for a piss."

"Since when did you get so bossy, anyway?" Lewis's glare was wasted on Brandon, who peered intently at the edge he was sharpening.

"Must be Jos. He likes all that kind of stuff. And when I say likes, I mean *really* likes."

The lascivious grin didn't leave Lewis in any doubt as to what Brandon meant. Well, who would have thought Brandon would get into the kinky stuff? Perhaps Jos was better for him than he'd realised. Lewis couldn't remember Brandon ever oozing this kind of confidence before. It suited him.

"Go on, then. Spit it out. What's bothering you?"

Lewis stared down at his hands where they hung between his knees, worrying the stalks of straw sticking out the end of the bale. "There's this guy..."

"There's always a guy with you."

"What do you mean?"

"Nothing, Mr. Serial Monogamist."

Ouch. But yes, that was probably fair. It wasn't like he'd ever gone for more than a couple of months between boyfriends. If that. "Okay, but this guy, he's a client, and he's totally fixated on me. I'm talking major transference. And that would be fine, but I've fancied him forever." Lewis pulled out a strand of straw and attempted to rip it in half. It refused to tear. "He's just so bloody tempting. I never should have given in to it, and now I think I've screwed everything up."

"Given in how, exactly? Come on, enquiring minds wanna know."

Lewis's cheeks heated. "It was just a frot in his garden, but pretty hot and heavy." And one of the most mind-blowing sexual experiences of his life so far, as his inability to put the brakes on had proved. "But now I think he's expecting a relationship of some sort. And I can't give him that."

"Not your type, then?"

"No. He's exactly my type."

"Oh God, another materialistic arsehole? You should steer well clear, mate. You do know you have terrible taste in men, right?"

"Oi! I've made a few bad choices, I know, but Jasper's different. He's the kind of bloke I can see me having a future with. Long-term. We've got loads in common, and he couldn't give a flying monkey's about material stuff. Well, except for all the books
162

he collects, but we're working on that."

"Is this that librarian fella Jos wanted to set you up with?"

"That's him."

"Oh, right. Yeah, Jos says he's a nice guy too. And I know he thinks that about everyone, but the way he described him, he sounded like the kind of person I'd get on with."

"You would. He's thoughtful. Kind of gentle. Majorly indecisive and a world-class procrastinator, but we're working on that too."

"So, let me get this right. He's a nice bloke, you fancy him, he fancies you, you had great sex, and you've got loads in common. Sorry mate, but you're going to have to spell out what the problem is, because I'm not seeing it."

"He's my client."

"So?"

"It's a total abuse of the therapeutic relationship."

"Who says? It's not like you have a boss who's gonna fire your arse. Go for it, I say."

"But his feelings for me aren't real. He's just experiencing transference. You know," he said, responding to Brandon's blank expression. "When someone going through the emotional upheaval of therapy starts to attach inappropriate emotions onto the person helping them."

"Inappropriate? Jesus, you should listen to yourself, mate. Who shoved the stick up your jacksie?"

"I'm not being anal about this. Transference is a real phenomenon. I think he's falling in love with me. I really upset him afterwards when I said it shouldn't have happened. He even offered to be friends with benefits, if that was all he could get from me."

"And you turned him down?"

"Of course."

Brandon shook his head. "I don't believe you sometimes. You fancy him, he's a nice guy, he's offering it all to you on a plate, no strings attached, and you turn him down? You sure you're not the one who needs therapy?"

"It's not that simple." Brandon was determined to make him spell it out, wasn't he? "Look, I know me, and I know I'm going to end up falling for him too. That would be a disaster. He's going through major changes, and he can't possibly know what he wants long-term right now. What if I fall in love and then he leaves me? I can't cope with another break-up." Not if it was Jasper doing the breaking up, anyway. Right now, he had the feeling he wouldn't care less if he were dumped by another Carlos. "It's best if we just stick to working together. Maybe the odd coffee as friends in the future. He lives near a great little café."

Brandon huffed. "So you're going to spend the rest of your life single, then?"

"No—"

"'Coz that's the way it's gonna go if you can't bloody well trust anyone," Brandon interrupted. "Listen, mate, I think you might be underestimating this Jasper bloke. Sounds like a pretty steady sort to me. Not likely to suddenly fall out of love just because you're not his head doctor anymore." Brandon stood, posing with the scythe. "I've just gotta mow the grass down around the edges. You can tag along if you want. Nice thing about scythes, you can still hear yourself think while you're mowing."

Lewis watched Brandon cutting down the long grass, mesmerised by the swish of the blade. The grass stood for a moment before toppling, releasing a heady, clean scent.

"Want me to help pick it all up?" he offered, but Brandon declined.

"Needs to dry out where it is, first. Then it'll be proper hay. Of course, we'll only end up bloody well composting it, which is a total waste. This little lot could keep a horse going all winter."

"You want to keep horses? Aren't they really expensive?"

"Just some old rescue nag. I'm not talking about a racehorse or anything. Just think how amazing that'd be for all the school kids who visit, though. Some of them have never been out into the countryside. They don't know one end of a cow from the other. Such a fucking shame."

"Don't reckon you did yourself six months ago, did you?"

"Watch it, mate. I've got a scythe, and I'm not afraid to use it."

"You planning on staying with this project, then?" Brandon's work tended to be short-term contracts with various right-on charities aiming at a fairer society, all of which fired up his passion, but Lewis had never seen him looking this at home. "It kind of suits you. The whole scarecrow look."

Brandon picked up a blade of grass and shoved it in his mouth. "Ooo arr. I be turnin' into a right old country bumpkin. Next thing you know, I'll be fornicating with sheep."

"So that's the real reason you want the livestock."

Brandon winked and thrust his hips forward. "Oh yeah. I'll get me a nice little harem going. A different kind of animal for every day of the week. You'd never get bored."

Lewis chuckled, and when Brandon joined in, it quickly turned into a full-on belly laugh. The tension melted from his shoulders, and he flung himself down on his back, staring up at the high, wispy clouds. Brandon landed beside him a few moments later.

"Maybe I should give it a go with Jasper. I mean, the friends-with-benefits idea. If I don't make any promises, then he won't feel he owes me and has to stick around even when his heart's somewhere else."

"Thought you didn't want him to leave you."

"I don't. But I don't want to start a proper relationship before he's dealt with all his issues. And I don't want to feel like I'm manipulating him."

"That'd be a first."

"What's that supposed to mean?"

"You always go after men you want to change. You start on their wardrobes, but I bet you get going on their heads too. Trying to solve all their little problems. Make them into the perfect man."

"That's not true!"

"Yeah? What about Carlos? You told me when you first met him that he'd be great if he could just learn how to relax, and that you were going to help him do it."

"He was a workaholic."

"I know. I'm not arguing with that. I'm just saying it's pretty dumb starting a relationship with a version of someone that doesn't even exist yet. You fell for the Carlos in your imagination. Not the real bloke, who, let's face it, was an egotistical bastard."

Lewis wasn't about to challenge that. "And that's why I want to wait with Jasper. Let him get his hoarding problem under control before we get serious."

"Fine. But no reason you can't enjoy a bit of sex in the meantime, is there? Might help motivate him."

Could it have positive benefits for Jasper? That was an angle Lewis hadn't really considered yet. "Maybe. He has agreed to a warehouse clear-out since we got it on." Whether the two facts were in any way connected was impossible to tell, but perhaps it had helped Jasper. "He does seem starved of physical affection. He's got no family, and few friends as far as I can see. When I touch him, just his hand, even, it's like he's drinking it up." He watched a wisp of cloud detach itself from the rest as an old song filled his head. "Like my skin is water on a burning beach. It brings him relief."

"You start singing Crowded House again, I'm gonna fucking well deck you."

"I'm amazed you even recognised the line." He'd always had a thing for the Kiwi band, but in their student days, Brandon had vociferously objected to being forced to listen to them.

"Couldn't help it. Bet I know all the lyrics to that album after you had it on repeat for three fucking years."

"I listened to other stuff too."

"Yep. And all of it was just as bland and mediocre. David fucking Grey. I ask you."

"Shut up. At least I'm not hankering after a brand-new combine harvester. You'll be singing the Wurzels before you know it, country boy."

"Oo arrr," Brandon agreed.

"You sound more like a pirate, now."

"Yo ho ho and shiver me fucking timbers. I've got a bottle of rum at home. We can have wine with chasers."

"Sounds good. You finished here?"

"Yep."

As Brandon went to lock away the scythe, Lewis turned the idea over in his mind. Him and Jasper, friends with benefits.

It scared him, but it was exciting too.

And better yet, it would make Jasper smile.

He couldn't think of a more worthy goal.

Chapter Nineteen

Jasper stared at the clear spot on his kitchen floor. All these weeks, and only one stack removed. But sometime soon, very soon, he'd agreed to have the whole lot taken out. It had seemed like such a good idea at the time, but now...

How the hell was he going to deal with all those empty rooms?

He sat heavily in his chair. His only clear chair. He should make some room for Lewis and move the papers off the others, he knew. There was even a space to move them to now, but somehow he couldn't summon up the energy. His limbs had turned into deadweights.

How on earth was he planning to achieve this clear-out? Even with Lewis's help, it would take months. There was just too much stuff. His gaze panned across the kitchen and slid over the fire extinguisher.

He should burn it.

The thought flared bright for a moment, tempting him. All his problems, dealt with by simply lighting a match and holding it to a stack of papers. He'd never have to go into that upstairs room again. Never have to confront that memory.

But he was too much of a coward.

Someone would have to order him or cajole him. He wasn't capable of taking independent action, that much was clear.

Jasper sank his head into the cradle of his arms and let himself drift. Lewis would know what to do. When he got here, everything would be fine again. It was only the times between Lewis's visits that everything went to crap.

Jasper must have fallen asleep there, because the sound of knocking on the front door had reached frantic levels before he lifted his head again. "Coming," he called out, doubting his voice would even carry that far.

He was halfway down the hallway when he heard his phone ringing back in the kitchen. Should he go back and get it? Which way? He stood there, his head whipping from side to side, unable to take a step in either direction.

Stupid, useless idiot. Every moment he dithered, Lewis would be getting more and more worried, picturing him buried under a pile of his own rubbish.

But he still couldn't seem to move. His feet had grown into the litter of junk mail on the floor. He'd finally taken root among his possessions.

"Jasper? Are you in there?" Lewis yelled. Jasper turned to see the letterbox open, and a torch beam shone through, wiggling around. The relieved sigh was quickly followed up by a frustrated sound. "What the hell are you doing standing there?"

"Sorry, so sorry," Jasper mumbled, almost tripping over his own shoes on his way to the door. He reached out to steady himself and knocked over a pile of books. They dashed his glasses off on the way down. "Oh God!"

"What? What's going on?" The torch beam swung erratically. "Shit! Are you okay in there? Jasper? Speak to me, Jasper?"

"Yes, I'm fine. I'm just... Umm... Some books went over, and I lost my specs."

"Can you still get to the door?"

"I think so."

Jasper eyed the floor ahead of him. It was covered in fallen books, and any one of them could be concealing his glasses underneath. But Lewis was worried, and Lewis was probably going to hug him when he got to the door.

Sod it. That was worth sacrificing a pair of specs for.

He trod carefully, the books' angled, slippery surfaces more hazardous than he'd imagined. It didn't help that his left eye was twitching like crazy, making what little light there was strobe distractingly. Without his glasses, it was tough to see what was underfoot in the dim light of the hallway. But there shouldn't be anything on the floor, should there? He should be walking on the marble, which lay solid and stable underneath all the shifting layers of paper. So stupid, living like this. It all had to go. All of it. Yes. Now.

Finally he reached the front door, and scrabbled at the last few books lying there so he could open it just enough.

"Are you okay?" Lewis shoved through, frowning. Didn't seem like he was pissed off with Jasper, though, because as soon as he got through the door, his arms enveloped him. More likely pissed off at the books or the whole stupid situation. "Jasper? I need you to talk to me."

"I'm... Yeah. I think so. Well, no, not really. But yes, I am now. Okay, I mean." God, he was really rambling. "Because you're here," he clarified, instantly wishing he could take the words back, because what could be more pathetic?

But Lewis didn't seem to think so, because he clutched Jasper even tighter. "I'm so glad. Freaks me out, thinking of you living in here."

"I think it's starting to freak me out too."

"How are you coping with that?"

Sitting around feeling sorry for himself? But he couldn't say that. "Not so well. It's...it's still frightening me. The idea of being in an empty house. But I don't know... I think now maybe I've become even more terrified by the hoard."

"How, exactly?" Lewis pulled back a little to look into Jasper's face, and he just wanted to bury his head to avoid that keen gaze. So much easier to talk that way.

Instead, he turned his head, looking down at the books

littering the floor. "It scares me, the way it's taken over my home. My life. Like there's nothing more to me than a big pile of books."

"There's a whole lot more to you than that. Believe me."

"But is there? I haven't done anything with my life. I'm still working in the same library I started out in. I've never had a boyfriend. I haven't even had a proper holiday since before Mama started getting ill. My boss normally has to order me to take a couple of weeks off every summer. You should have heard her when I called her up this morning and actually asked for a fortnight off."

"So you got it, then?"

"God, yes. Starting whenever I like. She said I had accrued holiday from last year too, so I can take a month off if I want to and still get back to work in time for the students returning."

"Whenever you like?" Lewis grinned, his smile like sunshine in the dark hallway. "How about tomorrow, then? I've rearranged my workload with Carroll so I'll be able to help you most days. The warehouse landlord said he could have it ready for us, and we can start with just a few vanloads. Hire a lorry for a day when we can get help roped in."

"Help?" Jasper's stomach plummeted. "Like who? I don't want strangers going through my stuff."

"Not strangers. People you trust and want to be there. Carroll, and anyone else you can think of to ask."

Oh. That sounded okay, then. His stomach climbed back up to its usual position again. "Yusef offered. And his two kids could help. I wouldn't mind letting them into the house." He glanced around again. "So long as we can get the hallway clear first. I don't want them seeing this."

"We'll do it tomorrow."

"But I need my glasses now."

Lewis fixed him with a gaze, and Jasper didn't know how to interpret it. Reminded him of how Lewis had looked lying in the garden. Something ardent and tender. Like a line from one of Shakespeare's sonnets written in his eyes.

"Okay, but there's something I want to do first." Lewis's hands framed his head, then, thumbs stroking his cheeks. Jasper stood perfectly still, transfixed as Lewis tilted his head and leaned forward.

Their lips brushed, the lightest pressure still electrifying every nerve ending in Jasper's body and stealing his breath.

He stood there, dazed, as Lewis regarded him with solemn eyes. "What was that for?" Jasper asked, touching his lips with his fingertips.

"A promise. I've been thinking about everything you said. Your offer. I'm not proud of how I acted last week, but I want to make it up to you. If you'll let me."

Jasper's heart leapt up inside him and started dancing the fandango.

"You mean..."

"I mean if you want to try being friends with benefits, I'm willing."

"Oh." Disappointment slowed his heart's dance into a waltz. But it was still dancing. Friends with benefits was better than nothing. Better than client and therapist. And it meant he'd get to have sex with Lewis. Perhaps even snuggle up afterwards. He smiled.

"Would that be okay?" Lewis asked, sounding hesitant.

"More than okay." Jasper kissed him back, but as he tried to deepen things, Lewis pulled back again.

"Not here. Not until it's cleared. Your house is a death trap right now."

"Yes, of course." Even more reason to get going on the clear-out. Jasper smiled. Life suddenly looked a hell of a lot more rosy, even without his glasses on. Thinking of which...

They stacked the books back up again between them, and it was Jasper who eventually uncovered them. "Shit. Sorry, erm, crap, I meant." He held them up so Lewis could see the broken lens, a single crack running down the middle of it. "At least they weren't glass lenses. Plastic's a lot tougher."

"Have you got a spare pair?"

"No. Didn't bother last time. Figured they'd only get lost anyway." He put them on. One lens was still okay, but the frame had been bent out of shape again, pinching the bridge of his nose uncomfortably.

Lewis pursed his lips and nodded slowly. Jasper could see him reaching a decision about something. Hopefully it wasn't that Jasper was too much of a clumsy muppet to risk shagging. He was fairly certain he wouldn't injure Lewis in the throes of passion. Not intentionally, anyway.

Lewis pointed at Jasper's left eye. "Those things make you look like you've been through the wars. I'm thinking *Lord of the Flies* right now, and Piggy really isn't a good look on you. I've got an idea for the rest of our session. How d'you fancy going frame shopping?"

"Right now? But shouldn't we be getting going on the clearing?"

"Can you see properly like that?"

Jasper panned his gaze around the hallway. The crack was distracting, all right, but it wasn't the end of the world. "I'm not blind. I can see fine through my right eye."

Lewis huffed. "And you've got a death-trap house to clear out? Yes, we're going frame shopping. I know you. You'll try to repair those things with Sellotape and a prayer, then wonder why you end up tripping up over everything. People have died buried under their own hoards, you know, and I don't think I could live with myself if something happened to you."

"You really mean that? I think that might be the sweetest thing anyone's ever said to me."

Lewis kissed him on the end of the nose. "That is a crying shame, because I can do much better than that. Now come on. I'll help you choose some nice ones. If that's all right with you."

"What's wrong with these?"

"You're squinting, and your left eye is twitching like crazy. Do you really need to ask?"

Jasper massaged his temples, aware of the ache building up behind his left eye. "Umm, no. Okay. I'm probably best off taking these off, actually. I think you might be right."

Lewis grinned. "Of course I am. Now let's go choose some that make you look like the super-hot nerd you really are."

"Oh. Okay."

After tipping out most of the contents of his bag and stashing just his phone, wallet and broken glasses back inside, Jasper trailed out the door behind Lewis. He was nowhere to be seen under the gloom of the trees, but when he reached the end of the garden path, there Lewis was, waiting for him.

His hand outstretched.

"Come on. You look like you need someone to show you the way. Don't want you trying to cross the road when it isn't safe."

Jasper bit back the urge to say he could see the cars fine; it was just the finer details of registration numbers and driver's faces he couldn't make out. Lewis seemed to be enjoying himself helping out, and if it meant Jasper got to hold on to his hand like a proper boyfriend would, that was fine by him.

"Let's go."

Chapter Twenty

Lewis walked Jasper down to the bus stop at the bottom of the hill, and they caught the bus into Bedminster. Lewis had been expecting one of those huge places like the ones you saw in the centre of Bristol, but this was more of a boutique optician and had a small selection of designer frames. Not like Jasper at all.

"What made you start coming here?" he asked as they walked in the glass door. A bell jangled above the door, announcing their entry.

"Here? Oh, I don't know. It was the closest place, and I like it. Not too much choice. I got overwhelmed the one time I went into a Specsavers."

"Makes sense." Decision making was such a difficult process for Jasper, Lewis could understand why this was the best option. "They've got a really nice range in here, though. Great choice."

"Thanks." Jasper beamed.

The receptionist frowned when she saw Jasper's mangled specs. "I'll see what we can do to make these wearable in the meantime, but it's going to take a few days to get you a new pair. Could be longer, depending on your prescription. When was the last time you were tested?"

Turned out it had been way too long, but luckily there was a slot free for an eye test in half an hour. Jasper sat on the chair by the door while Lewis walked up and down the display aisles, picking up various frames and peering at them. He even tried on a pair of horn-rimmed frames. The price tag dangling by his temple slightly detracted from the air of studious chic he was after, but they suited him.

"Wish I needed glasses," he said, turning to Jasper. "Something like this would be a great way of accessorising my face."

"Why would you want to accessorise your face? It's perfectly nice the way it is."

Lewis frowned into the mirror. "Oh, you know. Just to take attention away from all this." He gestured at his cheeks.

"All what?"

Did he really need to spell it out? Surely Jasper couldn't be that oblivious. "You know, the scarring. It's so ugly."

"It bothers you? Why? I think it makes you look rugged."

"Rugged? Baby, I'm so far from rugged, I may as well be dancing ballet in a pink tutu." Baby? Where did that come from? Friends with benefits. Not boyfriends. He really needed to keep the distinction somehow, for both their sakes. Right now, Jasper was looking kind of dazed.

Oh, the power of idle little words, uttered almost without thinking.

"I like your skin," Jasper said after a long pause. "It's kind of...sexy."

"Seriously?" Lewis turned back to the mirror and stared at the pitted scars. Carlos had hated them. "My last boyfriend encouraged me to look into plastic surgery for it."

"Your last boyfriend sounds like an opinionated bastard."

Lewis gazed into his reflection, strangely pensive. "I think perhaps you're right. It really doesn't bother you?"

"Not at all. Why would it? I'm the last person to criticise anyone else's looks. I'm no oil painting myself."

"That's not true. I'd paint you if I had the skills. Seems like Carroll hogged all the arty genes, though."

"I'm scruffy, and my nose is huge."

"Yeah, but you know what they say about men with big noses," Lewis teased. "All true in your case, I can vouch."

It took a moment for Jasper to cotton on to what he meant, and when he did, his cheeks heated. "Oh. Do they really say that? I thought it was feet."

"Feet, noses, ears, whatever. You've got pretty big feet too, you know."

Jasper stared down at his battered old trainers. "Must be why I keep tripping up over things, then."

Lewis grinned. "Well, I'm not saying it's big enough to mess with your centre of gravity or anything, but maybe. It's a respectable size." It was fun to watch the flush spread from Jasper's neck up to his cheeks. Flirting. He'd been struggling to hold it back all the time he'd known Jasper, but the man responded beautifully.

Jasper mumbled something incoherent and turned to look out of the front window. God knew what he could see without his lenses. Probably just a blur of blobby colours.

Lewis should look for some frames for him. Something to really suit him and bring out the colour of his eyes. Something... Oh crap. He was doing it again, wasn't he? Trying to dress a man the way he wanted. Trying to change him. Everything Brandon had accused him of.

He must have looked as stricken as he felt, because when Jasper turned back, he rose and took a tentative step towards him. "Hey, what's up? You look like you've just seen a ghost."

"Yep, and he was rattling his chains, warning me off."

"What?"

"Sorry. I just realised I was doing what I always do, and I need to stop doing that."

"Umm, you've lost me."

Oh, poor Jasper. He really didn't have a clue what Lewis was on about. Time to come clean and make some confessions. Lewis checked around the shop again, but no one else had entered while he'd been distracted by the frames. "I try to improve people," he said. "Always have done. Their clothing, their thoughts and feelings."

"So? Sounds like a pretty good goal to have."

"It's not, though. It's manipulative. It's part of why I've been trying to stay single. Get my own head in order while I figure out what I really want. There's no point in falling for my idea of what someone's like, rather than the real person. Sets me up for heartbreak every time."

Jasper nodded slowly, his eyes unfocused as if he was looking deep inside himself. Or perhaps it was simply that he couldn't see properly. "You sound like you have it all figured out."

"Wish I did." Carlos had accused him of having it "all figured out" several times, always in a sarcastic tone, but from Jasper the same words sounded wistful. "All I know right now is I need to avoid getting involved with anyone I'm seeking to change. It's not healthy."

"What if they want to change?"

"It's still not healthy."

"So you're not going to help me choose some frames that suit me?"

"I shouldn't," Lewis hedged.

Jasper peered at the display case they were standing next to and ran his fingertip down a row of lenses until he reached a boring pair of silver wire-framed oval ones. He picked them up and put them on. Lewis winced. Oh, so not right with Jasper's features. Wrong colour, wrong weight, wrong shape...

When Jasper began talking, his words were careful, deliberate. "Lewis, I'm asking you as a friend, and a friend only. Please could you help me choose a pair of frames that look good on me?"

"Why?"

"Because I trust your judgment, and otherwise I'm just going

178

to get these."

"Those are terrible."

"Right. But I can't see why, so I need you to help me out here."

"But if those frames are okay by you, then that's fine, isn't it?"

"No!" Now Jasper actually sounded exasperated. "It's not fine, because I want to have a pair that make you think I'm some kind of... What did you say? Sexy nerd?"

"You're a sexy nerd anyway, no matter which frames you wear."

Jasper's mouth twisted into a smile. "Thanks, but I'd really rather you weren't thinking how bloody awful my glasses were every time you look at me. So help me out? Please?"

Well, when he put it like that... Lewis let his resistance crumble, and euphoria rushed in. Oh, giving in to the urge to shop for Jasper was like a drug rush. His weakness. He gave Jasper a wry smile. "You do realise you're enabling my shopping addiction, don't you?"

Jasper's face fell. "Oh, I'm so sorry, I wasn't thinking—"

"No, no! Don't be sorry. I've been wanting to sort out your specs ever since I first saw you. Even back in school. You had this awful pair of gold-rimmed round ones. Who the hell told you those looked good on you?"

"You remember those?" Jasper's expression transformed into wonder. "I don't even remember those. You really noticed me back then?"

Was this really the time to confess it, here in a shop surrounded by glasses? Oh, what the hell. Jasper already knew about his shopping problem, so this couldn't be any more embarrassing.

"I fancied you like crazy at school. Used to hang around by the languages block at certain break times when I knew you'd be leaving the lab, just to get a glimpse of you between classes."

"I, er, wow." Jasper seemed at a loss for words, his mouth opening and closing. "I never…"

Lewis pushed his jaw shut with a fingertip. "You don't have to say anything. I already know you didn't feel the same way. Not back then. How could you? I looked a right state. Besides the zitty face, black and white really don't do anything for me. That school uniform couldn't have been designed to be any worse for me. Now you, on the other hand, looked hot as hell in it."

Lewis turned away to the nearest bank of frames, avoiding the intensity in Jasper's gaze.

"Dark, strong colours really suit you. You could get away with any of these heavier frames." He picked up a pair of black ones. They were rectangular, and the inside of the frame was white, giving an interesting two-tone effect around the lenses. Yes, they were plastic, but they seemed to be really well made. Should be at that price, anyway. "Here, try these on."

Oh yes, they were perfect. Jasper studied his reflection, frowning. "They're very…black."

"Yep. It's a great colour for you."

"Aren't they going to be all anyone notices about me?"

"I doubt it. Maybe if they didn't suit you, but as it is, they kind of blend in." No, that wasn't the right expression. "They enhance the rest of your features. Make you look about ten times more delicious."

"Oh." Jasper blinked at his reflection and pushed the frames back up his nose. "If you say so, then. They're pretty comfy."

"You don't want to try on any more for comparison?" Not that he wanted to encourage Mr. Indecisive to procrastinate.

"No. I trust your judgment."

Good thing somebody did, because Lewis was having major wibbles right now. Jasper was showing signs of becoming dangerously dependent on him.

After they got the house cleared, Lewis would have to find a way of drawing back gently. Easing away so that Jasper could stand on his own two feet.

Otherwise, what kind of relationship were they going to end up in?

Chapter Twenty-One

Lewis parked the van outside Jasper's house at nine a.m. the following morning. He peered out the window at the dark clouds on the horizon and checked the weather app on his phone. Thundery showers expected later. If they could load up at this end before the rain hit, they'd be fine unloading at the other end, as they could drive right into the warehouse.

It just remained to be seen how easily Jasper could bear to let his precious books out of the house.

Lewis pulled as much positive energy into himself as he could and, despite the muggy heat and the general grottiness of his jeans and T-shirt house-clearing outfit, was feeling pretty chipper as he walked up the garden path.

Jasper must have been waiting for him, because the front door was open.

Fully open. And there was Jasper, beaming at him as he added more books to the top of a pile on the path. He looked ever so slightly odd with his makeshift specs—one lens shining and the other missing—but it just added to his ragtag charm.

"Morning," Jasper called cheerily. "Thought I'd get going before you arrived. I didn't have any boxes to pack things into, but I wanted to clear the front door so we could get in and out more easily. I used bin bags for all the junk mail." He gestured at a couple of full sacks sitting by the front door. "I still want to sort through them, though. Hope that's all right."

"Of course it's all right. It's more than all right." Lewis let how very much more it was show in a cheek-straining grin, then pulled Jasper into a hug. "I'm so impressed you did all this before I even got here." Jasper was wearing only a thin T-shirt and jogging bottoms, so every inch of his body was tantalisingly apparent through the fabric.

Lewis let go before the sensation got him too excited to concentrate on the task ahead. "Boxes. I've got boxes in the van. I'll go fetch some."

"I'll get some coffee on the go too. Should I make a flask to take to the warehouse?"

"Good idea."

"Great." Jasper sauntered off inside, the twin mounds of his backside ever so apparent in his thin clothing. Lewis stifled a groan and adjusted his jeans.

Today did look like it was going to be challenging, after all. Just not in the way he'd imagined.

The first assault to Jasper's calm came when Lewis removed one of the stacks in front of the hat stand. Suddenly there they were: Mama's best winter coat and the scarf Yusef had knitted for her.

"Your mum's?" Lewis asked, turning towards him.

"Yes." He stumbled forwards, twisting to get around the half-packed boxes on the way.

The scarf was just as he remembered it, despite being festooned with dust, but the coat looked odd. Ragged, somehow. He pulled at the sleeve to get a better look, and the fabric tore at the shoulder. Dust billowed out.

"Oh my God!" He took a step back, horrified, and tripped. He landed heavily on a box and stared up at the coat hanging there with the sleeve draped over a stack of books. It looked like it was pointing at him in accusation.

"Are you all right?" Lewis asked, holding out a hand to help him up. "Looks like you've had clothes moths. Must have been a wool fabric. I'm afraid that will be ruined now. Not good for anything other than the bin."

"Moths? I had no idea."

"They were the bane of my life one place I lived in. They're little beige things. You're bound to have seen them flying around."

Had he? He'd always been more focused on the books, but now that Lewis mentioned it, he remembered seeing the odd one here and there. "Sometimes. But all houses have moths, don't they?"

"Not this sort. They're a real problem if you don't store your woollens properly."

"I had no idea. Are they going to have ruined anything else?"

"It's possible. They go for wool, silk, feathers and fur. All the natural, protein-based fibres. Your books should be fine, though."

"Even the leather-bound ones?"

Lewis's lips twisted. "I don't know. I hope so."

Jasper racked his brains, trying to think what else was hidden behind the books. Had his mother owned much in the way of wool and furs? Possibly. She had felt the cold keenly, always complaining about the damp chill of British winters.

"Jasper?" Lewis was standing up close to him, his voice soft, concerned. "How are you feeling?"

Jasper tried to force a smile onto his face, but his muscles wouldn't cooperate. "I don't know. I thought... I thought I'd be able to keep things. As mementoes. But now you're saying it could all be ruined... That coat can't be saved. Well, it kind of, it kind of—" He broke off, almost choking on the tears he was trying to swallow.

Lewis hugged him tight. "It won't all be ruined, I promise. It never is, even in the worst hoards."

"How can you be so sure?"

Lewis pulled back, only to return moments later. "Look, the

scarf is okay. A bit dusty, but nothing a washing machine can't deal with."

Jasper reached out gingerly, half afraid the delicate lacework would disintegrate when he touched it. But no, it stayed solid, and with growing confidence he handled it, brushing off the worst of the dust from the scalloped edges. "How come this didn't get eaten?"

"Must be made of something the moths won't eat. Acrylic, maybe." Lewis rubbed it between his fingers, like a true clothing connoisseur. "I don't know. It feels better quality than that. Perhaps cotton or linen. It's so soft."

"She loved this scarf. She'd wear it most of the year, even on days when everyone else was sweltering. Yusef made it for her." A love token, he now realised. He wanted to hold on to it, on to everything she'd loved, but perhaps there was someone who'd appreciate it even more. "He loved her. I only found out the other day. She wouldn't have him, though. Wanted to stay loyal to Dad. What a waste."

"Why do you say that?"

"They could have been happy together. Yusef's a lovely man. He'd have treated her well. Instead, she threw away all that time they could have had together over some pointless scruples."

"They probably didn't seem pointless to her," Lewis said, his voice strange. Defiant, almost. Before Jasper could figure out what he meant by it, Lewis started talking brightly, but his words sounded hollow. Forced. "We should carry on filling boxes. There's a storm forecast for later. Want to make sure we're finished up here before it hits."

But Jasper wasn't going to be thrown off the subject that easily. He toyed with the scarf again, tugging it gently so the stitches spread out and revealed their intricate beauty. "Do you think he'd like to have it to remember her by?"

He looked up then to find Lewis smiling, but pain still lurked in his eyes. When he spoke, this time his voice barely rose above a whisper. "I think that's a lovely idea."

They continued the packing in near silence, but to Jasper's surprise, it really wasn't awkward. Lewis was obviously in a subdued mood, but he was still Lewis. Still kind and attentive whenever Jasper needed him. The next time happened to be when Jasper began clearing the books from in front of the living room door. There hadn't seemed any point in leaving it clear when the way in was blocked anyway.

Blocked.

He stared at its blank white face. He knew a door couldn't possibly be mocking him, but it felt exactly like it was doing that.

"Oh crap."

"What? What is it?"

"I just realised, how are we going to get inside the rooms? There was a book avalanche behind this door."

Lewis came to stand next to him, rubbing his chin, and Jasper wanted nothing more than to lean against him and absorb his strength, his practicality.

But he stood firm, because he was buggered if he was going to lay out every little moment of weakness for Lewis's dissection.

"We can't get at the hinges to take it off from this side. Does it open at all? Even just a little bit?" Lewis asked.

They cleared the rest of the books away before trying. With both of them putting their weight behind it, they managed to get it open a couple of inches. Lewis wedged a folded-up piece of cardboard underneath to keep it from closing again.

Jasper could see the ends of the colourful spines of the neatly ordered stack of gardening paperbacks right by the door, but that was all. "This is useless. We can't reach the ones blocking it."

"We might have to get someone to cut through the door."

And damage his house. Jasper's throat burned with acid. "I don't want anyone doing that." He couldn't stand the idea of having a workman in here, seeing how he'd been living. Seeing how pathetic he was.

"What about the windows?" Lewis asked.

"What about them?"

"How would you feel about taking one out and getting into the room that way?"

That would be worse. Even with all the trees outside, the neighbours next door would still be able to see. He knew Mrs. Baptiste already considered him a nuisance neighbour and gossiped about him any chance she got. Yusef had told him as much.

"Jasper? Can you tell me what you're thinking?"

Lewis's voice was calm and patient, and it helped Jasper find a way out of the quagmire of his thoughts. "I don't want anyone else seeing in here."

"Okay. I understand." Lewis hummed a couple of times, then reached into the gap, right near the top of the door.

"It's pointless. I might just have to give up on that room. Use the ones that aren't blocked. At least if I can get those clear, I can live well enough. Kitchen, bedroom, bathroom, hallway. That's enough for one man."

"Don't be ridiculous," Lewis muttered, his face screwing up in concentration as he wriggled his hand around. "We're not going to let one stupid door beat us into submission. There!" he said triumphantly as his hand finally emerged from the top of the door holding a paperback copy of an old organic gardening book. "That's one off the top of this first stack."

Jasper stared at it. "Oh my God. How did you manage that?"

"Must be my dainty wrists." Lewis posed in a limp-wristed manner and winked. "Always knew they'd come in handy one day."

Jasper fought back the smile. He'd never been especially comfortable with effete parodies of homosexuality, but Lewis did look adorable, especially with that smirk on his face.

"Come on, cheer up. We've got a way in."

"What? One book at a time like that? It'll take forever."

"It'll get easier the more I remove, and once that stack's gone, we might be able to reach what's on the floor behind the door."

"I doubt it. There are more stacks behind that one."

"Then I'll remove those, one book at a time. We'll have plenty of help at the weekend, won't we?"

"Yusef said they'll all help on Sunday."

"Great. So while the rest of you are working on the upstairs, I'll be fighting my way into this room."

"It's not only this one, you know. The others are just as badly blocked." All except one room, but he didn't want to go into why just yet.

"One door at a time, Jasper. One door at a time. If you focus on the big picture too much, it can rob you of your energy. Little tasks are much more achievable."

"Little tasks. Right." There was nothing little about the job ahead, but as Jasper looked back towards the front door, he had to admit they'd already made a huge difference in one morning. The table by the front door was clear, the floor was clear, as was the section of wall between the front door and the living room door. Okay, so it was only six-foot-long stretch, but it was the first time he'd seen it in years. That Monet print Mama had loved still hung there, and he could see the poppies glowing under the shroud of dust.

"There's more light coming in already," he said.

"We're doing brilliantly. Trust me. I'm so proud of what you've managed to do today."

And when Lewis's hand landed on Jasper's shoulder, he could almost begin to believe it.

Chapter Twenty-Two

Lewis still wasn't entirely sure how Jasper would cope with the warehouse. He'd met the lettings agent there at seven that morning and spent the following couple of hours checking the place over and preparing for things arriving. He had to concede it was a fairly uninspiring place, bleak and somehow managing to feel chilly even on what had to be the muggiest day of the year so far. However, when he pulled Alice up outside, he did his best to project confidence, despite the run-down appearance of the exterior. The locked gate had meant it had avoided being tagged with graffiti, but it was now being taken over by the scrubby buddleia growing out of the chinks in the walls.

"Hold on," he said as they pulled up to the rusty gate in the chain-link fence. "I've got a key for the padlock."

Jasper's face had turned alarmingly pale, so instead of suggesting he get out and unlock it, Lewis killed the engine and did it himself. Good thing he did, as he'd forgotten to bring the WD40 to deal with the rust and it still took a bit of grappling to open. Jasper probably would have given up and sunk into a depression. It had almost happened twice already that morning, what with the coat and the blocked door, but both times Lewis had managed to talk him out of it.

It was tough to maintain his mental energy in this sultry heat, though.

He stared up at the sky. The clouds hung low and brassy, and the air crackled with ozone. Soon. He pushed his sweat-heavy hair off his forehead and sighed. The rain couldn't come a moment too soon.

The neighbourhood wasn't the nicest, so Lewis stopped the van on the other side of the fence and locked up behind them, before driving round the corner to be faced with the warehouse itself.

"Oh." Jasper's despondent expression spoke volumes.

Lewis tried to lift his mood with chatter. "I know it's looking pretty shabby, but it was the only decent-sized empty place we could find in a convenient location. We figured having it on the route between your home and work would help you find more time to sort through things. Hiring somewhere on the outskirts of town would have been a real disincentive. And it's not all that bad on the inside, really. I've got us a kettle sorted out and everything. Tomorrow I'll bring along a cafetière and some of that awful syrupy stuff you like to lace your coffee with." That last comment raised a twitch of a smile. "Come on. Help me open the doors. It's way too hot and sticky for me to be doing all the heavy work by myself."

The warehouse doors were huge, towering high enough to allow at least two lorries to pull in side by side. Lewis unlocked the padlock holding the giant metal concertina together before putting all his weight into shifting it sideways. It barely budged. Lewis frowned at it. He could see wheels underneath, so once it got moving it shouldn't be too hard to push back, but something was making it stick. The other side was just as stubborn. They could go in by the regular-sized door he'd used earlier, but it would be so much easier if they could park the van inside. "A little help?" he panted.

Jasper stirred from his stupor and stepped up to help out, shoulder to shoulder. The touch of their arms through the cloth of their T-shirts was intoxicating, and it inspired Lewis to push his muscles to the maximum. With a grunt from Jasper, the door began to shift, momentum carrying it forward at increasing speed until they were almost running to keep up with it. But then it folded up against the wall and crashed into itself with a bang. The two of them were thrown back by the impact. They landed on the concrete floor, side by side, breathless and bruised.

Lewis wasn't sure when he began laughing, but when Jasper joined in, it was the best sound ever. A choking, rasping wheeze that shouldn't have been sexy but somehow was. He rolled over to watch. Lines crinkled around the edges of Jasper's eyes, his forehead free of creases for a change.

If it wouldn't have killed the moment he'd have pulled his phone out to take a photograph, so instead he concentrated on every detail, storing it up in his memory.

When he'd finally calmed down, the smile Jasper gave him was almost shy. "Sorry. I've got a weird laugh."

"Who told you that?"

Jasper's forehead creased again, the habitual frown line back. "Can't remember. Lots of people, probably."

"None of them worth listening to." Lewis gave in to temptation and pressed a quick kiss to Jasper's lips. "Now take a look at this. I've been busy."

He offered a hand to help Jasper up, then refused to let go of it. Jasper was thinking too hard again. Worrying. Lewis could tell by the way Jasper's eye had started twitching away like he had an eyelash stuck in it. He'd just have to talk up the good points, ignoring the piles of rotting wooden pallets around the edge of the cavernous space and the cooing of the pigeons in the rafters.

"As you can see, we've got loads of room, so I've gone all out and marked up a floor plan of your house." He indicated the blue tape on the floor. "See? It's bigger than it is in reality, so we've got room to move around. The front door's here. We've got your dining room, living room and kitchen on the ground floor, and then over there is the top floor. Not actually sure what you call all those rooms and if the space I've allocated is in the right proportion, but we can always expand them if we need to. Nothing more complicated than moving the tape. This whole section is where we'll move all the boxes to as we bring them in, keeping them all in the right rooms so you know where things are."

Jasper's brow furrowed as he walked around the upper floor plan. "What's that over there, then?" he asked, pointing to the other floor plan Lewis had hastily taped out.

"That's where we'll move the things you want to go back to the house. It will let you see how much you've got in each room. Let you categorise and check out how much shelf space you'll need. I've also taped out some areas over by the far wall. We can use them to put things headed for different destinations. Recycling, charity, wherever you decide."

Jasper nodded slowly. Good. He wasn't bolting out the door in terror at the prospect. "I think I've found somewhere I want to donate my books. The fiction ones, anyway."

"You have?"

"There're a lot of homeless people in Bristol. They can't afford to buy new books, even second-hand, but I reckon they're more in need of the escape than anyone else. I spoke to a man at the shelter a few weeks back. He said they'd be happy to take them."

"That's great! How come you didn't tell me, then?"

"Just forgot." Jasper turned back, a guilty expression haunting his eyes. "That's not true. I just... I hated the idea of giving away my books to people who might lose or mistreat them. They'll get rain-damaged and grubby, won't they?"

Sugar-coating the truth was tempting, but it wouldn't do Jasper any favours right now. "I reckon that's pretty likely."

"Yeah. I thought so. But then I got thinking about what you'd said about needing to say good-bye to them properly. You know, cut all ties and let them out of my life. That means I can't control how they'll be treated after I let go of them. And I figured that even if each book only gets read once before it falls to pieces, that's still more times than it's likely to if it stays in my house. Books want to be read. They're pretty pointless, otherwise."

"Oh, I don't know. You've managed to build a fairly effective burglar deterrent out of yours, I reckon."

Jasper laughed again. A surprised huff of air, just stirring Lewis's sweat-dampened hair. "Shame they've been a boyfriend deterrent too, eh?"

"Jasper, I..." But what could he say when faced with that lost look in Jasper's eyes? The look that screamed *want me!* at the same time as it whispered *I'm worthless.*

The thunder saved him from having to answer. It rumbled close and loud. How had they missed the lightning? But then a flash illuminated them both standing there, staring at each other.

Jasper cleared his throat. "Your eyes glowed an amazing colour just then."

They were about to kiss. This was way too romantic for friends with benefits. Lewis glanced over at the open door and the strange, yellowish light outside. "I should get the van inside."

But even as he attempted to change the subject, the first fat raindrops landed. Dark spots splattered the tarmac outside. He jogged over to the open doors and gazed up at the sky. The clouds boiled alarmingly, the light behind them bruised and sallow.

A pink bolt of lightning arced down to earth with an ear-splitting boom, and Lewis jumped out of his skin.

"Shit!" Jasper exclaimed, right next to him. "Sorry. Hey, it's okay. Just a storm."

Lewis buried his face in the crook of Jasper's neck. "Always been a bit freaked by lightning when it's that close. Saw it strike a tree once. Half the bark sizzled away in an instant."

"You're okay here. It's fine. We're safe under cover."

"I know." But it didn't change the way his heart raced and his blood pounded. Being squished up this close to Jasper wasn't helping either. He smelled of their morning's exertions, all sweaty and masculine.

Thunder boomed again, even louder, and this time Lewis practically jumped up Jasper's body, clinging on for dear life. When

193

the rain began in earnest, he barely noticed, but all of a sudden Jasper somehow manhandled them both away from the door. When Lewis finally raised his head, he could see the rain hammering down outside, splashing up and wetting the ground a good five feet or so inside the open door. The sound it made on the warehouse roof was deafening, but at least it would dull any further thunderclaps.

Jasper slowly eased Lewis's grip on him. "You're drenched. We both are."

It wasn't too much of an exaggeration. His jeans were soggy from the knees down, and the top half of him was damp from the splashes. "I suppose there's nothing to stop me going and getting the van now, then. I mean, if I'm wet already." He had to raise his voice to almost shouting over the pounding of the rain.

"Don't be ridiculous. I'm not letting you out in that."

"Well, there's nothing else to do in here."

Jasper arched an eyebrow.

Oh. There was always that. And he had kind of promised, but he'd envisaged it being later. After their timetabled work hours were up. When Lewis was temporarily out of his role as therapist.

But how could he explain all that over the noise of the rain? Especially when Jasper's eyes had gone dark, inviting him to fall in and lose himself.

He leaned forward, meeting Jasper in a tentative kiss that quickly turned greedy. His adrenaline already pumping from the thunder, Lewis was more aggressive than he'd normally be, grabbing handfuls of clothing and flesh. He scrabbled under Jasper's T-shirt and down the back of his jeans.

Jasper matched him move for move, then wrested the upper hand by taking a firm hold of Lewis's cock through the fabric of his jeans and starting to jerk him off. Lewis moaned into Jasper's mouth, letting all his frustrated tension out with a strangled noise. Jasper felt so good, his chin just the right side of scratchy, his lips warm, his tongue wet and insistent.

And then there was his body, lean and long, bony but with just enough muscle to cushion the sharp edges. The grind of their hip bones together was surprisingly erotic.

But most of all, beyond the excitement of Jasper's body, there was the awareness that here was a man he could trust. Someone kind and loving who would never deliberately hurt him. No, he'd just drive him crazy by being irresistible and ill-advised.

Lewis almost protested when Jasper dropped to his knees. He wanted to be the one down there, giving head, but when Jasper pulled at his fly with such obvious enthusiasm Lewis couldn't deny him the pleasure. He let his wet jeans fall to the floor and twined his fingers into Jasper's surprisingly soft hair, losing himself in the sensations.

Jasper was good. Eager and a little sloppy with saliva, but clearly practised, as he could take Lewis deep and do something delicious with both his throat and the flat of his tongue. When had he been practising? And who had he practised with? Lewis should probably be grateful that he wasn't dealing with a complete novice, but it was excruciating to think of Jasper with anyone else.

Oh God, he had it bad. And he was about to come.

He needed to think of something else. Anything else. Lewis stared at the warehouse ceiling, the flickering light as the rain drummed on the dirty corrugated skylights, but it was no use. The warehouse reminded him of Jasper, because Jasper was the reason they were here.

He closed his eyes instead, but then all he could feel was Jasper's mouth on him, Jasper's breath against his groin, Jasper's hands clenching his buttocks and squeezing like he wanted to force Lewis even deeper. Impossibly deep. Lewis focused on his ragged breathing instead, till he couldn't hold back any longer.

"Touch yourself," Lewis groaned, not wanting to fall over the edge without company.

Jasper stared up into his eyes, and their gazes locked as Lewis shot down Jasper's willing throat.

The trouble with sex with Lewis, Jasper was discovering, was the aftermath. When all he wanted to do was to doze in the afterglow, Lewis got all twitchy. Was it nervous energy? Second thoughts? Jasper eased himself up from the floor, flexing his knees to work out the kinks, and watched as Lewis righted his clothing and paced over to the door.

"Rain's easing off," Lewis called. Jasper couldn't see his face, but at least his voice sounded normal. Not like in the garden. But he didn't want to think of a possible repeat of that awful scenario. This time it would be different. Even if Jasper couldn't control Lewis's reactions, he could control his own.

And so by the time he strolled over to join Lewis, he'd schooled his face into a casual friendliness. It was a mask slapped over the desperate longing he felt, but it helped a little. He could be normal, or at least learn to act normal. Lewis was teaching him that.

"Think we should start unloading?" Jasper asked, pleased to hear a matching casual note in his voice.

"Yep, we'd better if we want a chance to start sorting. I'll back Alice in. You wait here."

With a brief smile, Lewis clasped Jasper's hand, then dropped it and bounded off into the rain.

Jasper clutched his hand to his heart. He could hold these feelings in till Lewis was ready. He had to. After all, there was no telling how Lewis would react if Jasper told him how he really felt.

That he'd fallen.

Deeply, utterly, profoundly.

In love.

Chapter Twenty-Three

The clear-out was going smoother than Jasper had expected. Lewis and he worked on the hallway and kitchen over the week, filling up a vanload every day before unloading it over at the warehouse. They worked in the afternoons mainly, sometimes Lewis arriving in the van and sometimes Carroll turning up with it halfway through their session, when they'd stacked the front path with as many filled boxes as they could.

Boxes were at a premium, Jasper had discovered. He'd had no idea how many they'd need, but he balked at the idea of buying a job lot of them from a packaging company. No, wasn't it better to reduce and reuse? So the warehouse was looking even more like a strange, wall-less version of his house, piles of books and newspapers forming a kind of negative image of the rooms there. It reminded him of an art installation he'd once read about, when some trendy young Londoner had filled a house with concrete and then knocked the outside walls down.

But at least Jasper could see properly now his new specs were ready, and the sorting was underway. Lewis had encouraged him to get going with it when the prospect of returning to the house for another vanload got him down. Better to find something that energised him, Lewis said. And yes, strange though it was to discover, working through his books and papers was starting to feel productive. They'd even measured the newly cleared space and calculated how many metres of bookshelf space the hallway would eventually yield. Jasper had the measurements to hand, so he could keep track of how full his house was going to end up.

"How's it going?" Lewis asked him on the evening before their big session with helpers. He set a cup of coffee down on the old library trolley Jasper had borrowed from work. He was now using the length of the trolley shelves to calculate how much space the books he was keeping were going to take up. "Your system working out?"

"Not bad. It's going to take so long, though." An hour just on one small pile of books, and there were so many around him, still. And so many more to come. That was a problem, as he'd already saved enough books to fill up half of the available shelf space in his hallway. At this rate, he'd have to have bookshelves in the kitchen too. Not ideal because of the steam and cooking smells, but then again, that had never really bothered him about the newspapers.

Was he getting fussy?

"We could work out some rules if you like. Something you could delegate to others to sort. Yusef said he could help out some evenings too, didn't he?"

Evenings… Jasper glanced at his watch, then did a double take. "Bloody hell. No way is it seven thirty. What are you still doing here?" Because Lewis was pretty strict about leaving once his agreed working hours were over. A couple of times he'd stuck around for a quick handjob in the warehouse, but nothing more than that and Jasper hadn't liked to press. Now though, Lewis had a funny look on his face. Kind of awkward and hopeful all at the same time. "Wait a minute, it's Saturday. Shouldn't you be out doing something?"

"Like what?"

"I don't know. Seeing your friends?" What did your average gay man get up to on a Saturday night? Jasper only really had Mas for reference. "Clubbing?"

Lewis's mouth twitched at one side. "It's a bit early for clubbing, and I don't go much these days, anyway."

"Friends, then. Come on, you must have some."

"Not many that are close, and the others I kind of lost contact with when I was with Carlos."

"Oh. How come?"

Lewis shrugged unhappily. "I don't know, really. Carlos didn't really like my mates, and I never really gelled with his. It was easier just to stay in together most of the time. And then when he was away with work, I didn't feel much like going out on my own. It's not so bad during term time as a lot of my free time gets taken up with drama club rehearsals. It's just summer break when I'm at a loose end."

"So now you spend your Saturday nights hanging around in old warehouses?"

"Only when the company's up to scratch. And anyway, I was hoping you might want to do something. Not tonight. I'm too knackered. But tomorrow. My, er, my parents have invited you over for lunch." Lewis ducked his head and gave Jasper a look he could only interpret as bashful. "Nothing fancy. Just an average Sunday roast. Oh, except for the fact they've promised to keep their clothes on and not to spice up the gravy too much."

"Oh." Jasper blinked away the peculiar last sentence and tried to decipher Lewis's reluctant delivery. No, he'd just have to ask. "Do you want me there?"

"I'm a bit worried that it might all be too much for you, what with the big clear-out and everything, but of course I want you there. If you want to be there. If you don't, that's fine too." Now Lewis sounded overly defensive. Jasper caught himself going to crack his knuckles and made a conscious effort to keep his fingers flat on the pile of books.

"Sorry. You just don't sound all that sure. I don't want to embarrass you or anything."

Lewis sighed and dipped his head farther. "It's not you. It's them. They're weird. Both real characters, liable to say just about anything. You'll be asked all sorts of inappropriate questions, believe me. Then they'll start going on about how much freer life is without clothes on, and before you know it, they'll be naked. You too, possibly. I don't think I could bear it."

"You say that like it's a bad thing. Seeing me naked." Maybe that was why they'd not yet stripped off in their hurried, furtive fumblings. Was Lewis not that into his body?

"Oh God! No, not in that way. No, seeing you naked would be just fine. I'd rather not have it happen while my folks are there, though. That would be wrong." Lewis shuddered. "Seriously wrong."

Jasper breathed a sigh of relief. "Okay." He could handle this.

"Okay, what?" Now Lewis looked really worried. It was kind of cute on him, that little frown.

"Okay, I'll come, and okay, I promise to keep my clothes on."

"Really? I did mention what they're like, didn't I? The chilli thing? The conversations about homoeroticism in literature? They've driven previous boyfriends running for the hills, I can tell you. Carlos always managed to find an excuse to turn down their invitations."

"Yes, well, Carlos was a fool who couldn't see what a good thing he had going." It was then that Lewis's exact words caught up with Jasper. Previous boyfriends. Did that mean Lewis considered him a boyfriend now? Hope opened up inside him and fluttered, like pages riffled by the breeze.

"Thanks." Lewis finally raised his head and looked Jasper in the eye. "You might live to regret it, but thanks."

When he reached out for Jasper's hand, Jasper pulled him into a hug instead. It began all awkward angles and elbows, but eventually Lewis softened, melting against his body. Jasper tilted his head, aiming for Lewis's lips. He brushed the barest of kisses over them, but Lewis's eyelids quivered shut. Oh, that sight! It stole his breath and swelled his heart.

But then Lewis's eyes sprang open. "I should leave. Big day tomorrow. Me and Carroll are going to arrive early, say eight? We want to get going before Yusef and his kids arrive. Then lunch at my folks' at one. Then back to finish off the job in the afternoon."

"You really think we'll get it all done?"

Lewis drew off a few steps and threw his arms wide as if to take in all the surrounding piles and boxes. "Near enough. With that many pairs of hands, I'm convinced we can get all the downstairs and the landing finished. Maybe even a couple of the rooms upstairs. Just depends how energetic everyone's feeling. Maybe I should make a motivational playlist for us all. What do you reckon? Bit of Dire Straits' *Money for Nothing? We've got to move these refrigerators...*" Lewis began singing. His voice was pleasantly husky but not particularly tuneful.

"No, God no. Where do you know that from? My dad used to play that."

"Mine too." Lewis grinned. "Hey, I could raid his record collection and add in some Fleetwood Mac. Or maybe I could ask Brandon for a bit of hardcore drum and bass. What do you reckon?"

Jasper grimaced at the thought of his peaceful house polluted by music. "I reckon silence is golden."

"Spoilsport." Lewis stuck his tongue out, but at least he was smiling. And even if he did make his excuses and head off home without anything more happening between them, at least there was the family dinner to look forward to.

It had been a very long time since Jasper had experienced anything of the sort. Should he buy a gift? A bottle of wine, perhaps? There was still time to get to the supermarket before they closed.

But as Jasper's gaze roamed over the stacks of books an idea occurred to him. Oh yes, that would be much better than wine. With newfound purpose, he began scanning and categorising the pile in front of him.

The troops had arrived to help, and already Jasper was feeling paranoid. He tried to deny it, tried to hide away on the landing and leave the downstairs to the others, but they kept on coming up and trying to help out. This time it was Yusef.

"Hey, are you going to need all these doors unblocking like downstairs?"

"Not all of them. You can still get into the bedroom."

"You want me to start it now? We're all getting under each other's feet in the living room, and your Lewis is working on the dining room door. I feel like a spare part."

"Umm, okay." *But please leave me in peace,* he held back from adding. Lewis had warned him he might feel like this, hadn't he? Lewis had held him tight and spoken in a low voice, preparing him for the day ahead. Right before all the others had turned up and they'd had to step apart.

It had taken Lewis a solid hour to get the living room door open enough to start clearing in earnest, and Jasper had refused to enter the room until it was empty. He didn't want to see that tunnel through the books again. He didn't want to remember the tiny space surrounding his sofa, like an animal's nest. What had once been comforting was now frightening. A sign of psychological progress, perhaps—the only trouble being he was even more terrified of what the rooms would be like empty.

As Jasper turned to place another handful of books in the box, he realised Yusef was still standing there.

Standing there and staring at Mama's door.

"You're leaving this one till last, then?"

"No, I—" But when he looked at where he'd begun working, in the far corner of the landing rather than clearing the way to it in a more logical fashion, Jasper realised that was exactly what he'd been doing. He dropped his gaze. "I don't know if I'm ready for that yet."

Yusef steered his bulk through the maze of books and laid a hand on Jasper's shoulder. "We'll do it together, yes? You don't have to be alone in this. You have friends. Good friends."

"Thank you," he whispered, scared to speak in case his voice gave up on him.

"Right, then. I'll start on clearing here. No point emptying the rooms until the landing is clear, eh? We don't want to be tripping up and bumping into things. I don't know how you've coped with this for so long. Didn't you get sick of the twisting and turning to get anywhere?"

"Kind of, but I just got used to it, I think."

A protest rose in Jasper's throat as Yusef began on the book piles in front of Mama's door, but he swallowed it down. It had to be faced sometime soon, and like Yusef said, he was among friends. Besides, he definitely owed Yusef his cooperation after the man had closed the café and given up a day's takings just to help him out.

Jasper stood, walked over, and began filling the rest of his box with the books from the pile next to Yusef's.

Yusef smiled, and it was only when his hand gave Jasper's a quick pat he realised how he was trembling.

He glanced up at the top of the door frame.

Mama, please forgive me.

Chapter Twenty-Four

Lewis first noticed the change in Jasper when he headed upstairs with their midmorning coffee. The cheery "How's it going?" died in his throat when he saw the tense set of Jasper's shoulders and the furrows in his brow. Worse than that, though, was the way his eye kept twitching. The way he'd started clicking his finger joints again, only stopping when Lewis came and took hold of his hands.

"What's up?" he asked, softly. When Jasper didn't answer, he glanced over at Yusef, who was busy muttering to himself over a box. "Yusef, I didn't know how you took it, so your coffee's downstairs," he said, only half lying. Yasmina had told him exactly how her dad took his coffee, but he hadn't wanted to carry too many at a time through the house. It might be clearer than it had been, but with boxes underfoot, it was even more deceptively hazardous. Now he was glad he'd left it behind, as it gave him a chance to talk to Jasper on his own.

"Okay, okay. I'll leave you two lovebirds to it, shall I? I know when I'm not wanted."

"Is he bothering you up here?" Lewis asked once Yusef had disappeared down the stairs. "I could find something for him to do downstairs if you'd rather."

"No, it's not that. I think I'd be worse on my own."

"Jasper... You really don't have to come to lunch if it scares you. You won't hurt my feelings, I promise."

"Lunch?" Jasper scrunched up his forehead in confusion; then understanding dawned, smoothing the lines back down again. "Oh God, lunch. I'd forgotten. No, lunch is fine. I'm looking forward to it." The words sounded honest enough, but the smile Jasper gave was distinctly queasy looking.

"Okay, so if it's not Yusef and it's not the prospect of lunch with the Miller clan, what's got you looking so tense? Finding it tougher than you'd imagined?"

"Yes. No. I don't know. This is Mama's room." Jasper's gaze met Lewis's for a moment before skittering off again, but it was just long enough for him to see the fear lurking there. Fear, and something else that looked surprisingly like guilt.

No, not surprising, perhaps. The bereaved often experienced guilt about their loved ones. No doubt Jasper was running through a big list of "should haves" in his head.

"Do you want to talk about it?"

Jasper shook his head but wouldn't meet Lewis's gaze. Okay, he might not want to talk, but he probably needed to. "Want me to help you out for a bit?"

"Would you?" Jasper's voice vibrated with such need, Lewis almost took a step back. Oh God, it was just what he wanted and exactly what he dreaded. This need couldn't last. It was a temporary side effect of the emotional upheaval, and when it passed, what would be left in its place? Jasper was the kind of man who would never break a promise, Lewis knew, so he'd probably stick around long after the infatuation ended and see Lewis for who he really was.

That idea was even worse than being abandoned. Being doomed to live on in a sick relationship, both pining for something they couldn't have.

But he shoved down his own misgivings because Jasper was the one who was really suffering here. Lewis's fears for the future couldn't possibly compete with this level of distress. He crouched down and began packing up books.

Jasper's hand strayed over and clasped his own.

They'd reached the last layer of books in front of the door. Lewis sat back on his heels and stared up at them. He'd grown used to the mishmash of genres up on the landing, but these stacks were even more bewildering.

"Children's books?" Every single last one of them, and they all looked well-read too.

Jasper coloured, but when his hand ran over the spines, his touch was reverent. "I used to love this one," he whispered, pointing at the spine of Antoine de Saint-Exupéry's *The Little Prince*. "The illustrations, all those strange little planets. It wasn't till I grew up that I realised it was all about death."

"I always thought it was more about life," Lewis mused. "That's what Mum used to say, anyway. It was one of those books she said you could live by." He paused, looking for others. Oh yes, they were here in abundance. "Like *The Neverending Story*, or *The Secret Garden*. Hey, you've got loads of them."

"All my favourites."

As Lewis took in the titles and the faded colours of the spines, it dawned on him. There wasn't a single book that hadn't already been published by the time he was growing up. These books broke the rules Jasper had told him about the categorisation for the landing. Books up here were meant to be ones he hadn't read yet, but these clearly had been. Every last one of them.

"These aren't from charity shops. These are all yours, aren't they?"

Jasper nodded and chewed on his lower lip. The fear in his eyes now mingled with longing, making Lewis want to reach out and promise him anything. That it would all be all right. That he'd never have to hurt again. But that wasn't how life worked, and they both knew it.

"You put them here for a reason, didn't you?"

Lewis thought perhaps Jasper wasn't ready to share that reason, but eventually, after a bittersweet chuckle at a title he ran his fingertips over, he began to speak.

"I couldn't bear to look at them again. After she died. She used to read me a chapter, every night. Said it helped improve her English. I had to help her out sometimes, with the longer words. She could speak fluently, but writing and reading were tough for her."

"I bet she enjoyed it too. I know Mum did. She used to love doing all the different voices."

"Mama tried. Her growly monster voices always made me laugh. She'd pretend to be annoyed and tell me I should do them myself then, but she always gave in eventually."

"You really loved her."

Jasper's lips tightened, his eyes going bleak.

"Hey, it's okay. There's nothing wrong with feeling guilty about loved ones dying. We all do it."

"We don't all do what I've done."

"What? Barricade all the difficult things up behind books? No, we don't, but the feelings are there. Different people just find their own ways of dealing with them, that's all. This is the way you needed to cope. It was your way of staying sane under challenging circumstances."

Jasper shook his head, and whatever was bothering him, Lewis could see he hadn't managed to reach it yet. Perhaps when they got into the room. He glanced down at his watch, then sprang to his feet. "Blimey, it's almost twenty to one already. Mum and Dad will be sending out a search party. I'm surprised they haven't called me yet."

Just then, Carroll's voice called up from downstairs. "Lewis? I've got Mum on the phone. Says we need to get over there this instant or Dad's going to eat all the lamb and adulterate the roast spuds. He's reaching for the cayenne pepper as we speak."

Jasper blanched. "Chilli spuds? Seriously?"

"Didn't I tell you Dad puts it on everything? I wasn't joking. Come on, this lot can wait. We've got to go get our food while it's still edible. And save him from eating all that fatty lamb. He's meant to be cutting down on red meat, seeing as how it's clogged up his arteries. Did I tell you he's got angina?"

"No, I don't think so. Sorry to hear that."

"Oh, he's okay. Just takes some meds for it. Nothing to worry about." *Yet*, he added to himself.

Lewis tugged on Jasper's hand but managed to pull him away with one last wistful look at his childhood books. But two more steps and Jasper froze.

"Lewis? Are the rest taking a break too? I don't like the idea of them being here without me."

"They've got sarnies with them, and they were planning to work on through. We'd get it done much faster if you were willing to let them."

"No, I don't think so..."

"Are you sure? We could be some time at the folks', even if we do make our excuses after pud."

"Lewis?" The pleading tone in Jasper's voice made Lewis turn back. Jasper's gaze darted to the books again but higher. He was looking at the door. Oh God, Lewis had pushed too far. Jasper's face was ashen. "It's a ninety. The anxiety."

"Okay, okay. It's going to be okay." Lewis folded Jasper into his arms, troubled to feel the way Jasper's body tensed. "We'll insist they take a proper break. Doesn't matter if we still have some left to clear tomorrow, does it?"

Jasper nodded against the side of Lewis's head, and his breath snuffled. He sounded close to tears. What on earth was in that room? Lewis glared at the door as if he could bore a hole through it with his gaze. Whatever was on the other side, Jasper could count on Lewis's support. He hugged him fiercely, trying to put some of that security across using his body.

Eventually Jasper relaxed and mumbled a "Thanks," against Lewis's neck.

It was the sweetest thing he'd ever heard.

Chapter Twenty-Five

In the van, Jasper sat in the middle seat between Carroll, who was driving, and Lewis, who was staring out of the window with a troubled expression. Jasper held his bag against his chest tightly. It wasn't until Lewis eased his hand over Jasper's that he realised just how hard he'd been gripping it.

"It's okay. We don't have to go if you're not up for it," Lewis said.

"Bullshit," Carroll interjected from Jasper's other side. "I'm not going on my own and having them both interrogate me about why the two of you aren't there. Besides, if you don't turn up, I'm just going to tell them you're off doing something perverted in the warehouse. Maybe involving a giant roll of shrink wrap."

"Carroll!" Lewis complained, but Jasper laid a hand on his thigh. Lewis's eyebrows rose, but it shut him up for the time being.

"It's okay, I don't mind."

"What? The two of them thinking you've seduced my brother to the kinky side? Good luck to you, I say. Can't believe I shared a womb with someone so unrepentantly vanilla."

"You know what he meant," Lewis said to his twin, but now his hand was stroking Jasper's where it still lay on his thigh.

"Yeah, yeah." Carroll slowed the van, and Jasper realised this North Bristol suburb of modern, detached houses must be their final destination. Oh God. Lewis lived somewhere like this? What must he think of Jasper's crumbling wreck of a house?

"Here we are, out in Blandsville again," Lewis said as if in answer to Jasper's unspoken worries. "Don't be fooled by the generic exterior, though. Inside is a whole different experience."

Generic was hardly the right word for the front garden of neatly raked, multicoloured sand, spiny plants, and the centrepiece clay statue of a large-breasted woman with her arms thrown up in the air. No, this quirky garden seemed to be sticking two fingers up at its surroundings. Jasper wondered what the neighbours made of it spoiling the long sweep of green lawns and shade trees.

When they got out, Jasper hugged his bag even tighter, like a shield. Lewis didn't try to take his hand again as they walked up the path through the cactus garden, but at least he kept pace by Jasper's side, chatting in a relaxed manner about his father's tenacious attempts to grow plants that really weren't suited to their wet, Western climate.

A pot-bellied man with silvery hair and a trimmed beard opened the door. Lewis stepped forward to hug him. The man wasn't naked like Jasper had been half expecting, and instead wore a stripy apron over jeans and T-shirt. Professor Alan Miller, if that was who this was, studied Jasper over his son's shoulder with warm, intelligent eyes. "So, you must be the famous Jasper I've been hearing all about. Welcome to Casa Miller. Hope you don't mind barbecued food. I had a last-minute change of heart what with the weather, so I've chucked the lamb on the barbie."

"Not at all. Thanks, er, and hello." Jasper held out his hand in greeting once Lewis had been released, but Alan Miller ignored it, and before he could get too wound up about what was happening, Jasper was enveloped in a warm hug.

"No need to stand on ceremony here," Alan said, winking. "Anything goes, pretty much."

Carroll snorted. "You're not kidding. I tell you, Jasper, you're lucky they're even wearing clothes today."

"Yes, yes, don't remind me. It's far too hot for this right now. My crotch is getting horribly itchy."

"Dad! Oversharing much?"

"Don't you *Dad* me, Carroll Miller. Now come on. Cassie wants to see you all."

Lewis's mum turned out to be a willowy woman with a mass of tangled blonde ringlets, in a white dress that looked like something a country lass from a hundred years ago might have worn. Any pretence of sweet innocence soon evaporated when you caught the gleam in her eye or her dirty laugh, however. Jasper allowed himself to be enveloped in another squishy hug.

"Aww, you're a skinny thing, aren't you?" Cassie cooed. "Lewis normally brings them home with a bit more meat on them, but I think I'll enjoy feeding you up."

"Like you ever do any cooking," Alan grumbled, but he was smiling.

"You've got a bit of meat here, though," Cassie said, and Jasper stood there, mortified, as her hand squeezed his rear. "That's where it counts, eh?" Oh God. Lewis's mum was groping his arse. What was the protocol for situations like this? This really was the most touchy-feely family he'd ever encountered. No wonder Lewis could lay his hands on Jasper for comfort like it was the most natural thing in the world.

"Mum! Stop molesting the poor man. He doesn't bat for your team." Lewis steered Cassie away with an apologetic smile to Jasper, who stood there, mouth opening and closing. It wasn't till Alan pressed a bottle of beer into his hand that he remembered the contents of his bag.

"I, er, I hope these are appropriate gifts. I was going to bring wine, but then I didn't know what you liked and I'm not exactly a connoisseur myself, but then I thought I do know books and I've got a few too many, so, uh, yes. Here they are."

Cassie and Alan both smiled as he handed them over. "Oh, you sweetie," Cassie gushed. "How did you know? I keep losing my copies of this when I lend them to colleagues. No one ever seems to be able to return it." She flashed her copy of *Rum, Sodomy and the Lash: Piracy, Sexuality and Masculine Identity* to her children.

"Great choice," Alan said, beaming over his copy of *Plants of the Mexican Desert*. "These pictures are amazing. Hey, Cass, what do you think about growing one of these out front?" He pointed to a giant cactus towering above a man in a large hat.

"Darling, you really don't need to make a large phallic statement like that. You've got nothing to feel inadequate about."

"Mum!" Lewis and Carroll chorused.

Cassie grinned and winked at Jasper.

Jasper started to relax as Lewis led him out onto the back deck. Here too were more cacti in pots, strange nude sculptures and borders full of ornamental grasses. It wasn't like any garden he'd ever set foot in before, but despite the differences from his mum's cottage garden, he felt strangely at home. Perhaps it was because of the family vibe here. His gifts had gone down well, but even without them, Jasper had the impression he'd have been treated just as warmly.

Did Lewis even know how lucky he was to have a family like this?

Jasper walked over to where Lewis was standing, resting on the distressed wooden railing and staring out over the garden, beer in hand. "I really like your folks," he said.

"Yeah? I wasn't sure if they'd be a bit much for you."

"No. They're just right." And they were. Their easy acceptance and friendship was exactly the kind of thing he needed to relax. Jasper got the feeling he didn't need to worry about his own quirks, because here were two people who couldn't give a toss about keeping up appearances in any way.

Not like Jasper's mother had been. His heart sinking at the prospect of what their return to his house would bring, Jasper mirrored Lewis's pose and gazed out over the garden. There was a fountain in the centre of a gravel circle. A tall bronze column, but pitted and textured, like the original cast had been taken from roughly finished clay. The water trickled down gently from an ornate rosette set in one side of the column. "Did your mum make the fountain too?"

"Yep. That's her latest project. Not sure why it wasn't some naked satyr with a hard-on ejaculating water, but I suppose we should be grateful she abandoned the human form for at least one sculpture."

Jasper pondered the other artworks he'd seen inside the house. All of naked men and women, sometimes involved in carnal acts. He remembered the lovingly detailed genitalia.

That rosette... It looked like an orchid, all frilled and fleshy. In fact, it did look an awful lot like flesh.

"Um, Lewis? I think you might be wrong about that. I know the rest of the body isn't there, but I'm fairly sure that's erm, a representation of the, uh..." How to say it? His skin heated. "The female pudenda?"

"No it isn't— Hang on. Oh bloody hell. I think you're right. The sneaky woman!" The look of outrage mingled with a certain awe, and before Jasper knew it they were both laughing, the chuckles soon turning into full-blown belly laughs when Carroll asked them what was so funny.

"It's the... It's the..." Jasper said, "the fountain—"

Lewis wheezed, then hiccupped. "It's a twat!"

That set them both off again.

Chapter Twenty-Six

"He's a real sweetie, love," Cassie said as Lewis followed her into the kitchen, chilli-sauce-smeared plates in hand. "I'm so happy you've finally met someone nice."

"We're not together. I told you that already."

"Bullshit. Anyone can see you were made for each other. And you're clearly sleeping together. I can tell from your body language."

"You can tell? How?" It wasn't like he'd had an erection while they were eating or anything. He hadn't even touched Jasper any more than he'd normally touch a friend.

"Oh, it's easy. I pick up all these little signals. Can always tell when the other tutors are shagging one of their students. They think they're being so bloody discreet, but it's written all over them."

Lewis dropped his plates in the sink and began running the water, just to give himself an excuse not to look his mother in the eye. That woman could see far too much. "Okay, so we're friends with benefits. Occasional ones. And we haven't properly done it yet."

"Properly done it? What's that supposed to mean? I do hope you're not making the heteronormative assumption that penetrative intercourse is the only kind that counts? Honestly, love, it's all sex of a kind. Every little touch. Even just a look sometimes. Did I ever tell you about the time your father seduced me from across the dining table at a dinner party? Just a smouldering glance and a brush of his naked foot up my leg. It was one of the most erotic moments of my life. I nearly came, there and then."

"Mum!"

"What? Honestly, your generation's so prudish sometimes. Sometimes it seems like the sixties never happened."

"They didn't. Not for us. I was born in the eighties, remember?"

"Yes, of course I remember. Life under Thatcher's government and dealing with morning sickness. Dark days, Lewis. Dark days."

For half a second, Lewis contemplated changing the subject by getting her started on an anti-Thatcher rant, but they had to get back soon, and once she got started, it was hard to stop her. No, best he just explained the situation and got it all out in the open so she wouldn't do anything embarrassing—well, anything *more* embarrassing—in front of Jasper before they left.

"Listen, Mum..." He lifted the rinsed plates out of the sink and fitted the plug while trying to work out how to phrase it so she'd understand him. "Me and Jasper... It's complicated. He thinks he's in love with me, but he's just experiencing transference. I don't want to lead him on by making him think we're a proper couple."

"But you're happy to mess around with him?"

Lewis hung his head and felt his cheeks heat.

"Oh no, don't get me wrong. I don't disapprove. If two people fancy each other, they should have sex; that much is obvious. I just wondered how he was dealing with it."

"I don't know."

"Of course you do. What kind of therapist are you if you don't know how your client's dealing with things?"

"A bad one?" He was certainly an unprofessional one, at any rate. "I don't know, Mum. I just thought keeping him happy right now while he deals with the trauma of the clear-out would be helpful."

"Right now? So what are you planning to do when it's

finished?"

"Break it off." What else was possible?

"Don't you dare, Lewis Miller! That young man thinks the world of you, and he's the nicest one you've ever dragged home to meet us."

"You're only saying that because he complimented your artworks."

"At least someone finally noticed my yoni fountain. Honestly, I've been waiting for months for one of you to figure it out. That young man has smarts. And he's cute."

"And he's my client and therefore out of bounds."

"Oh puhleeze, darling. It's not like you're a proper therapist with memberships to professional bodies or anything. You're not working for the NHS. Who's going to complain? You get to make up your own rules."

Ouch. The proper-therapist barb stung, even though it was an old issue they'd hashed out plenty of times before. It wasn't that Cassie was materialistic, but she'd always liked the idea of him continuing his studies and gaining a string of letters after his name. Lewis's hurt made him more snippy than usual. "That's right. I'm my own boss, and I get to make up my own rules, and they say no romantic relationships with clients. This is just sex and friendship. Nothing more."

"Bullshit."

"Bull-true." That was a lie, and Lewis could see it written on his face as he stared down at his reflection in the dishwater. But the bubbles wouldn't tell on him.

Much to his relief, his mum just snorted, and the room filled up with Carroll, Alan and Jasper before she could pick up the thread of the conversation. He finished the washing up quickly; then they made their excuses and left.

"I really like your folks," Jasper said in the van on the way back. He sounded wistful, almost sad.

"They're all right," Carroll grudgingly admitted. "Even if they always have embarrassed the hell out of us. Remember that time I had my mates over for a sleepover, Lewis? Must have been when I was eight or nine. Well, they chose that night to have extra-noisy sex. Honestly, they were at it like rabbits back then. Thank fuck they've calmed down a bit since Dad's had his health scare."

"You really think so?" Lewis asked. He glanced over at Jasper. He'd never normally admit this in front of anyone other than Carroll, but Jasper was special. "You're kidding yourself, sis. I still hear them at it at least two or three times a week. And if anything, they're getting noisier. Thought Dad was going to holler the house down last week."

"Well, so long as he doesn't have a heart attack. God, but at sixty-nine? He must be swallowing Viagra like it's going out of fashion."

"Oh, that's not meant to be good if you've got angina," Jasper chipped in. "He should be careful."

"I've no idea if he's taking it." Lewis glanced at Carroll in time to see her scowl. When she got worried, Carroll tended to get angry. "I'll ask, okay? Discreetly." Although how he was meant to do that, God knew. Neither of their parents were the kind to go tiptoeing around a conversational point. If you didn't ask them something outright, they had no patience for verbal games.

He didn't realise he was frowning himself until he felt Jasper's hand land on his. He shot him a weak smile. It didn't do to be feeling sorry for himself about something so small when Jasper didn't have any family. Lewis clutched his hand back.

Both Yusef and Lewis had offered to accompany him into Mama's room, but Jasper turned them back at the door. "Please. Just give me a minute alone with her. Maybe ten." They'd both looked like they wanted to argue, but when Lewis nodded and said he understood, Yusef grunted a reluctant agreement.

The door opened on creaking hinges, and Jasper stepped forward, pushing it shut behind him.

Bright light dazzled him, but when he took a step sideways everything returned to darkness and he could see the single shaft of sunlight lancing in through the gap in the curtains, lighting up a beam of dust like the projector at a cinema.

"Welcome to the feature presentation," Jasper whispered to himself. "Jasper's Darkest Hour." He almost giggled then, not because there was anything funny about being back in here, but just as a way to release the tightness forming in his chest. "Oh, Mama," he began, and the words turned into a sob, which he swallowed back down.

Now that his eyes had adjusted to the gloom, he could make out her bed taking pride of place in the middle of the room. The mattress was gone now, that high-tech, constantly moving contraption that helped reduce, if not prevent, the bedsores she'd been prone to those last couple of years. Where had it got to? Perhaps the NHS had sent someone around to reclaim it. It wasn't like Jasper had any memory of those first few months after she'd died. He didn't have many memories of the last few years either. He'd pretty much stopped living right at the same time she had.

"Mama, I'm so sorry." He walked over to the empty bedframe. A memory surfaced. Tangled sheets wrapped around her twitching, wasting limbs. She'd stopped mentioning them towards the end, but Jasper had still pulled them straight every few hours when he was at home. The carers who popped in while he was at work had never bothered, so Mama had complained. But then again, she'd complained about everything back then.

No, he'd stopped living long before she went. He'd stopped living the moment she got into bed and refused to get out again. The day after he'd told her he was gay.

Jasper turned to take in the rest of the room, but it swam before his eyes. He walked blindly over to the curtains and tugged them open a little way, releasing a cloud of dust. He sneezed. There, he could blame his watery eyes on that now.

Better that than admit how he'd failed her. That because he could never give her the grandchildren she yearned for, he'd given her his entire life. Everything she asked for.

Even her death.

Jasper sank to the floor as the tears spilled over, sliding down his cheeks as he howled out his pain and guilt.

Chapter Twenty-Seven

When the inhuman wail sounded, Yusef and Lewis both froze, listening in horror. "Fuck," Yusef exclaimed, his expression mutinous. He gripped the doorknob defiantly, like he expected Lewis to stop him.

"Just open it," Lewis urged, and when Yusef did, he deftly pulled in front of him. It was hard to see anything in the dark chaos of the room, but the mournful keening sounds helped him home in on the huddled figure under the window. He crossed the room in two strides and gathered Jasper to him carefully like he was a wounded animal. The keening gave way to desperate sobbing. Easier on the ear but no less heartrending.

"Jasper? Hey, it's okay, I've got you. I've got you." Lewis repeated the words over and over, hoping that eventually they'd sink through into whatever dark place Jasper had retreated to. "Just let it all out. That's right. You've needed to for a long time, I think." He buried his face in Jasper's hair, inhaling the scent of herbal shampoo, its freshness at odds with the atmosphere of sorrow and guilt. As he sat there, rocking Jasper in his arms, Yusef pulled the curtains fully open. Bright sunlight bathed the cluttered space. Lewis gazed around him, trying to get a picture of the woman Jasper was so cut up about.

There were no piles of books here, but every piece of furniture was covered in stuff. It was the same kind of haphazard mix they'd uncovered behind the piles of books in the lounge. A china shepherdess figurine sat next to a plastic bag full of scrap fabric. An egg box filled with two decorated and two plain eggshells perched precariously on top of a wicker donkey wearing a sombrero. A half-finished weaving on a handheld loom rested against a wall covered in framed snapshots and embroideries. However, despite the rather chaotic nature of the space, the room had personality. Mrs. Richardson had clearly been someone who'd enjoyed travelling and collecting souvenirs, as well as all those craft projects Jasper had told him about.

There wasn't a book in sight, but it was evident where Jasper got his cluttering habit from. The only clear space in the room was the empty bed. It sat there, a plain utilitarian metal frame with a surprising lack of stuff underneath, its very nakedness drawing the eye.

Had she died in here?

Was Jasper remembering that? His sobbing had subsided to a series of hitched breaths now, his body calming and losing the stiff tension.

Yusef picked up a conch shell from the mantelpiece. "I remember when she found this. She was so proud of herself. Told me it was just perfect for this spot." He held it to his ear, then put it back down again with a wistful smile.

"I didn't know you'd been away together." Conches weren't local, were they?

"Huh? What do you mean?"

Lewis felt Jasper stir in his arms and resumed the soothing strokes on his back. "You said she found it."

"Oh, right. That wasn't on a beach or anything. No, she didn't travel. Not that I know of, anyway. This was from a charity shop somewhere. She stopped off for coffee on the way back and showed it to me."

"So if she didn't travel..." Lewis stared at a Delft china windmill. You could pick those up in every tourist shop in the Netherlands, and he guessed most travellers would want to keep them as a souvenir, but a fair few must end up as unwanted gifts to the friends and family who stayed behind.

"These are all somebody else's souvenirs." Yusef shook his

222

head, biting his lower lip. "She stopped living her own life when her husband died, but she took pleasure in surrounding herself with things from places she'd never go. Nothing from Egypt, though. Or not that I ever saw."

"No? Why not?"

Yusef just shrugged, but this time Jasper raised his head, revealing red-rimmed eyes and tear-streaked cheeks. His specs had fallen off in his lap somewhere. "She couldn't bear it. Being cast out. Having reminders of that. If she wanted to revisit Egypt, she'd take me up to the museum."

"Hey, you're back," Lewis teased, smiling gently. "Thought I'd lost you for a while there."

"I'm back," Jasper assured him and returned a wobbly smile.

It was impossible to resist kissing him then, even though Lewis knew he shouldn't. On top of the cosy family lunch, it would all mean too much. Raise Jasper's hopes too high.

But Jasper looked like a man who needed a kiss, and Lewis was a born helper.

Yusef cleared his throat loudly behind them, making Lewis jump.

"You want us to start clearing this room now?" Yusef asked. "It will be much quicker than the ones filled with books."

Jasper stuffed his glasses back on, and his eyes moved back and forth, gaze dancing over the room. He sniffed and rubbed his hand under his nose, then absentmindedly swiped it on his jeans. "Not this one," he finally said, his voice quiet but level. "Not yet, anyway."

"But we need to start somewhere up here. Come on, *canim.* We're staying for another four hours at least. We can clear a room. Maybe two, if they're not too bad."

"Not this one," Jasper repeated firmly. "My bedroom. You can start there. I want to make it less of a health hazard, and I'm going to want an early night. I think we all deserve one." The look he gave

223

Lewis then was one of both promise and pleading. How was he meant to resist those imploring eyes, still liquid with tears?

"An early night sounds like a good idea," Lewis croaked. Lust crackled in the air between them, and Lewis had to tear his eyes away before he jumped Jasper in front of Yusef. "Best carry on with it, then. If you're ready?" He held out a hand and Jasper took it, getting to his feet.

Jasper's bedroom looked totally different without the books. Oh, he still had a few paperbacks lingering around the perimeter, but they no longer blocked the window and they no longer crowded his bed. You could walk around it now. You could see everything in the peachy evening sunshine slanting in. Every mote of dust stirring in the air. Every scrap of rubbish they'd uncovered under the piles.

While the rest of the clearing team were finishing up downstairs, Jasper set to work with the vacuum cleaner Lewis and Carroll had brought with them. It was one of those cheerful red Henry ones with the smiley face. They had one at work and he'd always thought them ridiculous things, but he couldn't help grinning back at it while he transformed the floor from a layer of dust and detritus into an expanse of ugly beige-flecked carpet. Maybe he could get that replaced sometime soon, now the house was almost fit for outsiders to enter.

Mama wouldn't have approved, of course. She'd chosen that carpet because it was practical: didn't show the dirt and was hardwearing. Too hardwearing, really. It was expensive wool and would probably last another twenty years. He could hear Mama's voice in his head lecturing him about the wasteful ways of Western living, so different to how things had been back in Egypt. Of course, she'd loved that aspect of British life too—being able to pick up the spoils from charity shops. Living her life through other people's cast-offs.

Would it be wasteful to replace the carpet? Yes...but that didn't mean he couldn't, did it? Lewis had taught him that. That it wasn't evil to occasionally waste resources in the pursuit of harmonious living, and he did love hard floors far more than carpets. Carpets were... He scrubbed at a stubborn dust bunny with the vacuum nozzle. Carpets were dust traps, that's what they were.

He'd finally cleared the floor when he remembered the bed. He'd already pulled the pile of clothing off the end and shoved it into his newly unearthed wardrobe. When he'd opened it, there was a distinctly musty smell, but fortunately none of those clothes-eating moths. There were, however, garments in there he hadn't seen for years, and he wondered if any of them would stand up to Lewis's ideas of what he should be wearing. It would be good to have things Lewis liked him in. He didn't care so much for himself, but just to see Lewis look at him in that appreciative way. Yes, that would be nice.

But the bed still looked a rumpled mess, so he yanked off the duvet and straightened up the sheets. Yep, fresh ones were probably called for, but the ones in the drawer at the bottom of the wardrobe had smelled funny too. At least the ones on the bed only smelled of Jasper, rather than a vaguely unpleasant mouldy niff. Of course, he realised the moment he'd replaced the shaken-out duvet that he'd done things entirely the wrong way round. The floor was now covered with little bits again.

Housework, that was definitely something he'd need to put in some practice with. He'd managed okay when Mama first got sick, but she'd let him know when his efforts weren't up to her standards. Would he meet Lewis's standards? The man seemed easygoing, but he must have certain expectations.

Would he have expectations in bed? Would he want to top or bottom? Would he expect Jasper to take control? It was hard to answer any of those questions based on their limited mutual experience of hasty hand and blowjobs.

Jasper plumped up a pillow while he considered his tactics. Mas had always liked him to be more controlling and aggressive, but it wasn't his favourite way to act. But waiting for Lewis to make a move was excruciating. Lewis tended to flirt and make suggestions with his eyes, but he wasn't bold in coming forward. More of a tease. No, Jasper would have to take matters into his own hands in terms of actually getting Lewis into bed. Once there, though, perhaps he could ease up. Let them both discover each other at their own pace.

"You think he's going to stay?" he asked Henry's shiny plastic face, then slapped a hand over his mouth and stifled a chuckle. Talking to appliances, whatever next? He didn't want Lewis to find a single excuse not to stay, and Jasper talking to inanimate objects would definitely furnish him with a cast-iron one.

"How's it going up here?" Lewis called from the bottom of the stairs. "We're just taking the last load over to the warehouse. Thought you might want to stay behind and get things in order. Or just crash out."

Jasper raced to the top of the stairs. "Will you be coming back afterwards?" *Please-please-please-please-please!*

"Do you want me to?" In the half-light at the bottom of the stairs, Lewis's eyes were too dark to read.

"I want you to."

Lewis climbed up the stairs two at a time and stood, just inches from Jasper. Far too close for friends. Their chests almost touched every time they breathed in—something Jasper was starting to have trouble with.

Lewis reached out and cupped Jasper's jaw, rubbing him gently. His thumbnail scritched in Jasper's five-o'clock shadow.

"I'll be back, if that's what you want."

"I want..." Jasper shook his head and gave a wry laugh. If he couldn't admit this to Lewis, what chance did they ever stand of making things work? "I want so many things. With you."

"Okay."

"Okay?" Jasper's heart lurched. Did Lewis mean okay to the night or okay to the whole boyfriend thing? He didn't dare ask.

"Okay, I'll be back. And okay, we can do *things* tonight. If we're not too knackered. My arms feel like they're going to fall off after lugging boxes full of books all day."

Jasper smiled ruefully. Just an okay for the night, then. Right, he'd have to make it a good one so Lewis wanted more. "I should probably get cleaned up and shave."

Lewis's thumb rubbed the wrong way against his stubble again. "Don't bother on my account. It's sexy like this. Unless you meant shaving somewhere else, that is?" He waggled an eyebrow.

Oh, now that was just too cute.

Lewis cocked his head. "Do I take it by the silence you're thinking about shaving? Because if I'm honest, I like a man hairy. If I'd wanted smooth, I'd have been into girls, wouldn't I?"

"No, I uh, no, I don't want to shave. But some men are nice smooth." A memory of Mas's startlingly white, hairless buttocks flashed across his vision. When he'd asked, Mas had asserted that he felt more sensations when he was hairless, and that it was totally worth the pain of getting a back, sac and crack wax. "Erm, not that I'm suggesting you shave or anything. Not unless you wanted to. But, you know, no pressure. It's not a fetish or anything. Not even a kink. Er, should I stop talking now?"

Lewis was grinning widely. "You're pretty adorable when you get embarrassed, you know that?" He kissed Jasper quickly, then stepped back down onto the stairs. "I'll be back as soon as possible. You make sure you save your energy, yeah?"

"Okay," Jasper croaked, too embarrassed to come up with anything more suggestive and commanding. But maybe that didn't matter if Lewis found him adorable. Not that adorable was a particularly masculine or sexy adjective. Did gay men fall in love with adorable men? Did they want to move in and share their lives with them?

Or were adorable men only good for sharing a bed with? Someone you'd enjoy looking at now and again, but not the kind of appeal that stood up to the trials of day-to-day living. Mas was pretty adorable, and Jasper didn't want more out of him than a friendly, warm body to tangle with on occasion. And he didn't even want that anymore. Just the friendly part. No tangling.

Then again, Lewis wasn't Jasper. And, more to the point, Jasper found Lewis pretty bloody adorable too, and he'd be more than happy to find out whether that opinion stood up to the test of time.

As usual, he was totally overthinking this.

Chapter Twenty-Eight

Jasper gave himself a mental pep talk after he'd thanked Lewis and the others for their help and the front door had closed behind them. He needed to get ready, not hang around torturing himself with unanswerable questions. He should try some easier ones, like did he need a shower? He took an experimental sniff under his arm.

Right. He definitely needed a shower. First things first, though; he'd try to locate some clothes that didn't stink of shut-up wardrobe or sweaty pits. He eventually remembered the ones he'd hung out on the line several days ago, and went outside to retrieve them.

The evening light had turned golden, brushing the tops of the trees and hitting the veranda from a low angle so the whole back of the house was lit up. The garden itself was mostly in shade, the greens muted but every warm-hued flower glowing as if lit from within. Mama had loved this time of day. Even when she'd taken to her bed for good, she still asked to be helped out to the veranda every chance she got, a hot water bottle in her lap and a blanket over her legs.

Jasper smiled. There. That memory hadn't hurt. He wandered barefoot down through the garden until he reached the ancient rotary clothes line. Cool grass tickled his toes as he unclipped the pegs from a pair of soft, thin pyjama bottoms and an old V-necked T-shirt. They were both grey...or perhaps black. Lewis would probably call them something fancy like pewter or charcoal. They weren't clothes he'd go out in—even Jasper with his dubious grasp of fashion knew that some things were only suitable for sleepwear, and cotton that clung so close it showed every plane of his body was definitely included in that definition.

Still, beggars couldn't be choosers, and, along with the load of underpants and socks hanging on the line, these were the only clean clothes he had.

Jasper sluiced himself down in the shower as fast as possible, although his aching muscles did demand a slightly longer than usual time spent luxuriating under the hot spray. He then threw on his pyjamas and gathered up a large armful of clothes destined for the washing machine. At the top of the stairs, he turned his body sideways like he usually did, and then it hit him. He didn't need to do that anymore. Here was an unobstructed staircase, leading down to a clear hallway. What's more, he'd been reliably informed that all the downstairs rooms were now empty. Completely, one hundred percent empty.

He walked down in a daze. The house not only looked different. It felt different. His footsteps echoed. There was a cool draught around his ankles. That sweet smell of old paper had gone, replaced by something tangy and citrusy.

It wasn't until he'd set the washing machine going that he really took in just what the downstairs team had been up to while he emptied his bedroom.

The kitchen sparkled.

The taps gleamed, the tiles shone. Even the melamine doors were scrubbed clean of their usual grease marks. The vinyl floor still bore a few wet patches in the corners, and was cleaner than he'd seen it in years. He walked around the dining area. Okay, when they'd said empty, they had in fact left him his table and chairs, but they could have been a new set with the way they shone. A few stubborn white rings in the varnish remained from where he'd been placing his coffee cup, but other than that you'd never know it was the same table.

He turned around on the spot, scanning the walls, the ceiling, the shelves. Everything had been cleaned, at least superficially. There certainly wasn't that giant cobweb joining the lampshade to

230

the ceiling anymore. A funny part of him missed it. Or maybe he was just missing the books. But as he took in more of the room, he could see possibilities for storing them. The wall opposite the kitchen area had an old chimney breast in the centre, and on each side there was a perfect alcove for bookshelves. He stepped into one and guestimated the depth of his largest tomes. Yes, even they should fit in there without sticking out. Maybe it would be okay to have books in the kitchen. It wasn't like they'd be on a shelf over the cooker or anything.

He was still pondering the potential hazards of grease and paper when he heard the front door opening. It was an unfamiliar sound, now there wasn't a tonne of books to deaden the click of the lock and the protest of the hinges. Did he have any oil for those anywhere? Did he even care, when Lewis was just in the next room?

And they were just about to have sex?

Oh...fuck.

"Jasper?"

"In here." He couldn't move. His insides had transformed into seasick butterflies, and if he took a step, he just knew he'd probably spew. What had happened to his determination to take the upper hand? To seduce Lewis and convince him to stay the night.

"You look lost," Lewis said from the doorway, a tentative smile on his face.

"I don't recognise my own house." He wasn't sure he recognised Lewis either, in his soft loose shirt and trousers. He must have been home to shower and change, as his hair was damp too.

"Come on, I'll show you the rest." Lewis extended his hand, and when Jasper took hold of it, the butterflies settled. "You have Yusef and Carroll to thank for this. I never thought I'd see anyone who could take her on at speed cleaning, but that man has a talent."

"Must come from working in a busy café."

"That's what he said. Now, I reckon this room cleaned up pretty well and there's not going to be too much repair work needed. Maybe a fresh lick of paint as there was a bit of mildew on the outside wall, but the rest is in pretty good nick."

Jasper noted the niff of bleach and a faint greyish stain by the back door where Lewis indicated, but wasn't particularly perturbed. "Looks fine to me. I can live with it." He'd always rather liked the yellow his mama had chosen for this room.

Lewis gave him a lopsided smile. "That's fine, then, and it's going to make your life easier if you have a base room that doesn't need too much work doing to it. Have you looked into the front two rooms yet?" A frown creased Lewis's brow.

"Not yet."

"I'm warning you now, it probably looks worse than it is, so don't freak. You are definitely going to need to redecorate both those rooms, though. You might need to get in a plasterer too."

"Oh, okay." Jasper let himself be led through towards the living room. With his hand on the doorknob, Lewis shot him a worried look.

"Also, we took an executive decision and removed the curtains. Don't worry, we didn't chuck them. We moved them to the warehouse. But I don't think they'd be good for anything anymore."

Was it really going to be that bad? Lewis opened the door, and Jasper stepped inside.

"Oh God." He turned on the spot, taking it all in. The room was far larger than he'd ever remembered, but the wall around the window looked...ominous. Maybe it was simply the dim lighting making things look dilapidated. He went to flick the overhead light on and gasped.

"It's worse on the outside wall," Lewis said, tugging him in that direction. "I think you must have had a leak in the window frame,

232

so those might need replacing, which could be pricey, but as far as we can see, everything else is superficial damage."

Superficial? The wallpaper was bubbled and curling back at the edges all over the room, but on this wall it was almost falling off. And he was fairly sure plaster shouldn't be that blackish colour. When he got closer, the black resolved itself into patches of mildew. Ugh.

Jasper reached out and tugged at a strip of paper. The whole piece fell down, revealing damp plaster covered in blooms of mould.

"What are you thinking?" Lewis asked, his voice betraying a nervousness Jasper had never before heard from him.

"I've never seen so many different-coloured moulds before." He might have been familiar with the black mildew spots, but here were patches of mottled yellow, orange, blue, green and even some white fluffy stuff that looked like it should be growing on leftovers in the fridge. Not that he let the contents of his fridge get into that state. Well, not all that often, anyway. "It's kind of beautiful, in a strange way."

"Beautiful? I don't think I've ever heard anyone call mould beautiful."

"Sorry. It's just so colourful."

"Hey, no need to apologise. I like that you can see something special in everything. You really notice things. The details. So many people are so focused on the big picture they never take time to stop and look around them."

"And I just get stuck on the details." Like those times he'd tried to throw out newspapers and been distracted by reading the articles.

"You're getting better."

Was he really? Jasper supposed he must be if they'd even got this far. The prospect of working through all the contents of the warehouse, though? The very idea made dread settle in his guts. Then a thought wormed its way up into his conscious mind on a wave of bile. "Oh God, the mould. Did it spread? Is my stuff okay? The books?"

Lewis's face twisted. "I'm not going to lie to you. There were a few piles of books that I don't think are fit for anything other than landfill. And a few pieces of wooden furniture that were up against the outside walls are looking pretty bad, but I think they're salvageable. Also, some leatherworking stuff and an old slipper we found behind your sofa. Leather is one of those materials that just seems to attract mould."

Jasper listened with a sick feeling. "You chucked it all out?"

"No! Of course not. I promised we wouldn't, didn't I? We've taped out a new area in the warehouse for stuff that's badly damaged, but it's up to you to decide what goes. Hey, come on, it's not so bad, really." Lewis put an arm around Jasper's shoulders. "It's only stuff. There are much more important things out there."

"Like what?"

"Like people."

Jasper leaned his head against Lewis's, savouring the closeness. Yes, people were much more important. He hadn't had enough of them in his life for far too long now, and he didn't want his fear to ruin a chance at what he craved. He craned his neck to get a look at Lewis's face. "Lewis, I...I wanted to ask, will you stay. Tonight?"

Lewis's fingers plucked at the front of Jasper's T-shirt. "I think it's probably inevitable. I'm so knackered, I think I'm going to pass out as soon as my head hits a pillow."

"I'm kind of hoping you won't."

"Got plans for me, have you?" Lewis's tone stayed light, but his fingers kneaded the fabric of Jasper's shirt possessively, brushing his nipple in a most distracting way.

"I've got plans for both of us."

Jasper turned Lewis to face him, and slowly—slow enough for Lewis to stop him if it wasn't what he wanted—he leaned in to claim his lips.

For a kiss that started so politely, it soon turned messy. Teeth clashed and tongues grappled. Jasper's hands found their way down to Lewis's arse and lifted him. The pressure of Lewis's erection against his made him gasp. But when Lewis groped between them, Jasper grabbed his wrist.

"Not here." He didn't want another quick fumble in a ravaged room. He wanted to lay out a naked Lewis and take his time getting to know him. "On my bed."

Lewis nodded, spots of colour high on his cheeks.

Chapter Twenty-Nine

This time, Jasper led the way, pulling Lewis behind him.

"You want to look in the dining room?" Lewis asked.

"Not really." But as he hadn't been inside the room for years, he poked his head around the door. It was a square room with a bay window and two outside walls, and he always remembered it feeling cold, but perhaps he'd find a use for it one day. Right now, though, his mind was on other things. "Come on. Upstairs. I vacuumed my room for you and everything."

"I feel honoured," Lewis said, his solemn tones not giving anything away. It was hard to tell if that was sarcasm or a genuine sentiment, but Jasper didn't let the doubt slow him down.

When he opened the door, pink light flooded out.

"Wow," Lewis breathed, tugging Jasper over to the window and climbing up onto the bed to get a better view. "What a sunset."

The sky was strung with little puffy clouds and softer, gauzy ones behind them, all glowing shades of fiery peach, orange and gold. Lewis's hair shone like a corkscrew halo, picking up the warm light and dazzling Jasper. He could still see it shining even when he took his glasses off and laid them on the bedside table.

He climbed onto the bed where Lewis kneeled and moved behind him, fitting his knees between Lewis's legs and wrapping his arms around that lean waist. He pulled Lewis back a little so his weight was resting on Jasper's lap. Lewis's neck was right there, begging to be lavished with kisses. The skin was smooth, freshly shaven, and Lewis moaned as Jasper scraped his own stubbly skin over it in search of Lewis's pulse. He licked over the fluttering skin of Lewis's neck. Tasted warm man under the hint of shaving soap. Felt the rumble of Lewis's larynx as he groaned and arched back, pressing the crease of his arse against Jasper's aching dick.

Oh, that felt amazing.

Lewis's hands scrabbled around behind him as if trying to pull Jasper even closer against his back, but their urgency had to be resisted. Jasper wanted to take his time and make Lewis remember this night. He caught both Lewis's hands and pressed them down to the top of his brass bed frame. "Keep those there," he said, gently stroking each finger down so that it curled around the metal.

"Or what?" Lewis asked.

"Or I'll have to go find something to tie them there. Maybe my dressing gown cord."

"Mmmm, sounds hot." Lewis's eyelashes flickered, and he bit his lower lip as he arched back farther against Jasper's shoulder.

Blimey O'Reilly! He'd only been teasing, but now that he really considered tying Lewis up, he had to agree. It wasn't so much the vision of Lewis trussed up that thrilled him, more the idea that Lewis would trust him enough to be put in such a vulnerable position.

But not tonight. No, tonight it would be more than enough just to see Lewis fully naked at last. To have him there in his bed. To push inside him for the very first time.

To remember what living was all about.

Jasper tugged on Lewis's shirt, suddenly hungry for skin. The more of it, the better. Lewis obligingly lifted his arms to help Jasper remove the shirt, then placed his hands back on the bed frame.

Bare skin at last. Jasper sat on his heels to get a better look at Lewis's back. He was lean as expected, the knobs of his spine protruding in a way that tempted Jasper to run his fingertips down over them. Lewis gasped when he reached the crease of his arse.

"You're very welcome to keep going," Lewis rasped while

Jasper's finger paused there. "I've been kind of hoping you'd want to top the first time."

"God." It shuddered out of him on a wave of desire. He could. They could do it like this, kneeling on the bed by the open window, watching the sky blaze and dim. Or he could roll them both down onto the bed and take it slowly, face-to-face. That would be more loving, more memorable, surely?

Or maybe he could wait and do that in the morning.

"Please." Lewis ground his arse down against Jasper in a way that must surely have been calculated to drive him wild. "I brought condoms and lube and everything."

"Everything?" What else was there, exactly, without straying into the realms of the kinky? Jasper shifted forwards again to nuzzle Lewis's neck.

"Christ, that's good."

"You said *everything*."

"Everything? Oh, okay, just condoms and lube."

"I do have some here, you know."

"Yeah, but I wasn't sure they'd be in date."

Jasper pinched Lewis's nipple for that, pleased to feel him shiver in response. "They're perfectly in date, thanks. I've not been a complete hermit."

"Good, 'coz I'm planning on getting pretty carried away, and I don't think I'll have the presence of mind to talk you through technique."

"Cheeky. I'll show you *technique*." Because if all those tumbles with Mas had taught him anything, it was that, even if only in bed, he knew how to satisfy a man.

Jasper began with one earlobe pinched between his teeth, then licked and nuzzled his way down Lewis's spine while his hands got busy pushing those pesky trousers down and out of the way.

"Oh, oh shit, Jasper! Yeah, just like that." It was a buzz to hear the moans and half-mumbled curses Lewis let out. Who'd have thought the man actually had a dirty mouth on him?

Lewis had a cute little rear. Not all sticking out like a porn star's, but small, pale and firm to the touch. His skin was smooth—the light dusting of blond hair on his thighs having pretty much given up halfway up, like his arse was above the tree line. Jasper spent a moment admiring, massaging with his thumbs and gently drawing Lewis's cheeks apart. He blew experimentally over the rosy pink pucker, pleased to hear the whimper coming from above.

"God, Jasper, I didn't have you down for a tease."

Jasper smiled to himself, then oh-so-slowly leaned in and licked a trail up from Lewis's balls to his hole. His man tasted good. He'd known that already from sucking him off, but the flavour and scent here was subtly different. Earthier, despite the hint of soap. Jasper revelled in olfactory overload, ignored Lewis's groans of protest and moved back down to his balls. He'd not had a chance to really get to know them yet, so he took his time bathing them in saliva, sucking them into his mouth one by one.

Lewis's legs began to quake. Jasper craned his head to look up at him from beneath. Everything about Lewis burned. His skin and his hair caught the sunset and threw it back at Jasper, dazzling him. It was almost too bright for Jasper to catch the expression on his face, the grimace of ecstasy. Lewis looked like he was in danger of biting through his lower lip at any moment, so Jasper decided to move things along.

He got back in position behind Lewis and resumed teasing with his tongue, but this time he focussed on Lewis's twitching hole. The muscles fluttered under his probing, eventually letting him in, only to push him out again. By now Lewis was panting and pleading incoherently. Jasper had to dig his fingers into Lewis's hips to stop the man from shoving back at him and riding his face shamelessly.

Next time. For now, Jasper wanted to be the one setting the pace, so he drew it out longer, until his dick felt ready to explode if anyone so much as looked at it.

Lewis's hole was soft and pliant now, and since Jasper's tongue had gone numb he figured it was time for a change.

He moved back up, hugging Lewis around the waist and kissing his neck. "You ready for me?"

"So ready. Please."

It was the work of seconds to undress, roll on a condom and lube up. Jasper paused, looking down at the point where their bodies almost met, creamy white against darkly-furred tan. They looked great together. He gripped hold of Lewis's hips and nudged him with the tip of his erection. Lewis gasped, then turned his head, frowning endearingly.

"Please, just hurry up before I come all over your pillow."

Pillow? Oh yeah. He should probably go and get a towel or something to protect the sheets, but he didn't want to let go of Lewis even for a second. He flexed his fingers, enjoying the smoothness of Lewis's skin underneath them, and circled his dick against Lewis's entrance. He wanted in. What's more, Lewis's body wanted him in. Oh well. Pillow be damned. Jasper could just turn it over to sleep.

Jasper surged forward, and Lewis welcomed him with a throaty groan.

Chapter Thirty

Lewis clung to the bed frame, certain that if he let go he'd collapse.

God, Jasper really did know what he was doing. Even though Lewis's dick hadn't received the merest of strokes yet, his whole body shook from the effects of Jasper's attentions. That unhurried mastery had turned him to jelly. It seemed rash to start making comparisons to previous lovers based on just this one instance of foreplay, but Lewis couldn't remember ever feeling transported like this.

And now, with Jasper filling him up inside and Jasper's breath coming fast against his neck, there was absolutely nowhere he'd rather be.

"You can move now," Lewis eventually prompted, once the sting of entry had transformed into pulsing pleasure.

"I can't," Jasper groaned. "Not if you want it to last longer than ten seconds."

"Ten seconds would probably do me." Especially if someone actually touched his aching dick. Even rubbing it against the bedposts should work, although he'd rather have skin on skin.

"I want you to have a better time than that."

Lewis uncurled his fingers from the bed frame and pushed back, so he ended up pretty much sitting on Jasper's lap. He reached for Jasper's head and twisted, finally managing to meet his lips with an awkward kiss.

Jasper's forehead glistened with sweat, and his eyes were shut tight. God, he really did want to do his best. The thought wrapped Lewis up in perfect warmth. He couldn't remember a partner ever going to quite these lengths to stave off orgasm for his sake.

"Think of something boring. Think of... I don't know. Poetry. You know any poetry by heart?"

"Yeah, but I don't know any *boring* poems. It's all, you know, *sensual*. Shakespeare, Rimbaud... They're not going to take my mind off coming."

Good point. Why bother learning a boring poem? "Football scores?"

"As if."

Then it struck him. "The Dewey Decimal Classification System. You could go through that in your mind."

The furrow on Jasper's forehead deepened, then smoothed. "Okay. That could work. Is working. Thank Christ."

Lewis left it another minute before rippling his internal muscles to clench Jasper tight.

"Right, okay, yes. I'll try." Jasper's words came out in anguished pants. His hands gripped Lewis's hips even tighter and lifted him just a fraction, before thrusting back up into him.

"Oh fuck." Lewis grabbed hold of the bed frame again, his grip sweaty.

"You have a dirty mouth in bed," Jasper breathed before repeating the lift and thrust.

This time Jasper hit Lewis's sweet spot. He convulsed, his dick dripping precome all over the pillow. "Shit, that's it. Just like that."

"Never heard you swear before."

"I don't. Usually. Only with someone—fuck!—who knows what he's doing."

Jasper huffed in his ear. It might have been a laugh, but Lewis was too far gone to tell. Every jerk of Jasper's hips pushed a gush of precome out of him, and pleasure reverberated through his body. Every thrust turned into a mini-orgasm.

Lewis's hands began to shake, his grip loosening. His arms

slipped, and Jasper pushed him forward, up onto his knees. Now he could lean onto the top of the bed frame, his face almost touching the window.

And now Jasper really began to show him what he could do. Long, steady strokes in and out that were going to drive Lewis mad. Would someone please touch his dick? Jasper, preferably, as Lewis's sweaty hands were clutching on to the slippery bed frame for all he was worth.

"Please," he groaned. "Please touch me. I need to come."

"Not yet."

Lewis tried to swallow back the helpless sob in his throat, but it was a losing battle.

Jasper picked up his pace, hips pistoning. Balls slamming into Lewis's. The sound of skin slapping skin filling the air.

The sob became a howl.

Jasper's hands moved, hugged him tight. His mouth latched on to Lewis's neck. Sucking. Chin rasping.

Lewis was coming even before Jasper's hand closed around his cock. Jasper fucked him through it, his movements increasingly erratic and jerky.

Lewis's vision narrowed, static snow taking over the edges. His world was the bruising ache of Jasper moving inside him. The ragged gasps against his neck. The hand milking every last drop of pleasure from him.

"Lewis! Love this. Love you. Oh!" Jasper rammed in deeper than he had yet. So deep Lewis could feel it in his heart.

Jasper froze and groaned. His hips jerked.

Lewis was no stranger to sex, but never like this. Oh no. It had never felt like this. Ever.

With anyone.

Jasper tugged on him, and Lewis fell back against him, his head lolling. Jasper panted into the exposed skin of his neck. Felt good. So right. A moment of paradise, just for the two of them.

But the moment couldn't last forever, and eventually Jasper began moving beneath him, easing out.

"Ow!" Lewis winced, but the kiss on his neck made the withdrawal more bearable. It couldn't console him while Jasper left the room, though.

How could he ever make do with anyone else after this? Jasper had spoiled him. Screwed the stuffing out of him, and here he was, a limp ragdoll, unable to contemplate ever making love to anyone other than Jasper.

And it had been love, hadn't it? While you certainly couldn't believe everything you heard in the throes of orgasm (unless it was another man's name), he didn't doubt Jasper loved him. Really loved him. Which made what Lewis had to do even more impossibly tough on both of them.

He stared up at the ceiling, watching the violet shadows encroach as the peachy gold light dimmed.

The sound of the toilet flushing heralded Jasper's return.

"You have a lovely room," Lewis said. It was pathetic, really, trying to steer the conversation into safe territory. He knew they needed to talk, but he wanted to grab every extra moment of closeness he could. It was only a matter of time before the inevitable distance would open up between them. "Are you going to redecorate up here?"

"Don't know." Jasper landed on the bed beside him slumping into the mattress and pulling Lewis tight towards him. They touched, noses, chests, groins, knees, toes. Jasper was too close to focus his eyes on, so Lewis let his drift shut. "No sleeping. Not yet. I need to tell you...about Mama."

"You don't have to."

"I do!" The urgency in Jasper's tone surprised Lewis.

"Okay. Well, if it's what you need."

"I have to tell someone. I just... I just don't know how. Where

244

to start."

"It's usually best to start at the beginning." Lewis yawned but forced his eyes open to show he was paying attention. Jasper rolled onto his back but pulled Lewis's arm with him so he lay with his hand over Jasper's heart.

Jasper was quiet for so long Lewis would have thought him asleep, if it weren't for the fact his eyes were open and staring at the ceiling. When he did begin talking, his voice was so soft Lewis had to strain his ears.

"I suppose the beginning was when she got ill. I mean really ill. She took off to bed the day after I came out to her, and after that she didn't get up again without help. I had to care for her around the clock."

"Do you think that was deliberate?" She wouldn't have been the first person in the world to use an illness to manipulate the behaviour of those caring for her. "Like she was trying to stop you going out and finding a man?"

"I don't know. I don't think she was doing it consciously. She was just so depressed about the whole situation. Not having grandchildren. Said I'd never find a man to care about me in the same way a woman would. She wanted the best for me."

"The best would have been to let you live your life and love who you pleased."

Jasper's mouth twisted into a rough approximation of a smile. "It just wasn't that simple. Not when she was sick. She wasn't faking it. She'd just lost her reason to keep fighting the leukaemia. Anyway, that's not really the bit I need to tell you about. She kept going like that for another four years, just slowly sliding downhill. Her muscles wasted away with no exercise. She was in chronic pain. They gave her drugs, but she said they didn't work. She still ached all over. And it was terminal by then. It wasn't like she was going to live for very long anyway, even without..." Jasper gulped. "Even without my help."

Lewis's heart plummeted. "What exactly are you trying to tell me?"

"She begged me to help her end it. For almost six months. Every day, again and again and again. I didn't want to, but in the end... In the end, she wore me down, and I did it. I fucking well did it. I killed her, Lewis." Jasper's voice cracked, but he didn't start weeping. Perhaps he'd cried it all out of himself earlier.

"I...I don't know what to say." Possibly for the first time ever.

"You don't need to say anything. I just wanted to tell someone and not have them turn me over to the police. You won't, will you?"

"Of course not."

"Thanks. For listening and...everything." Jasper gulped, and Lewis watched as he drew himself together. It took a monumental effort of will, by the looks of it. That same willpower that had kept him going all those lonely years.

"Anytime," Lewis whispered, wondering if that was a lie. Was he really going to be around for Jasper, or would he stick to his guns and insist on the separation period he'd planned? Jasper's confession was troubling. No, more than that. It was frightening. Had he done it with a pillow over her face? Lewis shivered a little, imagining Jasper looming over a withered body, crying, perhaps, as he held the pillow down.

Poor bloke. Doing something like that... The guilt you'd have to live with. He wanted to talk it through now, but Jasper's breathing was already slowing, and they'd had such a long, hard day.

Lewis drifted off into nightmares, pursued through looming towers of junk by a creature he couldn't see but which reeked of death.

He woke with a shout, but Jasper was there to snuggle up to, and the weight of his arm across Lewis's chest helped to drag him back into an uneasy slumber.

Chapter Thirty-One

Jasper's morning began with a phone call from work, asking if he could come in and cover a shift as they were five down due to a nasty stomach bug doing the rounds. He stared at Lewis's sleeping form in the bed next to him as he heard himself agree. He was sure they'd fallen asleep together, but sometime in the night, Lewis had rolled away and onto his front and was now lying spread-eagled with his face buried in the pillow. Jasper could just see a slice of cheek and a whole load of rumpled blond hair.

Why on earth had he said yes to his boss? He was meant to be on holiday for another week. But then again, he'd always gone out of his way to cover shifts when necessary, and it had become a habit to just agree. Besides, it wasn't like he'd ever had anything better to do with his time.

Perhaps he needed to work on being a bit more selfish in future. If he had a reason to be, that is. A reason like the one that was lying next to him, snuffling softly. The first man he'd ever shared his bed with.

He lay back down again, and Lewis shifted, still half mashed into the pillow, but opening a bleary, unfocused eye. "Issat the phone?" he mumbled. "Wassa time?"

"Shhh, it's still early. Half seven." Lewis hadn't requested a particular wake-up time, that Jasper could recall. Or had he just forgotten during the stresses of yesterday?

Oh God. Had he really told Lewis his secret? He waited for the fear to kick in, but there was a strange wash of peace over his thoughts. What was that about, then? He could almost believe he hadn't told Lewis in the end, that it had all been a stress dream.

After all, the man was still here. He hadn't run away in disgust or turned him in to the police.

"I need to get going." Jasper attempted to hide his confusion by getting out of bed and rooting around in his wardrobe. Buggeration. No clean clothes. He'd put that wash on last night but then left it in the machine so it would still be damp. Was he going to have to buy a new outfit on the way in? No, he'd just wear some of the older stuff. The musty smell would wear off during the day, hopefully.

"Going where?" Lewis pushed himself up, revealing a splendid pillow print on his face. "Thought you, me and Carroll were sorting in the warehouse today."

"Work called. They need me to help out. It's an emergency." Because God forbid a university library was short-staffed for one day during the summer break. "Okay, maybe not an emergency, but my boss asked so nicely. Well...that's not exactly true. She kind of expected me to cover. It was hard to say no."

Lewis stared at him like he was a madman. "You have a job to do today. We've still got a couple of rooms up here to clear."

"Could you do it without me?"

"You'd let me? Really?"

"Yes. Just leave Mama's room alone. I'm going to deal with that one myself."

A look passed over Lewis's face. Haunted... Disturbed? Jasper couldn't quite place it, but he knew exactly why it was there. "I told you what happened?"

"That you, er, assisted her suicide?"

"Assisted her suicide?" Jasper choked back the bitter laughter those innocuous words called up. How could they explain the truth of what he'd done? "I murdered her. She drove me mad, and I murdered her."

"I'm sure it wasn't like that. There were mitigating circumstances." But Lewis didn't sound so sure. More like he was

248

clutching at straws.

"You don't know anything about it."

"Not yet. But you can share it with me. I won't tell anyone else, I promise."

Jasper glanced at his watch. "I don't have time now. I'll be finished at three, though." And then back to the warehouse with Carroll there too. No, that wouldn't work. "Could you come and meet me from work? We could go somewhere quiet to talk." A public place, where he wouldn't end up breaking down in tears or getting angry. Somewhere the both of them would be forced to be on best behaviour. Not that he could imagine Lewis ever shouting at anyone, but you never knew what stress would do to people.

"Yeah. I suppose. Me and Carroll will probably be finished by then."

"Thanks." Jasper started to give directions to the library, then rethought it. He'd have to introduce Lewis to everyone, and he wasn't sure he could take the sly teasing that was bound to ensue—especially if things didn't work out between them. "Hang on, how about the museum? It's close to work and it'll be cool in there."

Lewis nodded slowly. "Haven't been there in years. Used to love it."

"You'll love it even more now. They've improved things, but they haven't messed with any of the good stuff."

"They've still got all the stuffed animals?"

"Oh, yes."

"Count me in, then." Lewis gave a sleepy smile that made Jasper want to jump back into bed and ravish him.

Instead, he pulled on a khaki T-shirt and searched for the pair of cut-offs he was sure he'd owned once upon a time. He gave Lewis a quick kiss before leaving, but the man was already slipping back to the Land of Nod.

Later that afternoon, Jasper waited in the museum lobby, staring up at the aeroplane hanging above them. He'd been fascinated by it when he was younger, asking Mama how they'd managed to get it inside the building. Had they taken the roof off, he'd demanded to know, or had they just built the whole museum around it? She'd told him that must be how they'd done it, then dragged him into the Egyptian display.

Of course, eventually he'd figured out for himself that an old biplane like that could easily be dismantled to fit through the doors then rebuilt inside, but it didn't make it any the less magical for knowing how it had been done.

He felt a presence by his side and caught the scent of Lewis's now familiar aftershave.

"I used to love going up to the top galleries and waving at the pilot," Lewis said. "He looks so cheerful. Told the folks I was going to be a pilot when I grew up, right up until the point I realised how bloody precise and methodical you have to be."

"Nothing wrong with being precise and methodical. I have to be that all the time in my job." Jasper let his gaze run over the ornate ceiling and vaulted windows, evidence of other workmen with the same ethics.

"I'm better off with the imprecision of dealing with real people. Keeps me on my toes."

"You must love working with me, then," Jasper murmured.

"I do. I just wish we'd met under other circumstances. Ones where you weren't my client," Lewis amended when Jasper turned to stare at him. He had a shifty, guilty expression on his face.

Oh God, not that again. Just his pigging luck.

"I could stop being your client," Jasper offered. "Now the house is clear, I reckon I can probably cope with putting it back together by myself."

Lewis sighed deeply. "How about we discuss all that another time? You want to tell me about your mother, don't you?"

"Want is probably the wrong word. I think I need to, though. I owe you an explanation for what I said last night."

"Jasper, you don't have to tell me anything. I'm not going to judge you for it."

"I need you to understand," Jasper said doggedly.

"Okay. I hear you. Just, let's take it somewhere more private, yeah?"

"The Egyptian exhibit?" It would be dark, anyway, as they kept the lights low to protect all the antiquities. Lewis agreed, so Jasper led the way between the guardian statues on either side of the entrance.

Private wasn't really the right word for one of the museum's most popular attractions during the school holidays. Children were everywhere, breathing on the glass cases and enthusing about the gory details of mummification.

Death. Touch the screen to find out more, suggested one of the information points Jasper passed. How appropriate. He stared through the glass of the adjoining case at an intricately decorated sarcophagus.

"The ancients really knew how to do death properly, didn't they?" Lewis asked him.

Was the man a mind reader? "How do you mean?"

"All the ceremony. The grave goods. They might have believed it would help them on the other side, but I think it was more helpful to those left grieving. They could talk about death openly. Celebrate it, even. We can't do that anymore. It's all closed off behind funeral home doors."

Jasper rested his forehead against the glass and smiled bitterly. Yes. Clearly Lewis could read his mind. Or perhaps it was just all that therapist training he'd had. "Do you think it would help if we talked more about death?" Whether he was talking about the two of them or society as a whole, he had no idea.

"Absolutely. It's the only certainty in life, and it binds us all

251

together. Better to make peace with it while you're alive than live in fear."

"I'm not afraid of dying."

"But you're afraid of living, and that amounts to the same thing."

Did it? "Mama had to live with so much pain. She couldn't stand the morphine they had her on at the end. Said it made her head fuzzy, and she refused to take a full dose. Then she got this crazy idea in her head that she'd feel better on heroin. She used to beg me to go out and score her some."

Lewis gave the group nearest them a furtive glance, and Jasper realised belatedly that perhaps that wasn't the best topic for a room full of children. When Lewis suggested they move it upstairs to a quieter gallery, Jasper readily agreed.

There weren't many places to sit in the museum, but up in the deserted nineteenth-century French artists gallery they found a bench opposite a few lesser known Impressionist landscapes. Pretty enough, but not the ones that turned up plastered all over the calendars and tea towels his Mama had loved. Jasper studied the Pissarro garden while waiting for Lewis to speak. Perhaps Mama had modelled the planting scheme at the lower end of the garden on it, as there was the same preponderance of purple flowers. He'd never thought to ask, and now it was too late to ever find out.

"So? Did you score any heroin?" Lewis whispered.

"Of course not. Can you imagine me going out trying to buy drugs? I'd probably end up getting mugged for my trouble."

"I can just imagine you trying to speak street to a dealer." Lewis smiled then, lifting the gathering gloom for just a moment.

"Quite. It would be a bloody disaster. I don't know any of the proper slang, and I'm not sure I want to either. I'd have come home with the wrong thing entirely. Probably a bag of icing sugar, knowing my luck."

"Actually, H is usually brown."

"See what I mean? A disaster. Anyway, after a few months of begging for that, she changed her tune. Started asking me to help her end it all. Can you imagine what that's like? Someone you're caring for and giving your life up for, just begging you to kill them pretty much every time they open their mouth?"

He felt Lewis shudder beside him. "It's a good case for legalising euthanasia."

"Yes, well, I did look into a trip to Switzerland, but she wouldn't hear of travelling." If only she'd been willing. It could have saved him some of the burden of guilt, and everything would have been so much cleaner and quicker. Instead, it had dragged on for the best part of a year. "She kept on asking, though. She even asked her doctor, but he refused to have anything to do with it."

"So what happened to change your mind?"

"Just a long, slow war of attrition, I think. In the end, it was easier to give in than to resist." He shrugged. "I'm a weak person, when push comes to shove."

Now Lewis squeezed his hand. "You're one of the kindest, gentlest men I've ever met."

"Thanks, but isn't that another way of saying weak?"

"Not at all. It takes real strength to care for someone like you did. And the way you're starting to let go of your hoard. It takes guts and courage. Might not be the kind of strength the rest of the world recognises, but don't you go letting anyone tell you you're weak."

Lewis was so very earnest, it made Jasper smile despite himself. "Feels good to have someone on my side."

Another visitor to the gallery curtailed their conversation for a few minutes, but luckily she clip-clopped around the paintings with only a very brief pause to look before moving to the next. When she left for the modern art exhibition, Jasper exhaled noisily. "You want to know how I did it?"

"Only if you want to tell me."

"I do. I need to tell someone." Jasper kept his gaze fixed on the Pissarro as he spoke, because looking in Lewis's eyes would have made him feel too raw. Too exposed. "Her doctor took me aside one day and said on no account was I to accidentally double up her dose as that would be very dangerous and probably fatal. There was something about the way he said it, though. He kept nodding and fixing me with this stare, like he really needed me to understand something he wasn't saying, but I couldn't figure out what. I think I must have exasperated him in the end. When he was leaving, he said that of course it was highly unlikely in the event of her death that they'd bother with a post mortem as funds were tight and she was terminal anyway. So long as there were no obvious suspicious circumstances, he'd be happy to sign a death certificate citing natural causes."

"So he gave you permission?"

"A get-out-of-jail-free card."

"And so you did it? What he suggested?"

"Not straight away. Took me another few weeks to talk myself around. And then one day I realised that she couldn't enjoy anything anymore. It was a lovely September day. Warm and breezy. I'd opened her windows and picked a big bunch of her favourite flowers, but all she could do was complain about how she didn't want to live through another winter. And I got to thinking that maybe I was being cruel, denying her the peace she was after. And so I fetched her meds, and she must have known what I was up to, because she'd already had her dose that afternoon." He fell silent, remembering the way she'd looked up at him, the surprised expression that morphed into the first smile he'd seen from her in months.

"How did you feel, at the time?"

"Strangely peaceful. I sat and read *A Midsummer Night's Dream* to her, and it was just like she was falling asleep. Nothing so very unusual except for the fact she wasn't grumbling at me.

254

Afterwards...after I'd checked and knew she was gone... Well, I sat there for hours." He could remember that afternoon with clinical precision. The way she'd been smiling. The light slanting into the room. The bee buzzing around trying to find his way back out of the window. It was the last time he ever remembered feeling true peace. "Evening fell, and then I knew I had to ring the doctor or it was going to start looking suspicious. That's when the guilt kicked in."

"And you had no one to talk to about it."

"No one. Not till now."

Lewis's thumb ghosted over Jasper's knuckles for a few minutes as they sat in silence. "I think I'm starting to understand what got you started hoarding."

Jasper couldn't hold back a wry laugh. "Care to enlighten me?"

"You'd just let your mother go and were all alone. You didn't want to let anything else go. Couldn't handle the responsibility. And yet you didn't want to have to be reminded about her all the time, so you started stacking the books in front of everything. Covering it all up. Building walls around yourself. Around your heart."

"They're not there anymore." *You own my heart,* he wanted to say, but didn't quite have the courage.

"I keep thinking of you looking after her for all those years when you should have been out there, having a life. That's some strong sense of obligation you've got there. You need to look out for yourself more. You won't be any use at helping others if you don't take time out for yourself," Lewis said, his tone far more fierce than the words seemed to warrant.

It put Jasper on the defensive. "There's nothing wrong with having a sense of duty. I couldn't have left her like that, could I?"

"No, but..."

"But what? Now you're going to tell me there's some kind of

problem I have to overcome here as well? I'm never going to be perfect, you know."

"I know that!" In the hush of the gallery, Lewis's muttered words sounded more like a shout. "It's just... Oh crap. You really want to know why that bothers me? Fine. I'm just bloody paranoid that when you get your hoarding all under control, you're not going to need me anymore, are you?"

"I'll always need you."

"You won't. The therapeutic process will be over, and all these feelings you have for me, they're going to fall away. You'll see me for who I really am, and I'm warning you, I'm nowhere near as together as I look."

What exactly was the problem here? Was Lewis worried about being abandoned? "I'd never abandon you," he said, putting as much of his surety into his voice as he knew how to.

"Yes, exactly!" Lewis threw his hands wide, exasperation radiating from every line of his body. "Knowing you, you'll stay with me anyway because you feel obliged to. Then we'll be stuck together in a half-dead relationship, just hanging on for old time's sake. I don't want to put either of us through that."

Jasper stared into Lewis's eyes, trying to fathom the reasoning that had got Lewis to this scrambled assessment of their future together. "It's not going to be like that."

"You can't say that. You don't know how things will pan out."

"Well then, neither do you."

"Jasper, I've got a degree in this kind of thing. I know how transference works."

The man was every bit as stubborn as he was.

Jasper's stomach went into free fall. "Then what do you suggest? There must be something I can do to put things right." He wasn't going to give up on them. Not now. Not ever.

Silence reigned for what felt like hours, until Lewis opened his mouth. "Listen, please. I really, really care for you. You know that, don't you?"

Jasper nodded but didn't trust his voice to speak.

Lewis continued. "I know you want us to be a proper couple, and I do want that too. You've got to believe me. It's just... I need to know you can be strong enough on your own too. I need to know you're recovered before I let myself fall in love with you."

"And what does that entail, exactly? A full recovery."

Lewis looked down at his lap. "It means a time apart. Six months, minimum. And for you not to have slipped back into depression and hoarding during that time."

"I see." Anger crawled up from somewhere deep inside Jasper. He hadn't even realised he'd hidden it there, but the surge lent a bitterness to his words. "Is this something you've read in your therapists' manual, then? The six-months thing?"

"No. And most therapists would say it should be much longer than that before starting up a relationship, if ever. This is just what I would feel comfortable with."

"And what about what I'd feel comfortable with? You're abandoning me to fend for myself."

"Jasper, you're a grown man. I want you to feel strong in yourself. I don't want you feeling dependent. Like you have no choice but to be with me. That kind of thing is poisonous in the long-term. I really don't want us to be together if you still believe you couldn't cope without me."

"That's what you think I believe?"

"Well, don't you?" Lewis raised his head, and now Jasper could see the depth of anguish there. Okay, so Lewis was just as cut up about this as he was. Maybe it wasn't just a bit of pedantic rule-following after all.

Could he do it without Lewis? Could he manage for six months? It was the middle of August now. That would take them until the middle of February. The shortening days and cold weather would be a challenge, as that always got him down, but at least the autumn term was usually busy at work, what with giving all the new students their library-orientation sessions.

He didn't want to go it alone now he had Lewis in his grasp, but then again, he didn't want them to be in a relationship if Lewis couldn't trust in him.

Jasper thought of the long months ahead. Months filled with sorting his hoard and restocking his house. He sighed. It would be tough to do it alone, but hadn't he been alone for years now? In that respect, it wouldn't be so very different to life as usual. Just this time, with far fewer books. And maybe Lewis was right. He wouldn't need them in the same way now he'd made peace with Mama. "Okay."

"Okay what?"

Jasper lifted Lewis's chin and kissed him, ever so lightly. "Okay. I agree."

"You do?" Now Lewis really didn't sound like he believed him.

"I don't want you doubting me. I can prove it to you. I can do the rest of the clear-out by myself."

"Wait, I wasn't suggesting you go it alone straight away. You're going to need me over the next few months."

"I'm not. I can do it. You've shown me how."

"But, really, this isn't necessary. Not yet." Some people walked into the gallery, and Jasper made a shushing noise, but Lewis waved his hand irritably. "I thought we'd have longer together first. Getting to know each other. Building a bond." He leaned closer and breathed into Jasper's ear. "I want to wake up next to you again."

Oh God, Jasper wanted that too. But to do so knowing the days were numbered? That a six-month separation was looming? "Isn't that just going to make it even tougher to separate? I'd rather do it now."

"But I want us to be secure with each other first. To know what we're feeling is real."

"For fuck's sake, Lewis! I'm one hundred percent sure of the way I feel. Never been more sure about anything in my entire life."

Confusion and resentment washed over Lewis's face. Oh, so it wasn't merely that Lewis had doubts about Jasper's state of mind. He had doubts about his own. The knowledge tempered Jasper's irritation, and his voice dropped in pitch. "Maybe that time apart will be useful for you too. Absence makes the heart grow fonder, so I hear. Mama used to tell me that all the time."

Lewis half smiled. Anyone who didn't know him would probably think he looked composed, but Jasper could see the unshed tears in his eyes. "I wish I had your confidence."

"I wish you did too."

Lewis rose and walked over to the painting of the garden. Then he turned, crossed half the distance between them and halted. "I'm going to want Carroll to make regular visits and check in with you. Make sure you're getting any support you need. You'll need to talk through all this you've just told me, too. Your mother, I mean. There's still work to be done there."

"I thought the object was for me to go it alone."

"Not completely alone. The object isn't for you to go through life without help from others. Just to make sure it's a healthy kind of help rather than an overdependence on one person. Do you get the distinction I'm trying to make?"

"Of course."

"Good. Then...is this it? For now?"

Jasper looked up at the ceiling, but there was no help on offer there. "Dragging things out is only going to make it tougher on both of us."

"Can we meet up in a couple of weeks? Just for coffee?" There was an almost plaintive note in Lewis's voice.

"I don't think so. I think that's just going to make things more painful." Judging by the way he currently pined for Lewis when they were apart and spent almost every waking hour counting the minutes until their next meeting... Yes, it would be easier to find his equilibrium without that upset looming. "Cold turkey is going to work best for me."

"But I'm going to need to know how you're doing. You can't just abandon me like that."

"Carroll will keep you posted, I'm sure."

Lewis glanced at his watch, desperation in his eyes. "It's the fourteenth. So I'm not going to see you again till the fourteenth of February? This is good-bye? Here? Right now?"

It was hard to resist the pleading in Lewis's eyes, but damn it, it was his scruples that had resulted in this whole situation.

And worse yet, deep down Jasper knew Lewis was probably right to insist on it.

He pulled Lewis to him. There, in the gallery in front of the other browsers, and kissed the pout right off Lewis's face. Time to store up as much of Lewis as he could. The taste of him. The sensation of his lean body moulded to Jasper's. Those desperate little sounds he made in his throat. Jasper kept it up until the bittersweet pleasure of it all threatened to make him sob.

"It's not good-bye," Jasper said as he pulled back. He held Lewis's chin and rubbed the saliva from it with his thumb. Lewis's eyes glittered, and a single tear slid down his cheek. "Just *à bientôt.*"

He turned away before he wouldn't be able to.

It was the hardest thing he'd ever done.

He'd finally hit one hundred percent on that bloody scale.

Chapter Thirty-Two

A month later, and the memory of Jasper's slumped shoulders as he walked away from him still haunted Lewis every idle moment. He couldn't help trying to fix the memory, to go in there and say things differently. To explain it all so that Jasper would understand and see why things had to be this way. If he'd chosen his words differently, maybe Jasper would even have agreed to the occasional meeting together.

Being without him was miserable, Lewis decided. Not that he and Jasper had ever really been together, after all, but even just the chance to spend a few hours working with him had filled his need for meaningful human contact. No one else in his life seemed to be able to these days. Not even his twin sister, who was currently frowning at him from the driver's seat of the van. They were outside the Lehrmans' place, so at least he had an excuse for being miserable.

"Jesus fucking Christ, will you stop moping around with a face like a wet bloody fortnight in Wales. You've had a whole month to get over him."

"Over who?"

"Don't you dare! It's your own bloody fault too. Stupid men and their stupid pride."

"It's not pride!" They'd been over this so many times in the past five weeks, he was starting to feel like a broken record.

"Right, right. It's your *professional* duty, I know." Carroll glared at him. "Nothing to do with the fact you're still trying to prove to Mum you're a proper psychotherapist. I mean, God forbid she think you were like me. Just a glorified cleaner with a counselling certificate that's not worth the paper it's printed on."

"You're not a glorified cleaner," he began, but Carroll was already slamming the van door behind her. She stomped up the path. "I think you're amazing," he whispered to himself. Carroll knew exactly who she was and what she wanted, and she grabbed hold of it with both hands. He should be following her example, really.

Raised voices sounded from the front door. Carroll was using her brusquest, no-nonsense tones on Mr. Lehrman, which always ended up making the stubborn old git dig his heels in even more firmly. God help them both. Intent on damage limitation, Lewis set off after her.

"I'm still going through the process," Mr. Lehrman was whining when Lewis reached the front door. "Your brother said I don't need to get rid of anything till I'm ready, and I'm not ready, am I?"

When the old man turned his rheumy eyes in his direction, Lewis almost buckled and gave in again, like he always did, but glanced at Carroll first. She looked fit to murder someone, and very possibly that unfortunate person would be him if he didn't back her up.

"Actually, I do think you're ready," he began, watching incredulity wipe out Mr. Lehrman's self-satisfied smile. "You've been ready for a long time, as has your sister."

"She's always on at me about it. She's as bad as you lot. Always nagging and fussing. Well, it's my stuff, not hers."

"Yes, but it's her house." Lewis had checked, and it had been left to her by her late husband. "You should show her a bit more respect after she's put you up for so many years. And besides, that lot at the Council are this close to slapping a statutory notice to clear on you. If you don't start working with us, you'll end up having them clear the whole lot out in one go and chuck it all into landfill."

Mr. Lehrman gasped. Carroll continued. "That's right. We need to start seeing some results quick or they're going to get nasty. You think this is hardcore nagging, you've obviously never seen a legal notice to clear. They will come in and do it whether you give them permission or not."

Mr. Lehrman's mouth hung open as he looked from one to the other of them. "They couldn't. It's my stuff. My house." Even after his words trailed off, his mouth kept moving.

"Not your house, your sister's, and if you don't let them in, she will."

It wasn't particularly pleasant, seeing an elderly man cry, but Lewis felt a strange sense of satisfaction. Finally, a genuine emotional reaction rather than the habitual blocking and passive-aggressive silence. He watched the tears roll down Mr. Lehrman's cheeks for a moment, then stepped forward, arms held out.

"Uh-uh. My turn." Carroll pushed in front of him and enveloped Mr. L's bony shoulders in a hug. "There, there. Come on now, it's not so bad. You might even like it, being able to move around and see the walls again. Maybe you could take up dancing again. Your sister tells me you used to be quite the mover."

"No one will dance with me now. I'm too old."

"Utter nonsense. You can still shift some. I've seen you leap out of a chair when you think me or Lewis are about to make off with one of your treasures. I'd dance with you."

"You?" Mr. L looked like he didn't know whether to believe his ears, but at least it was better than the silent sobbing.

"You clear your dining room, and I'll dance around it with you. In fact, I'll treat you to a dance in every room I clear. How's that for a deal?"

"Just a dance?" The old man's eyes twinkled.

"Oi! Don't push your luck, buster. I'm practically married. Just a dance for you, but I could certainly help you get registered with an online dating agency if you want to find a more intimate dance partner."

Lewis shuddered at the idea, but then again, looking at Mr. Lehrman smiling, he had to concede he wasn't too bad for his age. Indeed, once you got past his stubbornness, he was almost likeable.

"Come on, then," Lewis chivvied, seeing Carroll squirming in Mr. L's clutches. "Better get going on that clearing if you want to dance with my sister. And I'm warning you, I'll be chaperoning her."

Mr. L grumbled as he disengaged and led their way back into the house, but Lewis grabbed hold of Carroll's arm as she tried to pass. "Listen, sis…"

Carroll jutted her chin out. "You going to tell me that was unprofessional behaviour now?"

"No! Not at all. I just wanted to say thanks. For getting through to him. Nothing I've been doing seems to have made the slightest bit of difference."

"That's because you've been sticking to the handbook, bro. Sometimes you've just got to wing it and find what's really going to motivate someone. Sometimes you need to stick with them too. Give them a chance. You know what I'm talking about."

"I am sticking with him. If he's keeping on top of the clutter and he still wants me in another few months, I'm his."

"But you're not going to offer him any help in the meantime?"

"He needs to do this on his own, Carroll. Bloody hell, six months is nothing, really. In the States, they say you should leave it at least two years after therapy ends. Other people say twenty-five years. Some say never."

She fixed him with a gaze as blue as his own. "And I think you're just using that as a justification because you're scared in case you screw it all up like you did with Carlos. Jasper's completely different, you know."

Before Lewis could reply, she was halfway down the hallway.

He did know. And he wasn't scared. Not really.

Merely terrified out of his wits.

After finishing up at the Lehrmans', Lewis decided to walk home. Carroll had offered to give him a lift back, but he knew the detour from Montpelier to Westbury on Trym and then back to Southville would have made her late for Jasper, and Lewis didn't want to do that to him. The man had enough stress of his own manufacturing already. Besides, it was a mild afternoon with a light breeze and scudding clouds, and it was only a couple of miles.

Lewis climbed the hill using the more picturesque residential streets, the bay-fronted Victorian terraces and leafy gardens reminding him of Jasper's home. Of course, prices were even higher on this side of the Avon where the sun warmed the south-facing hillsides. Lewis turned back at a spot where the city centre was spread out on view, all mellow limestone, orange tile, red brick, grey concrete and green trees jumbled together. His eyes found the spot on the horizon where Jasper's road must be. It was impossible from this distance to say which it was, but he imagined he could pick out Jasper's rooftop. The thought gave him a small measure of comfort, but it wasn't enough.

How the hell was he meant to survive another five months of this yearning?

Lewis sighed and kept on trudging up the hill. His thoughts kept returning to Jasper, so he attempted to keep them occupied by remembering past clients. They'd all had a breakthrough point like Mr. Lehrman had. Not always as dramatic as his, but there was still that moment when the mental blockage cleared. When they could finally not only see the logic behind letting go of the hoard, but to feel it too. It was the moment when clearing ceased being such a chore and energised them.

Jasper wasn't there yet, by all accounts. He'd learned some

sorting skills and wasn't acquiring new items, but his progress was slow and deliberate. Was that just the way it had to be with him? Or should Lewis have pushed more? Many clients had made their breakthrough after a nudge from him or Carroll. It would be fascinating to study that. To talk to other counsellors working with hoarders and find out if the same pattern was universal. To help refine the therapeutic guidelines for those working with hoarders.

So what exactly was stopping him?

The thought halted Lewis in his tracks, right in the middle of the pavement.

What, indeed? Lack of money? Time? Neither of those excuses washed. It really didn't cost anything much to read and phone people up. He had more free time than he knew what to do with, and he'd always loved studying. The only reason he hadn't carried on with it was because he'd felt he was doing more good immersing himself in the field and learning by first-hand observation. But now he had that experience, what was stopping him using it as the basis of further study? Okay, so if he were to sign up for a part-time PhD, he'd have to look for some funding and might have to knock the amateur dramatics on the head for a while, but there were other ways to study independently. You didn't have to be locked into a rigid course...

"Excuse me," a harried voice called from behind him. "Could you let me through?"

"Sorry," he murmured, flattening himself back against a garden wall to let the elderly woman in the mobility scooter past. She turned into the next driveway, and he continued on up the hill, ideas whirling through his head and assembling themselves into new patterns.

Lewis picked up his pace, suddenly desperate to get home and on the computer.

He had some serious research to be getting on with.

Chapter Thirty-Three

"Ready to go through some of this old crafting stuff?" Carroll called from the other side of a pile of boxes.

Jasper peered around cautiously. Carroll had been in a strange mood ever since she arrived, and while she said she was happy with a breakthrough she'd had with another client that morning, she seemed more angry and frustrated than anything else.

Jasper hoped it wasn't anything he'd done.

"I'm not sure," he said.

"It was your mum's, right?" Carroll was holding up a clear plastic bag full of tangles of yarn from the time Mama had taken up tapestry. There clearly wasn't any point in keeping hold of it, but the thought of letting it go made Jasper's palms sweat.

"I don't think I'm ready just yet."

Carroll's lips thinned, but then she shook her head and gave a dry chuckle. "Sometimes I just can't believe my idiot of a brother. How come he's left you to me when we all know full well you're never going to open up to a woman?"

What? Jasper realised his mouth was hanging open. He closed it again. "That's not true."

"Isn't it? Are you sure? Because the way it looks to me, you blame your mother for all your troubles, and by extension all women are suspect."

"I don't blame Mama!"

"Don't you? The woman who tricked you into giving up your own life so you could look after her? She wasn't even that ill to begin with, was she? She just refused to get out of bed."

Jasper gasped. "How do you know all this?"

"A little thing called case notes? You didn't think Lewis handed you over without filling me in, did you?"

Stricken, Jasper watched as she threw her hands up in an exasperated gesture.

"Fine!" Carroll declared. "If you can't work with me, then we'll figure something out. Although I've no idea what, seeing as how my brother's determined to be the stubbornest bastard to ever walk the face of the earth."

"I do want to work with you. I've been sorting books, haven't I?"

"It's not just about that, though." Carroll ran her hands through her hair and then came and sat on the box next to him. "Shit, I'm sorry. I didn't mean to lose my temper. It's not you I'm angry with, it's Lewis. I can't fucking well believe he left you to fend for yourself right after you told him about your mum. He's such a self-righteous twat sometimes."

Jasper's cheeks heated. "It wasn't exactly like that."

"Like what?"

"I kind of... Well, I insisted we start the six months straight away. The sooner we start, the sooner we finish? It seemed logical." It had at the time, anyway.

"Logical? Jasper, you have a mess of unresolved emotional issues to deal with, and Lewis is the only one you trust to open up to."

"I trust you too?" He meant it to come out emphatically, but it didn't seem to fool Carroll.

"You do? Prove it. Tell me how you feel about your mother." Carroll's fierce expression dissolved into a lopsided grin. "Oh God, I can't believe I just said that. It's such a bloody cliché."

Jasper smiled back briefly, settling into pondering her request.

How did he feel about Mama right now? "I don't know... I used to feel guilty most of the time, but I'm not sure if I do anymore." He stared down at the bag of tapestry yarn sitting between their feet. There was a burning lump inside his chest, which made it tough to push the words out. "I gave her everything I could that she asked for, but she still wanted more. More and more. She... Yes, you're right, she ruined my life. I don't think she did it deliberately, though."

Carroll just stared at him, her eyebrows raised in what looked uncomfortably like a challenge.

"She didn't! She was lonely. She loved my dad, and once he died, no one else was there for her."

"You were her child, Jasper. Not her husband. You hadn't made a vow to stick around in sickness and in health. You have every right to feel angry with her."

"I'm not angry. I'm just..." *Just what?* Was he going to spend the rest of his life making excuses for Mama's behaviour? Yes, she'd been sick. Yes, she'd had a hard life, being exiled from her family. But that didn't give her the right to manipulate him in the way she had. The ember in his chest blazed. "You're right. Fuck it. You're right." He kicked the bag of yarn, scattering them across the floor, then leapt to his feet. "I'm really pigging well pissed off with her."

"*Pigging* well?" Carroll sounded like she was suppressing amusement, and that got him even more annoyed.

"Fucking well pissed off. No!" He slammed his hand down on a pile of books, which toppled and crashed to the ground. "I'm not pissed off. I'm really fucking *furious*. Is that better? Is that what you wanted from me? You want me to admit how much I hated her at the end? I still hate her sometimes. Even though I love her. Shit." Jasper swiped at his eyes and looked down to realise he'd been stomping all over the yarn and it had tangled around his boots. He blinked, and it blurred.

Then Carroll was beside him, and her arm wrapped round his

waist made him want to howl at the unfairness of it all. That some were healthy and others sick. Some happy, others bitter.

Some rigidly sticking to a set of ethical guidelines that were making everyone miserable.

And no matter how good you were and how much you forced the complaints and resentment down, you still couldn't change your lot.

Maybe it was time to let some of those complaints out at last.

"You want me to tell you about Mama? Fine, I'll tell you. But maybe we should get some coffee first, because this could be a long one."

"I'll stay as long as you need me," Carroll said.

Jasper hugged her tight and started talking.

Jasper stood at the open warehouse door, watching Carroll pull away in the van. The September evening air had a distinct chill to it, and the twilight was starting earlier and earlier. Normally the return of cold evenings had him shivering in trepidation at the months ahead, living in a freezing-cold house. That wasn't the case now his radiators were all uncovered and his boiler serviced.

No, that wasn't the case, so what exactly was his excuse for feeling this bleak? He'd just exorcised all those pent-up feelings about his mother. Wasn't that cathartic enough?

Jasper sighed and turned back to the taped-out rooms. He tried to remember how big the hoard had been before he started sorting. Carroll had emailed him photographs, hadn't she? He'd have to check on his laptop later. But the hoard couldn't have been that much bigger than it was now. Over a month, and this piffling progress all he had to show for his time.

When he remembered how quickly he'd whizzed through the piles that week before Lewis left him... Well, when he remembered that, it made him...mad?

Mad, not sad. Jasper felt the sensation build behind his sternum, that coal flaring back into life. He started to pace. Felt like his body had had an injection of adrenaline. All those little reasons for keeping the books melted away. Why bother? They were only holding him back, keeping him stuck here in this rotten excuse for a warehouse. He should burn the lot of them.

A vision of a pyre of books burned behind his eyelids. Oh God, that looked like a totalitarian nightmare. No, okay, he wouldn't burn them. But he had to do something.

Even if Lewis never came back after his self-imposed exile.

Even then, Jasper didn't want to spend the rest of his life sorting through this never-ending pile of books. He could do it. He could get it done and put it behind him.

He could move on.

He strode over to the landing area where his empty trolley waited. Genre fiction. Right. That should be an easy place for him to start, as he didn't even read much of it. He picked a pile at random. A historical saga on the top, with a gushing recommendation from the *Daily Mail*.

The *Daily*-pigging-*Mail?* Right, that was reason enough to send it back to where it came from. He chucked it onto the trolley. The next was a lurid horror novel. Why had he brought this home? He didn't even like horror. The following book was one of those recent depressing Scandinavian thrillers riding on the success of *The Girl with the Something-Something* books. Well, he'd read the original and didn't think it was all that great, so why would a rip-off be any better?

Onto the trolley.

A Mills and Boon romance. Like he was ever going to read one of those.

Onto the trolley.

An Agatha Christie? That should be with the classics, surely? Oh, but then again, he'd read this one, and it wasn't like he wouldn't be able to pick up another copy somewhere should he get the urge to read it again someday. Christie wouldn't ever go out of print, right?

Onto the trolley.

Three hours later and a record twenty trolley trips over to the dispatch zone, the landing area was almost half clear, and Jasper was one hundred percent knackered.

Chapter Thirty-Four

"So exactly how far up the hill is this bloody café?" Lewis grumbled to Brandon. They were walking along Upper Maudlin Street, past the vast complex of hospital buildings on their right, and he was already heartily sick of the cold November drizzle and noise of traffic whooshing over wet tarmac. Seeing ambulances going past was never particularly cheery either. "You realise I could have driven here? I've got the Duchess back on the road. The coffee had better be as spectacular as you say it is."

"Or what, exactly?"

"Or...or next time I come round, I'll bring you Fosters instead of that fancy continental beer you like."

"Ooh, you fight dirty, mate. Well, Jos reckons it's the best coffee he's ever had in this country. You know I can't drink the stuff. Thought it might cheer you up now you're being too chickenshit to visit that Turkish bloke's café."

"I'm not being a coward. It's just completely out of my way now I'm not working with Jasper anymore." Anyway, that wasn't really why he was so upset at his self-imposed exile from Yusef's. The man did make great coffee, but it wasn't the best he'd ever tasted. No, it was more the whole package he was missing. The bits like sitting opposite Jasper and listening to his voice as he explained just what was so wonderful about some old book he'd acquired, knees brushing so they were joined under the table. Those were the things he really craved, and no matter how good a mate Brandon was, he couldn't give him any of that.

"Right, so you turning into a miserable fucking bastard and you stopping working with this Jasper fella have absolutely nothing in common, right? Even though they happened at exactly the same fucking time. Fuck, Lewis. You're such a fucking twat sometimes."

"Think you could stick a few more profanities into that sentence? I think you let a few nouns slip out without an F-word in front of them."

"F-word? For fuck's sake, mate. You're such a prude sometimes. And stop changing the subject. You're depressed, and it's all coz you've been a stupid, stubborn bastard."

"That's not why." Okay, it was, but he didn't want to admit it. Lewis kicked a bunch of leaves under one of the trees, but they just squelched, and one stuck to his wet boot. "I'm just sick of this dreary, cold weather. I hate November."

"Yeah, don't we all, but you started this pity party months ago."

"Okay. I hate having to walk up this bastard hill."

"That's an even worse excuse. Come on. I want my friend back. You." Brandon stopped and grabbed Lewis by the chin. "Weird, emo doppelganger, what have you done with my best mate?"

"Gerroff," Lewis twisted, but he couldn't help smiling. "I'm not even remotely emo. Look, I'm all colourful." He indicated his outfit of tastefully coordinated shades, even if it was all very last season now. He hadn't had the heart for shopping lately. Every last penny had been put aside for getting the Duchess back on the road and saving up for his future studies. "Not a hint of black."

"I dunno. Purples and greys seem pretty emo to me."

"Piss off. This is lavender and pewter."

Brandon screwed up his nose. "Now that just sounds gay."

"Takes one to know one."

"Yep. So my boyfriend tells me." Brandon grinned. "Hey, maybe you are Lewis after all."

Lewis raised his eyebrows and was about to make a smart

retort, when he spotted the shop behind Brandon's shoulder. An antiquarian bookshop. He'd forgotten all about it, if he'd ever noticed it in the first place, it being so long since he'd walked up this godforsaken hill. He stepped around Brandon, walked up to the condensation-fogged glass and peered inside. He couldn't see much, but there was a welcoming glow of halogen spotlights around the display, so he went to the door.

"Hey, this isn't it," Brandon said, but Lewis pushed on in anyway.

"Just want to have a quick look."

A wave of heat hit him when he opened the door, and a small bell jingled. He stepped in, wiping his wet feet on the sisal mat. Wooden bookshelves lined the lower halves of the walls, and above them were glass display cabinets with the more precious books on show, yellowing pages open to show the ornate illuminations and fancy text. An elderly, white-haired gent walked out from the back room marked Staff Only and wished them both a good afternoon. He fit the place perfectly in his mustard-coloured suit, complete with red bow tie and matching handkerchief sticking out of his pocket.

Jasper would love it in here.

Pain gripped Lewis's heart so fiercely he almost gasped. What he wouldn't do to have Jasper standing next to him, holding his hand as they browsed the shelves. Well, there was one thing he wouldn't do, which was back down from his plan before Jasper had had a chance to recover on his own. To prove to himself how strong he was.

And it might not happen. Even now, Jasper might be bringing back the old books and papers from his library and piling them up again, constructing a barrier between him and the real world.

But Carroll had assured him that wasn't happening, and Lewis couldn't give up all hope. Stopping at that spot and noticing this place felt like a sign. An omen of some sort. He just had to pray that it was the good kind.

He walked up to the counter, amazed to see one of those really old-fashioned cash registers with the little tabs that popped up on top. There was an iPad and a calculator sitting next to it, though, so perhaps it was ornamental rather than functional.

"Can I help you?" the shopkeeper asked, peering shrewdly over the top of his half-moon glasses.

"I certainly hope so." Lewis mentally ran through the contents of his bank account. Sorting out his beloved Mini with a new engine had used a lot of funds, and this looked like the kind of place where a book could set you back a fair whack. "Do you have any classic children's books, by any chance?"

"Of course. Quite a good collection too. I found a box at a house clearance recently. What an absolute goldmine, that was. It's staggering the way some people don't recognise the worth of what's sitting right under their noses."

"Reminds me of someone not a million miles away from me," Brandon muttered and pulled a book off a shelf. "Whoa! There're some crazy pictures in here. Hey, mate, don't suppose you sell any vintage erotic books do you? Bet they're good for a laugh."

"As a matter of fact, young man, I do, but they're not out on display for obvious reasons." The shopkeeper appraised Brandon with beady eyes and obviously liked what he saw, if the quirk of lips was anything to go by. "Would you be interested in a private showing? I have some photographs too. Of course, they're mostly of heterosexual couples or young women, but I do have a few of a more *specialist* interest."

Brandon's eyes almost popped out of his head. "Nah, thanks, I don't want to put you to any trouble. Anyway, we've got somewhere to be." He leaned in closer to Lewis and whispered, "Did he just offer to show me his *etchings* or what? Dirty old man."

"Shut up. If you can't be useful, just try not to break anything. I'm shopping, and I don't want any distractions."

Because sometimes, just sometimes, shopping was something

he didn't have to feel guilty about, and this was most definitely one of those times. He intended to savour every moment.

The trouble with putting books back on the shelves was in choosing the perfect order. Jasper sighed at the copy of *The Portrait of Dorian Grey* in his hand. Should he be alphabetising all the authors or separating the nineteenth- from the twentieth-century books before he alphabetised them? Would anyone other than him even care?

He was too much of a perfectionist, that was his problem. That and never being able to make a simple decision without seeing every single side of the problem first. Lewis had told him those things could be strengths too, but it was hard to see how when he still had a living room half full of boxes and two whole walls covered in empty shelves.

Coffee. That was what he needed. A trip down to Yusef's and some company.

As he entered the hallway, Jasper marvelled at the sensation of space. Almost four months since the clear-out, and it still caught him afresh every time. It wasn't that echoey, hard emptiness that had freaked him out at first, though. The shelves lining the wall opposite the staircase were now full of books. His unread paperbacks, which for some reason he hadn't felt the need to alphabetise. There was something comforting about searching for a new book to read on the unordered shelves. It reminded him of charity-shop browsing and helped keep a lid on the urge to go shopping for more.

He took a moment now to trace his finger along the spines, and when it came to rest on *Life of Pi*, he recalled how Lewis had described it to him. Yes, he'd take this one out with him. Reading it now would give them something more to discuss when Lewis had got over his cold feet and come back to him.

Cold feet? Where had that idea come from? Jasper held the book, his gaze sweeping over the bright cover but not taking in any of the details. He felt down inside himself for the tightness, the anger and resentment at Lewis for abandoning him. No, it was gone. At some point over the last week, it had melted away.

Strange.

Still lost in his thoughts, Jasper automatically reached for his coat and scarf, and the woolly hat Yusef had given him as a house-clearing present. December had settled in with a chill, and now the house was properly heated on the inside, the transition to outdoors could be dramatic.

The book forgotten on the hall table, Jasper made his way out and down the garden path. It was lighter now the trees had been pruned, but that wasn't what made him dawdle at the gate. He turned back to the house. What would Lewis see when he came back to him?

Because he was coming back.

Even if Jasper had to drag him back, kicking and screaming. He wasn't about to let the man run away from true love. That was what this was. It must be, if it had the power to inspire him to better things.

The house was definitely more cheerful than it had been, what with the freshly cleaned windows. He'd meant to paint the front door, though, hadn't he? As Jasper ran his gaze over the exterior, more and more ideas crowded into his head. Oh yes. He could prove to Lewis that he was ready now. All recovered and eager to move on.

To move on together.

As he strode down the hill, Jasper began whistling. He needed to start a shopping list, and it was going to be a long one.

He also needed to draft in a willing helper or two.

Chapter Thirty-Five

The text came while Lewis and Carroll were both at the Lehrmans' house. They'd finally cleared the kitchen and were working on the hallway when their phones both buzzed. Well, Lewis's buzzed. Carroll's screeched like an enraged chimp.

"Whoa! Coincidence or what," Carroll said, whipping her phone out of her pocket. "Mine's from Cassie. Who's yours from?"

Lewis fumbled with his touch screen. "Cassie," he said, and a heavy weight settled in his stomach as he read the first few words of the message in the menu screen.

Pls come to the hospital straight away...

"Oh, crap." He tapped on the message and read the rest. "Dad's had a heart attack. Oh, shit."

"Bloody, buggering fucknuts. This has got to be some kind of sick joke, right?" Carroll glared at her phone, her expression furious. "Hasn't it?"

"Carroll, it's not a joke. We need to go. Right now."

She nodded, biting her lip. "I don't wanna lose him, Lewis."

"Neither do I. Come on. We need to get there."

Carroll was shaking now, so he threw an arm round her and led her to the front door, calling out some kind of excuse to the Lehrmans. Something about an emergency, but his mind was somewhere else. His mind was hovering over a hospital bed, watching machines beeping and then flat lining. "Oh, Dad."

When Carroll went to the driver's side door, Lewis pulled her back. She was still shaking. "I'll drive us."

"You what? I can fucking well drive, thank you very much. I'm not some helpless woman."

"I know you can, but I want us to get there in one piece. You're too angry to handle Bristol traffic right now. It's not going to do anyone any good if we end up being admitted to intensive care ourselves."

Carroll scowled at him, but she thrust the keys in his direction. "Fine. You drive. See if I care." But even as she finished the sentence, she began to sniffle.

Lewis folded her into a hug. "I'm not ready to lose him," she choked out.

"Me either," Lewis said. "I doubt anyone ever is." His thoughts strayed to Jasper, as they so often did. Jasper hadn't been ready to let go of his mother, even after all those years of illness to prepare him. And their dad was so full of life. Surely death couldn't take someone that vibrant? It wasn't fair.

But he concentrated on rocking Carroll until her sobs subsided, then helped her into the passenger seat. His own feelings could wait. People needed him to be strong for them.

As predicted, the traffic was a nightmare, but eventually they pulled up outside the hospital, and Lewis let Carroll leap out of the van. "I'm going to find somewhere to park. You go find Mum," he said, leaning out the window. "Tell her I'll be right there, okay?"

"Okay." Carroll pulled a wobbly smile. "Thanks, bro. For driving. You're right. I couldn't have."

"Just go find her and give her a huge hug from me. And Dad, too."

Her lower lip trembled, but before any more tears could fall, Carroll had turned around and was stomping towards the entrance.

Finding a space wide enough for the van in the hospital's multistorey car park took longer than Lewis really had patience for.

Whoever designed the car park had obviously been keen to cram as many spaces in as physically possible. A dumb strategy when you considered how stressed most people parking there were already bound to be. He had to go all the way up to the top level before he found two empty spaces side by side. By the time he'd found his way back down to Accident and Emergency, Lewis was about ready to punch someone himself. He marched up to the main desk, demanding to see his father, but the woman there remained calm and unruffled. "Oh yes, cubicle eight. Just round the corner. Your family are already there."

Humbled by her gracious manners, Lewis mumbled his thanks and took the direction she indicated. There were two rows of curtained cubicles, and he strode down the central aisle, looking from side to side into the open ones.

There. There was Alan Miller in a hospital gown, sitting up in bed and laughing with the nurse, damn him.

"Dad!" Lewis dashed to his bedside. "You total bastard. I thought you'd had a heart attack."

"He did," his mum said from behind him. He turned to see her and Carroll standing there, both holding vending machine cups of coffee. "But it was only a small one. They just want to keep him in for observation this afternoon, and there'll be medication to take. And a new diet for you," she added, glaring in her husband's direction.

"Oh, come on, Cass. I want a second opinion on that. Chilli's meant to be good for the heart. It's not like they're dropping like flies from coronaries over in Mexico all the time now, is it?"

"It wasn't the chilli she banned. It was the fat. You can still have lean meat and all the kidney beans your heart desires."

"But it's not going to taste as good without the fat. Remember that time we went to Cancun? The food was incredible, the people were happy, and the tequila?" Alan kissed and flicked his fingertips in the manner of an Italian chef, wincing as the gesture nearly pulled the cannula out the back of his hand. "The tequila was to die for."

"Pretty tasteless joke, under the circumstances," Lewis said. But he couldn't help smiling as he stepped forward to take his father's hand. "Don't you dare do that again, okay? You're not allowed to go anywhere until you've taught me your recipe for enchiladas."

"Well, with the way you managed the last time I tried, I'll be sticking around till I'm at least a hundred."

"Oi, they weren't that bad," Lewis protested, before Alan pulled him down into a hug.

"Love you, son."

"Love you too, Dad."

The sound of the machine beeping in time to his dad's every heartbeat was the best music in the world right then.

Chapter Thirty-Six

"No fucking way!" Mas exclaimed, spinning on his heel in the middle of the warehouse. "You seriously telling me you had all this crap in your house?"

"It's not crap. It's books."

"And broken bits of furniture. And old papers. And, oh-my-fucking-God, is that a genuine 50s hood dryer you've got there?" He skipped over to the old bit of machinery and began cooing over it. It was one of those plastic-helmet-on-a-stand things women sat under in hairdressers for reasons Jasper had never quite grasped. He'd also never understood why his mother had dragged the no-doubt broken bit of equipment home, but if Mas could see the attraction too, then it just went to show that there was no such thing as worthless junk. Even old, mouldy food had its uses, as compost ingredients, biogas source material, and... Well, two uses were probably enough.

Jasper scanned across the bays of assorted objects ready to find their new homes. He'd thought it all looked more acceptable in the warehouse setting, what with the way the scale of the industrial space dwarfed the piles. Clearly Mas had much better spatial awareness than Jasper did.

"Anything you see there that you want, you can take it," he offered.

"You're selling it?"

"I'm giving it away."

"Are you serious? Wow, yeah, okay. This is like the ultimate eBay, you know? Where you actually get to touch and examine the stuff properly before you buy it. Except you don't even want any money for it, and I'm not going to be outbid at the last fucking second by some arsehole with nothing better to do than to sit at their sodding computer all day." Mas scowled, but seconds later the expression was swept away by a delighted smile as he spotted something else worth having.

"You don't have to buy second-hand stuff online, you know. There're charity shops, car boot sales and flea markets."

"Yeah, yeah, I know. But seeing as how I'm working most days while the charity shops are open, and I'm too fucking knackered to get up in time for the car boots and markets, I have to take what I can get. Anyway, it's much easier to find obscure stuff if you can type in a search. Bet you can't do that in your charity shops yet, can you?"

"Nooo, not yet. But when you get to know them, sometimes they hold back things they think you'll be interested in."

"Cool. Well, maybe I'll see if I can get out to some on my lunch hour." Mas tilted his head forwards until he was looking over at Jasper through his artfully mussed-up fringe. "Unless you want to pick me up one weekend and we'll go to a car boot. Or stay over first or something? That'd be best. I'm kinda grumpy in the mornings unless I wake up with a blowjob. Giving or receiving, I'm not fussy."

Oh buggeration. "Mas... I'm not... Listen, when I asked for help with this, I didn't mean I wanted anything else from you."

Mas pouted. "You mean you're not going to pay me in kind?"

Double buggeration with cream on top. "Erm, I'm really sorry. I obviously wasn't clear enough about what I meant. Mas... You're a really nice bloke, and I know we've had fun in the past, but I really don't think we should do anything else. I mean, I'm still in love with—"

"Okay, okay! I don't need to hear about this Lewis fella again, believe me. It's not good for the ego, you know?"

Jasper stared, stricken. "I'm so sorry. I didn't mean... I mean, I knew you used to feel something, but I thought by now you'd have... I don't know...moved on?"

"Chill, mate. I'm happy for you, really. And anyway, I'm like totally 'over' you now." Mas said the last in a parody of an American teenage girl, all air quotes and tossing hair. Jasper couldn't help snorting. "That's better. You really need to lighten up, you know? Most of what I waffle on about is utter crap anyway. Sometimes I don't believe the stuff that's coming out of my mouth. Told this bloke I'd pulled last week that I was a fucking ice-skater like that Johnny Weir fella. Turns out he used to skate and now he wants to take me to the rink down in Swindon. I'm going to make such a tit of myself if I get on the ice. Think I'm going to tell him I have my period."

"You didn't convince him you were a woman, did you?" Mas was cute but not that pretty.

"As if! You see what I mean, though? Utter rubbish. You should ignore most of it and laugh at the rest. That's what my other friends do."

"So... We're friends?"

"Well, duh! Isn't that why I'm here, helping you fill your house back up with books so you can impress this Lewis you've got a monster crush on?"

"We're not going to fill it. I've got shelves now. It's going to look good." Jasper turned back to the pile of waiting boxes, all packed and ready to transport. Two carloads, and then they'd return with the empty boxes to pack up the rest. He estimated eight carfuls still remained, so the two of them should be able to tackle it in a day. "Come on. The stuff that's going back is over here." He led the way, hearing Mas's footsteps behind him. "You can take anything you want from that lot when we've finished. After you've helped me with the lights, that is." And those were his real reasons for needing help. The carloads he could have handled himself, albeit in double the time, but the finishing touches to his freshly restocked home required two pairs of hands.

Jasper picked up a box and turned to find Mas standing, hand on hip, looking him up and down like he was an exhibit to be studied.

"Can't believe you were one of them hoarders. No, wait, what am I saying? Of course I can. The amount of stuff you carry around in that bag of yours. Anyone would think you were preparing for the end of the world. First time you turned up with it, I was fucking terrified it was full of gags and handcuffs and big knives. Or maybe just a few rolls of cling film like that Dexter bloke on the telly. You seen that? Fucking awesome series. He's hot in a geeky kinda way, just like you. 'Specially in those new specs. You've got that possible-serial-killer vibe, you know? Right up till you open your mouth, anyway. Then anyone can see you're just a big teddy bear in disguise."

Jasper opened and closed his mouth a few times, searching for an appropriate response. As ever, he felt blindsided around Mas's mile-a-minute commentary. "Umm, thanks. I think." He shook his head, trying to clear it of the excess words blocking his thought processes. "Do you want to load your car and I'll load mine?"

"You're the man with the plan." Eventually, Mas hefted a box, and despite his carefully cultivated air of waifish dissolution, he seemed to pick it up with ease. Well, Jasper had known he was stronger than he looked, or he'd never have asked.

"So," Mas continued as they trudged over to where the two cars waited, hatchback doors in the air. "You going to be inviting this mysterious Lewis over later?"

"Reckon so." It would be the first time he'd called Lewis since their separation and the very idea of pressing Dial terrified him. But not as much as another day without him. They'd stuck it for four months, after all. Lewis wouldn't be enough of a stickler to insist on another two, would he?

"Ooh, does this mean I'm going to meet him? Or will I be bundled out before he gets there, like a shameful one-night stand?"

"Erm, well, it might be best if you're not there. I'm probably going to want to say hello in private."

"Oh, I get it." Mas thumped his box down in the back of his car and got in on hands and knees to push it forwards. Why he hadn't just opened the side doors, Jasper couldn't imagine. The rest of his sentence was muffled by the car. "You're going to be all over each other and I'd end up feeling like the fairy godmother of all gooseberries."

If only. Jasper still didn't know if Lewis would even turn up, let alone want to get intimate. "I wouldn't want things to be awkward. For any of us."

"But I'm a total voyeur. Wouldn't be awkward in the slightest."

"Not for you, maybe."

Mas stuck his head out of the back of the car. "I getcha. Tell you what, though, when you two are all snuggled up and happy, don't you go forgetting me. Friends stay friends, yeah? I'm sick of being dumped when all my mates get boyfriends. Think they reckon I'm going to steal them away. I mean, do I look like a slapper? No, wait, don't answer that. Have I got home-breaker tattooed on my forehead or something? I think not." He hopped down onto the concrete, and Jasper could kind of understand why his newly coupled friends might not want him around. Mas was definitely eye-catching, and he had a slinky way of moving that oozed sex-appeal. He could resist it now, though, because what was inside Lewis's head was so much more intriguing than what Mas could offer him.

No, he'd much rather have Mas as a friend than a lover. And Lewis as a lover and a friend.

He'd take friend if that was all he could get, though, even if it crushed his heart to a pulp.

As they loaded the rest of the boxes, Jasper half concentrated on Mas's incessant chatter, while the rest of his mind wandered over memories of Lewis, daydreams of Lewis.

Lewis saying yes.

Lewis kissing him breathless.

Lewis down on one knee, asking him to... No, that was getting carried away. With a sigh, Jasper fitted the last box into his car, then stepped over to give Mas a hand with his.

Best not to think any more about what-ifs.

Best just to live in the moment, even if that did mean putting up with the worst case of queasy nerves he'd ever experienced.

One way or another, by the end of the day he'd have found out what Lewis wanted.

And if it wasn't what Jasper wanted, he'd just have to learn to live with it.

Later, after their dad had been transferred up to the cardiac ward for observation, Lewis and Carroll took a break in a ramshackle waiting room, littered with tawdry magazines, empty cardboard cups and torn sugar wrappers.

Lewis put his feet up on the coffee table and lay back in the chair. "I thought he'd gone and left us. I really did."

"Yep. Me too. Bloody Mum, not bothering to text once she knew he was okay. She should have known how worried we'd be."

"Don't blame her. She's really cut up about it." While Cassie had put her brave face on, both of them had seen her pallor, worry etched into her face. She'd aged ten years since Lewis had seen her over breakfast that morning. What must it have been like for Jasper, watching his mother slowly dying? And then having her plead with him to end it all?

"What are you thinking about?"

"Jasper."

"Oh. I was thinking about Dad. About how I didn't come over for lunch last week. I should have made up for it with a visit another day. I mean, they could just be gone tomorrow, couldn't they? How would I feel if that happened when I'd not visited them for a couple of weeks? We live in the same bloody town; it's not like I have a good excuse."

"Anyone you love could drop dead tomorrow."

"Yeah, thanks for that. So not what I needed right now." Carroll pouted and crossed her arms.

"I didn't mean it in a depressing way."

"Under what circumstances exactly could that not be depressing?"

"I meant... I meant you have to seize the day. Like you were saying, make every day count. Show them you love them. Spend time with them. Be there for them. Store up all those good memories, so that if they're taken away from you, you'll know that you didn't waste a minute of your time with them."

Carroll nodded slowly, her tightly crossed arms gradually easing down into a handclasp. "Yeah. I think you're right."

"I know I'm right." Lewis stood. He had somewhere he needed to be. A loved one who deserved a whole load of good memories building up to counteract the bad. "Could you let Mum know I'll call round later? Or maybe tomorrow morning, even. I bet Dad'll be tired tonight, but I'll phone to check if he's up for a visit."

"Where are you going?" Carroll asked. Her face was still blotchy, but at least her eyes were now clear.

"I need to let someone special know I love them. You're right. I've been a scaredy-cat and a selfish prick, and I'm just hoping he can forgive me for that."

The understanding dawned slowly, transforming her face into a radiant smile.

"You go get him, bro."

"I intend to. If he'll have me."

"I don't think there's any doubt of that."

He wished he had Carroll's confidence, but all Lewis could

remember was the look of abject misery on Jasper's face when at the museum. Lewis's insistence on their separation must have seemed like the ultimate betrayal after everything Jasper had shared with him.

But he'd crawl if he had to. Whatever it took to get back into Jasper's good graces.

He was worth it.

Chapter Thirty-Seven

When Lewis slowed to pull up in front of number sixty-four, the space was taken by a beat-up old Mazda, so he carried on down the hill until he found a free spot outside a house covered in an incredible amount of light-up crap. A Santa train comprised of coloured lightbulbs chugged away up on the roof, and the front garden was awash with light-up reindeer and a huge inflatable snowman.

Dear God, whatever sight met him at Jasper's house, it couldn't be as bad as all that.

Lewis patted his coat pocket to check his parcel was still where he'd stowed it and trudged up the hill. He was almost there when he saw a man walk out the front gate of Jasper's house. A young, slinky, attractive man. He was laughing, and as he lifted a box out of the boot of the Mazda, Lewis heard Jasper's answering guffaw coming from somewhere behind the trees.

Who the hell was this?

Horrified jealousy congealed the breath in his lungs. He watched as Jasper walked out, grabbed another box from the boot and said something that made Slinky laugh again.

Was this guy moving in? Did Jasper have a new boyfriend?

Had four months really been too long to wait?

As if he could sense the intensity of Lewis's stare, Jasper turned to look in his direction. His eyes widened, and his jaw dropped. "Lewis? Is that you?"

"Who?" Slinky asked, then turned to face Lewis as well. A delighted smile broke on his face. "Oh My non-gender-specific Deity. Is this *the* Lewis? The famous one?"

Lewis took an uncertain step forward.

Jasper stayed where he was, but Slinky began trotting towards him. "You would not believe how much he talks about you. I've spent the whole day hearing Lewis this and Lewis that. The man's got it bad. I hope you're going to treat him properly, or I'll break your legs. Well, not me, obviously. I couldn't even pull the legs off a fly. But I know people. One person, anyway. But he's big and butch, and he'd totally do whatever I asked him to if he thought I'd make it worth his while."

Who the hell was the chatterbox?

"Pleased to meet you," Slinky said, sticking out his hand awkwardly from around the side of the box. "I'm Mas. I doubt Jasper's ever mentioned me because I think he's made far more of an impression on me than I've ever made on him." Mas clamped his lips shut, eyes sparkling. "Oops, that sounded kind of filthy, didn't it? Well, you don't need to worry. There's nothing like that going on anymore. We're friends without benefits, unless you count me helping him lug his bloody books back from that fugly warehouse."

"The books?" Lewis stared past him. Now he knew Mas wasn't a threat, the man barely registered in his consciousness compared to the power of Jasper's silent presence. Standing, looking every bit as gobsmacked as Lewis felt. "Not all the books?" he asked, finally. "Jasper?"

"Okay, okay, I know when I'm not needed," Mas said with what Lewis assumed was only mock hurt considering the twinkle in his eye. "You can help Jasper with the last box, and I'll clear off. Not even a cup of tea for my efforts. It's a tough life sometimes, being a friend. Here." Mas shoved the box in Lewis's direction, and he had to take it or risk Jasper's stuff ending up on the pavement.

Jasper finally stepped forwards. "We'll have you round for dinner soon, Mas. I promise."

We? It hung in the air between them, tantalising and unexplained. Was Lewis included in that *we*?

"Well, toodle-pip, lovebirds. I'll leave you to make up by yourselves, since Jasper has banned me watching, the spoilsport. But I will hold you to that invitation, Jasper Richardson. Don't you forget it." The camp and coquettish tone dropped from Mas's voice just long enough for Lewis to hear the genuine emotion underneath. Needy. Lewis recognised it as the same feeling in his own chest.

The Mazda disappeared with a plume of exhaust fumes that surely shouldn't have been that brownish colour, and Lewis and Jasper were left standing there, both holding a box in front of them like some kind of antihug chastity belt. Maybe that was for the best, though, as now he was here, Lewis felt coy about stepping closer and taking what he needed. After all, he was a couple of months early. Maybe Jasper would insist on him sticking to the letter of his original terms.

As they stood there, staring at each other, something cold hit Lewis's cheek. Rain? But then he caught sight of a drifting white speck in the air. "No way. Snow?"

Jasper stared up at the sky, a dopey smile on his face. "Wow, it really did come. Saw it forecast, although they say it's too warm for it to settle. We got unpacked just in time."

"Unpacked?"

"Yep." Jasper looked inordinately proud of himself. "Come on in. We can drop these off. I'll make hot chocolate and take you on a tour of the house."

"Can I have a coffee instead? Hot chocolate makes me want to gag."

"No hot chocolate. Right. Better make sure I start buying more coffee. You like biscuits, though, right? Those rock-hard biscotti ones. Do you have to get them in a deli or do they stock them in the supermarket?"

"Are you making a shopping list?"

Jasper flashed a shy grin. "Maybe."

Okay, that was reassuring. Lewis returned his smile, watching Jasper's break wider and wider until you could see all of his teeth. Lewis's cheeks began to ache too. Then his teeth chattered.

"Right, inside," Jasper ordered. "Way too chilly out here."

"You first," Lewis said when they got into a front-gate-politeness standoff. Jasper apologised and went in ahead, while Lewis admired the cut of his jeans. Were they new? Oh, the front gate definitely was. Or freshly painted and repaired. But it couldn't hold a candle to the sight of Jasper's arse in indigo denim.

That was probably why he didn't properly notice the house until they were almost at the front door, when he finally spotted the Christmassy wreath hanging there and began to look around him.

"Oh my God. Jasper. This is... It's... You did all this?" The window frames were all painted the same shade as the front door and gate, a rich burgundy gloss. It reflected back the golden pinpricks of the fairy lights draped over the porch and around the two trees closest to the house. Now that he looked back, he could see the front garden had been cleared and beaten into submission. It was still like a woodland, but more of a mossy glade than a fly-tipper's rubbish-strewn thicket.

"All what? Mas helped with the lights, and I hired a couple of guys Carroll recommended to do all the decorating. I've had my work cut out for me sorting out the hoard."

"How's that going?"

"Why don't you come inside and have a look?"

The last time he'd been in Jasper's house it had been mostly clear and clean, but empty and with all the damage from neglect clearly on show. Now, though...

Jasper pushed open the front door and a wash of golden light fell over them. Lewis stepped onto a plush mat and stared at the entrance hall. The terrazzo marble floor gleamed, the banisters shone, and the bookshelves lining the wall between the living room and kitchen doors were packed with enticing spines of colourful paperbacks. He took it in for a moment before Jasper pushed the door to the living room open.

"Oh, Jasper!" Lewis stood on the threshold, staring, until Jasper came and took the box from his arms.

"Come inside. It's draughty with the door open."

Lewis stepped inside what had to be the warmest, cosiest room he'd ever entered. All three of the inside walls were lined with books from floor to ceiling, and a real fire blazed in the grate. There was a Persian rug with a geometric pattern of rusts and golds on the floor, flanked by a battered but comfortable-looking chocolate-brown leather sofa and a couple of green velvet armchairs.

The dark red curtains were still open, revealing a whirling profusion of flakes outside the bay window. But in here everything was comforting, the sweet scent and soft crackles of burning wood pervading the air.

"So, what do you think?" Jasper asked, nerves and pride battling for supremacy in his voice.

"I think it's the most homey room I've ever been in."

"Homely?" Jasper frowned. "Doesn't that mean ugly?"

"Hom-ey. Home-like. Cosy. Whatever you want to call it. This is it."

"You really think so?"

"I know so."

"So..." Jasper paused, biting his lower lip. "You think you could live somewhere like this?" The question had a hopeful lilt to it.

"Jasper, I..." He had to be honest, no matter how much he wanted to toss caution aside and agree to whatever Jasper asked for. "I'm not really in a position to be setting up a life with anyone right now. I'm going back to Cardiff Uni in the autumn. Just part time. I want to write a thesis on hoarders, but it means I'm going to be broke."

Jasper blanched. "You're moving away? To Cardiff?"

"God, no. I couldn't afford that. I'll be staying with Mum and Dad for the next few years, working with Carroll and going in on the train a couple of days a week. It's going to be tough, and I'll have no spare time, but I really want to do this. I think I can write something that's going to help more therapists have success with people like you."

Jasper had broken into a smile as Lewis spoke, and now he stepped forward and cupped Lewis's jaw. "That's wonderful."

"You sound sad."

Jasper's lips turned down at the corners. "I'm happy for you."

"But sad for yourself."

Jasper's shoulders twitched in what looked like an attempt at a shrug. "I'd hoped..."

He'd hoped? Lewis waited, aware of the gentle ticking of the clock on the mantelpiece and the hissing of the logs on the fire.

"Come on," Jasper said. "Let me show you the rest of the house."

Jasper opened the kitchen doorway. "I haven't had a new kitchen fitted yet, but it's pencilled in for the spring." He fought to keep his voice light. This wasn't the way it was meant to go. Lewis wasn't meant to be throwing more barriers up between them. Not now.

But he folded up and put away that thought, and concentrated instead on the look of wonder on Lewis's face.

"It looks fantastic." Lewis sounded genuine, anyway.

"It's not that different from when you saw it last, once it had been cleared."

"It is. You're really living in here now, aren't you?"

Jasper glanced at his laptop and books open on the table, and the empty mug sitting beside them. "I like it in here. I have tried setting up a study in the dining room, but it just doesn't feel as comfortable."

"Show me."

So he did, and Lewis spun on his heel in the near-empty room. "You just need more furnishings. A rug. An armchair. New curtains. Hey, was this desk yours before? It's gorgeous."

Jasper nodded. It had taken him days to scrub the heavy oak clean and wax it to its current finish, but he was proud of the work he'd put in. "Do you want to see upstairs?" he ventured.

"I'd like that." Lewis's reply was too soft to catch any hint of flirtation, and Jasper tamped his hopes back down again. The man was just looking at the rooms, that was all. He was congratulating himself on a job well done as a therapist. A project successfully concluded.

Jasper should probably show him the most impressive room first. Let him know just how complete that project was.

He turned left at the top of the stairs, towards Mama's old room. He ignored the overhead and flipped the switch for the reading light instead. The room was bathed in the blueish evening glow from the window and the warmth of the old-fashioned brass lamp.

Lewis's mouth hung open as he turned to take it all in. "Jasper! It's... I don't know what to say."

Good thing someone did. "I didn't want to make it into a shrine, but I wanted somewhere to go where I could remember the good bits, not just the end." It was simply furnished with a rug over the bare boards, an armchair, a footstool and a table, but he had fresh flowers on the mantelpiece and the walls were lined with shelves and pictures.

Lewis walked over to the bookshelves. "These are all children's books. And the pictures too."

Jasper had tracked down prints and framed them, covering

one wall with Tenniel's *Alice in Wonderland* illustrations. Stupidly sentimental of him, but it made him think not only of curling up as a child, but of Lewis and Carroll—and all they'd done for him. "This is my safe place. The whole house is now."

Lewis's eyes were wide, luminous, as he stared at Jasper like he was finally seeing the truth of him. He cleared his throat and blinked, and when he spoke, his voice carried a yearning to match Jasper's own.

"I want to be your safe place too."

They stepped towards each other, meeting somewhere in the middle of the rug. They moved as one, searching for each other with lips and arms. Jasper's heart pounded as he mashed himself closer to the man he loved.

Lewis tasted like home.

"I missed you," Lewis said when they finally came up for air.

"Me too. It was bloody awful at times."

"But you did it. All this. All by yourself."

"I had help."

"But not from me."

"Oh yes, from you too. Whenever I felt like giving up, I'd think of the things you taught me. It's like you never went away. Not really. Not when you were in here." Jasper pointed at his head, then smiled sheepishly and moved his hand to his chest. "And here."

"You're just an incurable romantic, aren't you?"

Jasper smiled. "Yep. And it looks like I got just what I wanted in plenty of time for Christmas. Hey, you can help me pick a tree. I mean, if you'll be living here, you should have a say in all that." He halted, remembering Lewis's words from earlier. What if he was serious about staying with his family? But no. Lewis had just kissed him, and that had to mean something. "You will be moving in, won't you?"

The dazed look on Lewis's face sharpened. "I don't know."

"You could study here just as well as at your parents. In fact, you can have the study downstairs, if you like it. Or one of the rooms up here, if you'd prefer. And I know you'll be busy, but at least this way we can still see each other at nighttime." *Please say yes, please say yes, please say yes.*

"I don't want to take advantage of you," Lewis whispered.

"You really wouldn't be." Jasper watched the hesitation waver on Lewis's face. Time to nudge. To tease? "If anything, I'll be the one taking advantage of you." He squished Lewis's bum with both hands, then realised how that might sound. "If you'll let me," he amended bashfully, turning the squeeze into a gentle pat.

Something flickered in Lewis's eyes. "Maybe I won't let you."

"God, I'm so sorry." Jasper drew his hand away.

Lewis grabbed it back. "What I meant was, maybe it's my turn to be in charge. I don't just like it on the bottom, you know."

All of a sudden, Jasper's buttocks were being groped, expertly and thoroughly, at the same time as his neck fell victim to a pair of hungry lips. He groaned. Oh yes, *this*. This was what he'd been after all along. But with Lewis it was something else. The contrast. Gentle, kind—Jasper jumped as Lewis pinched him through his jeans. Gentle, kind, *sexually aggressive* Lewis.

When Lewis pushed him towards the armchair, Jasper let himself be steered. He collapsed into the chair, under Lewis's weight. Lewis grinding down into him, kissing the breath out of him. Felt so right.

All except for that something hard poking into his side. Whatever it was, was in Lewis's coat pocket rather than his trousers. Jasper wriggled to move it out of the way.

Lewis stopped kissing him.

"Oh, hey, I got you a present."

"Later," Jasper insisted, his hand massaging Lewis's erection through his trousers.

"No. Now. Won't take long, I promise. Then I'll have my wicked way with you." Lewis reached into the coat pocket and handed Jasper a gift-wrapped parcel beautifully done up with ribbon and tasteful paper.

He pulled the ribbon and eased off the paper. "You really shouldn't h—"

Jasper fell silent as he realised what he was holding. "Lewis, is this..." He stared at the first edition hardback of *The Little Prince*. "Oh!" He stroked the cover reverently. The slipcover was yellowed and dog-eared, but that didn't matter. He opened it, releasing the sweet, heady smell of old paper. "Oh Lewis, this is beautiful."

The word was inadequate. The illustrated plates gleamed despite the spotting around the edges of the paper. It might have been well-loved, but it was still incredibly beautiful. He smiled at the picture of the fox peeking out of his burrow; then a thought made him frown.

"I hope you didn't go bankrupting yourself for this."

"Not really. It's the sixth printing, so it goes for considerably less than the earlier ones, so I've been told. Also, it's hardly in mint condition."

"But still, you really shouldn't have bought it for me."

"I should, and I did. Read the inscription."

Jasper turned to the beginning, to find Lewis's elegant handwriting on the title page.

Dear Jasper,

Please forgive me for letting you walk away.

All my love,

Lewis x

Jasper looked up, his eyes watery. "You're forgiven."

"Thank you." Lewis leaned down to kiss him then.

"And you'll move in?"

Lewis sat up straight and arched an eyebrow, a smile teasing his lips. "Just try stopping me." This time when Lewis leaned down, Jasper halted him with a fingertip.

"Of course, you do realise you've just increased my hoard again."

Lewis lifted his head and looked around. "This isn't a hoard anymore." He grinned and kissed Jasper on the nose. "This is a *collection.*"

About the Author

English through and through, Josephine Myles is addicted to tea and busy cultivating a reputation for eccentricity. She writes gay erotica and romance, but finds the erotica keeps cuddling up to the romance, and the romance keeps corrupting the erotica. She blames her rebellious muse but he never listens to her anyway, no matter how much she threatens him with a big stick. She's beginning to suspect he enjoys it.

Jo is a member of the Romantic Novelists Association and publishes regularly with Samhain. She's one of the organising team behind the UK Meet, an annual event celebrating GLBTQ fiction. She has also been known to edit anthologies and self-publish on occasion, although she prefers to leave the "boring bits" of the book creation process to someone else.

Visit JosephineMyles.com for more about her published stories, saucy free reads and regular blog posts.

Two plus one equals scorching hot fun.

The Hot Floor
© *2012 Josephine Myles*

Dumped by his boyfriend and reduced to living in a grotty bedsit, Josh Carpenter has gotten used to expecting the worst. Now he lives only for his job as a glassblower...and occasional glimpses of his sexy downstairs neighbors, Rai Nakmura and Evan Truman.

Every time he overhears the diminutive academic and the hunky plumber having loud and obviously kinky sex, Josh is overwhelmed with lust...and a longing for a fraction of what they have.

To his amazement, Rai and Evan find his embarrassing tendency to blush utterly charming, and the three men grow closer over the course of the long, hot summer. Despite Rai's charming flirtation and Evan's smoldering gaze, Josh is determined never to break his new friends' loving bonds.

On the night a naked Josh falls—quite literally—into the middle of one of Rai and Evan's marathon sex sessions, the force of their mutual attraction takes control. But just as Josh dares to hope, he senses a change. Leaving him to wonder if the winds of love are about to blow his way at last...or if history is about to repeat itself.

Warning: Contains one well-endowed stud with a sexy accent, one improbably toppy bottom boy with an unfortunate owl obsession, and one blushing naif who can't believe his luck. Also, the occasional indulgence in mathematical spanking and some shameless armpit sex.

Available now in ebook and print from Samhain Publishing.

SAMHAIN
PUBLISHING

It's all about the story...

Romance

HORROR

www.samhainpublishing.com

CPSIA information can be obtained at www.ICGtesting.com
Printed in the USA
BVOW05s2151091214

378711BV00002B/59/P

9 781619 219557